Colville Manor

Shalene Marie

This book is a work of fiction. Although some historical events and persons have been referenced, many details have been adjusted for the benefits of the story and are in no way intended to be construed as facts.

First edition, 2023

Contributors:

Editing: Krista Venero @ mountainswanted.com
Cover design: Marta and David DaSilva
        @ artbook_illustration@hotmail.com
Author: Shalene Marie @ shalenemarie.space

Acknowledgments

I have many thanks to send out to all those who have helped me with all the facets required to make the leap into the world of self-publishing:

First, to my long-time friend, Angie Cain, thank you for your support and for putting me in touch with another author who has mastered the self-publishing world.

Second, to my new friend, Melissa Sinclair (author), who has been very patient and informative with all my questions when it came to the technical aspects of making the transition from personal to public, thank you a hundred times over for everything. Everyone, please check out her books on Amazon!

Third, to my knowledgeable and thorough editor, Krista Venero, for all of the hard work to help update my words to ensure they are logical and technically correct, I appreciate all you do and will continue to do!

And, finally, to all the friends and family who have offered me nothing but support throughout the years as I've worked nights and weekends on a hobby I truly enjoy, thank you for everything, and know that I appreciate you all.

Caution!
This book contains trigger warnings. For the full list of what those
are please see the author's website at:
https://www.shalenemarie.space/trigger-warnings

Prologue

November 1359, England

Lord Viktor Colville was awakened from a deep sleep by the sound of a scream ringing in his ears. From his position on his stomach, he hastily flipped onto his back and sat up, looking for the cause of the noise.

His black eyes fixed on a female servant standing in the open doorway. Her mouth was agape, her voice ringing in horror. The confused man followed the direction of her stare until he spotted a pair of delicate bare feet at the foot of his bed. His gaze slowly rose up slim legs, generous hips, a small waist, and an ample bosom. They settled on a familiar face.

Lady Golly, his stepmother, lay next to him without a stitch of clothing on, but far more shocking was the fact that she was irrefutably dead. Her emerald eyes were covered with a milky white film, staring without direction. And her skin was a ghastly white, with ugly bruising around her neck, shouting to anyone who looked upon her that her life had been successfully extinguished. Clearly, she had been strangled to death.

"God's teeth!" he cursed under his breath.

Even though his heart was pounding in stunned disbelief, Viktor rose from his bed with a calm that belied his inner turmoil. As he stood there, overwhelmed by confusion, a group of curious onlookers began to gather in his bedchamber doorway.

His mind began to race, combing his memory for answers to this disturbing enigma. But when he tried to recall the events of the previous evening, his mind was incredibly hazy.

The previous day, he was wed to a woman he had never met before in his life. That was followed by supper, which was an uncomfortable affair, but most of that was clear in his brain. It was after the third tankard of ale when his memories began to falter. He was given the barest impression of consummating his marriage to Reissa, but after that, there was nothing else at all.

He glanced down upon his own figure and saw he was still fully clothed in braies and a tunic. His gaze touched on the corpse, and he was struck with a startling thought. Had he murdered his own stepmother?

He certainly had good cause to do so.

He shook his head. He could not have, but if he had not, how had she come to be in his bed? And why was she nude?

Viktor searched his soul, needing an answer to his questions. As he thought of the evening when he had placed his hand around her neck, he knew he could not be guilty. He had been unable to terminate her then. His morals and sense of control had stopped him from doing so, which told him he could not have committed murder, even in his altered state of intoxication.

So, knowing he could not have done such a despicable crime, he was assaulted with another string of inquiries. Who had killed Golly? Why was she stripped of clothing? And why was the guilty party so obviously framing him for her murder?

Chapter 1

October 1359, England

It was early morning. The dark of night lingered due to thick cloud cover, casting shadows upon the gathering of somber spectators watching from England's shores. Viktor observed in muted silence as the log raft transporting his father's body floated into the open sea. Flames licked the tiny wooden vessel, biting the hemp lashing that held each individual log together. Chalky smoke billowed upon an autumn breeze and then dissipated as it climbed into the overcast sky. A myriad of orange and yellow coloring reflected off the seawater, creating a mirror glow that danced with the movement of the waves.

Viktor's eyes were dry, but his heart was heavy. His father, Lord Collin Colville Senior, had exuded the life of immortality, in health and in temperament. Therefore, it was a stunning blow to all of his loved ones when he abruptly clutched his chest at supper three days ago. His body slumped over the trestle table, and his face fell limply into a full trencher of food. All breath was expelled, his pulse nonexistent. Collin Senior was a man of strength, a noble, a baron. To complain was not in his nature, but it was clear he had been favoring his left arm prior to the incident that terminated his life.

Collin Senior had not been the warmest man in creation, but a single soul could not deny that he had been a good father. He was stubborn, unyielding, and often chilling in nature. He drove his boys to exhaustion in their daily drills of mock battle. Compliments were few and far between, while criticism was constant. He continuously raised his standards of discipline when it came to their duties to their holdings and to their king. The man showed little affection, if any at all, yet his love was spoken through his loyalty to their well-being and his highly protective nature. He would have given his life before allowing anyone to hurt his family.

His wife had succumbed to the Plague in 1348, leaving him the only remaining parent of two sons. Lady Margaret Colville was known as a kind and gentle-hearted woman, and she had also been the biological mother of his two boys.

As was typical, Lord Colville had not been a faithful husband, but, atypically, he had never sired any bastards with the numerous wenches he tumbled outside of the marriage bed. His sons were legitimate, and that created the illusion of fidelity. His eldest, Collin, was ten and nine years of age when Lady Margaret passed, and his youngest, Viktor, had only been ten and six years of age. At the time of her death, both sons had been men by any standards, but Viktor had still been in the midst of training to be knighted.

Now, eleven years later, in the midst of the Hundred Years War, both of his children had seen and participated in enough bloodshed to last two lifetimes. The Treaty of Bretigny was signed in recent years, marking a hiatus of uncertain peace in Europe. Collin Sr. and his sons had finally been able to return to their respective holdings in northern England, following years of absence.

After Margaret's passing, Collin Jr. was given lordship over a flourishing estate in the northern province of Westmorland, Moorestone, deeming him Collin of Ender, while Collin Sr. and Viktor remained in Colville Manor, several hundred miles north in the same province. However, now that their father had met his death, the lordship of Colville Manor fell to Viktor, identifying the man as Viktor of Appleta.

The elder son took after their mother in appearance, whereas the younger was a mixture of both parents. Collin possessed a crown of fine chestnut waves that dusted his wide shoulders, with eyes so dark that the retina and iris nearly blended into one. His tanned cheeks were concealed with a beard that was kept neatly trimmed, and his brows were bushy. The lord's build was lean and muscular, and he stood over six feet tall. Overall, the man was rather striking in his attractiveness, and his jaunty personality only added to the allure.

Viktor possessed the same black eyes, their father's eyes, but his crown of thick midnight waves belonged to their mother. The raven hair was shorter than his brother's, curling boyishly at his nape; however, the man was anything but boyish in appearance and demeanor. His chiseled jaw was usually clean-shaven, but because they'd been traveling for days, his chin sported black stubble. His brows were two slashes of menace, and his full lips were thinned with feeling as he continued to witness an unforgettable scene. Viktor may have been the younger of the two brothers, but his build was ever so slightly more muscular. His height also towered well over six feet.

Viktor was a man of mixed temperament. His smile was swift to arise, but his frown turned down with much more ease. His dark figure was extremely frightening when he was enraged, yet stunningly handsome when his mood was light. The softer, virtually nonexistent side of the man was reserved for those he was closest to, such as his brother, and that was only because Collin was able to draw it out of him with his mild disposition.

As sunlight began to stream through the breaking clouds, two brothers stood side by side as the burning raft continued to drift. Collin placed his arm around his wife's shoulders, seeking silent support when the lashing began to deteriorate. Lady Moira hugged her husband close as the logs gave away, sinking into seawater. The flames hissed as they were extinguished.

The couple had been married nearly two years prior, and the lady was currently carrying Collin's first legitimate child. An announcement of the babe had been shared mere days before Collin Senior's death. The Lord had been good enough not to take him before the sharing of this glorious news. All of the family had been invited to Moorestone for that particular reason. Moira was barely four fortnights along, making travel possible for quite some time yet. In fact, it would be a while before the lady began to show the truth of her condition.

Collin had also sired one bastard child before his marriage. The beautiful little girl was not yet six and lived with her servant mother in Scotland. According to Collin, he hadn't had any desire to dally with another once he'd bedded his wife, but Viktor refused to believe that that was possible. He could not even conceive of the idea of monogamy. No man could desire one woman for the rest of his life. The word seemed to be a curse on his tongue, but then he set eyes upon his new sister-in-law. She was positively beautiful and charming. Seeing her had put a dent in his disbelief of monogamy; however, admittedly, it was a sliver of a dent.

Viktor soon learned that Lady Moira Colville was only twenty and one years old. Collin was thirty and two, but the difference in age did nothing to diminish their feelings for one another. Her height was a mere two inches over five feet. Her head was defined with jet-black curls and large sparkling blue eyes. The color of her eyes was outstanding, the reflection of a clear summer sky. The lady's curves would draw any man's eye, not too voluptuous or too slim, an outstanding complement to her lovely face.

Viktor was drawn from his reverie when the remaining flames fizzled out, effectively putting an end to the ceremony of farewell. Hearing a loud sniffle at his side, the lord's gaze shifted to the woman on his right. He observed the tears glistening upon his stepmother's flawless cheeks and could not help but roll his eyes.

His father had married Golly during their last visit home from the battles in France. The couple had mere months together before he was needed once again to wear his armor and wield his sword, as was the case with his sons. In that short period of time,

Viktor had seen little of his stepmother. While she was in the castle tending to her matronly duties, he was out in the bailey maintaining the shape of a warrior by doing daily drills. She remained a virtual stranger, and to that day, even though they'd been home for several months' time, that detail held true.

The only occasions that brought them together were meals, and even then, they said little to one another. Viktor had no real interest in knowing the lady who had replaced his mother's status in his life, and she gave the impression of feeling the same. She may have only been six years his senior, but he didn't see her as a woman. He saw her as a liability, a resentment.

Any other person would have made an attempt to draw his loved ones together, but Lord Colville Senior was not any other person. He knew his sons had an aversion to the lady because she could not replace a mother they had both adored. Not once did he push the issue of reconciling the relationships between Golly and Collin and Viktor. So he allowed them their distance. Collin was slightly more welcoming of the woman into their family, but not much more.

What little Viktor did know of the woman did not place her in his favor. She exuded a haughtiness that was beyond rude, a self-righteousness that was infuriating, and an unnecessarily heavy hand with the servants. That would have stamped a frown on his mother's serene face.

Any man would be hard-pressed to say that she was not an appealing woman in appearance, because she certainly was. Her ash-blond tresses were naturally straight. She usually left them free-flowing around seductively curved hips. Her emerald eyes were brilliant with color but dull with life. Blond brows were gracefully arched, and her mouth was a pink bow.

She was extraordinarily tall for a female at five-foot-eight, causing her eye-catching face to stand out in a crowd like the North Star. And her luscious, voluptuous curves would weaken a saint's resolve. At thirty and three years of age, she had the beginnings of lines around her eyes and mouth, but that did nothing to detract from her loveliness.

However, her grating personality certainly left much to be desired. Once one met her, her beauty failed to overcome an ugly disposition. Only God himself knew how Collin Sr. and Golly had become a willing match for marriage, because his sons were dumbfounded.

When at last Viktor wordlessly turned to retrace his steps to his mount, he was annoyed to feel his stepmother's arm hook around his, assuming he'd escort her to her own. The lady's presence was suffered in silence as he led her to her enviable thoroughbred. He gritted his teeth as she waited for him to help her into the saddle.

If it had been any other day, he would have left her to her own devices, uncaring that it was not the gentlemanly thing to do. Viktor behaved in polite fashion only to those he respected and to those who deserved it, society be damned. But on this day, the day of his father's funeral, he made an exception, refusing to dishonor his memory by initiating a squabble with his widow.

Colville Manor

Unaware of the weight of his hauberk, he hoisted her cloaked figure into the saddle with ease, then, without waiting for her praise of thanks, he turned and walked away. As Viktor climbed his massive mount, a warhorse with the same black coloring as his own, the lord noticed the remainder of his party was also preparing for departure. In addition to the family of mourners, squires, fifteen men-at-arms, and a handful of knights, all of whom wore the Colville colors of navy and gold, accompanied them. Their tunics were marked with the family's coat of arms, as were their mounts.

Viktor's closest and most beloved friend, Sir Alden Kilgour, was among the knights in attendance, as was Alden's younger sister, Lady Edith. The men had been confidants for as long as either could remember. For so long, in fact, that neither ever made any attempt to recall their first meeting. To do so would be an impossibility.

The Kilgours originated in Scotland, a titled family of noble class. Unfortunately, they were unusually poor for their rank in society. Alden's father squandered their wealth and created a scandal when he was caught stealing from another member of the noble class. After his hand had been severed for his crime, the entire family was banished from the country.

They fled to England, where Alden and Viktor had met as babes in the village mere miles from Colville Manor. Despite their opposing backgrounds of wealth and poverty, the boys were inseparable. And when the Black Death stole Kilgour's parents in the same year as Viktor's mother, Collin Senior, knowing the siblings well, was more than willing to accept Alden and Edith into his home. The boys were knighted on the same day.

Observing his friend's taut expression, Alden left his sister in his squire's care and thread his horse through the crowd. The chestnut mount ground to a halt beside Viktor's.

"When I felt the shift in temperature, I surmised I would find a scowl upon your face, my friend. Is anything else the cause, or merely the burden of this day?" As he spoke, a cool October breeze lifted the golden blond curls upon his pate, his amazing amber eyes alight with curiosity.

In coloring, the boys were comparable to the contrast of night and day. Viktor was night with his black locks and eyes, and Alden was day with his blond curls and yellow eyes. However, there was much they had in common. Both stood well over six feet tall, and both were quite brawny and robust. Both were also the same age at twenty and seven years.

Viktor glanced in the direction where he knew Golly to be. His brow creased in vexation. "The burden of a stepmother."

Chapter 2

The whole of the Colville entourage arrived at Moorestone rather late the next evening. Anticipating the party's arrival, Collin's steward had a meal awaiting his lord's return. The nobles and knights were seated at the table situated on a raised dais at the far side of the keep, while the men-at-arms, squires, and all others were seated at the long trestle tables below, running perpendicular to the platform.

The kitchen was built within the keep, behind the dais. Two massive fireplaces lined the wall, enabling the servants to prepare gigantic feasts and immediately serve them, while also warming the residents from the chilling weather outside. Another fireplace was situated in the left wall upon entering, where several smaller tables and benches were set up for recreational activities following the meal, such as chess and dice and needlework. The right wall contained a wide-open staircase that led to the occupants' chambers above.

When the owners were in residence, musicians, minstrels, jesters or mimes generally visited on the weekends and on special occasions, creating entertainment for the spectators. The vast space in the far-left corner remained open for those people to set up and play. However, as it was a Wednesday, that corner was cold and empty. The noise in the hall mundanely consisted of its occupants, the servants busying themselves in the kitchen, and the sound of three crackling fireplaces.

After receiving all pertinent news during his short absence, Collin was seated at the head of the table, Moira to his right, and Viktor at his left. Golly had taken up the open chair next to Moira only after seeing Alden on Viktor's left. Lady Edith was also present, as was Collin's steward, Lyonel. Lyonel was a ghost of a man with an ashen pallor that was normal for the man. He was rather petite for a male at only five-feet-four, with a diminutive bone structure, but his gray eyes were intelligent, and he exuded an authority that one failed to question in spite of his minimal size.

"Lady Edith, your medicinal hand was in dire need last eventide. A child in the village was struck with an inordinate case of the colic," Lyonel informed as he clutched his tankard of cider. The meal spread out before them consisted of loins of beef, pork, and venison. Several types of poultry and eggs. There were cheeses and breads and various kinds of vegetables. To wash down their sustenance, they had ale, cider, and wine.

The woman frowned. "Do you not have any others to consult on such matters?" Edith Kilgour was a female version of her elder brother, possessing the same blond curls and amber eyes. At ten and nine years of age, she had reached her full height of five feet. She was a particularly lovely girl; however, her modest beauty was distorted with an excess of weight. She was what many would term as pleasantly plump.

Possibly because of that detail, the lady was extremely sweet, almost sickeningly sweet at times. Some would question the overt kindness as an act, a well-put-on performance to conceal a tempestuous side, but most accepted her disposition at face value.

"A surgeon and a midwife are not of any use on such matters, milady. The poor child was forced to rely on improvisation."

"'Tis a pity. I have contrived a tonic for that particular ailment," she voiced with obvious regret.

"I must issue an apology for the burden of our ailing community, Lady Edith. My husband has been lax in his duties to commandeer a primary physician for his people," Moira inserted while throwing Collin a disapproving glance.

"Aye, I must speak my gratitude for sharing your knowledge of healing herbs as our guest. The whole of the village will regret your departure on the morrow," Moorestone's owner announced with an easy grin.

"I thank you, but your gratitude is misplaced. I merely share the knowledge the Lord has gifted upon me. 'Tis a duty, not a chore."

"My dear sister is much too modest," Alden remarked, placing an arm around her shoulders. He gave her a quick squeeze, showing his brotherly pride in her abilities. After taking a gulp of ale, his amber eyes shifted to his host. "Pride in our younger siblings grows simply, does it not, Collin?"

Collin laughed in jest. "I know naught of what you speak, Alden." He gestured to Viktor as brown liquid sloshed from his tankard. "Have you met my brother?"

Viktor gave the man on his right a baleful glare but remained silent. There was no need for serious offense when Collin was dishing out good-natured ribbing. It was a well-known pastime amongst the knights, needing humor to cut the eternal days when they were surrounded with nothing but war.

Knowing Viktor well, the men at the table shared in the comedy with loud guffaws.

"Aye," Alden chuckled, "my good judgment must have fled."

"To hear him speak it, the only pride is in his way with maids," Collin continued the jest, momentarily forgetting that well-bred ladies surrounded him. His words were only partially false. Never had Viktor spoken of his dalliances with women, but Collin shared with Viktor that he had heard much from the women themselves, singing his brother's praises until his ears were ready to fall off from overuse.

Upon hearing the comment, Golly's emerald eyes shot Viktor with a hard stare, while Moira and Edith gasped scandalously.

"This conversation is highly inappropriate. Collin, your father would have disapproved of such behavior," Golly reprimanded.

"Our father may have been a serious man, but he favored the ability to speak one's mind, Lady; whether in truth or in jest, it mattered not to him," Viktor was quick to defend his kin.

The lady's chin rose a notch. "Very well, speak crudely of your conquests. But I refuse to dignify this with my presence," their stepmother hissed. With that, she jumped to her feet and departed with her nose in the air.

Viktor knew Moira and Edith were not fond of the elder woman, but they agreed with her wholeheartedly by their actions. Silently, they followed suit, causing many of the men to stare after them with regret, damning their lord for chasing away the fairer sex.

Collin was clearly kicking himself for behaving so callously before the ladies and his wife.

Viktor, however, had finally broken into a roar of laughter, enjoying the display. "Ah, wenches and their delicate sensibilities," he remarked to no one in particular.

"You may see the humor in this, little brother, but I fear I will be barred from my bed this evening."

Collin's comment only succeeded in elevating Viktor's laughter.

"If you do not cease that cackling, I will not furnish you with a willing bedmate this evening," the man at the head of the table threatened.

Viktor immediately sobered. "I ask not for your hospitality, brother. I am more than capable of securing a companion for my pleasure."

"That I know." It was Collin's turn to scowl. He glanced at the feminine servants in the kitchen, three of whom hadn't taken their eyes from his younger sibling since they'd marched through the front entrance. One was new, and two of them had already warmed his bed on previous occasions.

"For future reference, 'tis best to threaten what he cares for, Collin, not what comes easily to him," Alden chimed in with a grin.

Both brothers threw glares his way. Kilgour's grin widened. "I believe I shall join the women," he returned happily, then rose from his seat and also departed.

Moira and Edith had taken up a game of chess in the lounging area, and Golly was nowhere to seen, so it was assumed by all that she had retired for the evening. For lack of paid entertainment, a few of the knights had decided to amuse themselves with an archery contest in the empty corner where the minstrels usually played. Seeing that, Alden didn't hesitate to join them.

Collin and Viktor were the only two remaining. Two pairs of black eyes surveyed their empty table, and, realizing they had driven everyone else away, they looked to one another and broke into fits of amused laughter.

Chapter 3

Viktor never invited women into his bed. When he desired the release of his baser needs, he found it within the arms of a willing wench, but the act took place anywhere and elsewhere, with the exception of where he slept. Once he tumbled the woman he lusted after most on a particular evening, he preferred to sleep *alone*.

He would take them whenever and wherever the mood struck him: in a shadowy corner, an empty tower, gatehouses, and, rarely, the women's own quarters. Then he would return to his chambers and sprawl out on his empty bed, using the vast space to sleep without distraction. During the few occasions when he had made the mistake of sleeping beside a female, he would wake in the night by their screams when he rolled over, nearly crushing them with his weight.

Or he'd be thoroughly annoyed when they embraced him in slumber, effectively waking him with the suffocation of someone holding him close. After the last time, when he'd accidentally pushed the wench onto the cold stone floor and received a sound scolding for his insensitivity, he had ordered the maid from his room, slammed the door, and vowed "never again!"

So, once he had bedded the new kitchen servant in a darkened corner out in the bailey, he returned to his chamber, thoroughly sated and mellowed. He stripped down to nothing and poured himself a goblet of wine from the bottle on a tiny table in the corner. It had been opened to breathe. The bed had been turned down with heated bricks at the foot and the fire stoked for maximum heat, assuring his comfort. He seated himself in a wooden chair before the fireplace and stared into the jumping flames.

His father was gone forever.

In all of his years on earth, Viktor had never been witness to his father's laughter. In fact, the man had seemed incapable of such extensive feeling. He had barely smiled, for Christ's sake, yet Golly's comment earlier in the keep had rattled him far more than he cared to admit. It should not matter that Collin Sr. failed to give them a softer side of himself, yet it did.

When Viktor reflected inwardly, analyzing the toll his father's personality had taken upon his sons, he was startled to see much of his father in himself, and more of their mother in Collin. Viktor knew he wasn't as cold in the extreme as his father was, but he knew himself to be a hard, withdrawn man. He gave little of himself to loved ones, refused to let them in, yet he knew no other way to be.

The sound of his chamber door creaking open interrupted his pensive reverie, instantly drawing his attention. His knight's reflexes sprang into action. He jumped up from the chair and grabbed the dagger he always left on the mantel for emergencies.

His gaze shifted to the figure quietly shutting the heavy oak door. He was irritated to see his stepmother turning toward him. Her mouth opened to speak, but when she saw that he was nude, her jaw dropped, and she simply gaped in silence.

Viktor cared not that he wore no clothing; however, he did care that his privacy had been intruded upon.

"I fail to recall offering an invitation into my personal chambers, lady. Remove yourself afore I do so for you."

His gravelly voice snapped her from her shocked state. Rather than moving to leave, she stepped farther into the room. Viktor returned the dagger to the mantel while keeping a wary eye on the widow.

When she continued her approach, he held up a palm to halt her obvious intent. She wore nothing but a sea-green-hued cotte, a lady's undergarment with a tight bodice and a free-flowing skirt, and linen drawers underneath that. On her feet, she sported matching satin slippers, designed for wear around one's room to ward off a chill. In her state of undress, it would be impossible for him to mistake her reason for inviting herself into his chamber.

"Denial is in poor taste, Viktor. I desire you as you desire me." Her arms lifted to slide around his neck, but he easily caught her wrists in a bruising grip.

"You are under an outlandish misconception, lady." He spoke with unyielding determination as he pushed her into a forced retreat.

"I have felt our connection. In all this time, we have avoided contact out of respect for your father, but—"

Viktor cut her off with a throaty grunt of fury. "You show my father outright disrespect with this lurid display on the eve of his burial." To make his rejection clear, he pushed her up against the wall next to the door, then released one of her wrists to open the thick structure.

"Viktor, please, you know not what you are doing; you are addled with sorrow." She clutched at his biceps pathetically, but he dismissed her pleading. When she decided that he really was going to throw her from his chamber, she resorted to desperation. "I will scream rape if you fail to grant me a moment."

His expression became as black as his eyes. His forearm pressed to her slender neck. "You will feel the point of my dagger afore I allow you to shame me with such lies." The man growled, feeling his fingers itch to slap her. "Speak what you must, then begone."

Golly ignored the discomfort of his arm against her neck and grabbed his free hand. She placed his palm against one of the mounds beneath her bodice and asked, "You do not feel any desire for me, Viktor?"

Their eyes locked.

"Do you jest, lady?"

"I never jest over pleasure, my lord," she responded seductively.

His face inched toward hers, his mouth a hairsbreadth from touching hers, then suddenly the pressure to her throat increased, nearly cutting off her air supply. "I do not feel any desire for you." He paused, causing the tension to rise. "The Lord's honest truth is that I despise you. If you proposition me a second time, I give you my word, Golly, I will not show mercy."

With that, he yanked open the door, shoved her into the dank corridor, then shut it in her face. And then, to add insult to injury, he dropped the plank in place to securely lock the door, knowing she would hear it.

Chapter 4

Golly formulated her plan of revenge as she lay awake that evening, licking her invisible wounds. She decided on a simple but effective resolution. She would marry off her stepson to a woman he was certain to despise, ensuring that the remainder of his life would be led in misery.

In the months following his return to England, Golly had been watching him closely, obsessed with the man she could not have because she had married his father. Collin Senior's passing had been a stroke of fortune, plain and simple. His death had opened the path to hidden lust, and she traveled it without hesitation. To be rejected with such fervor had torn her pride to shreds, and now she was grateful for all of her observations. She knew exactly what type of woman ignited the man's passions, and it enabled her to choose precisely the opposite.

The irony was that Viktor preferred females much like herself. And knowing that only twisted the hypothetical blade he had already sheathed in her flesh. There was no mistaking it, the man was attracted to beauties. To her knowledge, every woman he bedded was a maid with outstanding looks. It mattered not what hair color or eye color, because there had been many of all types.

But when she stopped to run a mental list, she realized, more so than not, the women had been brunettes. Very well, no brunettes. Coloring had little influence over Golly's final decision, but body type was a detail that became clear when she thought back to her many observations. He liked a woman with curves, a woman with ample flesh in all the right places. So, she would have to choose someone with very little to offer, or far too much.

In terms of personality, he favored a maid with a voice, someone who could spar with the best of them, someone who had no qualms about speaking her mind. He enjoyed an outgoing, seductively aware female, a woman who used her wiles with years of know-how and experience. The type of wench who knew what she wanted and wasn't afraid to act. One who was willing to do what was necessary to obtain the unobtainable, aggressive, perhaps even feisty at times.

Viktor could be a frightening man, so he chose women who did not scare easily, women who didn't flee when he looked at them crossly. Golly knew she possessed each and every one of those qualities. She also knew there weren't many females out there who did, which meant her stepson often settled for wenches who were available, or an easy tumble. And rarely did he seek the same woman twice. Clearly, he enjoyed variety; monotony was not his forte. But monotony was what he would have. The same woman for the rest of his life.

As Viktor's stepmother and only remaining legal guardian, she possessed the authority to choose his wife. However, if he disapproved of her choice, and he certainly would, he had the option to seek a reprieve from their overlord.

Lord Rynearson's word was their law, and if he approved the match, Viktor must bend to his will, his desires be damned. There was no going against their overlord, not unless he was prepared to start a war that would anger their king, and one did not anger the king. King Edward III had chosen Rynearson as Baron of Westmorland, and if Rynearson was offended, he would take the matter to the king.

Lady Golly had met their overlord but once; however, in that short span of time, she was well aware of his silent appraisal of her beauty. His eyes had followed her every move, but she assumed he hadn't made any sexual overtures because her husband had been at her side every moment. Rynearson was a man of power, but her husband would have been a formidable opponent. He wouldn't have given permission for the use of his wife without a battle, and somehow Rynearson seemed to guess as much, because his desire remained unspoken.

But now that Collin Sr. had passed on, she had no doubt she could buy the approval of her stepson's bride-to-be with her body. Rynearson was not a particularly attractive man—he was rather plain, in fact, but she could summon the will to bed him if it meant the success of her vengeance.

The next day, with her escort and several men-at-arms in tow, Golly rode into the village several miles from Moorestone in search of the perfect mismatch for Viktor. The skies were gray; the cloud cover appeared swollen with gathering rain, yet the moisture held off. Countless chickens scattered in all directions as horse hooves pounded the main dirt path leading through the little community.

A plump woman was seated on the stoop of her hut in front of a large wooden tub, laundering a frock that had seen better days. Seeing the exquisitely adorned lady on a chestnut mount, she gave a tentative smile. Golly dismissed the warm greeting, as well as the woman, and looked to the smithy shop. Sounds of heated metal being cooled and pounded into shape rang through the air and then doubled in intensity when the entrance was opened to take advantage of the autumn breeze.

Hearing the commotion in the street, an extremely soiled man peered out. Many other doors were also opened, the occupants curiously watching as the lady led her protective entourage around a curve that brought a barren schoolyard into view.

Golly pulled her mount to an abrupt halt when she noticed a gathering of small children with their hands clasped together. They were moving in a circle while singing a lively tune that appeared to be some sort of game. The tiny figures were smeared with mud from their heads to their toes from playing in the dirt yard. Despite their unwashed bodies and soiled clothes, every last one of them had healthy grins on their faces. They broke into peals of laughter as they collapsed to the ground with happy purpose.

A girl among them began to clap, leading them all into a round of clapping for their sport. As Golly watched closely, she realized the girl was a young woman. An authority, not a child. The lady decided she was either the teacher or perhaps an assistant. Golly didn't realize her mouth had fallen open in shock.

The young miss had blended so completely into the group, it was amazing she had noticed her at all. Her face was just as smeared with brown dust, her worn gown practically a rag that hung on her rail-thin body, a body that looked like a child's, not a woman's. Her petite frame and short height of five feet had only added to the easy misconception that she was nothing but a child.

As the miss kindly helped some of the children to their feet, Golly took stock of her appearance. Despite the dust covering her figure, it was a simple matter to see that there wasn't a single outstanding feature about her. She was plain, boring. She had the type of face one forgot mere moments after seeing.

Her strawberry blond locks were limp, straight, and dull. The youth's face was narrow, with sunken cheeks, delicately arched brows, thin lips, and even white teeth. Her complexion was fair, with a smattering of freckles concealed beneath the dirt. A distance of fifty feet separated them, yet Golly was able to distinguish a pair of ash-gray eyes that reminded her of the chalky dust remaining in the fireplace after an evening of spent fire.

In terms of appearance, the wench could not be more fitting for her plan; however, she must yet meet her to determine disposition. As the woman broke away from the children to ring the bell to resume the school day for all, including those who had not partaken in the game with their teacher, Golly dismounted and approached.

"You there!" she raised her voice across the distance. When Golly noticed the tiny figure give a start, she had to bite back a grin.

Cautiously, the petite figure turned and greeted her unexpected guest with a wary expression. "Aye, milady," was followed with a meek curtsy.

"I seek directions to Moorestone; do you know of it?"

Those gray eyes tentatively glanced at the foot soldiers on the path, then turned east, where the castle was located. She gave a spiritless nod.

"If you follow the sun, milady, you will reach the destination you seek." Her hands were clasped together, her posture submissive.

A slow, sinful smile spread across Golly's mouth. She had chosen her victim. "Your aid is much appreciated." With that, she dismissed the youth and returned to her mount. She watched as the teacher entered the small hut of a schoolroom where her students awaited.

When one lagging little boy entered her vision, running for the structure so as not to be late, Golly called out to him. Having gained his attention, he stopped so suddenly that he almost tripped over his own feet. Fearfully he looked to the extravagantly dressed woman. She beckoned him with a smile and a pearl that she'd plucked from the deep pockets of her cloak. Ever so slowly, he trudged forward, dragging his feet in the dirt.

"You shall keep this pearl if you reveal the name of your mistress and the whereabouts of her home, child," Golly offered with a fake smile.

He looked uncertain for a moment, then abruptly said, "Miss Maitland lives with her papa," he pointed to a crumbling hovel on the opposite side of the road, "there." The wooden roof slatted with hay was caving in, and the walls appeared to need much repair, yet their tiny yard was clearly well tended.

A real smile formed on the Lady's lips. She tossed the pearl at the boy then spurred her horse into a hasty gallop, kicking up dust in the child's soiled face. He coughed and rubbed his eyes as the lady traveled a hundred yards to his teacher's home.

With two of the foot soldiers at her back, she walked the flower-lined path to the door. Anticipating her intent, one of the men knocked for her so she wouldn't have to dirty her hands by touching the poverty-ridden shelter.

Within moments, the door was thrown open, nearly yanking it off its rusted, squeaky hinges. Golly was presented with a man rather unlike the girl she'd just met in the schoolyard.

He was somewhere around six feet in stature, with a solid, lean build. His complexion was permanently pockmarked from the imperfection of youth, giving him a ruddy, harsh appearance. The raven tresses on his crown were sprinkled gray with age, yet he couldn't have endured more than forty years of living. It was only after she looked into his ash eyes that she realized this man had to be Miss Maitland's father.

Clearly, he was brought up short to find a noble woman standing on his doorstep, because his eyes widened to shocked bulges. His mouth opened to demand their intent, but Golly spoke first.

"I am Lady Golly Colville of Appleta. I live in Colville Manor to the north with my youngest stepson, Lord Viktor Colville of Appleta. I have come to your home on this day to extend a proposition of marriage for your daughter to said stepson," she announced in a pleasant tone.

"Reissa?" he asked with a furrowed brow.

"The teacher in the school over yonder?" She extended a finger down the road.

The man nodded.

"Aye," she confirmed.

Maitland stood there, dumbfounded for close to a minute before he smiled and opened the door to offer entrance.

Chapter 5

Less than an hour later, Golly departed the Maitland residence with a stunning smile on her face. Bernard had promised his daughter's hand to Viktor Colville without any qualms or concerns. He had asked nothing of his future son-in-law's age, appearance, or disposition. He seemed to care not who the man was.

However, he had been extremely interested in what would be granted to him if he agreed to her proposition. The lady had offered the father residence in Colville Manor, where Reissa would be living with Viktor and herself, a handsome dowry, and, in exchange, he asked for a single requirement: the assurance that his daughter conceive an heir within the first year of their marriage.

Now that she had secured the word of her victim's father, she had but one final confirmation to acquire: Rynearson's.

***

Viktor's pleasant intoxication was interrupted when Golly entered the keep with a blinding smile on her beautiful face. The extensively smug glint in her emerald eyes caused a hint of unease. Then his unease elevated into pure annoyance when those green gems settled on his masculine figure, and she began a determined approach.

Viktor, Collin, and Alden were all seated at the trestle table on the dais. Noticing his brother's abrupt shift in mood, Collin looked to the woman crossing the hall. Seeing Collin's passive stare, Alden's head also turned. The trio was unusually silent as they watched the folds of her skirts swish as she moved nearer.

Their lady was wearing a royal blue overtunic of velvet, shot through with silver threading. The gown was detailed with floor-trailing tippets at the elbows and a trim of pure silver. Her chin was held proudly as she lifted her skirts to climb the steps onto the dais. She moved to stand over them, looking down on the seated gentlemen from the head of the table. She smiled happily then gazed out over the lingering occupants in the Meeting Hall. Once again, Edith and Moira were crowded over a chessboard.

The foot soldiers who had accompanied the lady were now seated at the lower tables munching on bread and cheese leftover from the evening meal. And several knights, intrigued by the ladies' long-standing game of chess, were gathered around observing their play.

"Lords and ladies, I bring good tidings!" Golly shouted over the din, gaining everyone's attention. She placed a possessive hand on Viktor's shoulder. "I am pleased to announce the imminent marriage of my beloved stepson to one Miss Reissa Maitland. I ask all to share in the celebration of his betrothal!"

Her words were met with an uncertain silence. Heads turned, looking to others for confirmation, and when no one provided support, they looked to Viktor. To his credit, he remained oddly calm. Seeing that he had not exploded with a denial, whoops and cheers erupted all around. The servants busied themselves pouring extra tankards of ale and silver goblets of wine. As the conversation hummed, Viktor rose from his seat and turned turbulent eyes on Golly.

"I will have a word in private," he ordered in a soft growl. With that, he clutched her arm in a way that appeared she was voluntarily being escorted from the massive hall rather than forced. Viktor ignored the hearty slaps on the back and words of congratulations as they crossed to the front entrance, leaving those to whom he was closest to stare after them, shocked by news of his wedding.

Once they stood out in the bailey, Viktor dropped her arm, disgusted by the contact. "If your words are true, I will have your head, lady."

"You may now be the Lord of Colville Manor, but I fear nothing from you, Viktor. My men will protect me," she returned with unwavering confidence.

"Your men are *my* men, wench. You have everything to fear from me."

"The maid arrives in a month, with a ceremony to follow. If you desire another match, you will have to take the matter to Lord Rynearson; however, I have informed the man, and he has assured me of his choice to support my decision. You will meet nothing but resistance."

He took a menacing step forward without warning. The sudden movement was no comparison to the deadly look in his black eyes.

Golly was so startled by his action that she tripped over her skirts in fearful retreat. She fell hard on her backside, causing her to grunt in pain from the force of the fall.

Once again, he moved forward, towering over her from his monstrous height. Then he knelt before her and wrapped his hand around her throat. "You will see to our lord and rescind this decision. I order it, or I shall be forced to terminate you," he remarked with a piercing glint in his eyes.

He glared at her, watching as the color drained from her face. A furious grunt vibrated in his chest.

"'Tis done, Viktor," she stated.

"You vengeful, spiteful bitch! You go too far!" he shouted in response, his grip around her neck tightening slightly.

"I am unable to deny that," Golly returned as she gave him a haughty smile, her hands only loosely holding onto his wrist.

The scowl he turned on her would have chilled a weaker woman's blood, but she giggled, sadistically taking pleasure in his tirade.

"She lives in the village. A rather plain, thin girl. I found her meekness quite endearing."

"I will not hear any more!" he roared then rose and stomped back into the keep.

He thundered across the stone floor, his expression scaring away any thoughts of more congratulations from Collin's men. His hard figure climbed the dais where Collin, Alden, Moira, and Edith awaited to hear the truth of the matter. However, no one needed to hear the words because his face said it all.

Viktor threw himself into a chair and promptly downed an entire tankard of ale. Several drops rolled down his chin and onto his charcoal-gray tunic.

"She does not jest," Collin remarked, his eyes on his brother.

After slamming down the heavy mug, he confessed, "I could've killed the wench." His gaze touched on Alden's sister. "Edith, she may be in need of your gentle ministrations."

Wordlessly, the lady nodded, then rose to do his bidding.

"She has been beaten?" Moira questioned in disbelief.

"She has been warned," was his only reply.

"Yet the marriage stands?" Alden wondered.

"Aye," Viktor nearly choked on the word.

"What is her cause, Viktor? You have shared but few words with your stepmother in as many years, but 'tis now clear that she is vexed, and you are her target," his friend quizzed.

Turbulent eyes glanced at Moira, and he shocked all with his civility when he said, "I will say nothing in front of the lady."

She smiled, appreciative of his unexpected thoughtfulness. "Speak it, Viktor. I shall not take offense."

The man sighed, then sipped from the tankard that a servant had punctually replenished. "The lady made a candid overture of desire. I dismissed her."

Moira's cheeks blossomed with color, Collin cursed, and Alden appeared stupefied.

"Golly would lead you to unhappiness because she has been rejected?" his sister-in-law was first to inquire.

"'Twould seem as such."

"Father has turned in his watery grave," his brother muttered.

"His widow has shamed him," Alden mentioned.

Viktor shook his head. "The widow has shamed herself."

"What of Rynearson?" Collin tested, changing the subject.

"She has seen to him."

"Is it possible she lies?" Moira put out.

"It has come down to the hope that 'tis so. Reissa Maitland best be an aberration of her addled mind."

"Reissa Maitland?" Collin's brow rose.

"A wench from your village," Viktor supplied with another scowl.

"An untitled maid without any lands or holdings?"

"Aye. And Golly has chosen a wench I am assured to dislike in every way."

"You must plead your case to Rynearson, little brother."

Viktor nodded. "I depart at dawn."

***

Viktor stormed from his overlord's castle as he had stormed across his brother's Meeting Hall the previous evening. The man had been unyielding in his stand, refusing to give over. Viktor had gone about it several ways. He tried being polite; he tried being friendly.

When he was firmly rebuffed, he tried being cunning, then finally, he was inspired to fury. He actually felt his hand move to the hilt of his sword, considering cutting the man down, but at the last moment, he came to his senses and marched from the monstrous stone dwelling, seething.

It seemed he would have to resign himself to an unwanted wedding.

Chapter 6

Reissa Maitland clasped her delicate hands together to still their quaking, but doing so only emphasized the trembling within the whole of her tiny body. On that day, her life would forever be changed. On that day, she would be wed to a complete stranger. Her ash-gray eyes would not be set upon the man who would be her husband until she began the terrifying journey down the aisle in Moorestone's extensive chapel.

As she stood outside what was about to become her former home, waiting beside her father for their escort, she appeared externally calm, but her mind was humming with thought. Despite all she knew she should have been fretting over, she could think of only one thing: her husband's inevitable disappointment when he looked upon his bride.

Reissa was well aware that she was no beauty. To know anything to the contrary was an impossibility when her tyrant of a father shoved those insecurities down her throat for the entirety of her twenty and one years on earth.

Even now as he stared down at her from his towering height, she felt the weight of his silent reprimand, warning her not to do anything to tilt fortune's scale. A month prior, Bernard had announced that she was to marry Lord Viktor Colville. She knew he would never consider asking her feelings on the matter because he cared nothing for her feelings. Only his own were of any worth, and he coveted the riches that would accompany her wedded union.

Reissa accepted the news with a shock that she had been unable to hide from her only remaining parent. Then her shock swiftly shifted to familiar horror when he thundered across their crumbling dwelling and raised his hand to her without a hint of moral conscience.

The youth had grown accustomed to the violent ways of her ruthless father. She knew the warning signs of his outrageous temper and had cultivated a quiet meekness that usually flew below his radar of anger. But one never grew accustomed to being beaten. She had raised her arm to instinctively ward off the blow, but his brutish hand mercilessly struck her cheek. It was impossible to ignore the pain that radiated throughout her head. Ash-gray eyes watered from the stunning force of a backhanded slap.

She accepted his abuse with as much dignity as her petite figure could muster, yet the following day, she still bore the marks as a constant reminder of his punishment for reacting innocently to the news of her upcoming marriage. Thirty days had passed, allowing more than enough time for her to heal, but she would carry the memory of it for too long. She could clearly recall every beating he had ever dealt.

Refusing the marriage was *not* an option. Bernard raised his hand to her over the slightest of circumstances, but to anger him over such an event, the lady closed her eyes, imagining that he would be capable of beating her to death. So, she had accepted the burden without complaint; in fact, the marriage inspired a bud of hope.

Colville Manor

According to the oral agreement between her father and Lady Colville, Bernard would reside with Lord Viktor and herself, but she desperately hoped she would fall under the protection of a conscionable husband who would keep her safe from her own parent.

Of course, that brought her thoughts to the question of her husband's disposition. Looks were of no importance to her; neither was age, for that matter, although her father had been kind enough to impart that the lady shared his age of twenty and seven. The only detail that truly mattered was temperament. Every evening when she knelt beside her pallet with the knowledge of the pending marriage, she prayed for a man with a gentle disposition, a man who was not comparable to her father.

Once again that brought her thoughts full circle. If her husband was disappointed in her appearance, he may not give one whit for her troubles. The years of her father's verbal abuse over a plain face came crashing down upon her. Slender hands unclasped to clutch her ragged skirts in a tense grip. She was a plain woman for a plain man, so that was what she needed her husband to be if she was to have any hope for a content future.

Bernard had also imparted the stipulation that she was to conceive an heir within a year. Her mind had barely dwelled on the apprehension of consummation on that night, her wedding night, because, when she realized all she had suffered at the hands of her father, the task of shedding her innocence seemed slight in comparison. She had not spent any time dwelling on a physical act she was certain she could easily withstand.

She had, however, dwelled on the delightful prospect of birthing a child. Reissa loved children; in fact, without any close friends her own age to share her time, because her father had scared them all away, she lived for children. Her days were spent teaching. It was her only love, her only passion. Teaching children was all she had to cling to in this miserable life.

Marriage would not change that. And even though she would become instantly rich through her wedded union, she would never give up teaching, not for anything or anyone. Bernard, sadistic bastard that he was, hated to see his daughter with a smile upon her face, yet he allowed her to continue the occupation she loved because it was their only source of income.

An advancing entourage of men on horseback caught her eye, ripping her from an unpleasant reverie. Her heart began to pound in nervous anticipation. They had been informed that Viktor's brother was to be their escort to Moorestone, so Reissa found herself searching for the leader of the party, for the man who would be her future in-law.

At such a distance, features were indistinguishable, yet her gaze was riveted upon the display of power topping the rise. Her mouth parted in surprise when she realized her escort was the lord of their village, the Lord of Moorestone. She was growing increasingly nervous. She wiped her clammy palms on her skirts and tried to maintain an air of polite welcome despite her desire to flee.

As if sensing her thoughts, Bernard clutched her elbow in a biting grip. "You will be wed, girl," he ordered harshly. "There is nothing you will do to displease me on this day."

Her eyes lowered to the ground, refusing to meet his probing gaze. She knew if he saw the instinctual rebellion of self-preservation within their gray depths, he would likely strike her before their escort rounded the curve of the dirt road.

"I do not have any wish to displease you, Father. I will wed Lord Colville," she assured in a quiet tone as the entourage rounded the bend. The young woman pasted a light smile on her lips in silent greeting as the party drew nearer. As Reissa was able to make out the features upon their faces, she noticed that one was not a man at all.

A woman accompanied her escort, an incredibly beautiful woman with stunning blue eyes and ebony curls secured in a gold coiffe. Reissa's already insecure nature took a sharp dive, causing her to feel positively homely in comparison. Her eyes would have meekly lowered to the ground in the face of such loveliness, but the man riding beside the lady distracted her.

A conscious effort had to be made not to gape in awe. He was nearly as stunning as the female. She saw that he was an amazing specimen of manhood despite the chestnut beard concealing the lower half of his face. His most outstanding feature was his eyes, black as a moonless night.

The couple led the party, so common sense told her the man was her escort, Lord Colville, and she knew their lord to be married, so it was likely that the lady was his wife. All horses were reined to a halt in front of their tiny shack as Reissa and Bernard strolled out to welcome them. The handsome man dismounted, then gave aid to the lady while the others remained dutifully seated upon their extravagantly armored horses.

The couple turned to them, and her gaze automatically shifted to the dirt. Reissa felt two pairs of noble eyes settle on her, clearly assessing her person. When the moments began to stretch in stark silence, she felt her cheeks begin to go up in flames of mortification. Before she could embrace her embarrassment, the perceptive noblewoman noticed her state and stepped forward to divert her discomfort.

"Miss Maitland, I presume?"

The woman's words demanded Reissa's attention. Her ash-gray eyes lifted to find the lady smiling warmly at her.

"I am Lady Moira Colville," she touched Reissa's forearm lightly in an obvious attempt to dispel her tension, then gestured toward the man at her side, "and may I present my husband, Lord Collin Colville, your escort and future brother-in-law."

Collin threw a frown at his wife for usurping his duties of introduction, but then he quickly recovered with a genuine grin for Reissa. He clasped her hand in a light grip and politely brushed his mouth over her knuckles.

"'Tis a pleasure, Miss Maitland."

She smiled shyly, and her voice was a mere whisper when she spoke. "'Twould please me for you to call me, Reissa, my lord," then she looked to Moira, "my lady."

"And you shall use my given name, my dear; do call me Moira."

Her husband was quick to follow with a genuine grin. "My brother's bride will not embrace formalities; do call me Collin."

When Reissa nodded in heartfelt agreement, the Colvilles turned to Bernard. As the trio shared civil introductions, Reissa was slightly surprised and thoroughly honored that the attractive couple had gone against propriety in greeting her first rather than her father.

As she observed their easy smiles and warm demeanor, she realized she liked them both immediately. They exuded an air of class, yet they were not haughty. They possessed a considerable fortune, but they were not condescending to the Maitlands' poverty. And they boasted looks beyond any Reissa had ever seen, but they were not conceited in the least. Was the Lord finally smiling down upon her?

Her gaze shifted to Bernard, and the warmth that had spread through her mind quickly dissipated. It was replaced with cool disdain. Her father had embraced a façade she knew to be untrue. His kind words and tight smiles were that of a man she had never been subjected to in all her life. The man she looked upon did not truly exist. His disposition was a front for their guests. Reissa had no doubt that his rough exterior would return the moment the clergy announced the legality of her marriage to a nobleman.

With a wave of his hand, Collin's squire was summoned forward. He presented two saddled mounts.

Reissa's nerves returned full force, and her apprehension must have been written clearly on her face, because Moira questioned softly, "Do you not ride, my dear?"

"I have never been graced with the privilege, my lady," she returned timidly.

"Tsk, tsk, Reissa, my dear," she corrected in the most charming way, then lightly gripped her elbow and drew her forward. "Your fears shall be alleviated momentarily. My loving husband will be delighted to personally escort you to Moorestone on his mount."

Startled eyes flew to Collin. Without missing a beat, he reassured her with a handsome upturn of his mouth. He mounted his horse with fluid grace. His squire aided Reissa's mount from the ground while Collin was sure to steady her once she was seated before him. He directed her to hook her knee over the pommel as ladies of nobility were taught to ride, then an arm lightly encircled her narrow waist to maintain her sense of safety.

With a knowledge of horseflesh that minimally surpassed his daughter's, Bernard hoisted himself onto the other horse. His posture was rigid, but he assured all that he could handle himself quite well.

Collin snapped the reins, and the animal beneath them began a mild trot.

As if sensing their guest's rising fears as they journeyed to Moorestone, Moira engaged Reissa in idle chitchat to distract her from the day's pending events. She prodded her into talking of the children she taught and the goings-on in the village. When they arrived after a short duration of time, she was thankful to her female escort for keeping her mind preoccupied.

It was midday when the entourage passed under Moorestone's portcullis. With the ceremony pending until dusk, there was not much time for the bride to be readied for her wedding. So, immediately after Reissa's feet touched the cobblestones in the bailey, she was ushered into the monstrous stone dwelling. She was awed by the massive Meeting Hall, but they didn't make any stops.

Moira escorted her to the upper chamber where the family members slept. Reissa was further struck with wonder when the lady escorted her into a suite of rooms that she was informed were to be her own during her stay at Moorestone. Several maids awaited them in the bedchamber with a steaming hot bath, an extravagant gown, and rich accessories, prepared to turn the miss into a fitting bride by sundown.

Chapter 7

Viktor had looked out upon the bailey from the window embrasure in his antechamber as the entourage arrived at Moorestone. As a man of little patience, he had held out extremely well in the prior days. He was desperate to know the woman who would be his wife. The temptation to visit the village had been great, simply to steal a glimpse of Reissa Maitland, but, with difficulty, he had resisted the urge. His days had been steeped with activity and his nights filled with women. He worked and played to exhaustion in an attempt to distract his mind from the inevitability of the wedding.

Finally, when his bride had accompanied Collin into the bailey, he gave in to the overwhelming need to set eyes upon her.

Now, he was seated before the cold fireplace in his bedchamber with a goblet of wine, damning his stepmother to everlasting hell. She had taken his future in her hands and crushed it like a mound of crumbling earth. Admittedly, Golly had not chosen a homely individual, but the wench had made certain he would not be attracted to his wife in any way.

Reissa Maitland was not hard on the eyes, but she was not easy on the eyes either; she was simply, there. Bluntly, she was a face that took up space. The distance to the ground from the upper level made it impossible to see her eyes, but he had no doubt they were as unremarkable as the rest of her.

Not only was she plain, she was also too skinny, too petite, and appeared far too fragile. The wench did not possess a single attribute he found desirable. However, she was not so unattractive that the thought of bedding her sickened him. The simple task of using his imagination in the dark would aid his duty. There was certainly no danger of him losing control of his passions when he carried out his husbandly duties in her bed, so he could not unintentionally shatter that delicate body with his excessive strength. Generally, he enjoyed feeling slightly battered and bruised from his exertions between the sheets, but unfortunately that would not be the case with that one.

As he sipped from the metal goblet, his thoughts took a mild turn. Viktor grudgingly accepted his fate, but he would not give in to being bound to another. Reissa Maitland would be his wife in the barest sense of the term. He would do his duty by implanting his seed in her body, he would visit her bed out of necessity, but he would find true pleasure elsewhere.

Women he desired were always within reach, and, more so, women who desired him were in abundance. To follow in the footsteps of many generations before him, he would not remain faithful to his unwanted, undesirable wife.

A head full of ebony locks shook negatively. He should've terminated his stepmother when the opportunity presented itself.

Chapter 8

Reissa stood before the closed chapel doors with her father hooked on her arm. Bernard was the study of a proud parent as he glowed at her side; however, his illuminating smile was in no way related to his daughter's wedding. It was related in every way to the fact that the man was about to inherit an impressive dowry for a daughter he considered less than worth it.

Miss Maitland pushed such heavy thoughts aside. She had more significant worries at the moment. Her heart beat in her throat, and she was nearly ill with nerves. As she waited for the double doors to open, a trembling palm smoothed over the rich material of her wedding gown.

The castle maids had diligently transformed her into the picture of a blushing bride. Unfortunately, they were unable to produce the beauty to correspond with her glorious attire.

She had been stripped of the linen rags she wore, and then her petite body had been scrubbed clean. Years of dirt from inadequate sponge baths behind a broken-down screen in their shack had been washed away, ridding her sun-kissed skin of a perpetual cloak of dust.

After she had been dried of the lavender-scented water, one of the maids draped her in a dressing gown while another began to detangle the knots from her strawberry blond tresses. Once the gold-handled comb was able to flow through her waist-length hair without obstacle, the locks were interwoven with silver ribbons and divided into several slim braids. Then they were arranged in a circular fashion atop the crown of her head. With that done, a modest silver crown was placed, fitting around the braids to perfection.

At last, the dressing gown was discarded for a white cotte, an undergarment with a tight bodice and a gauzy, flowing skirt, and linen drawers. The ribbons were laced up the back of the cotte, then a snug lavender underdress, with full-length fitted sleeves adorned with tippets, was donned. Finally, a sleeveless cotehardie of white, shot through with silver threading, was the last to be worn. Because the top layer was minus sleeves, the tippets of the lavender underdress were allowed to fall nearly to the floor, creating a generous sight of fabric that emphasized the female form.

Unfortunately, Reissa did not have the endowments to fill out the garments. Nevertheless, the gowns greatly improved her figure in comparison to the shapeless sacks she usually wore. A single accessory was the finishing touch to her appearance: a large opal pendant that rested between her slight bosoms.

When Reissa was finally able to take stock of her appearance in the large standing oval mirror in her antechamber, she was assaulted with an overwhelming feeling of disappointment. After watching numerous maids flit about her, busying themselves with the chore of improving her appearance, she expected to witness a miracle when she gazed in the mirror. But there was no miracle to be found. She saw within the same plain face, the same dull hair, and the same stick of a body.

There was no doubt that the garments were absolutely beautiful, but extravagance merely seemed to emphasize the fact that she was not worthy of them. She was still Reissa Maitland, a plain, poverty-ridden girl who did not deserve to wed a man of noble birth.

So, as she stood outside the chapel, clinging to her father's arm, she felt on the verge of tears. In no way would her husband be pleased with his bride; she knew it was as certain as she knew the sun would rise the next day.

At long last, two footmen opened the doors for the Maitlands, and the youth was met with the sight of her future husband. Reissa nearly fainted dead away. The only thing that saved her from collapsing to the cool stone flooring was her father's arm. Noticing her swaying figure, he clenched her elbow in a painful grip, causing her to cling to consciousness.

Her eyes fell to the floor. She shook off the fog and steadied herself, but her mind continued to spin in disbelief. How could the Lord be so cruel? That gorgeous creature at the end of the aisle could not be the man she was to marry. Not only did she feel unworthy of Colville because of her common birth, but now she was forced to suffer the added burden of feeling completely inadequate due to his unrivaled appearance.

Reissa had considered Collin to be one of the most attractive men she had ever set her eyes upon, but Viktor Colville was clearly the victor on that matter. He possessed a beauty resembling a woman's, with his long, sooty lashes and sharp cheekbones, but there was also an overpowering masculinity that cut through the beauty with his razor jaw and slashing brows announcing he was pure male. His overpowering presence conquered the whole of the room even though he stood in stark silence.

The woman summoned every ounce of will to lift her eyes. They settled on Viktor, and her heart stalled. Not only was he the most stunning man she had ever seen, he was also the most frightening. Dear Lord, his menace caused her trembling to intensify. Her nerves were replaced with genuine fear. She was horrifically mesmerized, like stumbling upon an accident scene. She desperately wanted to look away, yet she was unable to tear her eyes from him.

Viktor's dark vanity, his unruly black waves and glittering black eyes demanded attention without effort. His lips were compressed into a thin line, and his brow was creased as he observed her approach. She was given the impression that he was struggling to appear indifferent, yet his hard expression belied such feeling. Clearly, he was displeased, and Reissa knew she was the object of his foul mood.

His intimidating figure was cloaked in an ebony tunic and braies, overlaid with a matching mantle that was shot through with silver thread to match the details of her gown.

She was unaware that Bernard had inconspicuously dragged her down the aisle until, suddenly, Viktor's height was towering over her tiny figure. She jumped in her skin, losing ten years off her life when he abruptly stepped forward and dutifully offered the crook of his arm.

Without hesitating, Bernard handed his daughter off to a complete stranger. Tentatively, Reissa slid her hand under his arm and hooked her palm over his elbow, all while her eyes remained meekly on the chapel floor. As they stood before a vicar with graying hair in white robes, she could not help but be incredibly aware of the figure standing at her side. She felt like a child next to him, vulnerable and defenseless.

He stood over a foot taller than she. If Reissa dared to glance up, she would have to raise her head toward the ceiling just to gain sight of him, but she did not dare. She was too terrified. Feeling the strength in his forearm beneath her palm and the danger exuded by his mere presence, she could not help but be reminded of her father.

All hopes for protection were vanquished. In fact, additional fears were heaped onto the lot. Already she lived under Bernard's cloud of inhumanity, but now her husband brought thunder and lightning into the rain of her depressing reality. It seemed she was destined for abuse no matter the circumstances.

Reissa suffered the ceremony despite the frantic urge to escape the man she was being joined to for all eternity. Her voice was a wisp of a sound when she was prompted to speak, "I will," while Viktor's deep voice echoed throughout the cavernous chamber brimming with knights and nobles. And when it came time for the groom to kiss his bride, Reissa closed her eyes, raised her face, and braced herself for the unknown.

A pair of warm, dry lips barely touched the corner of her mouth, causing her to feel nothing in response. Then he hooked her arm around his and guided her to face their audience as the clergyman announced their union as husband and wife. The assembly of spectators thundered to their feet, and applause drummed in Reissa's ears.

It was done. She was legally Lady Viktor Colville. Her father had sealed her fate to a man she had yet to converse with, but she was already terrified of her own husband. As they walked down the aisle together, she found it impossible to conjure a smile for their onlookers. Her stare remained locked on the floor, avoiding eye contact with anyone and everyone.

Viktor silently led her into the Meeting Hall, where the servants were bustling about preparing the wedding feast. Unfamiliar with such extensive skirts, Reissa stumbled up the stairs to the dais. When her husband easily steadied her balance by curling an arm around her slender waist, startled eyes darted up to him in surprised gratitude. But the words died on her lips when she found him frowning down at her.

After years of abuse, the lady was conditioned to expect violence when such an expression was bestowed upon her, so she reacted with stealth, fleeing what she could not prevent. Her feet carried her quickly down the dais, and when she found there was an abrupt end to the platform, she was forced to halt. Frantically, she looked about for an escape, but when nothing presented itself, she was forced to calm her surging emotions. With a quiet dignity that concealed her consternation, she turned to face her judgment.

Her stalled breath rushed past her lips when she found Collin gesturing toward a chair he had pulled out for her. Viktor was already seated, paying her no heed. Once again, she was dumbstruck by his outrageous good looks, but when that receded, she was stunned by disbelief. He had thrown a dark expression her way, but he had no intention of raising his hand to her?

Then she noticed the guests filing into the hall and decided he must just be biding his time. Perhaps it was a matter of witnesses. He chose not to publicly strike her. She desperately hoped that was the case. It was difficult suffering the misery of a beating in private, but to suffer such before others was a humiliation one could never wash off. It stained the soul.

As Reissa seated herself in the chair Collin offered, she recalled the one and only instance when her father had physically abused her while eyes looked on. Bernard did not possess the courage to accost her when the audience consisted of adults, but he had no qualms about showing the finer points of his sadistic nature in front of children.

One beautiful sunny morning, he had found chalk dust on his finest pair of braies. The man had stormed into her schoolroom, placed his hands on her chest and heaved, launching her off the dais in front of the chalkboard. She broke her leg that day. She had been fortunate that it healed quite well, although the bone ached horribly when it rained or when it was exerted beyond endurance. On such days, the pain was so great that a limp was revealed. But the youth was able to conceal it when she thought to do so.

Reissa glanced up to take stock of the others seated around her, then returned her eyes to the chalice of wine at her elbow. Collin sat at the head of the table with his wife on his right. Golly was on Moira's right. Viktor was seated at Collin's left. Reissa had been placed beside her husband, and her father was on her opposite side. A handsome man and a plump woman, each with blond hair and amber eyes, were situated across from Bernard, and strangers occupied the remainder of the seats on the dais.

The young woman, seated between the men in her life, realized her appetite for the wedding feast was nonexistent. She felt as though she was suffocating, and when a trencher of food was dropped onto the table before her, she was overcome with a sudden bout of nausea. Reissa swallowed hard, then clutched the goblet and took a gulp of wine.

When she felt her husband staring at her from the corner of his eye, she realized her sudden movement had caught his attention. Quickly, she returned the goblet to the table, feeling as though she had been caught committing a mortal sin.

Viktor leaned toward her, and with a well-placed fist in front of his mouth to hide his dialogue, he said to her under his breath, "Drowning your woes in spirits will not save you from consummation, wench."

Reissa gasped, utterly shocked by the first statement the man had spoken directly to her. He was unconscionable. His words confirmed her fears. He was as tyrannical as her father. She had the urge to snap an angry retort, but apprehension stilled her tongue. She adhered to the meekness that was her sole protector from violent confrontations.

"I merely had need to wet a dry throat, my lord," Reissa explained softly without turning her eyes in his direction.

A monotonous grunt was his only reply, then he shifted focus to the conversation between Collin and the blond man she had heard being referred to as Alden. Having been dismissed from her husband's attention, she expelled the tense breath she had not realized she was holding.

While Reissa picked at the food in her trencher, she listened to the table conversation with half an ear. Although, when she heard Moira mention that the wedding celebration was to continue with three days of activities, she felt her heart plummet in dissatisfaction. She was already mentally and physically exhausted from the day's events, so the thought of another three days of endurance tugged at her meager will power.

In the morning, she had planned to spend the hours curled up in her massive canopy bed and simply feel sorry for herself. But her desires would go unfulfilled. She would have to present the dutiful wife by clinging to her husband's side. Against her will, her eyes rose to glance at Viktor.

Physically, she nearly jumped from her chair when she found him gazing at her expectantly. An icy shiver of unease rolled down her back even as she acknowledged the stunning gold flecks in those hard black eyes.

Then she gradually became aware that the others were also looking at her, telling the lady they were waiting for her to answer a question that had been put to her. Her palms instantly became clammy with moisture as she searched her memory. Oh, dear Lord, what had been said to her?! Her mind went blank. She had to confess to inattentiveness. She looked to Alden, who had been the one to ask a question of her.

"Begging your pardon, Sir Alden, what do you ask of me?" Her voice was a squeak.

"Would you fancy a riding lesson afore the hunt, my lady?"

She scanned the table to find that all were curiously awaiting her reply. At the mercy of so many inquisitive pairs of eyes, she could hardly say no.

"I graciously accept your offer." She made an attempt to smile but failed miserably.

The knight bestowed a polite grin upon her then looked at her father. "Would the lady's father care to join us?"

"Unfortunately, I must decline. Lady Golly and myself have a previous engagement to tour the grounds," he firmly refused the offer, then shot Golly a haughty grin.

Reissa would have snorted her disgust if she were not surrounded by a platform of lords and ladies. The villain had already taken to high ground, so to speak, and she was not married an hour.

She knew he considered her a waste of breath, but he was quite blind to the truth that she held him in the same regard. True, he was her father, but the man had successfully beaten the love from her heart years ago. The only feelings she harbored for him were an irrational sense of loyalty and pure resentment.

Many had finished their meals and began rising from the table to partake of the music struck by a band of minstrels in their designated corner. Several knights moved into a circle and began to dance to a lively tune.

Moira grabbed her husband's hand, and with a brilliant smile on her lovely face, tugged until he rose from his seat to join her in the celebration.

Alden turned to his sister. "Shall we dance, Edith?"

She nodded prettily and placed her hand in his.

Bernard and Golly hastened away as well.

Before Reissa knew it, the only occupants remaining at the table were herself and her husband. She couldn't help it; she took another hearty gulp of wine. During the meal, Viktor had imbibed two tankards of ale and was now working on his third.

"You are certainly a lady of few words," Viktor abruptly spoke with an intonation that told her he was displeased.

She clutched the chalice to distract herself from staring into those beautifully frightening eyes. "I only speak when 'tis necessary, my lord."

The man sighed heavily. "We are now husband and wife, Reissa; you will not use formality with me."

"Aye, my lord," she slipped, then immediately cringed. Her hand moved to the arm of the chair to push herself to her feet. But foreseeing her intention, Viktor dropped a large hand to her shoulder and exerted the slightest pressure, wordlessly telling her to remain seated.

"Calm yourself, wench, I will not throttle you for such a minor error," he assured, although he sounded thoroughly irritated with her behavior.

She nodded meekly. The mere sound of his deep voice caused fingers of fear to pull at her neck and shoulders.

Viktor shifted in his chair, turning to face her so he didn't have to strain his neck while he spoke. His hand remained glued to the tankard of ale on the table as his eyes drilled into her. "As my wife, I do not require more of you than your station outlines. We are both well aware that this marriage is a loveless arrangement. You will provide an heir, and in return, I will provide the protection of my home."

Aye, but who will protect me from you? she thought solemnly.

"I will not tolerate disobedience, disrespect, possessiveness, or jealousy," he continued his dictating tirade, causing her to feel smaller and smaller within her seat. "I expect promptness in my requests and a tight lip to my faithlessness. Do you understand?"

When she merely nodded in acceptance to his commands, he slammed his fist onto the tabletop. Reissa was so startled by the noise and his dark expression that several drops of red port sloshed from the goblet onto her white gown. He clutched her quivering chin firmly in his fingers and lifted her face, forcing her to meet his probing gaze. "And you will look me in the eye when I speak to you," he added angrily.

"Aye, my lord."

His lips thinned, and his brows creased in disapproval. "My given name is Viktor, wench. I will not bring this to your attention a third time."

Because he was holding her chin, she was unable to respond with a simple nod. "I shall not forget again," she said tentatively, "Viktor."

His hand fell away from her face, then he gulped from the tankard, emptying the last of the contents.

"If that is all, I believe I will retire."

He waved a dismissive hand without giving her his eyes. "Begone, but do not slumber. I will visit your bed, Reissa," he warned in a hard tone.

"Aye, Viktor." With that, she traveled to the staircase, just short of running to seek escape.

Chapter 9

Viktor tried to keep a tight rein on his raging temper as he watched his wife retreat to the staircase. He had entered into hell, not a marriage.

Upon finally seeing her close up in the chapel, he remained unimpressed by her exterior qualities. Certainly, the wedding gown was lovelier than the sack she arrived in, but the rich material did nothing to increase a plain face. The cut of the dress clung to her tiny figure; unfortunately, she did not possess a figure to display. The snug material only emphasized her childish body.

And at last, he was able to determine the color of her eyes. They were an average shade of gray that did not contrast well with her dull strawberry blond locks, leaving him to hope that there was something within her personality to covet.

But the wench was absolutely infuriating in her meekness, and her obvious fear of him only added to his irritation. She reacted to his every move as if he would upbraid, humiliate, or strike her. And if she had any opinions whatsoever, they remained unspoken. She was severely introverted, with a wall built high around herself to keep others from crossing into her world.

She was firmly resolute in her need to remain invisible, but at the same time, extremely susceptible to outside forces. Her guard was kept erected, yet she was delicate in heart and body. He found within himself the urge to shake some life into her, but he knew to do so would only elevate the wench's fright in relation to him.

All in all, Lady Reissa Colville inspired only one desire in him: avoidance. He had resigned himself to the task of consummating his marriage, but now he dreaded visiting a bed that was likely to be cold and uninviting.

He had to give Golly credit for her thoroughness of finding him a wife he was sure to dislike in every way, because she had certainly done a spectacular job in her vengeance. Her act of retribution had successfully ruined his life, so he also found himself overrun with thoughts of exacting his own vengeance. Never had he despised another person with such intensity.

Unable to help himself, Viktor had glanced at Golly during the ceremony. The triumphant smile on her face made his blood boil. And then, during supper, he could not help but notice she was watching them, savoring every awkward moment he and his wife shared. Golly had won their battle, and she knew Viktor knew it too.

A snap of fingers before his face yanked him from his pensive state. He looked up to see that everyone had returned to the table, and a fresh tankard of ale sat before him. The only people who had not returned were his wife and his father-in-law. Without thought, he sipped from the heavy mug, and when he set it down, Golly's smiling face came into view across the table.

"Smile, Viktor, you have just been wed," she chirped, taking immense pleasure in his foul mood.

"'Twould be best if you removed yourself from my presence, lady, afore I break your neck," he seethed, uncaring that they had an audience.

His anger only spurred her on. "Are you not pleased with your bride?" she wondered with feigned hurt, then a glorious grin turned up her lips.

"Perhaps 'twould be best if you retired," Collin suggested to their stepmother, also obviously growing irritated with her brazen smugness.

"'Tis early, my son," Golly returned, then picked up her goblet and downed the contents in one healthy swallow.

"Your bride may not be a beauty, but she is a darling," Moira chimed in. "I do believe I like her, Viktor."

"And I do believe you are mad, my lady." Colville's voice was grating in his annoyance.

"Be easy, little brother, I will not allow you to offend my wife," Collin protected, although his words held minor threat.

Moira ignored their slight interaction and continued her point. "Aye, she is timid, but she is kind."

"The wench is terrified of me, and I do not have any patience for her fear." He was blunt as a spoon.

There were several hearty laughs to that comment, but Moira's was the richest of all. "Perhaps because you are a terrifying individual, rather like her father, I imagine."

"And I do not have any patience for your analytical nature," Viktor mumbled, then drank from the tankard.

She sighed in defeat and rose from her seated position. She moved to stand beside her husband and placed a palm on his shoulder, giving it a tender squeeze. "Have a care with Reissa,

Viktor; she deserves naught but kindness." With that, her sky-blue eyes flicked over the people at the table. "I will retire now. Enjoy the evening."

Now Collin was the one to watch his wife take to the stone staircase; however, the eyes that followed her were steeped with admiration and hunger.

"I quite agree with my wife, little brother. I find naught disagreeable in your bride."

Viktor gave him a sharp look. "Perhaps you should marry the wench."

Collin chuckled. "I have zero interest in taking two wives. The one I have is quite enough to fill my hands." The hidden innuendo was not lost on his companions.

Hearing his words, Edith's cheeks went up in flames. Despite her size, she rose gracefully from her chair and excused herself.

"Viktor is unable to speak the same," Golly joyfully pointed out Reissa's shortcomings, once again bringing attention to the fact that she was the cause of her youngest stepson's misery.

He glared at her, although his mind was beginning to swim with unusually turbulent thoughts, and his limbs felt slightly sluggish.

"The hour grows late, and your duty as a husband grows near," Golly practically sang. She looked to Collin and Alden. "You boys must escort our groom to his marriage bed."

As Viktor's thoughts hazed over, he jumped up from his chair and began to stalk toward the lady. He acted on feeling alone, unsure what his mind planned once he had her within his grasp, but suddenly two sets of strong hands gripped his upper arms and held him back.

"Your anger will subside; leave her be," Alden ordered reasonably.

"The wench is in need of a sound lashing," he growled, although he made no attempt to break from his brother and friend's hold.

Golly audaciously approached. "Sweet dreams," she breathed happily then pressed her lips to Viktor's taut cheek. With that, she retired while a trio of eyes observed her departure.

Viktor made one attempt to break away and go after her, but Alden and Collin held strong. Once Golly had disappeared from sight, the man shook off his human restraints. Uncaring that his mind was already altered with drink, he downed the remaining ale in the tankard, threw a fiery glare at his male companions, then marched from the platform alone.

As he made the journey to his wife's bedchamber, his mind was swirling with such a fog that he was unable to string two intelligent thoughts together. He felt severely intoxicated, yet there was something odd about the buzz. Typically, he required numerous tankards to bring him to such a state of drunkenness, but he had only consumed four mugs below.

The math did not add up; although, at that point, addition only confused his already taxed brain. And on that occasion, the ale seemed to be affecting him in capricious ways. He was plagued with a sharpness in his movements, although his limbs felt heavy, causing him to exert more strength than was needed to accomplish a task. And his judgment was skewed, distorting his sense of reality like a man rapidly going insane.

Viktor was vaguely conscious of the task to consummate his marriage, but beyond that, he was rather unlike himself. He burst into Reissa's room, causing the tiny figure in bed to bolt upright in terror. A single candle burned on the bedside table, casting shadows upon her face as she desperately clutched the bed sheets to her chest.

A pair of black eyes located his wife's form within the massive canopy structure, which was a simple task because the bed curtains had already been drawn aside. His gaze scraped over her face, feeling nothing at all as he did so.

"Disrobe," he barked as he kicked the door firmly shut. Without hesitating, he began to remove his mantle. In his deteriorating state, he failed to see her eyes bulging in fear as she took in his gracelessness and glazed vision.

She rose from the feather mattress and placed her bare feet on the cool stone floor. "May I douse the candle, Viktor?" she inquired in an unsteady whisper.

"Aye." His eyes remained on the floor as he responded and continued to clumsily undress.

Reissa, seeing him lifting his tunic, revealing the tanned skin of his torso, quickly blew out the flickering flame, dropping a blanket of darkness onto the scene. She swiftly divested herself of the white cotte and drawers, then jumped back into bed, covering her naked, trembling body with the covers.

Viktor did not completely disrobe. His braies remained, clothing the bottom half of his lean figure. He merely opened the laces, which would allow him to free himself when the moment finally arose. Uncaring that his eyes had yet to adjust to the darkness, he stalked in the direction where he knew the bed to be situated. Suddenly his toe stubbed against a solid wooden post, and he cursed emphatically into the night.

As his mind spun out of control, he felt for the edge of the bed sheets. When he did so, he jerked them from Reissa's weak grip, causing her to let out a startled whimper. The sound barely registered in his ears as his hands circled her slender ankles and roughly pulled her feet toward the side of the mattress, forcefully changing her position so that she lay parallel to the headboard.

With the image of a beautiful woman trickling through the staccato of thoughts in his head, he freed himself from his braies. His hands clutched her thighs in a bruising grip and yanked her body toward the edge of the bed, causing her legs to dangle above the floor. He leaned forward and braced one palm on the mattress beside his bride's head, while the other crushed her hip, holding her in place. Then he took himself in his hand and with one violent movement, he thrust into her, causing a shriek of agony to echo throughout the room.

The sound bounced off his bubble of indifference, allowing him to initiate a rhythm that quickly mounted into a pounding of pleasure that gave him the release he sought. His hoarse gasps filled the air, mingling with Reissa's quiet tears.

When the convulsions finally eased, he backed away and wordlessly tied the laces of his braies. All thoughts and feelings failed him as he turned and meandered to the door. His lean figure stumbled back to his bedchamber. He tripped across the vast space, then fell into the yielding structure of his mattress and promptly passed out.

***

Reissa lay in the darkness, unable to staunch the flow of tears from her red-rimmed eyes. She had not moved an inch after her husband had completed his degrading duty more than an hour ago. She was paralyzed with pain and shame. The lady made no effort to cover her nudity, certain Viktor would not return.

Originally Reissa was convinced she could withstand the intimacies between a man and wife. She knew little of such things, but she decided it could not be worse than a beating. However, after meeting her husband, the modicum of courage she possessed failed her. As the hour grew late, she grew increasingly more nervous of consummation.

Viktor was a terrifyingly cold man, so she had expected a certain amount of unpleasantness, but in no way could she have prepared herself for the brutality she just suffered. She felt dehumanized, broken, and humiliated. Her thighs still throbbed from his grip, and her insides felt like they had been ripped apart.

As Viktor had used her body for his pleasure, she had curled her fists into the mattress beneath her, praying for a swift end to her pain. When the time stretched and he remained within her, the tears began to fall. Utter relief had flooded her mind and body when the man finally exited.

If that was all sex had to offer, she could certainly do without. In fact, the mere idea of enduring the act on another occasion brought on a whole new round of weeping. How would she ever be able to face her husband again? How would she ever be able to look him in the eye?

As she finally acknowledged the shivers racking her body, she wiped away the moisture from her face with the back of her hand. Gingerly, the lady sat up, her face contorting as she felt the smarting she could not ignore.

A match was struck and flared to life, then the candle on her bedside table was relit. A dark stain on the bed immediately distracted her gaze. She looked to the edge of the mattress and gasped in dismay when she took in the puddle of crimson. Thoughtlessly, her eyes shifted to her legs, and she was further shocked to see streaks of dried blood on her thighs.

Slowly Reissa rose from the bed and crossed to the washstand. She wet a rag and wiped the dark patches away. As she did so, she also noticed the bruises that were quickly growing visible under the pale skin of her thighs. A sob filtered through the room as she finished with the objectionable chore.

In a state of never-ending misery, she pulled on her discarded cotte and drawers and crawled onto the clean side of the mattress. It was hours before she fell into an exhausted slumber.

Chapter 10

Viktor was awakened from a deep sleep by the sound of a scream ringing in his ears. Positioned on his stomach, he hastily flipped onto his back and sat up, looking about for the cause of the noise. His gaze fixed on a female servant standing in the open doorway. Her mouth was agape, her voice ringing in horror. The confused man followed the direction of her stare until he spotted a pair of delicate feet at the foot of his bed. His eyes rose up slim legs, generous hips, and an ample bosom until they settled on a familiar face.

Golly lay next to him without a stitch of clothing on, but far more shocking was the fact that she was irrefutably dead. Her emerald eyes were covered with a milky-white film, staring without direction. And her skin was a ghastly white, with ugly bruising around her neck, shouting to anyone who looked upon her that her life had been successfully extinguished. She had been strangled to death.

"God's teeth!" he cursed under his breath.

Even though his heart was pounding in stunned disbelief, Viktor rose from his bed with a calm that belied his inner turmoil. As he stood there, overwhelmed by confusion, a group of curious onlookers began to gather in his bedchamber doorway.

His mind began to race, combing his memory for answers to this disturbing enigma. But when he tried to recall the events of the previous evening, his mind was incredibly hazy. He was given the barest impression of consummating his marriage, but there was nothing else at all.

Stunned eyes touched on the corpse, and he was struck with a startling thought. Had he murdered his own stepmother? If he had not, how else had she come to be in his bed? And why was she nude?

Viktor searched his soul, needing an answer to his questions. As he thought of the evening when he had placed his hand around her neck, he knew he could not be guilty. He had been unable to terminate her then. His morals and ethics had stopped him from doing so, which told him he could not have committed murder, even in his altered state of intoxication.

So, knowing he could not have done such a despicable crime, he was assaulted with another string of inquiries. Who killed Golly? Why was she stripped of clothing? And why was the guilty party so obviously framing him for her murder?

***

Reissa also awoke to the sound of screaming. The pain in her body slowed her intentions, but she managed to pull on a navy bed robe and a pair of slippers a servant had laid out for her the previous evening. With that done, she rushed into the airy corridor and hurried down the hall toward the assembly of people she saw crowding into someone's open doorway. Her petite figure aided the ease with which she slipped through the whispering masses, and she was brought up short to find her husband standing beside his bed in nothing but his braies.

Immediately, her eyes were drawn to his naked chest. The man possessed a pair of uncommonly broad shoulders that eased into the bulk of strong pectorals. His chest was covered in a thin mat of curly black hair that tapered down to a narrow washboard stomach. The sight of him unexpectedly impressed Reissa, but that budding feeling was plucked before it had the chance to grow into anything significant, because she noticed he was staring at his bed.

Her gaze shifted, and the floor nearly dropped out from under her.

If Reissa had been frightened of the man before, now she was positively petrified. Her husband had murdered his stepmother, and, judging by the number of people looking on at that moment, the whole castle was aware of his crime.

The lady stood frozen to the spot. As Viktor's wife, she knew it was her duty to aid him in any way she could, which meant helping to disperse the crowd, but her fears were crippling. She could not move, much less take on the burden of authority. It was also her duty to stand by his side, giving unquestionable support, but how could she defend a man who had clearly committed the ultimate of crimes?

She was torn and scared, and… her gaze returned to Viktor. He appeared quite unaware of the people looking on. It was either that, or he simply had no care for them. However, seeing that he was not going to act any time in the near future, she summoned every ounce of will power to turn and speak.

"Everyone begone! 'Tis not your affair!" Her shout rose over the din of shocked voices.

Many pairs of eyes jumped to her, including her husband's, who stood at her back. When the servants saw the fierce expression she wore, they uniformly began to disperse.

Reissa watched them go in silence until a hand on her shoulder caused her to jump in terror. She swung around and instinctually began to retreat from her husband's huge, intimidating form, but his firm grip halted her.

"Your assistance is appreciated, Reissa," he remarked in that deep voice that seemed to reach inside and squeeze her stomach every time he spoke.

"'Tis my duty, my lord," she gasped, then quickly corrected herself, "Viktor." Against her will, her eyes strayed to the body in the bed. Her skin began to crawl with renewed consternation.

Observing his wife's open expression, his hand fell away to replace gratitude with impatience. "Calm yourself, I am innocent of this crime, lady."

"My opinion is not of any consequence, Viktor," she muttered. After his mistreatment of her the previous evening, trusting him was an impossibility. She was unable to believe his claim.

"The matter will be dealt with when we go below to break our fast." He tossed her way as he turned to glance at his stepmother.

Suddenly Collin and Moira raced through the open doorway and ground to a halt. Their clothing was mussed as if they had haphazardly pulled the garments on when they heard the scream.

"So 'tis true," Collin breathed incredulously. "A passerby informed us, but I did not believe."

"Golly has been murdered," Moira stated the obvious, too shocked to say more.

"I awoke to find the lady beside me, in that lifeless state," Viktor explained to his brother.

"Who is responsible for this atrocity?" Collin wondered, unable to tear his eyes from the victim.

"Unfortunately, I must plead ignorance; however, I am anxious to learn the identity of the guilty party. Clearly this person has a grievance with me," Viktor growled while Moira padded over to the bed and draped a blanket over the deceased's nude figure.

"We must have her removed," Moira spoke rationally and then departed to collect servants to deal with the body, leaving Reissa alone with the brothers.

As if feeling her sudden vulnerability due to Moira's exit, Viktor glanced at his wife and issued a quiet command. "Prepare yourself to greet the day; the morning meal will be served shortly." With that, he dismissed her from thought.

Reissa was thankful for the reprieve. She nearly bolted from the room. Once she was safely within the confines of her chamber, a drawn-out sigh of relief steeped the large space. Her knees felt weak, and her hands were trembling uncontrollably. She was overcome with the need to cry, but a soft knock upon the door interrupted her emotions.

She opened it to find a maid looking to aid her toilet. As Reissa wordlessly moved to seat herself at her vanity, she became aware that the bloodied sheet from the bed had been removed and replaced with clean linens. That told her the servants had displayed the sheet, the truth of her abolished maidenhead, as was tradition the day after a wedding ceremony.

Her cheeks fused with embarrassed color, and it had not completely receded by the time she was ready to descend to the Meeting Hall. Her straight strawberry blond locks had been tucked into a gold coiffe adorned in emeralds, and her tiny form was attired in another white cotte and a relatively plain overdress of matching emerald that hugged her slim curves.

When she entered the hall, all the trestle tables were filled to brimming, including the one on the dais. Clearly everyone was anxious to hear what their lord and his brother had to say about the murder of their stepmother. She crossed the cavernous room and climbed the miniature staircase to the platform. Seeing that the seat next to her husband remained empty, she cautiously approached.

Collin, who was the first male to notice her arrival, swiftly rose from his seat and graciously pulled out her chair. She nodded her thanks, then ever so gently sat down on the hard wooden structure. A wince of pain flitted across her face, but she was quick to recover a hollow expression of contentment. Catching her grimace from the corner of his eye, Viktor glanced at his wife but said nothing.

"Now that everyone has arrived, I believe 'twould be best if you said something, little brother," Collin suggested after settling into his chair.

Viktor's lips turned down in a frown, yet he grudgingly nodded in agreement. He stood and circled the table, standing beside Moira to face the room full of occupants.

"Lords, ladies!" he called, gaining the attention of every last person in the room. Instantly, a hush fell. "Due to the dawn's tragic events, I feel compelled to profess my innocence to all." His brow creased, creating a dangerous display. "The unfortunate truth is that Lady Golly has been slain. As I am guiltless, 'tis clear there is a murderer and a traitor among us who intended to guilt me with this crime.

"This person has dishonored and betrayed my trust. I am deeply angry, but forgiveness may be obtained if the guilty party collects the courage to step forward and is willing to confess his or her offense." Silently, observant eyes scanned the crowd while the knights and men-at-arms looked around amongst themselves, waiting for someone to stand and admit to guilt.

Tense moments stretched, but no one announced themselves, prompting Viktor to continue, "This has not concluded the issue. The king will be notified, and Lord Collin and myself shall personally follow up this matter until the villain has been identified." His expression grew terrifying. "You have been warned," he spoke to the anonymous murderer, then marched around the table and gracefully folded into his chair.

Reissa glanced at her father, the object of blame for her marriage to a murderer. She was brought up short to find him staring at his trencher as if in a preoccupied trance. When his gray eyes made no move to lift to reality, she was given cause to wonder what he was thinking of.

With the speech concluded, the hush of talk continued along with the meal.

Alden was the first to speak. "Lady Reissa, due to the morning's circumstances, I shall be most understanding if you wish to forgo the riding lesson."

Reissa tore her gaze from Bernard and sent the knight a kind look, ever so grateful for rescinding his offer. Her body was far too battered and bruised to subject herself to the torment of being jostled on a horse, so she jumped at the opportunity to back out.

"May I have your word that we shall reschedule at a later date?" she inquired quietly.

"Aye, you have it, my lady." He smiled.

"'Til then." She nodded politely, then turned her attention to the trencher of bread and cheese that had been placed in front of her, but her appetite was nowhere to be found. She was ignorant of the scowl on her face until her husband's breath fanned against her ear.

"Eat, Reissa, you are far too thin. A bag of bones fails to ignite my desires," he drawled with harsh honesty.

The words were out before she could think twice. "I shall be certain to remain a bag of bones then." Her hand flew to her mouth to stifle a gasp, instantly contrite. She stared at Viktor, wide-eyed, fearing his reaction.

The man had strangled his stepmother to death. He was an unconscionable brute. So, she was most perplexed when the corners of his mouth twitched with something akin to humor. Had he no intention of taking her to task for her insubordination?

"My wife has spirit after all," Viktor remarked quietly to himself. However, Reissa heard it, causing her confusion to rise.

The couple was quiet for a moment, listening to the conversation around them. All were cautiously stepping around the subject of Golly. Her empty chair was a constant reminder of her untimely demise.

The air was charged with tension even as Moira and Edith discussed the interior design of babe Colville's nursery and Collin and Alden spoke of horseflesh. Bernard was ensconced in dialogue with one of the knights over sword techniques, leaving the recently wedded couple to their own thoughts.

Suddenly, Viktor broke the silence between them. "We shall have a private word following the meal, Reissa," he commanded in a tone that brooked no argument.

Battling her husband was the furthest thing from her mind. His order had inspired such fear that she could not find her voice, much less summon the will for combat. She was certain the man intended to punish her for her recent outspoken remark, and anticipating a beating from him was like facing a firing squad.

She could barely withstand her father's abuse, but her husband's build was more impressive. As she stared at him in fearful silence, she could not help but wonder if she would survive the pummeling of those stone fists. And as he observed her cowering form, she saw his hardened expression rapidly darkening with fury. He was about to make a raging retort when—

"Viktor, we must address the issue of Golly." Collin broke into their troubling reverie, causing Reissa to fall in love with the man for redirecting her husband's focus. "We have planned three days of celebration for your wedding, but now a funeral must take place. How do you propose we manage the affair?"

"We shall carry out the celebration as planned. I do not have any desire to disappoint the guests, then we shall travel to the coast to commit the lady's body to sea. Following the burial, my wife and I will return to Colville Manor. I must see to my home in the wake of father's absence. Alden and Edith shall accompany us, certainly, but I would like to extend an invitation to Moira and yourself to be our guests until the birth of your child."

Collin's brow rose with heartfelt surprise, then he looked to his wife for confirmation. When she returned a genuine smile and a nod as her eyes touched on Reissa, Collin clapped Viktor on the back and said, "We would be delighted, little brother!"

With the meal concluding, several people rose from their seats and departed the keep.

"If you will excuse us, my wife and I shall prepare for the hunt," Viktor explained as he gripped Reissa's elbow and drew her to her feet. He guided her from the platform and across the hall.

As they mounted the cold stone staircase, Reissa felt her legs grow heavy with fear. The lady lifted her skirts with one quaking hand, because in her terror, she clung to the one person she feared most. Yes, she feared this man more than her father. At least with Bernard she knew what to expect; with Viktor, she faced the unknown.

Knowing she could not go against her husband's order, she put up little resistance. Nevertheless, her instincts turned on, causing her to move in a snail-like fashion. Doing so contrasted with Viktor's swift, long-legged gait, forcing him to drag her to the upper level.

He opened the door to her antechamber and practically shoved her inside. The door was slammed with a vengeance, and Reissa cringed as she turned to face her death sentence.

Her insides quivered, eyes on the floor. Viktor's footsteps were heavy as he angrily approached and gripped her chin uncomfortably between his thumb and forefinger. He raised her head, forcing her to look up into black eyes that were shooting sparks.

"We must address the issue of your constant terror, Reissa," he gritted. "I will not tolerate it."

"Please, Viktor," her bottom lip quaked, "hasten with your punishment and be done."

He stared at her for several tense moments before understanding dawned. His hand fell away, and accusation entered his expression. "You foresee a beating?" he demanded.

"Is that not how a husband chastises his wife?" she asked softly.

He waved his hand in disgust. "You have done nothing to warrant such a punishment, lady." Coal-black orbs returned to her as an idea occurred. "Is that the reason for your irrational fear of me? You expect I will raise my hand to you?"

"A wife is meant to obey her husband, and he may punish her as he sees fit," she said timidly without really supplying an answer to his question.

"You must discard this fear you possess in my presence, Reissa. I cannot abide such foolishness every time I look upon you crossly," he grated, presenting the frightening image of his words.

She nodded unconvincingly. His eyes narrowed, then abruptly he stepped toward her, testing the sincerity of her gesture. When she instinctually retreated in horror, he threw his hands up in furious defeat and stormed from the room.

Chapter 11

Everyone congregated near the stables in preparation for the fox hunt. Reissa, dreading the prospect of pulling her aching body onto a horse, dragged her feet as the sun poured down onto the bailey. It was unusually warm for a day in late November, yet all the leaves had already fallen off the trees, and it was clear that winter was swiftly rolling in.

The lady wore a thin velvet cloak of charcoal gray over her maroon overdress. Sir Alden was hooked on her arm. She had come across him waiting in the keep, and he had escorted her outside. He deposited her at her husband's side, then politely moved off to aid his sister's mount.

Viktor spared her the briefest of glances and continued readying his horse. Reissa stood back, watching his figure as he secured the saddle and reins. He was without armor, allowing his coffee-colored tunic to reveal the muscles bulging and flexing beneath the material.

Her eyes appraised the sight. As they traveled over his broad back, they halted upon firm buttocks, then moved down to long, strong legs. She felt her stomach tighten with an odd feeling of warmth.

Abruptly, he turned around, and the blood rushed to her cheeks as she acknowledged the fact that she had been ogling a man she was deeply afraid of. She fought for calm as he grabbed the reins of a chestnut mare grazing nearby and led the animal to Reissa.

"This is Hornet. She is extremely gentle. You have nothing to fear from her." The inflection in his tone told her he recalled their earlier interaction, and his ire had yet to cool. But he stood patiently, waiting to aid her mount.

Reissa lifted her skirts enough to tuck her toes into the stirrups despite the pain that shot down the inside of her leg. She gritted her teeth in an attempt to block out the throbbing in her body, then clutched the saddle tightly in both hands. She felt those dark eyes taking stock of her posture. Her breath caught when he reached down to move her booted foot onto the ball at the top of her arch. As he did so, he thoughtlessly placed a palm on her bruised thigh for leverage.

A gasp of pain escaped her mouth against her will, and she tore her foot from the stirrup. She averted her face to hide a grimace as a palm automatically cradled the smarting flesh, attempting to soothe her misery.

Her husband grunted unhappily. "What are you about, woman?"

"A moment, Viktor, please," she muttered while her face remained turned away.

He eyed her suspiciously. Ignoring her request, he clutched her slender wrist, denying her inevitable withdrawal from his presence. Curious eyes shifted to her torso, then he reached down from his extensive height and pressed his fingers to her thigh through voluminous skirts.

When he heard a sharply indrawn breath and felt a tiny hand clutch his tunic, his head rose to survey their surroundings. With the mare concealing them from one side, he turned his broad back to the crowd milling about, effectively shielding Haley from any curious onlookers. An arm slid around her waist to balance her figure, then his free hand hooked behind her knee and raised her leg in one fluid movement. Without hesitation, he whipped up her skirts, revealing the pale skin of her thigh to his probing gaze.

Reissa bowed her head in abject humiliation as he took in the ugly purple patches marking her flesh. Would the man forever treat her so brashly? But then she heard his heavy sigh, and her eyes curiously rose to his handsome face, wondering at his unexpected response.

As he stared at her, his expression was filled with self-loathing. "I am the cause of this, am I not?"

Her uneasy stare supplied answer enough.

He muttered an oath that burned her ears. He dropped her skirts and turned away, showing her his back.

"Return to your chambers, Reissa. I will make your excuses," he threw at her over his shoulder, his voice curt.

The lady did not hesitate to comply.

***

As Viktor's recreational horse pounded across open fields and entered the forest, searching for the prize of their sport, the sight of an abused thigh distracted his thoughts. He awoke that morning to find his stepmother dead in his bed, yet in that moment, he could think of nothing other than the comparably meager fact that he had hurt his delicate young wife.

Initially he tried to pass the blame onto the fact that he had not been himself, but guilt still flooded his being. Yes, it was true Reissa was in no way the wife he would have chosen for himself. He cared nothing for her, felt nothing in the form of attraction, and resented the whole of the marriage, but never did that timid female deserve to be treated in such a brutal fashion.

Trust needed to be built in the union between a husband and wife, but his behavior assured that Lady Colville would never be able to trust in him. She had been frightened of him right from the start, but his cruel use of her body could have only increased her terror. Her feet would constantly be walking upon eggshells because she was sure to dread his next visit to her bed.

As his mind continued to dwell on their situation, his mood grew increasingly foul. He was furious that he felt such guilt. She was his wife, and he had the right to treat her in any fashion he chose, yet he could not dismiss the self-resentment, no matter how hard he tried.

By the time they returned for the midday meal, he was a mass of pent-up rage in his self-disgust. He snapped at anyone who dared to speak to him, including his brother. He effectively drove everyone away, leaving him to his churlish thoughts.

Chapter 12

"Has the ache in your head abated, Reissa?" Moira asked after the lady had been seated at the trestle table for supper.

She glanced at her husband's sharp profile, realizing he had pleaded a headache to dismiss her from the day's events.

Picking up on his ruse, she nodded lightly. "Aye, thank you."

"You should have sought me out, my lady. I have a remedy for such an ailment," Edith commented sweetly.

"My sister is a medical marvel," Alden remarked with obvious pride. "I do not know any other who has such an intelligence for herbs."

"Lady Edith will attend to me during the birth of our child," Moira added. "And when you birth your first child, she shall attend to you as well."

Reissa shifted in her chair, feeling physical and mental discomfort. The reference to a babe was an unfortunate reminder of conception, and the pain in her body spoke of the intent to avoid conception at all costs. Yes, the result would be a miracle, but the events leading up to it would be abhorrent.

"I shall be grateful to be in such capable hands," Reissa returned, her words genuine.

Edith smiled in gratitude.

"Golly spoke of your teaching responsibilities in the village. Do you miss the children?" Collin questioned with sincere curiosity.

"Aye, I miss them terribly. I love children. I would love many of my own," she admitted honestly.

"Perhaps Viktor will allow you to continue teaching after you have returned to Appleta," Moira suggested, looking at the man who was quietly listening to the conversation.

Reissa peered at her husband with hope in her eyes, but the negative shake of his head was instantaneous, giving the idea no consideration whatsoever.

"She will not."

Her face fell, her hopes dashed like waves crashing upon a rocky cliff.

"I will not have a wife doing menial labor in the village. 'Tis an insult to myself and our King."

"Viktor, clearly 'twould please the lady. Perhaps you might reconsider," Moira fought for her.

"You forget your place, lady," he charged.

"And you forget the ability of kindness," she dared.

His balled fist slammed onto the table, causing the contents to rattle and the room to quiet, gaining the attention of all. His mouth opened to upbraid the lady, but Reissa quickly spoke up.

"I appreciate your lobbying, Moira, but this issue is not worth removing yourself from my husband's good graces. I shall accept his decision forthwith." Even as she said it, she felt the tears stinging her throat, threatening her calm composure. She fought their appearance; unfortunately, she failed miserably.

When the moisture began to fill her eyes, she looked at her lap and whispered, "Please excuse me." With that, she promptly rose from her seat and hurried from the hall, despising her husband beyond comprehension.

Reissa threw herself onto her bed and wept.

***

Moira threw a glare at her brother-in-law and said, "You are a fantastically cruel man, Viktor."

"If I desired your opinion, I would request it," he returned in irritation as his eyes wandered to the empty staircase. His wife had fled with tears in her eyes. And those tears were a result of his cold heart.

With a disdainful expression on her beautiful face, Moira wordlessly rose from her seat and followed Reissa from the room.

"Do not be swayed by her tears, my lord. My daughter is faint of heart, but she will abide your decision," Bernard spoke with the arrogance of knowledge.

Viktor spared him an indifferent glance but said nothing. He had barely shared two words with his father-in-law since they met, yet there was something about the man he simply did not like. He didn't know why; he just felt an unexplainable aversion to him.

***

A knock sounded softly on Reissa's bedchamber door, then Moira entered without being beckoned in. She crossed to the canopy structure and perched on the edge of the mattress. When Haley's tears continued, she gently stroked her strawberry blond locks in an attempt to soothe her sorrow.

"You despise him now, but he remains a stranger to you, my dear. I have known Viktor for greater than two years, and I admit, it was some time before I witnessed the good in him. He is a good man."

Reissa's head popped up, her face contorted in awesome disbelief. "A good man?" she repeated. "He is cold, harsh, and unfeeling."

"Aye, but he is also loyal, strong, and commands respect," she defended despite the fact that she was extremely cross with him.

"You speak of loyalty, yet he ordered me to turn a blind eye to his faithlessness." She breathed with an acrid taste in her mouth.

"'Tis common knowledge that husbands stray from the marriage bed, but when I speak of loyalty, I refer to the assurance that he would give his life in defense of his loved ones."

"I am not a loved one," Reissa said with absolute certainty as she wiped the moisture from her face with the back of her hand.

"You are his wife, and that status is held above any other."

Reissa was thoughtful for a moment, then she asked, "Is Collin faithful to you?"

"Our marriage is of a rare breed; 'tis a marriage of love. If Collin were to bed another woman, 'twould destroy me," she announced baldly. The mere thought of it caused her face to set in lines of pain.

"I will never know such a marriage," Reissa said sadly.

"That 'tis not a certainty, my dear. Once you have surpassed your fear of Viktor, you may find yourself falling victim to love for him," Moira claimed with a ghost of a smile.

"I shall never surpass my fear of the man. He is a true terror." Reissa was racked with a sudden chill as she thought of the possibility of his visiting her bed that evening.

"I was also afeared of the man when we first met, but not any longer. He is not as cruel as he seems."

"As the victim of his brutality, I assure you, Moira, he is," she muttered softly.

Misunderstanding her remark, Moira said, "Do not give up your desire to continue teaching, Reissa. His word is not law. In time, he may give in."

"I shall wither and die if I am denied teaching, Moira." Her tears returned to wet her copper-toned cheeks.

"Do not give up your hope. I am confident you will teach again."

"I must pray for your optimism, for I am confident he will remain firm in his stand to deny my wish." Reissa thoughtlessly removed her coiffe, causing her strawberry blond locks to tumble around her slender waist.

"I will not allow this topic to rest," Moira stated with a stone resolve.

"I cannot allow you to take on my battle. 'Tis my own. And I shall fight it," Reissa declared while praying for the strength to do so.

"I shall give you my full support then." She smiled.

"You are too kind."

Moira squeezed Reissa's hand, then stood and crossed to the door.

"Moira?"

She turned back with an inquisitive expression.

"Is—is there any doubt in your mind that my husband did not s-strangle his stepmother?" Reissa tentatively asked.

The lady stared at her for several long moments, then smiled. "Rest yourself." With that, she departed.

Chapter 13

It was near dawn when Reissa fell into an exhausted sleep. She lay in bed for hours, her posture rigid with tension as she waited for her husband to visit and carry out his duty, but he failed to appear. When she was certain he had no intention to bed her that evening, she was unexpectedly stung with a new layer of tension.

Her mind raced with questions, and it was the lack of answers that prompted her to toss and turn until the sun began to rise. *Why* had he failed to arrive? Had he been so repulsed by her that he could not dredge up the will to bed her a second time? Or had he chosen to pass the night in another woman's bed?

She told herself to be thankful that he did not desire her, be thankful he would rather take his pleasure in another woman's bed, but she was perplexed to find herself extremely disheartened by the possibility of either. Unbidden, a picture of him giving some wench a tumble slithered into her thoughts, and a feeling resembling jealousy shook her to the core.

She could not understand it. She had no desire for him to visit his brutality upon her, but the idea of him satiating himself with another caused an unsettling feeling in the pit of her stomach. Finally, she decided it must be her sense of pride that caused her to feel so strongly. She knew she was no beauty, but she still possessed dignity, and his sinful behavior struck at the heart of her being.

When she came to that resolution, at last she began to doze, but suddenly she was ripped from her fatigue when an outrageous insight bashed her over the head with as much force as a physical blow. Could it be possible he had stayed away because he had seen the bruises and knew bedding her would be too painful? Was he exhibiting an ounce of compassion? Her head automatically shook from side to side. Certainly not, the man was incapable of compassion. He was a cold-hearted brute. The idea was ludicrous.

The only reason why he had excused her from the hunt was because he had no desire to suffer her presence. Clearly, he had used her bruises as an excuse, but she knew it was a self-serving act. He found her unattractive, timid, and he was continually angry with her. He made no pretense of caring for her, so at least she had to give him credit for being honest.

When her eyes opened to greet the morning, she was stunned to find the sun high in the sky. The morning meal had long since passed, and her slumber had gone on undisturbed. Reissa could not recall the last time she had been allowed to sleep beyond the dawn. The lady had been chastised early on in life if she slept too late. Bernard would wake her with a swift kick to her hip, quickly conditioning her into rising at dawn.

On that day, she had slept well into the morning, but her father made no appearance. She was ever so grateful for that, yet she was annoyed with herself for staying abed longer than was acceptable on a day of celebration for her own wedding. Immediately, she rang for a maid to aid her toilet.

As she was helped into a gold underdress with floor-length tippets and a navy sleeveless overdress with gold satin trim, she heard the clanging of swords out in the bailey. The noise told her the day's activities had already begun. Her long tresses were swept up into a plain gold coiffe, and the finishing touch was a navy cloak of crushed velvet.

Reissa hurried out into the bailey and weaved through the crowd in time to see her husband and her brother-in-law facing off at the center of the circle. Their heavy swords were held easily within strong, callused hands. She was brought up short when her heart jumped into her throat, unsettled by the sight. She could do nothing but watch in silence as Viktor and Collin began an interaction that could result in a loss of life. She believed neither brother would intentionally cause a fatal wound, but mistakes could be made, and accidents happened. She felt short of breath. Reissa's hands clutched her navy skirts so tightly that her knuckles turned white.

Both men were encased in their armor, but as Viktor began the combat by quickly claiming the offense, she felt the blood drain from her face. Glare from the sun glinted off the metal of their blades. A ringing echo of their battle bounced off the curtain walls and stone of the castle. The crowd was deathly silent. They were so engrossed in the sight of their lord and his brother striving for blood that no one noticed her entrance.

Even as Reissa feared for both men, she was entranced by the awesome display of power and skill. It was obvious by their graceful footwork and remarkable endurance that both were accomplished in the art of war. The offense and defense passed back and forth for nearly an hour.

Finally, Viktor noticed a gap in Collin's stance and thrust his sword into the shoulder joint of his armor. The elder brother gasped, and his sword dropped to the ground. The horrifying sight of crimson glimmered on Viktor's blade. Instantly Viktor and Moira moved to help Collin with his armor. When they determined the wound was just a scratch, the crowd broke into an uproarious applause.

Reissa was still too engrossed in feeling to slap the palms of her hands together, so she simply stood there, making a desperate attempt to regain her breath.

"Lady Reissa, are you ill?" Edith's soft voice broke through her haze of nerves.

"Pardon me?"

"You are rather pale; are you feeling unwell?"

The lady tried to conjure up a smile for her spectator, but it came off as an obscure thinning of her lips. "I am well, merely fatigued."

"You have only just arrived, my lady, have you not?" Alden wondered, standing at his sister's side.

"I witnessed the battle," she returned.

"Your first?" the knight questioned.

"Aye."

His alluring amber eyes lit with understanding. "I believe I know the cause of her pallor, Edith," he explained. "One must grow accustomed to the entertainment of swordplay. Our new Lady Colville is awed, and perhaps slightly taken aback. Am I correct?"

Reissa nodded, embarrassed by the sharp wit that easily dissected her feelings.

Over Edith's shoulder, her eyes were distracted by the tall dark figure approaching. As was typical, she was overcome with the urge to flee.

She gave in to that urge.

"Please excuse me," she mumbled, then turned and rushed into the castle. During her journey up the back stairwell, she nearly ran headlong into her father's unyielding figure on the upstairs landing. Instantly, her insides cringed with the knowledge that they were incredibly alone.

"Ah, my daughter," he purred with transparent affection. "In the midst of escape, are you?" His question was rhetorical, insulting her with sarcasm she knew all too well.

He was in a tempestuous mood, and that did not bode well for her. It would be best if she withdrew as swiftly as possible. Yes, she had been in the midst of escape from her husband's presence, but now, as she was assaulted with the presence of her father, she felt the irrational need to seek out and take shelter behind her husband's broad back.

"I must return to the celebration, Father," she said breathlessly, then spun on her heel and rushed across the landing.

"I have not dismissed you, Reissa," his voice was dangerously low.

A shiver of fear rolled down her back as she slowly turned to face him. "What is it, Father?"

Gray eyes, the mirror image of her own, raked over her body as if he knew what lay beneath her clothing, the abuse of consummation. "How goes the marriage?"

Had he witnessed her husband lifting her skirts in the bailey the previous day? Or was he simply making an educated guess? Upon meeting her husband, it was not much of a stretch to assume he was as frightening in bed as out.

"You ask a question you already know the answer to," she said through gritted teeth, resenting him with every word she spoke.

"How so?" he quizzed, crossing his arms over his chest.

"You have sold your only daughter into the hands of a brute." Reissa was unable to halt her rising anger.

"I have married you to a noble, which is far better than you deserve," he growled softly.

After days of constant terror, her thread of patience finally snapped. She could suffer no more. "You have married me to a murderer, Father! How could you?!" she hissed under her breath.

"You ungrateful little bitch!" he seethed.

Reissa saw it coming, almost as if in slow motion, but she was unable to escape it. His open palm cracked against her cheekbone. The rough skin of his hand scraped her flesh raw, as a ripple effect of pain throbbed throughout her face. Instantly, her left eye began to water as she tried to steady her body from the force of the blow.

She caught herself, supporting her slight weight by pressing a hand to the cold stone wall nearby. As she glanced over her left shoulder, she realized she was fortunate she had not tumbled down the staircase at her back.

"I am kind enough to give your hand to a wealthy noble, and you dare to chastise me, girl!" he raged quietly, mindful that a raised voice would echo into the hall below. His hand rose, preparing to strike her a second time.

"Reissa!" Viktor's voice called to her from the Meeting Hall. He must have seen her entering the castle and followed. The inflection in his tone told her he was also irritated with her.

Upon hearing his call, Bernard stopped dead. He threw a glare at his daughter, silently blaming her for her husband's untimely intervention. Then he whirled around and fled down the hallway.

A second pair of footsteps sounded, moving toward her from below. Despite the smarting in her cheek, Reissa reacted quickly. Recalling her clumsiness as she ascended the dais steps on her wedding day, she knelt down and rubbed her cloak and skirts into the dirt on the landing, needing an excuse for the red patch on her cheek.

Never would she admit to anyone that her father used her as his own personal punching bag. The fact shamed and humiliated her. To preserve what little dignity she possessed, it would remain her secret until death.

The lady was just rising to her feet when Viktor appeared on the staircase.

"You are lax in your duties to provide your presence for our wedding celebration, Reissa," he accused as he climbed onto the landing. Those dark eyes took in her disheveled appearance, and his brow furrowed. She stood in the shadows.

He clutched her wrist and pulled her into a shaft of light streaming through a high window embrasure. His gaze moved over her soiled skirts and then shifted to her face. Wordlessly, his hand lifted.

He firmly pushed up her chin and turned her head with the crook of his index finger so he could get a better look at her cheek. His hand opened to cradle her chin, allowing him to look into her eyes for answers, even as he demanded, "What is the meaning of this, woman?"

Extremely intimidated by his probing gaze, she could do nothing but stare back for several moments. At last, his voice rose, scaring her from her silence. "Reissa?!"

"'Tis a result of my clumsiness, Viktor. I caught my toe on the hem of my skirts," she lied.

His lips thinned as he compressed them together in thought. Quietly, he gazed at her for many long moments, as if pondering the truth of her words, but then—"Best take greater care, Wife," he ordered in a monotone.

Ever so slowly, she let out a sigh of relief. Reissa knew she was a terrible liar, but she was fortunate in that respect, because he believed her.

"Aye, I shall," Reissa agreed. Her fear had only increased when the presence of her father was replaced by that of her husband, but she noticed an unusual contrast in her fears. She was frightened of Bernard's harsh touch, while, at the same time, she was frightened of Viktor's touch as a whole.

Whenever his fingers held her chin in a firm grip, she felt a surge of unexplored feeling bolt down to the tips of her toes. There was an awakening in her body that she could not understand or explain. He had only harmed her once, but it was that single occasion that kept her terror from abating. Yes, he was frightening in appearance when he was in a foul mood, but she was beginning to grow accustomed to his beautiful frowns.

"You will join us for the evening meal," Viktor ordered, but he was also excusing her from the celebratory events until then.

"You have my gratitude for the temporary pardon," she thanked him meekly.

He made no remark upon her words, merely gave a curt nod, then turned and retraced his steps down to the bailey.

***

He had sought his wife out to upbraid her for her extended absence during their swordplay, but when he found her in less than

106

perfect condition due to her clumsiness, he was reminded of the abuse he bestowed upon her on the eve of their wedding. And that thought only spurred his anger for feeling unnecessary guilt over the treatment of his wife.

She was his wife. He had the right to treat her in any fashion he chose. Yet he was still guilt-riddled because he knew he would not have treated her so cruelly if his judgment had not been skewed.

As he stalked out into the lush green courtyard, he teetered between guilt and anger and back again. What was it about that uncomely little waif that inspired such extreme feeling within him?

Chapter 14

Lady Reissa was forced to give her lie a second time when Moira inquired about the bruise on her cheek that evening at supper. Bernard had audaciously decided to fill Golly's empty chair without consulting the lord of the castle, yet no one seemed to mind that he had done so. And because of his shift in position at the trestle table, Reissa became ever more conscious of her father.

With him seated directly across from her, she looked to the hands clasped in her lap. Quietly, she explained tripping up the staircase and scraping her skin on the stone flooring. She felt his stare drilling into the top of her head, then felt the weight of his eyes leave her when he realized she was going to support the pretense of an accident, rather than offer the truth.

The food was served, and she ate her meal in invisible silence, merely listening to the talk of countless challenges that had taken place that day. When she wordlessly considered retiring, Collin targeted her with a question.

"My quiet sister in law, we have yet to speak in depth. May I interest you in a game of chess?"

Reissa was pleasantly surprised by the request. She was honored that the man was making a genuine attempt to know her better, so the thought to refuse him never even occurred to her.

"You may." She nodded kindly and rose from her chair.

Collin accompanied her to a small table situated near the fireplace where a chessboard was a permanent fixture in the hall. He displayed consideration by pulling her chair for her, then seated himself on the opposite side of the board.

Reissa took stock of the wooden chess pieces and was brought back to the age of seven. It had been over fourteen years ago, but she could recall being taught the intricacies of the game as if it were yesterday. One would assume that Bernard had been the mentor to instruct her, but he was not; it had been her mother. The lady had been a fountain of patience and understanding until her young daughter was able to best her. In chess, they were no longer mother and daughter; they were equals.

"Shall we dance?" Collin grinned in reference to the game.

Inspired to return the smile, she agreed, "Aye, we shall."

He gestured toward the board, offering her the first move, but his gaze settled on her, and he was pensive for a moment. Collin observed, "Ah, Reissa, you have a lovely smile. 'Tis unfortunate that we do not inspire you to bestow it upon us more often."

The receipt of such a genuine compliment caused her face to flush with color. Never had she known the wonder of praise from a man, and certainly never from a man who possessed such outstanding good looks. Consequently, unnerved by his words, and quite unsure how to deal with a commendation, she shifted her focus to the board. Reissa moved one of her chessmen, then sat back to wait for her opponent to do the same.

Collin also moved a pawn forward, then he leaned against the chairback. He propped an elbow on the armrest with a fist clenched near his jaw, then casually studied her, the game forgotten.

"Marriage suits you, my lady," he remarked with obvious sincerity.

Reissa nearly dropped the pawn she held between her fingers. "'Tis a prison," she choked with disdain before she could think twice.

Collin chuckled heartily. "Viktor has failed to capture your heart?"

The lady stared at him mutely, pondering the possibility of sharing her thoughts with him. Could she trust him? Could she confide in him? He was her husband's older brother, yet she knew he was a man of his own mind. He would defend his sibling upon principle alone, but he could also formulate his own opinions.

If he could not understand her aversion to her husband, perhaps he could at least introduce her to the man beneath the darkened exterior. Moira had attempted to do just that, but her avoidance of the all-important question pertaining to Viktor's guilt of murder had only caused her terrifying suspicions to rise.

"Forgive me, but your brother is a terrifying individual," she confessed, glancing across the distance at her husband, who was partially turned away from them. He was involved in a conversation with Alden and quite unaware that he was the subject of her discussion with Collin.

"You shall grow accustomed to my little brother in time, Reissa," Collin guaranteed with a supportive grin.

Her expression was pure doubt.

The lord sat forward, braced his elbows on his knees and rested his chin on his folded hands. He stared at the chessboard, appearing to ponder his strategy, but his words told her he was focused on their dialogue.

"I have known him from birth, known him at his best, and worst. Nary a day has passed when we have not shared words or silence. I was witness to his suckling from our mother's breast and his floundering as he took his first steps. We have stood together while battling for the king's reign, besieging castles and villages. Viktor and I have confronted horrors beyond your imagination, my lady. Therefore, I believe I am able to speak with all due confidence in knowing the man you wed," he said conversationally.

Reissa held up a hand to halt any continuance. "Your wife has traveled this path, Collin. She has assured me of my husband's shining attributes. However, I do not look for you to place him upon a pedestal simply to conquer my fears of him; in fact, I do not look for you to convince me of anything at all." She sighed heavily, making no attempt to hide her misgivings and her frustrations.

"Will you speak to me of the brother you know, as you know him, if only to help me understand the man's heart? We are husband and wife, yet I know nothing of his past, of his life."

"And he knows nothing of you," her handsome companion replied, then moved his rook several spaces.

"I am given the impression that he does not have any desire to know his wife."

"He resents the marriage, Reissa; 'tis not a reflection upon you." He scratched the beard on his chin as the fireplace popped loudly.

"My husband and I remain strangers; therefore, I do not take exception to his feelings on the matter. Yet I seem to be the target of his resentment, nevertheless."

"I would do anything for my brother, my lady, but I am unable to defend his discourteous behavior toward you. His temperament is volatile, an unfortunate character flaw he inherited from our father, who has only recently passed," Collin explained quietly, his demeanor distracted by memories.

Curious to know the nature of another's father, she found herself intrigued by the mystery of Collin Senior.

"You have my sympathies for your loss," she offered respectfully. When he merely nodded as a show of gratitude, the meek woman was prompted to continue. "Will you speak of him?"

He took a deep breath and leaned back in the straight-backed chair. His stare shifted from the board to her. "You have only to look upon your own husband to know my father."

"Collin Sr. was a temperamental, frighteningly cold man?" she inquired frankly.

"Precisely." He moved one of his bishops to take the place of her only remaining knight.

Her eyes scanned the small wooden figures scattered across the game board as contented silence fell upon them. The hall was slowly growing vacant of occupants as their game continued endlessly. Only a couple of maids remained in the kitchen area, cleaning up.

Suddenly Collin spoke. "I do not believe he has shed a tear in all of his life. Even as a child, he was immune to mournful sentiments. Our greatest tragedy was the death of our mother. She was a victim of the Plague, yet he remained dry-eyed throughout the funeral."

Reissa was startled to hear this. It was rather unexpected to learn that she shared the same tragedy; however, as her mourning never ceased to abate, she was quite unwilling to speak of her mother's death. She missed Grace with every breath in her body, yet she felt a never-ending guilt inside because she also felt a certain amount of joy in her passing.

The Plague had been a blessing in disguise, terminating a life of misery. Before Grace made the journey up to heaven, she was the focus of her father's abusive raging. Not once had he raised his hand to Reissa. Grace had made certain of that by taunting Bernard's ire to ensure his anger was always directed at his kind young wife rather than at his daughter. In no way was Reissa grateful for the beatings she suffered, but she could be thankful that Grace was now in a better place, no longer at the mercy of an unmerciful husband.

"His heart is ice," Reissa commented softly, utterly deflated.

Collin shook his head in disagreement. "A man with a heart of ice does not display such a tendency for anger. He is merely strong-willed." The man took a deep breath and stared at her for a moment, seemingly pondering a decision. A callused hand moved a chess piece, placing her in check.

As she studied the board, his masculine voice said, "I have never spoken of this to another."

The words instantly gained her attention.

"And my wife is not an exception," he went on. Those black eyes shifted to the fire, and he stared into the flames as he spoke of the past. "Our mother's name was Margaret. She was a beautiful woman, perhaps the loveliest I have ever known. Following her death, she was laid out in the chapel at Colville Manor to await the priest's blessing for the afterlife.

"'Twas near dawn, and I was unable to sleep. Without direction, I found myself standing at the entrance to the chapel. The candles were nearly spent, casting shadows upon the room, but Viktor's figure was easily discernable. He knelt beside the pedestal, his head bowed over her body. I began to grow concerned when he remained still for an indiscernible period of time.

"When the sun rose over the horizon, lighting the dim interior, he finally lifted his head, and never have I seen him in such a state. Tears were absent, but his eyes were so forlorn that I felt moved to tears myself. I left him to his sorrow, but I have never forgotten that expression of grief." His gaze returned to her. "Nay, his heart is not ice. He simply guards his feelings well." With that, he placed her in checkmate, winning the game.

As Reissa stared at the game board, she felt her throat begin to burn with unshed tears. Her husband's grief in relation to his mother was all too familiar.

With a heavy heart, she thanked Collin for the game, then politely retired to her chambers.

Exhausted from the day's events, she fell into an immediate slumber.

Viktor did not visit her that night.

Chapter 15

The third day of celebration was to be jousting. Reissa stood beside Moira as they watched their husbands, clad in full armor, mounting their horses in preparation of sport.

Collin guided his chestnut stallion to the rail and faced off against Alden.

"Sir Alden is undefeated; he excels at jousting," Lady Moira announced, her nerves clearly visible. She was unable to tear her gaze from her husband's knighted form.

"If your husband is in need of care, I shall collect a balm for his aches," Lady Kilgour commented from her place beside them.

"You are a dear, Edith," Moira returned with a smile of thanks.

"Dare I ask of my husband's record?" Reissa put forth quietly.

"Viktor is undefeated in all, with the exception of jousting," Lady Moira admitted with a certain amount of pride in her brother-in-law.

"In jousting he falls in second only to my brother," Edith offered in her sweet voice.

"I need your hand," Moira said in a tight voice as her husband lowered the shield of his metal helmet.

Without thought, Reissa placed her petite hand within the lady's larger one. But she was quick to regret compliance when

Collin spurred his horse into motion and her knuckles were crushed together as Moira squeezed in a state of fearful anticipation.

Eight horse hooves pounded the dirt as they charged toward one another from opposite sides of the wooden rail, their lances tucked firmly underarm.

Reissa heard Moira take a deep breath then hold it in as the trio of women avidly watched the equestrians race toward each other. Suddenly their lances connected, and the force of the blows caused an ugly sound of splintering wood as the weapons bounced off unyielding metal armor. Both of their upper bodies were knocked back on their mounts, but only one figure managed to stay seated.

Collin teetered in the saddle for a horrifying moment before freefalling onto the hard-packed earth.

"God almighty!" Moira breathed with feeling, then she dropped Reissa's throbbing hand and rushed out into the circle to take stock of her husband's condition. He was already rising from the ground when she moved to take his arm. His helmet was discarded, and he bestowed a brilliant smile upon the lady, wordlessly telling her he was unhurt.

He waved a hand to the crowd, a sign of a graceful loser, and then exited the circle with his wife at his side. Moira took up her place at Reissa's side with the addition of Collin, who was now a spectator.

Viktor gently kicked his mount into motion and halted at the rail as Alden moved to do the same. Suddenly Reissa was longing for a hand to hold. Her fears of yesterday were reinstated. As her husband flicked down the shield of his helmet, she tried to rationalize her apprehension away. Viktor was a virtual stranger to her, and for the duration of their marriage, he had only succeeded in frightening and hurting her, so to feel fear when he was placed in the path of danger was illogical.

The only explanation that stood up to reason was her sense of human compassion. She had no desire to see another hurt, no matter the person or their disposition. She knew this man was of a strong temperament and a strong will, and she knew he was capable of murder, yet she could not hope for him to suffer at the hands of fate. Never did she want to see him in pain.

Tiny fists curled into her violet skirts as horse hooves dug into the earth and kicked up dirt. The best friends set out at a reckless pace toward one another. Reissa barely noticed the feminine hand that came to rest upon her shoulder and gave a reassuring squeeze as she took in the unsettling scene in muted silence.

The events seemed to carry out in slow motion even as it all happened swiftly. Two knights set aside their personal closeness in the name of sport. They targeted one another with the points of their lances and charged headlong into danger.

Reissa pressed her eyes shut a split second prior to their violent meeting. Once again, she heard the distinct sound of their weapons breaking upon contact and the heart-stopping bangs as they nearly punctured one another's protective metal with force and momentum. With the exception of pummeling hoof beats, there was a deafening silence that followed before the unmistakable crash of an armored body thunderously dropping to the dirt.

As a roar of applause filtered through the crowd, the lady took a deep breath and opened her eyes, expecting the worst. Instantly, she sought out the figure on the ground. The metal-clad body was painfully but slowly rising to a sitting position. She was distracted when she noticed the opponent stripping off his helmet. A haze of euphoric relief flooded her being as a pair of familiar black eyes and a head of raven locks were revealed when the helmet was lifted and thrown aside. Long strides carried him toward the man on the ground.

Viktor graciously helped his fallen friend to his feet. Alden also removed his helmet, and, after a moment's hesitation, his mouth turned up in a defeated grin as he waved to the crowd.

Not only relieved that neither man had been injured but also proud of her husband's outstanding accomplishment over an undefeated man, she thoughtlessly lifted her hands and clapped in support of Viktor's victory.

After the applause died away, everyone began to disperse in preparation of the dinner hour. Reissa was no exception. She hurried from the bailey as quickly as possible, avoiding every possible contact and confrontation with her husband.

Chapter 16

Lady Colville yawned and enjoyed a thorough stretch as she surfaced through her unconscious state. However, her contentment was effectively shattered when she recalled the dinner hour. Her petite figure bolted off the bed, and she glanced out the window embrasure only to find that darkness had long since fallen.

Reissa was still clad in the dressing gown she had donned after bathing, and her strawberry blond tresses were still damp. Uncaring that her hair was unbound, she mumbled an unladylike curse as she struggled into clean clothing, not willing to waste precious time by waiting for a maid to arrive to aid her toilet. After donning an off-white cotte, drawers, a royal blue underdress, and a gold overdress without sleeves, the candles were doused, and she rushed into the corridor, praying she was not tardy for the evening meal.

In her haste to reach the hall, she lifted her skirts and broke into a hearty run. With her eyes taking care to watch the ground, she failed to see the massive figure turning the corner in front of her. Reissa collided with what felt like a stone wall, but when she bounced off the warm structure and a pair of iron hands clutched her elbows to save her from a painful fall, she realized she had struck a person.

Startled eyes quickly rose, and the lady was frozen with fear when she found a black gaze glaring down at her from a towering height of greater than six feet.

"Viktor," she croaked.

"The dinner hour has gone, wench, and, as you have missed it, you shall go without," he announced irritably.

"I apologize," her voice quivered, knowing he was wroth with her. "I have only just awakened."

"Must I visit your bedchamber afore every meal to assure you will attend?" he demanded in an unforgiving tone.

"Nay," she returned quickly, too quickly, "I shall not be tardy again." The thought of the man in her bedchamber thrice a day was far too disconcerting. She had learned to avoid any and every threat at all costs, and her husband was most certainly the greatest threat of all.

***

Viktor's jaw clenched in anger upon hearing her emphatic desire to bar him from her chambers. He was well aware of his lack of attraction to his wife, but to learn of hers struck at his male pride. Yes, she was terrified of him, but it was possible for lust to exist along with fear.

However, that was not true in this case. His wife was an exception to the countless women who desired to be bedded by him.

That thought was accompanied by an unusual surge of anger, but he suppressed it because other matters needed tending.

Uncomfortable with what must be done as a requirement of the marriage agreement, he sighed heavily, bracing himself for her horror. If he did not secure her in an embrace, Viktor knew she would attempt to flee.

***

Reissa felt her heart stop when he abruptly lifted her feather weight into his powerful arms and began to carry her toward her chambers. She clutched his forest-green tunic and stared up at his hard jaw as he looked straight ahead. Fear of the unknown caused her hands to tremble. Would he finally punish her for her shortcomings? Or would he carry out his animal duty as her husband?

"Viktor, I would know of your intentions," she requested desperately.

"Unfortunately, immaculate conception is not a reality, Reissa. If you are to conceive an heir, I must implant my seed within you," he announced with bald honesty.

The consequences be damned, she would not suffer the pain and humiliation he had subjected her to on their wedding night. Reissa immediately began to fight for freedom from his arms, but he held her fast, denying escape.

"Calm yourself, Reissa; I shall be gentle," he said, evidently trying to soothe her misgivings. He passed through her open bedchamber door and kicked the oak structure shut with his foot, casting shadows upon the unlit room. The only illumination was a shaft of moonlight streaming through the single window embrasure in the vast space of her chamber.

"My body would have to disagree, my lord." She gained a sliver of courage, unable to see his gorgeous face in the darkness.

"I cannot account for my behavior on the eve of our wedding, woman. I was sotted with drink," he explained as he cautiously crossed to the canopy. His movements were slow, clearly allowing his eyes to adjust to the night.

"Spirits were the cause of your—" she floundered, uncertain how to label his savagery, "—your lack of mercy?"

"Aye." The word was clipped, his vexation clear.

Reissa sensed his tight nod in the darkness as he placed her on her feet and drew aside the bed curtains with one swift motion.

"I have very little recollection of the events of that evening," her husband admitted, his deep voice causing gooseflesh to spread on her arms and legs. She knew his clarification was meant to smother her fears, but as she acknowledged the fury burning below the surface, the lady was renewed with the need to take flight.

When she heard him removing his tunic, her feet began to move of their own accord. She bolted in the direction of the door, but Viktor must have anticipated her actions, because he easily caught her slender wrist while he tossed the tunic aside. His heated palms closed around her forearms, and he spun her around and lowered her onto the mattress with one swift motion, causing her skirts and hair to fan out with the force of the momentum.

Caught off guard by the ease of his dominance, she gasped in a mixture of surprise and apprehension. A heavy leg was thrown over her knees as he held her wrists to the mattress on either side of her head. He rested upon an elbow for leverage, allowing him to rule her figure by only touching her in those two chaste areas.

Now, completely at his mercy, Reissa's startlement faded, leaving nothing but pure terror. She could barely see the outline of his face hovering near hers; nevertheless, her eyes squeezed shut, anticipating nothing but misery.

"Reissa, does your pain remain?" Viktor inquired with little feeling in his voice. He slid her hands up until he was able to close one hand around both of her delicate wrists. With that done, he lifted her skirts and gingerly touched the sensitive flesh of a bared thigh.

Two nights had passed since he had taken her maidenhead, but the lady no longer felt her pain. As the victim of years of abuse, her body had miraculously conditioned itself to heal with a speed that defied reason. Unbelievably, the scrape Bernard had administered to her cheek was already beginning to fade, and the bruises on her thighs were simply yellow-green patches, no longer tender to the touch.

Reissa would love to plead injury to gain freedom from the act, but she would not lie. She only lied to cover her father's abuse, and even then, she was overwhelmed with guilt for doing so. Silence and honesty were her forte. And as she felt his palm on her thigh, her throat began to burn with feeling.

"Nay. Please, make haste," she begged as tears flooded her eyes. Knowing she could never escape his strength, she resigned herself to suffering the act.

She heard his grunt of frustration and then felt his palm slide up her thigh. Her flesh shrank away from his unfeeling touch as he roughly pulled down her drawers and a gasp of horror filtered through the darkness when a finger intruded into her body.

"You are not ready for me, Wife," he said softly as he removed his finger.

Following his unwanted intimate touch, her instincts screamed at her to fight. And she listened.

"I insist you leave me!" Reissa shouted through her tears as she made a furious attempt to disentangle her wrists from his superior hold.

Her struggling only caused his grip to tighten. His free hand clutched her chin, and she felt the warmth of his breath near her ear. "I do not have any desire for your battle, or for you," he hissed, "but you must conceive an heir, Reissa. 'Tis a chore that must be done."

"Then be done and begone!" she ordered angrily, forgetting herself.

***

Viktor heard the uncontrollable emotion in her voice, and even though he did not like her tears, he acknowledged a certain amount of admiration for the sudden display of courage. Perhaps there was more to the woman than meekness and fear. However, she certainly did not possess any attraction to him. Her body would not receive him without protest, and he would not force her.

As the lady's tears became hiccupping sobs, he knew he was unable to go through with his intent. Not only was she not prepared for him, but he was also no longer prepared for her. Their daunting interaction and her extreme aversion to him smothered any arousal he had sustained for the necessary task of bedding his wife.

"I cannot," he admitted as his hold on her wrists loosened and the leg imprisoning her knees was removed. "To take you now would be sadistic at best."

He heard Reissa's drawn-out sigh of relief and was overcome with the urge to throw his fist through a stone wall. Viktor was in a fine rage as he pushed himself to his feet.

"Arise early. We depart for the coast at dawn." His order came to her through the darkness, then he stormed from her chambers without another word.

Chapter 17

The journey to the coast was blissfully uneventful.

Due to Moira's delicate condition, and, Reissa was certain, also due in part to her husband's aversion to her and her inability to ride solo, Collin arranged for the ladies to travel in an elegant carriage while the men rode on horseback.

Five days were filled with continuous transport, excluding one morning where they said farewell to a woman who was not well liked. The aesthetic scenery consisted of rolling hills and trees marked with the final colors of autumn. The nights were spent at inns, their separate rooms rented for comfort and sublime avoidance of each other after the uncomfortable night when husband and wife failed to carry out their duty to conceive an heir.

Reissa saw less of her husband in those five days than she had during the entire course of their union as husband and wife. He did not visit her in an attempt to conceive in all their time on the road, for which Reissa was eternally grateful. Following the evening when Viktor had stormed from her chamber, she had been unable to meet his direct gaze without her cheeks burning in humiliation. His handsome figure was a constant reminder of his obvious disgust in their marriage bed, and those dark eyes struck her down with her everlasting fear of him.

The only occasions in which they actually shared company were during meals. And then few words were exchanged, if any at all. And those few words were typically curt orders, given from husband to wife.

***

Reissa's gaunt cheeks and rail-thin figure prompted Viktor to take up the task of monitoring her food intake. When he had lifted her into his arms for a tumble, he realized how petite she truly was. Her delicate bone structure left her defenseless, and that detail only added to his frustration, because he was forced to take great care when dealing with her in any physical capacity.

So, he kept watch over her meals, refusing her to leave the table without eating all that was given to her. He was determined to put some weight on the wench. His wife complied without complaint, and for that he found himself feeling admiration for the woman he had wed. It was rather pleasant to be married to a woman who did not fight his every turn.

***

Dutifully, Reissa had stood at Viktor's side while the wooden raft supporting Golly's body carried her away, but husband and wife were as strangers. Knowing little of Golly and Viktor's relationship, she could offer no words of understanding or empathy, so she provided what little she could: her presence.

Any onlooker would have been confused by the gathering of mourners because every last pair of eyes were dry as they watched a family member's body float into open waters. The crowd felt little for the deceased as their clergyman spoke of a life taken before her time.

Reissa found herself looking to her husband when there was an indirect mention of murder. A shiver of apprehension coursed through her body, and she instinctually took a step away from the man. Her charcoal-gray skirts were clutched in small fists as a strong wind ruffled her clothing. The sun was shining, yet there was an eerie chill in the air.

The crowd dispersed without speech and began the extended journey to Appleta.

Now, three days later, darkness was falling as they crested a rise. Reissa's new home, Colville Manor, became visible.

She looked upon the marvelous stone structure in awe. The concentric castle was massive. The keep itself was grander than any she had ever seen. Her new home contained several circular towers connected by shallow stone walls. The outermost curtain wall was extensive in height and outlined by a deep moat. Two tall gatehouses upheld the portcullis, and as they approached, the drawbridge was lowered to admit entrance.

The carriage made a hollow sound as it crossed the planks of the drawbridge, then quieted as they moved on to the bailey. The men dismounted, and their carriage driver opened the door for the women. Collin was the first to appear, and he helped all three ladies step down to the ground.

Reissa felt a heavy stare and glanced up to find Viktor approaching, his expression the mark of stoicism. Silently, he held out his arm in escort and waited for her to take what he offered. Her eyes shifted meekly to the hem of her skirts, and she hooked her fingers around his bent elbow.

Viktor led her into the keep, and Reissa was surprised to find that the interior was nearly the mirror image of Moorestone. The kitchen was built within the massive room, behind the raised dais, and there were three monstrous fireplaces, two on the far wall, and one on the left. The only exceptions of difference were the rows of trestle tables placed parallel to the dais rather than perpendicular, and the staircase leading up to the chamber was enclosed rather than wide open.

The servants, seeing that their lord had arrived without prior warning, jumped into motion, quickly preparing a meal for the travel-worn occupants. As their companions moved off to freshen up for supper, Viktor halted and gazed down upon his wife with questions in his eyes.

"You appear rather weary, Reissa. Would it please you to take your meal in chambers?" he asked quietly, surprising her with the unexpected kindness.

"Aye, Viktor, 'twould," she returned softly, her lids heavy with fatigue. The journey had been grueling, and she felt every lost hour of sleep.

He nodded, then led her up the staircase and down the coolly damp corridor to a massive antechamber. They passed through into a smaller room that was inviting in its coziness yet furnished for a queen.

As Reissa took in the beautiful four-post bed with silken bed curtains, a wardrobe with elaborately carved doors, an exquisitely detailed oriental rug, a gigantic fireplace, and a remarkable vanity with an oval mirror, Viktor made quick work of lighting several candles to rub out the shadows of sunset.

Then he moved to start a fire. Typically, the servants tended to such duties; however, because they arrived without warning, the lord of the manor took the duties on himself. When a knock sounded on the door and a young girl hurried in to take over, Viktor dismissed her to the kitchen to prepare a tray for Reissa.

After the fire was crackling, giving off heat, the petite lady instinctually moved closer to stamp out the chill in her body. Viktor turned and glanced at her wrinkled attire. Abruptly, he began a determined approach, and Reissa felt her insides shrinking, desperate to maintain distance. She claimed a step in retreat, and he frowned down upon her.

"Present your back, Reissa," he ordered in a clipped tone.

Her eyes lifted to stare up at him in paralyzed terror.

"God's teeth, lady, I will not ravish you," he growled his frustration through gritted teeth. "I have sent your maid away; you will need aid with your gown," he explained as he gripped her shoulder and roughly spun her around. With jerky, angry movements, he unbuttoned her gown and loosened the laces of her cotte so she could easily slip from the garments without further help.

Reissa pressed her palms to her upper chest to save the material from falling to the floor as Viktor flung open the wardrobe doors and yanked out a bed robe for her to change into. He practically pushed it at her, forcing her to struggle as she held up her clothes and took the nightdress from him simultaneously.

"I require your presence in the stables at dawn to provide a tour of Colville Manor," he commanded as his gaze bore into hers. There was no mistaking that it was not a request. "Drills are a majority of our daily routine; therefore, my time is precious. I expect punctuality, Reissa. Do not be tardy, or I shall wake you myself." The threat was indirect but clear. He made no mention of how he would wake her, but she was certain it would not be pleasant.

"Aye, Viktor."

After acknowledging her acceptance of his order with a nod, he turned and stalked from the room without another word. Reissa stood frozen, apprehensive he would change his mind and return to bed her, per their marriage contract.

Minutes passed as the bare skin of her back grew bumpy with gooseflesh and her body ached with rigid tension, but when it appeared he had indeed left her for the evening, she let the day's garments fall to the floor and pulled the bed robe onto her arms. She quickly removed her slippers, then she sprinted across the cool stone flooring beneath her feet and jumped into bed.

A soft knock sounded on the door, and Reissa immediately regained the tension in her body, certain her husband had returned. She summoned every effort to prompt her guest to enter, but she breathed a sigh of relief when the young maid walked through the door. She carried a tray of bread, cheese, and a glass of wine. The girl was modestly pretty with mouse-brown hair and a pair of shining blue eyes. She was as petite as Reissa, if not smaller, with tanned skin, and she announced her name as Gert, short for Gertrude.

"Will you be in need of anything else, my lady?" the maid inquired politely.

"Nay, Gert, thank you," Reissa dismissed her with a kind smile then began to pick at the contents on the tray. After Viktor had forced her to eat more than she was used to during meals, her appetite had increased slightly, so, before she knew it, every last crumb was gone. She sipped the red port then lay back in the massive bed and shut her eyes, willing sleep to arrive.

Despite her overwhelming fatigue, slumber eluded her. Her buzzing thoughts kept her awake. However, it was a single thought that she found her mind returning to time and again. She was now in her new home, and she had left her children behind. Of course they were not *her* children, but she had been a prominent adult in their little lives, and the idea of being ordered not to teach any longer was flooding her heart with resentment and regret.

Children were her precious lifeline; she needed them to survive. How could she accept her husband's command without a fight? How could she allow him to dictate her only possible chance for happiness? The answer was clear. She could not. She must gather the courage to confront Viktor with her dissatisfaction over his decision. She must request his reconsideration and not falter if he denied her a second time.

She knew Viktor was a hard, unyielding man, and she also knew that if it came down to it, she would get down on her hands and knees to beg him for permission. Reissa wanted it that much. She would suffer the weapons of his fists if she angered him to the point of abuse. She would submit to anything for the company of children.

The abrupt sound of another soft knock on the door jolted her from her thoughts. Reissa sat bolt upright in bed. She took a deep breath and squeaked permission for her guest to enter.

The lady was extremely relieved to see Edith stroll into the chamber with a tankard clutched in her thick hands and a shy smile tacked on her round face.

"Edith, 'tis a pleasant surprise," she stated with genuine sincerity.

"As this is the first evening in your new home, I thought you may have difficulty finding slumber. I brought you warm milk sprinkled with a pinch of my own personal sleeping powder."

Reissa grinned in gratitude. "Ah, Edith, you are too generous for words," she breathed as she accepted the tankard from her and took a sip of the soothing substance. "I *have* experienced trouble finding slumber this night," she admitted.

"You will grow to love this castle as Alden and I have, I assure you. Soon you will sleep the days away in contentment."

She ignored the comment, unable to believe the truth of her words. "I appreciate your care, Lady Kilgour," Reissa said in reference to the tonic, then took a healthy swallow.

"'Tis my pleasure, Lady Reissa."

Reissa began to feel the effects of the sleeping agent almost immediately. Her body was slowly growing languid, and her eyelids were heavy with sleep. The tankard in her hand felt as if it weighed a ton, and she was forced to place it on the bedside table before she dropped it in her weakness.

Reissa lay back on her fluffy feather pillows, and as she gazed up at Edith, she felt the mystery surrounding the lady. They had scarcely exchanged words in the short time since their meeting, even though they more than likely shared much in common. Both were cursed with an average vanity, her own as clear as day, while Edith's was made so by her excess weight. Not only did they pale in comparison to Moira, they were both timid and quiet. Reissa attributed her own meekness to her father's lack of kindness, but she knew not why Edith was so closed off. She was curious to learn more about the girl, but she would not pry. If Lady Kilgour chose to open up, she would allow her to do so, and allow her to choose the moment.

So, rather than inquiring of personal matters, she pointed to the tankard and offered, "Would you care to sample your own remedy?"

"Thank you, but, nay, I have promised my brother a game of chess. I must have my wits about me to battle Alden. I have yet to be the victor." Her smile was soft around the edges. "I will leave you to your slumber, Lady Reissa. May your dreams be pleasant." With that, she gave a slight curtsy, then made a quiet departure.

The door was still in the process of closing when Reissa swiftly drifted into unconsciousness.

Chapter 18

Reissa awoke long before dawn, and, recalling Viktor's threat that he would wake her if she was tardy, she rose immediately. Because of that, she beat Viktor to the stables by nearly an hour. In minutes, she became a student to the stableman. When he learned she was ignorant of horses and of her inability to ride, he took it upon himself to show her a mount's accessories, and he was not vague by any means. He went into great detail over every single item, right down to the curing of the leather reins.

Despite her boredom, Reissa was patiently polite. She listened to his every word, giving him all of her attention, but she was almost thankful when Viktor's deep voice broke through the monotone of the elder man's discourse.

"You may saddle a single mount for myself and the lady, Dax," he ordered conversationally. He merely gave her a curt nod then turned and rudely ignored her presence as he petted a beautiful thoroughbred's muzzle.

His chaste movement drew her gaze to the flexing biceps beneath the material of his teal tunic. And that in turn caused her eyes to drift across his broad shoulders, over the flat plains of his back and down to a narrow waist.

From some shuttered room in her being, she was accosted with the image of her fingers smoothing over the taut skin of his spine and lower. As she imagined that hard body in her bed, she felt a shiver course through her limbs. Through that fear, a mysterious feeling was warming her blood, and that feeling created confusion.

As if sensing he was the object of her focus as she stared at his buttocks, his head swiveled, and he pinned her with a penetrating look.

Instantly, her eyes fell to the ground, and her cheeks began to flood with embarrassed color. Without realizing it, she began to back away, instinctually needing to remove herself from an uncomfortable situation and a man who always seemed to dominate her world.

Because her eyes were on the ground, she failed to see her husband's expression change from one of passivity to frantic determination. He rushed forward and reached out for her.

Reissa felt the edge of the wooden trough full of water strike her calves, and panic surged through her veins. The momentum of her retreat rocked the petite figure off balance. Her head automatically lifted, and her hands flailed as she helplessly fought against a fall into the horse trough full of cold water. She looked up to find Viktor suddenly before her, his arms closing around her back and shoulders in iron bands of rescue. He caught her to him, saving her from herself and her clumsiness.

Despite the identity of her savior, she clutched his tunic to steady herself. With the support of his powerful arms, she quickly regained her balance, but the moment she became aware that the danger had passed, she simultaneously realized Viktor held her in his arms. And he held her in his arms because of her extreme lack of grace.

Her humiliation over gawking at his male form was hastily replaced with humiliation over her physical blunder. She felt like a fool. She wanted to crawl into a hole, never to come out, but all she could do was bury her face in the rough material of his tunic while trying to hold her self-pitying tears at bay.

"Reissa, have you been hurt?" Viktor asked when she did not immediately withdraw from his hold.

She shook her head against his chest. With that, he gripped her nape and gently drew her away to gaze down into her crimson-stained face. She quickly averted her eyes to his chest.

"You must take greater care, Reissa. I am unable to watch your every movement to ensure safety from yourself," he dictated, anger causing his words to sound in harsh tones.

"Aye, Viktor. Thank you," she responded softly, his scolding only causing her cheeks to burn with more heat and higher color. Reissa knew she was generally not a clumsy person. It was her husband's intoxicating presence that caused her to lose control over her grace, but she could not confess that to him. Not only would it speak of her unease around him, but she needed carelessness as an excuse when she was subjected to her father's foul moods. Bernard's fists never failed to leave marks, and lies were her only cover.

He stared at her for a moment, evidently wondering at her thoughts on the matter. Something in the lilt of her voice prompted him to demand, "Do you mock me, lady?"

Startled gray eyes lifted to meet a flashing pair of dark orbs flecked with a beautiful shade of gold. She emphatically shook her head in the negative, but his gaze narrowed in doubt as his callused fingers lightly moved over the skin of her neck.

As Reissa met his piercing stare, she knew he was unaware of his subtle actions. However, the brush of his fingertips across the sensitive skin of her nape caused shocking waves of heat to roll over her shoulders and down to her breasts. Perplexed by the unfamiliar reaction to her husband's touch, she became desperate to remove herself from the strength of his arms.

The clop clop of horse hooves sounded. Reissa's gaze shifted to see the stableman leading a saddled mount toward them. She was so grateful for the timely reprieve that she could have kissed the gray-haired little man.

Viktor clutched a slim upper arm and led her over to the animal. Reissa felt his hands circle her tiny waist, and suddenly she was hoisted onto the thoroughbred's back. As Collin had taught her, she rearranged her emerald skirts and quickly hooked her knee over the pommel.

She held on tightly, frightened she would fall from the height of the horse's back. Without pause, her husband climbed into the saddle at her back. The palm of his hand slid around to her abdomen as he snapped the reins and spurred the mount into a steady canter.

Even though Reissa disliked being so close to the man, she clung to the pommel and leaned back against his chest, welcoming the support of his body.

The trio rode from the stables. The sun had recently broken over the horizon, so the light of day was still dim. Shadows of night slowly faded as they crossed the moat and continued beyond the outermost curtain walls. There was a thin veil of cloud cover in the sky, allowing the sun to peek through in stages, and there was not a hint of a breeze, yet the day was bitingly cold.

As Reissa gazed out over the rolling hills of her husband's lands, she noticed faint white flakes drifting through the air. It was not a steady snowfall, merely flurries, which meant there would be no accumulation. However, it was a solid sign that winter was swiftly bearing down upon them.

The lady pulled the edges of her white ermine cloak together to ward off the chill. She was rather comfortable within the confines of the heavy outer layer, yet her body continued to shake. She knew the height was partially to blame. But she was afraid that being so close to her husband was more to blame. Long ago, she had mastered her fear of heights, but on rare occasions it struck her with a vengeance, reminding her of the day when she had toppled off the dais in front of her students.

Reissa was far too aware of Viktor's arm around her waist and his voluminous chest pressing against her back. In their stark silence, she tried to ignore the man, but forgetting he was near was impossible.

Suddenly, her gaze caught sight of smoke off in the distance, and her already elevated pulse jumped. "Oh!" she breathed. "Viktor, 'tis smoke." A slender hand lifted to point toward the north.

Abruptly, he yanked on the reins and brought them to a halt. He followed the direction of her finger, and she felt his heavy sigh of relief, followed by the shake of his head. "Nay, Reissa, 'tis our hot spring."

Her brow lifted in surprise. "A hot spring?" she repeated.

"Aye, 'tis warm as bath water. There are many in this area."

"Mmm, sounds heavenly," she said in a melodious purr as she imagined stepping into one.

Her inviting fantasy was interrupted when Viktor's arm suddenly pressed her close, and his clean-shaven cheek touched to her temple. Reissa sucked in her breath, startled and unsettled by her husband's movements. She desired to ask his reasoning, but she was unable to do so. Her mouth opened, but no sound erupted.

"You are trembling, wife," he observed, his heated breath fanning her brow. He dropped the reins and folded her tiny figure in a warm embrace. She was so small, she nearly disappeared within his thick arms. "'Tis not a wonder when you are stick thin," Viktor growled softly.

The lady summoned every ounce of will to speak. "'Tis not the cold, my lord." In her paralyzed state, she reverted to formality and was unaware that she had done so. "I am terrified of heights."

His hold instantly slackened, yet his arms remained loosely around her. "Is there nothing you are unafraid of, lady?" he questioned with a hint of irritation.

Hurt by the truth of his words, her head bowed in self-disgust. She knew she was a coward, but to hear it spoken aloud by her husband was sincerely deflating.

"God's teeth, Reissa, you must temper your sensitivity. 'Tis not my intention to insult you."

"Nay, your question holds truth, Viktor. I fear much." However, she could not say that he was her greatest fear.

His gaze dropped to the greenish-brown grass. "We are but five feet from the earth, Reissa," he rationalized, obviously unable to comprehend her apprehension.

"'Tis no matter, I am afeard," she whispered.

Seeing her genuine terror as he gazed at her profile, his arms instinctually tightened around her. "Is there a cause for your aversion to heights?"

Numbly, she nodded. She was loath to speak of the reason, but she was well aware that Viktor simply tolerated her presence because she was his wife, so it was useless to conceal her never-ending list of faults. "I fell from the platform in the village schoolhouse. 'Twas a short fall, but my right leg was broken. I would give anything to forget that day, but I am plagued with a limp during days of rain or snow. 'Tis an incessant reminder."

***

Viktor was caught off guard by her tale. Immediately, his eyes shifted to the leg that was not hooked around the pommel. Her skirts and cloak concealed it, yet he imagined the slender limb beneath, and he was assaulted with a myriad of emotions. The first one he addressed was confusion. "I have never observed a limp in your gait."

A ghost of a smile touched her lips. "I hide it well."

He gazed at her for a moment, then looked to the overcast sky. "Does it pain you on this day?"

"Mildly," she said with a dismissing wave of her hand.

His callused fingers gripped her chin and turned her head to meet his questioning gaze. "Has your clumsiness been the cause of any other broken bones?"

He couldn't help but think back to her misfortune in the stables and his reaction to it.

It was clear that she had been mortified by her blunder, but he could not ease her shame with kind words because her clumsiness had started his heart with fear. The unexpected surge of concern over such a trivial event was rather perplexing, but he did not analyze his feelings on the matter because fear spawned anger, and he had not hesitated to unleash it on her. Perhaps he had been overly harsh with her, but the lady inspired extreme emotions within, and he couldn't explain why that would be so.

***

Reissa did not make any attempt to correct his false assumption, yet she could not meet his eyes as she said, "Nay, only my leg has suffered a break."

Viktor looked to the ground, then sighed heavily and shook his head in obvious frustration. But he didn't chastise her carelessness a second time that day; in fact, he dropped the subject entirely.

"Let us go now, Reissa. I would like you to see the Wallingham ruins afore we return for the midday meal." He picked up the reins, and rather than urge their mount into a swift pace, he prompted a moderate trot.

Reissa was unsure if the slowed pace was because of her confession to a fear of heights, but whatever the cause, she was grateful. Her hold on the pommel was not as desperate, and she was better able to enjoy their autumn surroundings. Unfortunately, she still felt her insides trembling. She remained far too conscious of the man at her back.

As they rode, Viktor painted her a picture of the neighboring estate's history. The Wallingham family had consisted of nearly all men. Lady Wallingham was the only female member. Over the years, every last male had been called away to serve the king, and every last male died serving their king. When the lady of the manor learned that her only remaining son was killed in the line of duty, she hung herself from the upraised portcullis. Her death brought about the desertion of the castle. For a century, the structure stood alone, falling to ruin without occupants to care for it.

"'Tis a horrible tale," she groaned when he had concluded.

During his dialogue, the sun rose higher in the sky. At one point, they crossed a wooden bridge that had been built over a modest river. Several times their mount waded through shallow streams. The trees were nearly bare, with very few stubborn leaves clinging to their branches, and even though the day was progressing, the temperature seemed to be slowly dropping.

"Unfortunate, aye. Nevertheless, the ruins are absolutely beautiful." As he stated it, the stone dwelling became visible over a gently sloping rise.

Wallingham Castle was a solitary structure with a single defensive curtain wall that had long since toppled to the ground. The structure itself had partially crumbled. A portion of the roof had caved in, and one of the corner walls was no longer standing, leaving a gaping hole that allowed for viewing of the overgrown interior from the outside.

Reissa was so preoccupied with the aesthetic beauty of the castle that she failed to notice their halt and Viktor's aid as he lowered her to the ground. She did not wait for his guidance. Her feet carried her forward without him. She picked her way around the stones resting on the ground and entered through the open space.

Her eyes were mesmerized as they moved over the vines clinging to the walls and the tree that had punctured the stone flooring. It had grown to fruition, its branches reaching through the hole in the roof. Moss was scattered in a random pattern throughout, breaking through every last crack. Leaves had blown inside, their volume greater near the missing corner.

A rabbit scampered away in fright as her slippers sounded on the stone beneath her feet. The little white figure fled through an open doorway on the opposite side, but Reissa did not follow. As she peered up into the second level, she moved toward the stairway attached to the wall on her left. Because the staircase was only enclosed on one side, she stayed well away from the drop on the other.

Aside from the massive gap in the floor, which Reissa walked around, the chamber level consisted of decaying rooms that were blanketed with more leaves and cobwebs. Then she found another staircase that led below. The lady began her descent, then rounded a corner and was brought up short to find that one of the window embrasures had collapsed onto the landing.

Carefully, she crawled over the pile of stones and continued down to the hall. She found Viktor sitting on one of the window seats overlooking the front entrance. His left foot remained planted on the ground as if he was braced to rise, a warrior forever prepared for battle. Seeing the sword strapped to his slim waist effectively erased the smile from her face. It was a stark reminder of what he was capable of, and what he had done to his stepmother.

When he heard her tentative approach, he looked up and asked, "Shall we return?"

Chapter 19

While Reissa lay in bed that evening, she realized the morning spent with her husband had been far less unbearable than she imagined it would be. The incident in the stables was confusing. And the ride they shared had been unsettling, thanks to old fears resurfacing. But not once during that entire time had she been genuinely afraid of *him*.

In a cruel slap of irony, the lady's bedchamber door opened without warning, and the star of her thoughts walked in, making a liar of her. There could be no mistaking the reason for his arrival. Despair made her desperate, and desperation made her act without thought for the consequences.

She jumped up and stood in the middle of the bed, clutching the coverlet to her breasts to hide the fact that she wore nothing more than a white cotte. The bed curtains were already open because she liked to see the door at all times. It was a habit she had grown accustomed to in their little shack in Ender.

"Viktor, is this really necessary?" she squeaked.

"Aye, I have been neglectful of my husbandly duties for too long, Reissa. We must conceive an heir," he announced firmly as he stepped away from the closed chamber door. He placed a small metal container on the bedside table, then he began to unhook the sword belt around his waist.

The lady's face drained of all color. Her eyes darted to the door, gauging the distance between it, her husband, and herself. There were no thoughts for tomorrow, only that night and her need to flee. Horrifying memories of the eve of their wedding washed over her vision, and she stifled a cry. The consequences be damned, she must escape.

When Viktor lifted the teal tunic over his head, baring his tanned skin to the waist, she did not hesitate a moment longer. She dropped the coverlet, fearing it would hamper her actions, then jumped off the bed. Reissa ignored the sharp pain that shot up her lame leg and bolted toward the door as quickly as her short stature would carry her.

She became hopeful as the exit drew nearer, and even felt freedom in the shape of the brass door handle. But suddenly Viktor's arms snaked around her shoulders from behind. His hands clasped together. Corded forearms pressed over her modest breasts. She was imprisoned in his unyielding embrace, her upper arms pinned to her sides, her back flush against his chest. His head dipped, and warm, humid breath caressed her ear.

"Reissa, I know I was merciless on the eve of our wedding, but I shall not hurt you this night; I give you my word," he said with quiet determination.

"I am unable to discard my fear," her quivering voice upheld the truth of her statement.

"I assure you of haste and physical care, Reissa."

Her cheeks fused with heat as she thought of the last time they lay in her bed. She was loath to speak of it, but curiosity won out over social consciousness. Tentatively, she said, "L-last time you claimed I was not r-ready for you—"

"That will not be an issue this night," he interrupted. "I have a cream to aid our union." With that, he moved to lift her into his arms, but the moment Reissa realized his intent, her instincts kicked into gear.

She could not trust his vague assurances. And she was suddenly reminded of Golly. It was impossible to ignore the fact that he was a cold-blooded killer. Reissa renewed her struggle with every ounce of strength in her petite figure.

Her urgent need to escape his attentions only succeeded in raising his ire. He nearly crushed her in a frustrated hold as he marched over to the bed and unceremoniously dropped her onto the mattress. She was not given a moment's respite. Hastily, a heavy leg was thrown over hers, and her wrists were pinned to the pillow beside her head. Viktor glared down at her, his intense eyes flashing in the candlelight like a beautiful demon sent to do the devil's work.

"You have a marital duty to accept me into your body, Reissa," he hissed. "You will not deny me."

She stared up at him, positively horrified. Her eyes closed of their own will, and she turned her head away, knowing she could not fight his masculine strength.

"Please douse the light, my lord," she begged, longing to darken their surroundings and the view of the man above her.

Seeing her eyes squeezed tightly shut and the trembling of her pink lips, he complied without argument. His head rose, and, with one forceful gust, he blew out the single flame burning on the bedside table, casting the room in total blackness.

Left to her remaining four senses, Reissa was still too aware of her husband leaning over her, imprisoning her by force, and a contract that must be upheld. She was still frightened beyond her imagination, dreading his next move and his unwanted touch. She wished it was morning, then the whole terrible ordeal would already have passed.

"Thank you," her whisper was no more than a breath. That breath stalled when she felt his hand raising the skirt of her cotte, baring her legs to the cool night air. Frightened flesh shrank away from his unfeeling touch. Her limbs trembled as she waited for the inevitable piercing of his body into hers.

She heard him working loose the laces of his braies with one hand while he continued to imprison her to the bed. Then the tin sounded, followed by his deep voice. "Be easy, Reissa, 'tis time," he warned softly as his hand fell to her naked hip, releasing her wrists from their bonds.

She could not squelch the whimper that slipped past her lips.

Viktor grunted angrily, then voiced his frustration aloud, "Curse you and your never-ending fear of me, woman." With that, he gently pushed into her.

Reissa clutched the mattress beneath her, expecting the tearing agony she felt on the eve of their wedding, but it did not arrive. There was nothing but a tight pressure as her body stretched to accommodate his excessive size within her petite frame. He filled her, uniting them, yet their bodies barely touched.

He was braced above her, holding up his heavy frame with one arm while the other hand pulled her hips to him. Viktor was still for a moment, and she wondered if he was assessing her adjustment to him. If so, when he was certain she had accepted him into her body without discomfort, he began to move.

The lady lay there, startled by a dull sensation that was slowly building as he broke into a rhythm inside her. Her husband was climbing to an unknown precipice that caused his breathing to labor and his voice to vibrate in his throat as he crested the heights of this act.

Suddenly he let out a shaky groan as he gave a few final thrusts, spilling his seed deep inside her body, then fell away from her, rolling onto his back beside her on the bed.

Aside from a strong ebb coursing through her veins, Reissa was virtually unaffected by their intercourse. She remained still, barely able to breathe as she was assaulted with a mixture of emotions. His assurance had been the truth, he had not hurt her. There had not been the slightest amount of pain, yet somehow, she felt hollowed, used, and violated just the same.

She was merely a vessel to birth his heir, a body that provided access to Viktor's marital rights despite his lack of affection or attraction. Reissa was accustomed to poverty, but she felt cheapened; she felt invaluable. That only proved to knock down her self-esteem to its lowest level yet.

The urge to weep was strong, but her husband's presence forced her to blink back salty tears. As she maintained a sense of composure, she realized Viktor was lying there next to her in the darkness, regaining the normality of his breath. His lack of speech was disconcerting. The lagging silence riddled her with acute discomfort and tension. So, she distracted herself by sitting up and pushing down the skirts her husband had pushed up.

At last Viktor's voice sounded. "Have I hurt you, Reissa?"

The lady cleared her throat to gain strength. "Nay, you have not."

The mattress shifted, signifying that he also sat up. "Now that you have received proof that 'tis not my intention to hurt you during the need to conceive a babe, I will not tolerate disobedience in our marriage bed, do you understand?"

Reissa nodded absently, but the darkness concealed her response. She was so distracted by her deflating thoughts that she failed to realize she had not spoken aloud. A bit disoriented by the darkness, she rose from the bed and picked her course across the room to stand before the window embrasure. She looked out into the cloak of night but saw nothing through the blackness.

Suddenly a match flared, and the wick in the bedside candle was lit. The action gained the lady's attention. She looked up to find Viktor stalking toward her. His braies had been replaced, but his broad chest was still bare, and it drew the focus of her eyes. Her husband gripped her chin and forced her to meet a shadowed gaze that was glittering with fury.

"You will not turn away from me in our marriage bed, Reissa; I will not have it," he ordered through gritted teeth.

The frown on his handsome face was so thick that her blood ran cold. Thoughtlessly, she nodded, and the moment his hand fell away from her face, her eyes fell meekly to the floor. Viktor's gaze followed hers, which drew his eyes to her bare feet. His frown darkened. Without warning, he lifted her into his arms and started for the bed.

She stared up at his stubbled jaw, wide-eyed with questions, but in her frozen state of fear, only one word erupted. "Viktor?"

He glanced down at her, and when he took in the terror written clearly on her plain features, he scowled deeply. "You wear nothing on your feet, woman; you will catch your death from cold." His scolding supplied an explanation that left her dumbstruck.

He cared nothing for her; she was nothing but a liability to him, so why would he chastise her for a matter such as that? She failed to understand.

Once again, he dropped her unceremoniously on the mattress. After recovering from the slight fall, Reissa scurried to the head of the bed and pulled the coverlet around her. As Viktor marched over to the fireplace and tended to the dying coals, she belatedly realized her feet were chilled, as was her entire body.

Her eyes lifted to stare at her husband's broad back. She was immersed in a state of confusion. The man seemed to be more aware of her wellbeing than she was, and that was extremely odd. How could a man such as he, a terror, a killer, concern himself with her cold feet?

A ready answer eluded her. Then she became distracted yet again as the rekindled fire burned and Viktor stood and swiveled to face her. His naked chest shifted her thoughts to what had recently occurred in her bed. She must conceive his heir within a year. And the thought of having their child reminded her of her desire to continue teaching. And with that, her intention to speak with Viktor about it.

He took in her seated figure, securely wrapped in the bedclothes, then crossed the chamber, snatched his tunic from the floor and wordlessly began toward the door.

"Viktor," Reissa spoke so quietly, she was certain he had not heard her. Therefore, she was startled when he turned, and those dark eyes locked on her curiously.

The lady took a deep breath, gathering every ounce of courage she possessed to confront what she knew was going to be an extremely unpleasant scene.

"I understand the issue has been addressed, but I must ask you to reconsider my teaching in the village," she requested delicately.

Viktor grunted unhappily. "Aye, the issue has been addressed, and it has been decided upon. You will not teach, Reissa," he stated in a hard tone, then turned back to the door.

"Viktor, please," she pleaded, "I cannot suffer the days without children to care for."

"In time, we shall have our own," he supplied as his hand reached for the door handle, his head turned from her.

"'Tis not enough, Viktor, I must ask more of you." The lady shifted onto her knees and sat back on her haunches, prepared to spring from the bed to stop his departure if necessary.

"I have made my decision," he ground out, then turned the door handle and yanked open the wooden structure with a vengeance.

Prompted by his hasty exit, she sprang into frantic action. She jumped from the bed and bolted across the chamber. A slender wrist hooked around his elbow and tugged. "Viktor," she begged as tears burned in her throat. "Please, grant me a moment."

He stopped and sighed heavily, making no attempt to hide his irritation as he turned to her in the open doorway and crossed his arms over his chest.

"Will you not consider a compromise?" she questioned with feeling.

"Nay," he said automatically, clearly not giving the idea any thought. Once again, he moved to leave; however, Reissa was not going to give up so easily.

She clutched his forearm and cried, "Please wait!"

His gaze glanced at the shadowed corridor with the obvious desire to be elsewhere, but he did not leave her just yet. He glowered down at her, his voice hoarse with fury. "My patience has met its end, lady." With that, he gripped her upper arms and swung her around to press her slender form firmly against the door. "You will not work, and 'tis the end of it."

Reissa held her fists up near her face, readying herself to fend off blows. She was absolutely horrified at that point, but she had vowed she would not back down until she said all there was to say on the matter. Her courage was quickly fading, but she would not accept defeat yet.

"I shall volunteer my teaching services; I shall refuse payment," she offered, knowing he was opposed to a working wife. His high-class nobility was positively conceited with wealth and power, and she was suffering as a result.

She felt her hopes growing when he seemed to think on it for a moment, but then: "Nay." And, as if suddenly recalling her bare feet, he grunted and tossed her over his shoulder. He threw her onto the bed with little effort and spun around for the door. The mattress cushioned Reissa's landing, allowing her to quickly regain focus.

"One day a week?"

He continued on as if he had not heard the generous offer.

She pushed herself onto her knees with the intent to rise again, but, guessing her game, he whirled around and stood over her with an expression of such menace, the lady raised her forearms to shield her face from his fists.

She was rewarded with the sound of his disgusted grunt. "Be damned, Reissa, your face will not suffer the punishment of my fists;

however, I will turn you over my knee if you insist on pursuing a dead issue."

Despite the presence of fear, her temper took over. He was denying her only chance for happiness. She lowered her hands and glared up at him. "I hate you, Viktor," she hissed quietly.

He sneered, "There are few who do not." With that, he spun on his heel and stormed from her chambers.

Reissa sat up and glared after him. The man may not have changed his mind, but she still refused to accept defeat. She would have what she wanted, but first she would have to learn how to ride.

Viktor need never know of her plans.

Chapter 20

"Sir Alden, has your generous offer to teach me to ride expired?" Reissa requested when she spotted him in the chamber corridor the next morning.

"Certainly not, my lady. When would you like to make use of my services?" he questioned with a smile, then held out his arm to escort her below to break their fast.

She hooked her arm with his, and they leisurely strolled down the shadowed hall toward the front stairwell.

"Would this morn be an imposition?" She asked tentatively, not wanting to overstep her bounds in any way.

"Not an imposition a' tall," he returned with an inconsequential wave of his hand. "Shall we meet in the stables an hour after the morning meal?"

"Aye, 'twould be a pleasure."

The pair crossed the keep in contented silence and ascended the dais. He politely pulled her chair, then moved around to seat himself in his designated place. After they were both settled, they scanned the table and realized Viktor and Collin were absent.

Reissa's gaze lifted and caught Moira's perceptive stare.

"I believe your husband joined mine in a perverse indulgence of spirits last eventide, my dear. Collin is still abed; therefore, I assume Viktor is as well," she supplied, answering the question

Reissa had no intention of voicing aloud. She did not want her curiosity to show.

"Is that so?" was her only response. The other occupants at the table had taken up conversation, leaving the women to discuss such matters without spectators.

"'Tis a rare event; however, the brothers generally share a night of intoxication when one has suffered a taxing day. Unfortunately, Collin and I quarreled last eventide; therefore, he sought Viktor's welcoming presence," Moira admitted without a hint of modesty. "The man needed an outlet for the fury I ignited."

Following her sister-in-law's lead, Reissa added under her breath, "Viktor and I also quarreled last eventide."

The lady's stunning blue eyes bulged in shock. "And you survived?"

When Reissa's expression changed into one of utter terror, Moira reached across the table and touched her hand, giving an apologetic smile. "Forgive me, my dear, 'twas a terrible jest." She gazed at her for a pensive moment. "May I ask what the two of you quarreled over?"

Reissa picked at the contents of her trencher, her appetite waning. "I asked him to reconsider my teaching in the village."

"Were you able to persuade him into giving over?" the mother-to-be wondered as she began munching on her third piece of cheese.

"Nay, the man is a bloody tyrant, intent on exerting his will."

"Aye, he is that. Much like my own husband at times."

"I do not see any resemblance in disposition, my lady. Your husband is a pleasant presence. Viktor is—" she broke off, unable to find the appropriate words to describe the man. She glanced at the staircase entrance, fearful that he might appear at any moment and overhear their talk.

"You need not go on, Reissa; I am well aware of Viktor's ways. Aye, he is a difficult man, but he is also my husband's brother; therefore, I must accept him into my life without regret."

"He is my husband. I must do the same. However, 'tis a rather grueling task to wed a stranger who cares nothing for marriage."

"I love the man I married, but there are occasions when I feel what you are feeling, my dear. Last eventide is a prime example."

Reissa gazed at her for a moment, her curiosity rising. "May I inquire as to your quarrel?" she asked softly.

"I feel that not enough has been done to seek Golly's murderer. Not enough have been questioned; zero action has been taken. I will not suffer the presence of a murderer when our child has been born, and I informed him of this. Suffice it to say that he was not pleased." Her smile was sad as she relived the harsh words that had passed between them the prior evening.

"Has the issue been resolved?"

"Aye, temporarily. As Viktor stated the morning when Golly was found, a messenger has been sent to inform the king of our unfortunate tidings. Until we learn of our king's decision on the matter, I must be content to accept our present circumstances," she explained, although her fury clearly had not dissipated.

Neither Viktor nor Collin appeared during the course of the meal. When Reissa did not see either of the brothers as she made her way to stables for her riding lesson, she was stricken with a mild case of concern. She walked out into the bright light of day. The sun was shining, and the air was cool, but she noticed none of it because her mind was preoccupied with thoughts of seeing to her husband's ailments. She had a strong desire to check on his state, but she brushed off the feeling as Alden entered the stables and greeted her with a smile.

As a teacher, Kilgour's tactics were to be admired. He was extremely knowledgeable, patient, and determined not give up on a student he learned was fearful of heights. He never left her side. He was present every step of the way as she became familiar with being seated alone in the saddle and the perfecting of her skill. When the hour of the midday meal struck, Reissa had grown comfortable enough to get into the saddle without aid and spur the mount into a leisurely trot. Certainly, she had much to learn. There was need for much more experience to be considered an accomplished rider, but she now knew enough to further her plan.

In the morning, while the men were preoccupied with their daily drills, she would make her way to the village.

Despite her resentment of their quarrel the previous evening, Reissa decided to act on her concern over Viktor's ill state. She told herself that she was his wife, and it was her duty to see to his needs, but Reissa knew it was just an excuse to check in on him. Yes, she feared him, but for reasons unknown to her, reasons she could not explain, she suddenly had the need to surround herself with his presence.

Her slippered feet were quiet on the staircase as she ascended to the chamber and moved down the corridor to his quarters. Never would she have considered entering his bedchamber without announcing herself in some fashion, but the door to his antechamber was slightly ajar, so she did not hesitate to enter without knocking.

She walked in tentatively, while simultaneously scolding herself for intentionally seeking him out. But Reissa was brought up short by the unexpected and disturbing sight of Edith standing over a chair of Viktor's discarded clothing. She held one of his tunics to her nose, her eyes were closed, and there was no mistaking the scene. She was breathing in his scent.

Reissa was unable to stifle her stunned gasp.

Hearing the intrusive sound, Edith dropped the tunic and turned, her expression marked with guilt for her trespassing. "My lady!" she cried.

"Lady Kilgour, you should not be in my husband's personal quarters." Reissa stepped into the room, a frown upon her face. Typically, because of her poor background, she had difficulty upholding her role as a woman of noble class, but now, in protection of her husband's interests, she had no trouble donning the noble cloak. "I believe an explanation is in order."

Her round face fell in shame, eyes lowering to the floor. "Forgive me, please."

"I know not what I am to forgive, Edith. You have failed to supply the explanation I requested."

Edith's sigh was unsteady. "'Tis my secret, my lady; I cannot speak it."

"You shall, or I will be forced to take the matter to my husband," she threatened, although something in the lady's demeanor touched her heart with pity. When the frantic shimmer of tears became visible in those amber eyes as Edith hurried forward and pressed her palms together in earnest, Reissa had to hide her empathy.

"I beg of you, do not speak of this to Viktor." Her puffy cheeks grew wet with moisture, eyes pleading.

"Your secret?" Reissa refused to dismiss the scene without learning the truth.

Edith's eyes closed as she gave in. "I care for him, my lady."

She shrugged, misunderstanding. "You may not share his blood, but you are a member of this family nevertheless; 'tis natural for you to care for him."

"My feelings for him are not that of a sister," she confessed in a whisper.

At last, Reissa was able to comprehend the lady's meaning. The question was immediate upon her lips. "Do you love him?"

"Aye." She nodded as she broke into heart-wrenching sobs.

Even though the information greatly unnerved her, Reissa could not help but put her arms around the larger woman and fold her in a soothing embrace. "'Tis an unfortunate affair, Edith; I am truly sorry."

"An apology is not necessary, my lady. 'Tis my load to bear." She hiccupped in an attempt to stop the flow of tears.

"You must despise me," Lady Colville perceived as she tried to see the picture through Edith's eyes.

Kilgour abruptly pulled from her arms and emphatically shook her head from side to side. "Nay, my lady, never."

"I shall understand if you resent my presence in your lives."

"I do not. I am convinced my feelings shall fade in time, and I understand my fate lay elsewhere. One day when I have gathered enough courage, I will leave Appleta."

Reissa gazed at her, uncertain how to respond. How could she tell her to stay when it was clearly tearing her apart to love Viktor, yet unable to indulge in that love? She could not. But was that the only reason why she did not speak up and convince her to stay? She feared it was not.

Chapter 21

A brilliant smile marked Reissa's plain face on her return trip from the village the next afternoon. She had secured a position as a teaching assistant two days a week, Tuesdays and Thursdays. The elder lady she would be assisting was a kind, friendly woman with graying hair and big blue eyes made more so by the spectacles perched precariously on the end of her nose. She was constantly pushing them up into place. And the children were a delight.

She met them briefly when Mrs. Sandborne introduced her before class let out for the day. A lively bunch, full of laughter. She had watched as they departed, going their separate ways home. One little girl caught her attention when she halted near the road and simply stood there, looking both ways, as if she had forgotten where to go.

Reissa approached and politely asked, "Is anything wrong?"

When those big brown eyes lifted up to meet her inquiring gaze, her heart was stolen. Instantly, she knew Maisie would be her favorite in class. With a scrawny little figure, mousy hair, and smudged cheeks, she was reminded of herself at that age. Hell, even at her present age, before her marriage.

Maisie nodded shyly. "Mama is not here."

"She walks you home?"

The girl nodded a second time.

"Would you like me to walk with you?"

Another timid nod. Reissa smiled and offered her hand. The meek little girl took it, and she walked a mile to her home.

Thinking of the change in her life, she felt as if some of the spirit had returned to her soul. Even the bulging snow clouds overhead did not threaten her happiness. However, as her thoughts returned to the previous day, her smile dissolved. After Edith's confession, it had been extremely difficult to go below and partake of the midday meal with her husband.

She knew he was still angry with her over the previous night's argument because he said not a word to her during the entire course of the meal. Nevertheless, her eyes shifted between her husband and Edith with a will of their own. As she ate her food, she could not help but wonder how Viktor would react if he knew of Lady Kilgour's feelings.

Aye, Edith may have been cursed with an excess of weight, but the face beneath was truly lovely. Did Viktor see it? And if so, if he saw the presence of her love for him, would he go to her?

Her good mood dipped. As her mind imagined her husband visiting Edith's bedchamber, she could not help but recall his order to overlook his faithlessness. Had he bedded another since their wedding?

The possibility that he had soured her mood until she actually felt herself trembling with feeling. She tried to soothe her buzzing emotions with the rationale that she would prefer he bedded another rather than be subjected to his attentions herself, but that did nothing to calm her.

In an effort to distract her thoughts, she lifted her eyes to the sky and was startled to see that darkness was falling.

"Oh dear," she breathed. Escorting Maisie home had eaten up more time than she could afford to give in her position. The dinner hour would soon arrive, and she was not yet halfway to her destination. If she failed to appear for the meal without an excuse for her absence, it was likely that Viktor would seek her out. And if he sought her out, he would learn that she had taken a mount hours ago and had yet to return.

A shiver coursed through her body as she foresaw his temper over her act of insubordination. The man would be irate. Would he strike her? If he struck her, would she survive it? She shivered.

Despite her inexperience, Reissa spurred Hornet into a steady canter and held on tight. The remainder of the ride was filled with nothing but prayers for his understanding as night settled around her. When she finally entered the stables, the dinner hour had long since passed. She knew there was no way her absence had been overlooked. As she dismounted and exited the massive building, she was overcome with fear.

When she heard the sudden pounding of footsteps moving in her direction, she lifted her gaze and saw an army of armored men moving toward her.

Reissa stopped dead. Her breath stalled when she noticed Viktor led them. She knew the moment he spotted her because his sober expression instantly turned black. His eyes drilled into her, shaking her with their intent. He marched up to her and clutched her upper arm in a merciless grip, ensuring she could not escape him. He dismissed his entourage of soldiers with a few curt words and a wave of his hand, then looked to her as if she had committed a mortal sin.

"Where have you been, lady?" He demanded through gritted teeth.

She would not lie to cover disobeying his order. She would face the consequences despite her paralyzing terror.

"The village," she choked out, unable to meet his penetrating gaze.

"The village. What necessitated a visit to the village?" he growled, although she feared he already knew the answer to his question.

"I—" she floundered until he gave her a rough shake. "I sought a teaching position."

"You disobeyed a direct order?" His sudden calm was more horrifying than his temper.

"Aye." Her face grew crimson in shame.

He grunted with feeling then turned to the castle and ruthlessly dragged her toward the towering structure. His long legs and swift gait forced her to run to keep up; otherwise she would have fallen to the ground, and she had no doubts he would not have been good enough to stop to allow her to return to her feet.

He entered the keep and dragged her across the vast Meeting Hall for all occupants to see, causing her to lower her head when she noticed they had gained every last person's attention. Without a care for his angry display, Viktor bellowed for his squire to hasten to his quarters.

Reissa stumbled once up the staircase. The heartless man surprised her by yanking her from her knees without a word, then continued on, not sparing his wife a glance. He entered her bedchamber and roughly guided her inside. He stood in the open doorway. She turned, expecting him to be bearing down upon her, but she was confused when he pointed a finger at her and ordered, "You will await my return, Wife. 'Tis necessary for me to discard my armor for what I must do." With that, he slammed the door, leaving her to fall to her knees, weakened by the threat of violence.

She sat back on her haunches on the cool stone flooring, uncaring that a chill swept through her clothing and into her diminutive figure. She rested an elbow on the pine chest at the foot of her bed and buried her face in the crook of her arm, desperate to keep the tears at bay. All the fears that had mounted since first meeting her husband were about to come crashing down upon her. As a result, she was a pathetic, quivering mass.

If she possessed any courage at tall, it failed to give her the strength to rise when Viktor abruptly burst into her bedchamber and once again threw the door shut. Her head felt like it weighed a ton when she lifted it to take in her husband's masculine figure. His armor had been removed, leaving him in navy braies and a matching belted tunic. She looked at his chest and arms and flinched when she saw the dark material clinging to the hard muscle beneath.

When he spotted her kneeling on the floor, his raging expression did not falter. He marched into the room, grasped her upper arms in a tense grip and yanked her to her feet. Reissa felt her stomach turn with nausea when he moved toward the bed.

"What are you about, Viktor?" she cried despondently.

"I will execute your punishment, lady," her husband announced in an inarguable tone, then sat on the edge of the bed and guided her to stand beside his knees. His beautiful face was impassive as he unhooked the clasp at her throat and drew aside the heavy cloak. He dropped it onto the bed beside him, took her hand in his, and gazed up at her. His hard features softened almost imperceptibly when he noticed the trembling she was unable to hide.

"I am regretful for your fear, Reissa, but you must learn to obey my orders. I do not do this to be cruel; I do it for your protection," he said quietly.

Her mouth gaped. His words sparked her temper in spite of an elevating apprehension. At least her father had the decency to act swiftly in his beatings, without plying her with rubbish before he did so. "I fail to understand how abuse is a form of protection, my lord," she remarked defiantly, hating him in that moment for what he was about to do, and for his transparent apology.

When she saw his jaw clench in irritation, she closed her eyes, expecting to suffer an unforgiving fist to the face. Instead, he tugged on her hand and forced her face down across his lap, causing her eyes to fly open in startled surprise. The shocked retort upon her lips was cut off when he lifted her skirts and pushed down her drawers, baring her bottom to his gaze.

After she muddled through pure humiliation, finally she realized his intent, and her pulse stalled. Reissa was unable to analyze her feelings in that instant because his palm connected painfully with her derrière, and her eyes squeezed shut, attempting to block out the throbbing wave that passed through her tiny figure.

She gritted her teeth to the whimper that vibrated in her throat as the second spanking registered with her mind and body. It was quickly followed with another, and another. His harsh administrations continued until she could no longer feel her backside. Even as she suffered his punishment, she found she was grateful for it.

Several spanks were trivial in comparison to her father's merciless fists. She would survive without a mark, and that certainly was not the case when Bernard was angry with her. Her father struck her without the slightest provocation, yet she had incensed Viktor with her insubordination and constant fears of him, and that was the worst she had been subjected to in his anger.

It was cause to wonder, was he not the type to beat a woman after all? Or did he reserve punches and slaps for his worst punishments? But then she recalled Golly's strangled figure and realized death was a result of his worst punishments. Another shiver coursed through her body.

At last, he pushed down her skirts. She knew it would be days before she could sit comfortably, yet she had survived, and she was proud of herself for not giving in to tears.

Viktor gripped her arms and lifted her to stand while he erected himself from his seated position. Those dark eyes looked down upon her as he aided her unsteady stance. He was pensive for a moment, then said, "You risked my ire to teach, and I know how much you fear me. Does it mean that much to you, Reissa?"

"Aye, Viktor." She suffered his punishment without crying, yet the unexpected gentleness in his voice prompted a floodgate of tears that spilled over before she could avert her gaze.

She quickly brushed them away as she peered at the floor, but he refused to let her look away. He held her chin in a firm grip and stared into her shimmering gray orbs. The tiny flecks of gold in his were more visible than she had ever seen.

"Tell me of the agreement," he suggested lightly.

"I am to aid the principal teacher in the village on Tuesday and Thursday afternoons," her voice was a soft quiver.

"How did you intend to explain your absences?" he wondered.

"I will leave following the morning meal and arrive home prior to supper. You have drills all day. I believed you would never learn of my absences."

His lips thinned, clearly not liking that answer. But he didn't share his thoughts and asked another question, "Will you be paid for your services?"

"Nay, I refused payment."

He gave a nod of approval. "Very well, you may continue your dealings in the village."

Reissa's mouth fell open in stunned disbelief. Had she heard him correctly?

"However, I require a five-man escort at all times. I will not see you going alone, as you did this day; do you understand?"

"Aye," she was quick to respond, although she was still shocked by his sudden accommodation to her happiness.

With that, he tenderly wiped a stray tear from her cheek with the pad of his thumb, then turned and exited without another word.

Chapter 22

An entire week passed without incident. Reissa saw little of her husband. Not once did he visit her in request of his marital rights. When they were together, which was typically during meals, he treated her with distant familiarity. They only spoke when it was necessary, and those occasions were rare.

As more days passed, somehow word spread through the servants, and then on to the nobility, that Viktor hadn't entered his wife's bedchamber in nearly a fortnight. Clearly the man did not give a fig for gossip because he was not prompted to put an end to his absence simply because of the talk.

And due to his extended hiatus, Reissa felt unwanted suspicions growing within her. Had he taken a mistress? A lover? Was he seeking pleasure elsewhere; was that the cause for his absence? Or was his aversion to her so strong that he simply could not bring himself to return to her bed?

Viktor had become the focal point of nearly every thought, shadowing her every breath, even when he was not nearby. She was plagued with desolate images of him taking another woman into his bed and imaginings of him laughing with his faceless lover about his plain wife. The lady hypothetically beat herself up for her unattractive face and stick-thin body, knowing she would never be the beauty he should have on his arm.

Of course, he was on her mind one Tuesday after she returned from the village and entered her room to dress for the evening meal. However, she was brought up short to find Bernard waiting in her antechamber.

"Father?" She breathed, then glanced into the corridor, praying for a passerby to intrude upon them. Hell, she would have welcomed Viktor's presence in that moment.

"Shut the door, girl," he ordered as he paced back and forth with a tankard of ale clutched in his hand.

Reissa did not shut the door completely. She left it slightly ajar, deciding she would not suffer a beating that day. Today she would run from him. So, she stood with her back to the door, poised to bolt if he came near.

"Why have you sought me out, Father?" she questioned, keeping her voice low.

"I have heard the rumors, and I have come to speak of my displeasure," he grated as he placed the tankard on a table in front of the brocade sofa.

"I know of your displeasure, Father." She wanted to ask him when he was not displeased with her, but she knew doing so would be tantamount to raising his fist for him. "Please, I must dress for supper." She hoped he would take the hint and leave, but he ignored her plea.

"'Tis a stipulation of the marriage contract that you provide an heir within a year. I want that heir, Reissa, but 'tis an impossible feat if your husband refuses to warm your bed," he accused with a disgusted curl of his lip. "You are a failure, girl."

He began a determined approach. Memories of past cruelties flooded her mind, temporarily paralyzing her. Instinct told her to flee, but her feet refused to comply. She could do nothing but watch in horror as he lifted his arm and cracked the back of his hand across her pale face. The force of the blow unbalanced her. She rocked on her feet before crumpling to the floor in a helpless heap.

Her father would know one blow had rendered her defenseless, but he paid her state no heed. He was a merciless devil. He pushed the door shut and turned back to her.

"You homely, worthless piece of baggage," he bit out under his breath before kicking the vulnerable flesh of her side.

Reissa bit her lip to keep from crying out. She knew her screams would draw the curiosity of many, and she would rather die than suffer the humiliation of others learning her secret.

So, when Bernard balled his fist and callously struck her cheek while she was down, she quickly covered her mouth to drown out a shriek of pain. The door may have been shut, but she knew the screams would carry if she didn't staunch their noise.

"My life would have been greatly bettered if you had never been born." The monster actually pursed his lips and spit on her.

The clear liquid splashed onto her temple and mingled with the tears that were trailing down her ashen skin. She clutched her skirts and wiped the insult from her face, then stared up at him in a frozen state of fear. The throbbing in her left cheek was unbearable, but she could do nothing to stop the hurt, physically and mentally.

"You will give me an heir, or I shall be forced to beat the life from you," he ordered with overt menace. With that, he opened the door and casually strolled from the room as if nothing out of the ordinary had occurred.

After he had gone, she lay there, unwilling to move, knowing the pain would be horrendous. Warm blood trickled from her nose, and her cheek was quickly swelling, but she cared not. The true blow had been to her sense of self. She felt as worthless as he claimed.

Every time he hurt her, she felt another loss of control. Her life was not her own, and it seemed it never would be. Bernard would forever be there to remind her that she had ruined his life, simply by living. And because of that, he would forever make hers a living hell.

Ever so slowly, she rolled onto the side he had not kicked. She curled up into the fetal position and gave in to the need to weep quietly.

※ ※ ※

Reissa pled fatigue as an excuse for her absence from the evening meal that night, and she was rewarded with privacy from everyone, save the maid who had relayed word. No one knew of her state because she had turned away, using only her voice to dismiss the girl from her chambers after her meal had been brought up.

As the days had passed, Lady Colville had almost longed for Viktor to visit her when night fell, but on that night, she prayed for him to stay away. And he did. And she was grateful.

Unfortunately, she could not stall time. Morning arrived too soon, and she knew she could not plead continued fatigue without someone checking in on her. So, she conjured up a lie to tell when the question was asked about her injuries and rang for Gert to aid her toilet.

After the girl helped her don an emerald underdress, a navy overdress with green hemming, and netted her strawberry blond locks, she took a deep breath and stepped into the shadowed corridor.

"Reissa," a familiar voice broke through her tense reverie, causing her head to lift without thought. She looked up to find Viktor moving toward her, but he halted when his gaze touched on her bruised face.

"Dear Lord," he mumbled, then hurried forward and pressed his palm to her cheek, turning her face so he could study the ugly patch of color trailing down the side of her face. The lighting in the darkened corridor was inadequate, yet there was no mistaking that she had been struck, and by the extent of her bruises, clearly she had suffered more than one blow. "Who has done this, Reissa?"

"'Tis not as 'twould seem, Viktor," she explained, shifting her eyes to the floor. "Two men were engaged in a quarrel in the village yesterday afternoon. I stepped in to break up the combat and was rewarded with two accidental fists in my face."

"Who were these men?" he tested. "Why did they not accompany you and deliver a personal apology for their unacceptable behavior?"

"'Twas an accident, Viktor. I told them 'twould not be necessary to do so."

He gazed at her skeptically, then, "Why have my men not informed me of the matter?"

She had to think fast. "They were not witness to the event; in fact, they know nothing of the matter. The bruises became visible to the eye only after I retired for the evening and slept."

His sigh was heavy with feeling. "Are you in need of medical attention? Shall I summon Edith?"

"Nay, I am well. It looks worse than it feels, I assure you." It was only a partial lie. In truth, the blow that had the greatest lingering effect was the kick to her side. Her ribs smarted with every step, although she was certain her father had not done any permanent damage.

"Nevertheless, you are confined to your chambers for the length of the day to rest," he ordered, gently gripping her elbow. "I will make your excuses to all."

"Thank you, Viktor."

His features softened for a moment, then abruptly filled with fury. "Never again will you behave so recklessly, Reissa. If you are ever confronted with a like situation, I forbid you to intrude. Do you understand?"

She nodded, consumed with guilt for her lies.

As Viktor led the lady back to her chambers, she realized he had gained her gratitude for the second time in a fortnight. She was not yet ready to confront a Meeting Hall full of observers with a face marked by brutality. He had delayed what was certain to be a tense scene, and she could not deny that an added day of rest would greatly speed the healing process along.

However, that gratitude quickly plummeted when he followed her directly into her bedchamber without breaking stride.

She halted near the window embrasure and watched as he rang for her lady's maid. Then he moved over to the wardrobe and extracted a modest cotte for Gert to help her change into.

Finally, he glanced at her and said, "Despite your assurances to the contrary, I will send Edith to look after you." Then he departed before she could speak a word to stop him.

Chapter 23

Viktor stepped into the darkened corridor and ground to a halt. He let out a heavy breath, supremely disturbed by the illogical feeling coursing through his veins. Seeing the sharp discoloration upon his wife's face had rivaled a punch in the gut. A deeply rooted anger gripped him. He demanded a culprit, and when she admitted her bruises were the result of an unfortunate accident, that anger only dissolved a fraction.

Against his will, he had imagined the pain she suffered, and he grew desperate for someone to blame. He desired an outlet for his irrational fury, wanting to throw his fists into the flesh of another man's face.

As he ascended the staircase, he told himself that the only reason behind his heartfelt reaction was because Reissa was a member of his family, and he protected his family at all costs. As he took his seat at the trestle table, he sent one of the maids to collect a tankard of ale to soothe his raging emotions.

Well attuned to the clues of his brother's quieter moods, Collin turned a pair of curious eyes in his direction and put a voice to his thoughts. "Spirits at dawn, little brother. What has passed?"

"My wife will not be joining us."

"Is she unwell?" Moira asked in concern.

"She is not ill. However, she has suffered a rather intense beating," he explained while staring at the food that had been placed in front of him. He did not move to eat it.

The group was so enraptured by their lord's tale that they failed to see the obvious expression of guilt that Bernard quickly transformed into one of feigned concern.

"Two men in the village erupted into violence, and my timid little wife stepped in to avert their battle." He glanced at Lady Kilgour. "I would like assurance that Reissa has not been seriously injured. Will you see to her, Edith?"

"Of course, Viktor." She moved off to do his bidding immediately.

"Are the consequences of her actions visible?" Alden quizzed with a creased brow.

"The entire left side of her face is marked with bruising." Viktor took a healthy swallow from the tankard a maid placed directly into his awaiting, open hand.

"Would you like to seek out the guilty parties, little brother?" Collin suggested. His carefree countenance had been replaced with dark seriousness.

"I would like nothing more," he growled softly. "I would like to fault those men for what they have done, but I cannot. 'Twas not their intent to harm her; therefore, I shall let the matter rest. My anger stands nevertheless."

A tense silence stretched for some time before Kilgour interrupted it with lighthearted banter. "I pity the man who is first to face you on the battlefield this day, my friend."

"As do I," Collin added, quickly regaining his humor.

"The exercise is much needed following a mere eight hours on the field yesterday," Viktor said in an attempt to change the subject, ignoring their jests. "We may have need for extended drills if the rumors circulating Ender are correct." His words gained the attention of every occupant at the table.

"'Twould seem the future may see a period of civil unrest within our provinces. There has been talk that our good friend, Rynearson," sarcasm dripped thick as molasses from his tongue, "may have gained an ally in Cumberland."

"Rynearson and Bennington have been on the verge of war for nearly a decade," Alden inserted with a frown.

"'Tis common knowledge that our overlord and Cumberland's overlord are sworn enemies; therefore, the speculation of sudden allegiance does not bode well for our territory, perhaps the whole of England."

"Rynearson is a greedy fop. 'Twas only a matter of time afore he sought war for more power," Collin mentioned.

"'Tis also common knowledge that the king is considering dispatching Northumberland's overlord. Rynearson created tension with Edward during the Treaty of Bretigny, demanding another territory for himself, but I am certain you are well aware that Edward refused," Bernard entered into the conversation.

"Aye, Maitland," Alden acknowledged. "If summoned, Rynearson is certain to enter into an allegiance with Cumberland."

"Do you believe they seek to overthrow the throne?" Moira asked of her brother-in-law.

"I would wager the manor on the matter," Viktor drawled with suppressed rage.

"Bennington is a sworn ally to our king, but above and beyond that, they are confidants," Lady Moira pointed out to the men.

"The man is spineless; he is not above treason," Collin spoke in harsh tones; however, his hard eyes grew gentle when they touched on his wife's lovely face. In spite of the worry the conversation created amongst loyal members to the crown, Moira possessed a pregnant glow that only added to her beauty.

"If such rumors are true, battle with our overlord is imminent," Alden remarked unhappily. "We must seek the allegiance of our neighbors."

"We cannot act upon mere speculation." Collin was the voice of reason. "There is a margin of error we must take into consideration. If the rumors are incorrect, we risk angering a loyal overlord, and action toward him is also treason to the throne. We tread on a fine line of peace."

"Is the king aware of the talk of civil unrest?" Bernard requested of no one in particular.

"'Tis a certainty," Viktor responded, then took a healthy pull from his tankard. "Edward maintains informants within every territory."

"Then 'tis possible he is in preparation of war within England's shores?" Moira wondered.

Viktor brushed a stray lock from his eyes. "Edward is in preparation of war at all times."

A gatehouse horn abruptly sounded, informing the castle's occupants that a guest awaited outside, requesting entrance into Colville Manor. The horn sounded when the visitor was unknown to the guards securing the outer curtain wall. Members of the family and close personal friends were generously escorted into the keep with prior permission from the lord of the manor.

Viktor rose from the table and crossed the keep. He mounted a saddled horse beyond the castle doors and made the lengthy journey across the bailey to the south gatehouse, where one of the guards awaited to inform him of the visitor's identity. When he learned that the man was a royal messenger of the crown, the portcullis was elevated, and the drawbridge lowered.

The man and the animal wearing England's colors were clearly exhausted as they ambled across the drawbridge to meet the nobleman they sought. His dismount was stiff, then he collected a miniature trumpet from leather saddlebags and played a tune that Viktor knew all too well.

"By order of the royal crown, I have been sent on to inform you that King Edward III will arrive at Colville Manor within days to address the issue of Lady Golly Colville's murder."

Chapter 24

Reissa could not have been more grateful for the distraction of teaching in the village than she was on that Thursday. She had suffered all of the pitiful looks she could bear two mornings prior when she descended for the morning meal. Her bruises had already begun to fade, but despite her prayers for the discoloring to disappear entirely, it had not.

Perceiving her desire not to discuss it, everyone had been kind enough not to speak of the occurrence, but she knew all thoughts had touched on the matter, including her father's. When he turned to watch her approach from where he was seated at the trestle table, his covert expression of warning could not be mistaken. Silently, he told her that if she spoke of the truth behind her injuries, he would end her.

As had become their normal routine in the recent fortnight, Reissa and Viktor barely spoke while the meal commenced. She only listened with half an ear over idle chitchat until the discussion broke into the king's impending arrival. Initially, the lady was startled to learn she was going to meet the King of England, but the palpable tension emanating from her husband's form caught her attention.

The crime of Golly's murder had been sent to the king, and he was arriving to look into the matter personally. Was Viktor nervous that Edward would learn of his guilt? Was he feeling the pressure of his crime?

That same question had swirled around her mind countless times since breaking her fast two days ago. Now, with Viktor at her side during the journey into the village, the issue of Golly's death once again plagued her.

It was late December, and as Lord of Ender, Viktor needed to fulfill his responsibility to the community by visiting his judgment upon others. On that day, he must conduct court. He would provide his presence in the extensive jailhouse at the heart of the village and hear each and every case until he had seen the last of its occupants, deeming them guilty or innocent of their criminal charges.

Reissa glanced at her husband's stunning profile and marveled at the morbid irony of it. In her opinion, this man, a murderer, was not fit to pass his judgment upon others. He possessed the legal rights to oversee his citizens, but, morally, he had lost all such rights when he cut his stepmother's life short.

Her gaze fell to his hands. She could almost see them tightening about Golly's slender throat, see her limbs flailing in desperation. Her fear of the man, which had ebbed of late, reaffirmed itself with full force. Never had she forgotten the sight of Golly's ashen body in her husband's bed. Never had she forgotten the picture of him standing over her, his face a mask of stone. Yet, in spite of it all, he had her believing him to be a human being rather than a monster.

Nearly every moment they had spent together proved to be to the contrary of his obviously volatile nature. The only scene that upheld the truth of his violent capabilities in relation to her was the eve of their wedding. Certainly, she had been apprehensive of him in many moments since their meeting, but to give him credit, he had never raised his hand to her.

Yes, he had doled out a physical punishment for defiance of a strict order, but even Reissa knew he was bound to act as he had. She did not harbor any resentment toward him for that day. And, yes, the man possessed an extreme temperament, but in actuality, the eve of their wedding and Golly's murder were the only instances in which she held him in an immoral prison.

Such crimes were of the utmost horrors, never to be locked away or forgiven. The simple knowledge that this man was able to murder without hesitation or regret would forever be the cause of her fear of him.

Reissa pulled the hood of her gold cloak against the biting cold. Winter had set upon them with a vengeance, but the ground was absent of snow. There was a dusting of white flakes, but as the sky was pure blue on that day, it would seem there was no need to worry over the weather.

They crested the rise near the village, and the entire party came to a halt.

Viktor looked at her. "I shall collect you when I have concluded my business at the jailhouse," he announced and directed several of his men to escort her to the schoolhouse.

Reissa merely nodded, then husband and wife urged their mounts into motion, parting without a backwards glance.

***

Lady Colville attended to a small group of children who needed special attention with their studies, while Mrs. Sandborne followed the remainder of the students out the door to watch them off at the end of their school day. As anticipated, Maisie had become the most favored of all her charges.

Reissa found herself adoring the girl's meek nature, and there was a kindness that sprouted from a warm heart. She happened to be the brightest of any child she had ever met, but she had an unfortunate tendency to neglect the schoolwork she took home. Because of that, she fell behind in her lessons, and because of her lagging, she was placed in Reissa's tutoring group.

They spent a couple hours going over the fundamentals of learning to read, but when the lady glanced out the window and saw that the sun was quickly dipping in the sky, she dismissed her students for the day.

***

Viktor saw the child trip down the last step of the schoolhouse entrance, but he was unable to save her from the fall as he observed from a distance of approximately fifty yards. The girl held her hands out to break the fall onto the frozen, packed dirt, but she struck the earth hard and immediately broke into high-pitched wails of pain. The lord was about to spur his mount into a hasty gallop when he witnessed his wife hurry through the open doors to give aid.

Thoughtlessly, he drew nearer as Reissa knelt next to the child, uncaring that her elegant skirts were trailing in dirt.

"Maisie, dear, are you hurt?" his wife demanded in a maternal tone as she scanned the little figure for serious injury. In response, the girl jumped to her feet, threw herself into the arms Reissa automatically opened for her, and proceeded to cry with more intensity.

The pair was presented to him in profile. He was positioned down the road, his men patiently waiting behind him, and watched in motionless silence as his mount slowly carried him closer. He was quite unable to tear his eyes from the scene playing out before him, and quite uncertain as to why. Viktor knew Reissa was too preoccupied with her tiny dilemma to hear the horse hooves approaching, yet he did nothing to make his presence known.

"Shh, darling," she said in a calming voice while her palm smoothed over the girl's back. "You have taken a tumble, but you are alright."

Maisie's cries turned into hiccupping sobs, and Reissa finally pulled away to thoroughly look her over. She spotted blood on the girl's skirts and lifted them to reveal scrapes on the child's knees. Her mouth turned down in a frown.

"Oh," she breathed, "let us go inside so I may tend to your wounds, Maisie." Reissa stood up. When she looked down upon the child, clearly intending to lift her into her arms so her bruised charge would not have to climb the steps, the frown deepened, knowing she did not possess the strength to do so.

Now, mere feet away, Viktor dismounted and reached the pair in ten long strides. He scooped the child into his arms and waited for his startled wife to precede him into the building.

After her initial surprise, her eyes shifted to the sniffling girl as she explained, "Do not be alarmed, Maisie, 'tis Viktor, my husband." With that, she lifted her skirts and hastily ascended the wooden flight of stairs.

Reissa crossed the room to the teacher's desk at the front. She collected a tiny wooden box containing first aid supplies while Viktor seated the girl on the edge of the structure. He stepped back, giving Reissa space to carry out the task of bandaging the child's wounds. Thoughtlessly he leaned back against the wall and crossed his arms over his chest, once again watching the scene in muted silence.

Reissa wet a clean rag from the water in the basin in the corner, then gingerly wiped the dirt and excess blood from Maisie's skinned knees. Feeling the pain the contact caused, the child's tears returned.

"I know that hurts, but I must prevent infection," she explained as her gaze held the child's attention. "Listen to my voice,

Maisie; I shall tell you a story." With that, she bestowed a loving smile upon the girl.

Viktor's breath caught as he took in the first real smile he had ever seen turn up the corners of his wife's mouth. It was not spectacular by any means, yet he felt the barest hint of sparked interest. Yes, his wife was plain, forgettable even, but when she smiled, a miraculous transformation had taken place. Her whole face became brilliant with light and life. There was a sparkle in her generally overcast eyes, a shimmer that could not be mistaken for unshed tears.

The woman standing before the child was a stranger to him. She was alive with meaning because of the girl's need for her care. He observed a happiness within that had been absent ever since they met.

The sudden realization produced a disturbing frown. The lady he knew was a meek, soft-spoken, and oftentimes forlorn individual. Clearly, she was unhappy in their marriage, and in her life. But teaching, being needed and caring for others were her only causes for joy.

Viktor bore next to nothing in knowledge of his wife, but he did know this: she had only one person in her life, and that was her father. Any other family or friends whom she had once loved were now gone. He was aware of it because the only person present for her wedding was Bernard. She spoke of no one, and no one had come to visit her, either at Moorestone or Colville Manor. And the relationship he speculated between father and daughter was purely a bond of blood and none other. If they felt love for one another, he had yet to see any display of it. They spoke little, and when they exchanged words, they were icy and formal.

In seeing her display of joy, any lingering feelings of resentment he harbored for allowing her to teach were gone. He felt an extreme degree of satisfaction in knowing that his grudging willingness to give in to her intent resulted in her pleasure. Capriciously, he was struck with the desire to be the cause of her happiness whenever an opportunity presented itself.

"—and she let down her long golden locks," Reissa told the story of Rapunzel as she extended her own strawberry blond tresses. The lady conveyed the complete story with vivid animation and gestures that mesmerized the tot while she simultaneously bandaged bony, skinned knees.

Not only was Maisie spellbound, but Viktor also found himself just as taken with her telling of the tale, absolutely intrigued by the transformation in his wife. Her brilliant smiles, soft melodic voice, and hand gestures held his attention, inspiring a new liking for a story he had heard countless times in his youth yet never really cared for.

Finally, Reissa finished her task and the tale, then looked up to the open double doors. She stared outside.

"Maisie, your mother has failed to arrive." Then those overcast eyes glanced at Viktor meekly. "We shall escort you home." When she saw that her husband made no objection, merely met her gaze passively, she looked to her little charge, grinned, and asked, "Have you ever ridden a horse?"

Maisie gasped with excited anticipation and shook her head from side to side. She put her arms out and waited for Reissa to pick her up. Lady Colville looked to her husband, and, without hesitation, he moved forward and lifted the girl into his arms. The trio exited the building, and Reissa mounted Hornet.

Viktor hoisted the girl up to sit in front of her teacher, then he climbed into the saddle of his own mount. Their escort of men followed at a meager distance as the Colvilles set out at a steady pace.

The sun was rapidly descending in the sky. Night would fall upon them before their return to the manor, but the couple, wordlessly deciding that Maisie's safe journey home was their first priority, continued on without reconsidering.

Viktor remained silent during the short journey down the dirt road, quietly listening to the sweet interaction between his wife and her student as they played word games. The game was meant to teach, but it was done with such fun that children knew not that they were learning.

Lord Colville's eyes were comfortably settled on his wife's profile when he noticed her gaze narrowing upon something in the distance. Viktor looked up and saw a labored woman hurrying toward them, her tired eyes pinned to Maisie's little figure. The woman was ragged, her skirts wrinkled and soiled, with dark shadows under her eyes. A distinct feeling of pity struck the lord upon seeing her fatigued form.

"Mama," the child's single word explained her identity.

When the woman reached them, the couple pulled their horses to a halt. Viktor swiftly dismounted and rounded to lift Maisie and his wife down.

"Please forgive my tardiness, my lady; I slumbered on despite the hour," she apologized as she knelt next to her daughter and placed a loving kiss upon her brow.

"I understand, Mrs. Michaels," Reissa said politely, failing to notice her husband's slight flinch at the mention of the woman's last name. "But 'tis not any trouble; Maisie is truly a joy. However, I have unfortunate news to impart. Your daughter tripped down the schoolhouse staircase. Do not be alarmed; she was not seriously injured, I assure you, but she has suffered minor scrapes to the knees. I have disinfected and dressed her cuts, but they will need added care."

Mrs. Michaels lifted soiled skirts, looked over her daughter's bandaged knees, then gently ran a hand through Maisie's tangled locks. She stood up and nodded her gratitude. "I appreciate your tender care, my lady." She shot the girl an affectionate smile, then shifted her gaze back to Reissa. Her expression was outlined with sadness. "I admit, my daughter is rather accident-prone."

"I suffer the same affliction," Reissa confessed.

Viktor scanned the dimming sky, then his large hand delicately palmed Reissa's shoulder.

***

The jolt of sensation that shot down her back was startling. She looked up to find her husband gazing at her intently. Another shock of sensation rolled through her.

"We must return presently, Reissa," he suggested firmly.

She tore her eyes from those beautiful black orbs and also glanced at the sky. Mindlessly, she nodded and returned her focus to mother and daughter.

"Once again, I must apologize for my tardiness. I have been rather exhausted of late," her excuse was punctuated with a hearty cough, "but I assure you, I shall be punctual in the future." With that, she took her daughter's hand, and after Maisie waved farewell, they turned and headed home.

Reissa stood there, looking after them, lost in her own world of thoughts, which prompted Viktor to give her shoulder a slight shake. She broke from her maternal thoughts, then glanced at the masculine hand resting on her shoulder and once again stared up into her husband's dark eyes.

"I have news to impart, but we shall discuss it during the journey." His hands closed around her waist and easily placed her in Hornet's saddle.

After he mounted his horse, they set out at a swift pace. Not only was night quickly descending upon them, they also needed to return in a timely fashion for the celebration of Collin and Moira's second wedding anniversary.

With their escort of mounted soldiers following at a safe distance, Viktor tentatively shifted his gaze to his wife.

Feeling the weight of his eyes upon her, Reissa put forth a question without looking at him, "What is it, Viktor?"

"Mr. Michaels appeared afore my court this day," he confessed in a hard tone.

Reissa's head turned to him, her expression wary. "Maisie's father?"

"I believe so."

Her eyes closed, sending a short prayer to the sky, then she spoke aloud, unable to hide her desperation. "Please impart his innocence."

"I cannot, Reissa; his guilt is a certainty."

"He has been sentenced?"

"Aye."

The lady thought of that woman who had greeted them in an obviously unhealthy state. And a helpless little girl living in a tiny shack. Both without the benefit of a husband and father. Her heart immediately went out to them.

"How long will they suffer his absence?"

"Forever." He took a deep breath. "He will hang, Reissa."

She gasped, instantly shaken by the brutality and finality of his decision. In spite of her fear of him, her spirited temper exploded, yet at the same time, she fought to keep it in check.

"You heartless wretch of a man," she muttered, only half wishing he would hear her scorn.

When he responded, her heart lurched with the realization that he had, in fact, heard her epithet. "You go too far, woman, as you are ignorant of his crimes. Perhaps 'twould be best to judge only after you have learned of the man's sins."

"Do tell," she spoke softly, but her words were curt.

"During my extended visit to Moorestone, a band of thieves was robbing travelers passing through Ender. I have learned that their leader, one Mr. Michaels, ruthlessly bludgeoned two such victims to death when they refused to give over their valuables."

Reissa cringed when she heard the word "bludgeoned." It was so graphic that she could not help but picture a bloody scene of mercilessness. Her head bowed, resenting her impulse to be angry with him for sentencing the man to the gallows. When she imagined a man such as that fathering Maisie, she felt fairly certain a person in possession of such a tempestuous nature could not have withheld his hand from his delicate wife and daughter.

"I recall my insult," she said simply.

"How gracious," he snapped.

"Give over, Viktor," she gave in to frustration, "that girl is now fatherless. What will they do?"

***

His gaze touched on a figure now painted by the shadows of twilight. Once again, he felt an unmistakable desire to aid in her happiness. Generally, he would have assigned one of his men to look in on his more poverty-ridden citizens from time to time, but in that case, knowing Reissa cared for the girl, he decided he would see to the Michaelses himself. "You need not concern yourself, Reissa; I will see that their needs are met."

"You will look after them?" she asked hopefully.

"Aye."

"Thank you, Viktor."

The lord shifted his gaze and observed that his wife's head was bowed in submissive gratitude. He was struck by the reality of her delicate form, not only in body, but in mind as well. She was a woman to be treated with care, and he knew he was not such a man.

He knew himself to be hard, unyielding, and rough, yet as his eyes lingered on Reissa's face, he decided to make an effort in relation to her. He would know what lay underneath a plain, unintriguing exterior to the mystery he sensed existed within.

"Your gratitude is unnecessary, woman; 'tis a responsibility to my people and nothing more," he remarked modestly.

"Many do not fulfill that responsibility, Viktor. Many care for nothing but themselves and their wealth and power." She observed.

"I am not many, Reissa," was his evasive response.

"'Tis certainly an understatement," she spoke before thinking twice.

He sent her a sideways glance, his expression masked. "Shall I accept that as a compliment or an insult?"

***

The lady gathered her strength and boldly stated, "Both."

The corner of his mouth twitched with a tremor of a smile before his head turned to stare straight ahead. It was the first Reissa had seen a snippet of humor in the man; therefore, she was startled to learn that he possessed such a facet in his personality.

Prior to that moment, she truly believed there was no existence of a softer side. Yes, she had deemed him to be human rather than a beast. And as she thought of him lifting Maisie's slight weight for her, she now knew that idea was likely. Could it be possible that a sense of humor and a sliver of kindness were present inside this killer?

"You have gained courage in the days following our marriage, Reissa. I must commend you for that," he commented seriously.

She stared, pleasantly surprised by his compliment, but insecurity budded modesty. "Courage is a trait I do not possess, Viktor, but I thank you for the approving remark."

"You possess more than you know, Reissa," he returned quietly, although there was a hard inflection in his voice as he continued on. "You defied a direct order and faced your punishment without making an attempt to flee." He nodded. "Aye, you possess courage."

Reissa was warmed by his praise, but as a woman unfamiliar with compliments, she was also embarrassed by it. So, she disregarded his words and made an abrupt subject change.

"Did the other members of Mr. Michaels' crew appear afore your court as well?"

"I am not at liberty to discuss such details. I have made an exception in Mr. Michaels's case because I know you care for his daughter."

His statement effectively put Reissa off. She turned her head, gazed out over the shadows swallowing England's rolling hills, and sighed, acknowledging the tense discomfort passing between her husband and herself. However, as the minutes stretched, she brushed it off as a question formed in her mind. She did not hesitate to voice it aloud. "Did you receive an impression of Mrs. Michaels' ill state?"

"Aye."

His immediate confirmation elevated her concern. "I would like Edith to see to her."

"Do you seek permission to accompany Lady Kilgour?" Viktor quizzed.

"Aye, with all due haste."

"Very well, you may return to the village on the morrow. Of course, I require an adequate escort of armed men." He pinned her with a commanding gaze.

"Aye, of course," she willingly agreed, grateful for his assistance on the matter.

Chapter 25

When Viktor and Reissa arrived at Colville Manor, they entered into a Meeting Hall that was bustling with activity. A group of minstrels occupied their designated corner. Couples surrounded them, happily dancing to a lively tune. And in the opposite corner, countless men were milling about, spectators of a friendly swordfight between two knights. Many were gathered in front of the fireplace. Some were playing chess, others were socializing, but all were consuming large amounts of ale. The trestle tables were spilling over with food and drink and diners, including the main table on the dais.

Taking notice of their return, Moira rose from the dais and hurried over to greet them. She nodded politely at Viktor, then took Reissa's hand and said with a smile, "Gert awaits you in your chambers to aid in your swift return to the celebration." Then, to the both of them, she said, "The meal will not commence without our hosts."

With that, the Colvilles ascended to the second level and parted to their separate quarters to dress for supper. Reissa entered to find a full bath of warm water waiting and Gert patiently biding her time. She bathed quickly then donned a golden cotte. A fitted underdress of matching gold with tippets at the sleeves was the next layer, and finally an overdress of navy blue velvet was the last. Her strawberry blond locks were left unbound, excluding two small braids that were woven into a perfect circle around the crown of her head.

When she emerged from her bedchamber in under an hour, she was brought up short to find Viktor dozing on a chaise near the window embrasure in her antechamber. He was dressed in a marvelously tailored navy blue tunic and braies that hugged his masculine form to perfection. A wide leather belt that sported a gold buckle with the Colville coat of arms accessorized the tunic. An ever-present sword hung from his hip, contrary to the innocence of his slumbering expression. Shiny ebony locks were tousled from his relaxed position on the chair.

Hearing her entrance, Viktor's eyes snapped open without pause. He jumped up, and his hand instinctually moved to the hilt of his sword as his gaze scanned the room for danger.

When she saw his offensive stance, Reissa froze, fearing he would cut her down before he realized it was she who stood there. But when he spotted her standing in the open doorway of her bedchamber, wide-eyed, the set of taut lines in his handsome face receded. He sighed, and his hand fell away from the hilt.

The lady was so relieved by his awareness that she felt guilty for startling him from his state of rest. "I apologize for disturbing your slumber."

"A full day of court is rather taxing, but we have a celebration to attend," he returned as he offered an arm, then dutifully escorted her from the room.

A hush fell over the crowd as they entered the Meeting Hall, respecting their hosts with silence as they crossed the vast space. Viktor pulled his wife's chair after they mounted the dais. Before taking his seat at the head of the table, he raised his tarnished chalice of wine, signaling his intent to toast the evening's celebrated couple. Only when he was certain he possessed the focus of every last pair of eyes did he speak.

"As Collin's younger brother, 'tis my honor and my privilege to toast the second anniversary of his union to a woman who has entered into our family with the ease of being born into it. This remarkable couple is to be admired, praised, and loved. In tribute to the lord and lady, I expect every occupant in this room to celebrate their years by draining Colville Manor's reserves of spirits."

Hearty laughter erupted from the crowd, and Reissa's pulse tripped when her husband's rosy lips turned up in a radiant grin.

"Let us drink to Collin and Moira," he ended, lifting his goblet toward them in a symbolic gesture, then took a healthy pull of the red port. The crowd followed by doing the same, then there was an uproar of applause and sharp whistles.

At last Viktor folded into his chair, giving the cue for everyone to begin eating. Reissa looked to the trencher before her, but her mind was lingering on the mesmerizing image of her husband's smile. The reveal of even white teeth had only added to an already devastating appearance.

Her eyes lifted and openly gaped. As she watched him conversing with his brother, she was once again overwhelmed with the truth that she was married to a man who was far too attractive. In spite of her elegant attire, she felt dowdy and deeply unworthy to grace the arm of one so handsome.

She had to force her thoughts to travel in another direction. When she regained a modicum of control, her mind hastily touched on Maisie's mother. Overcast eyes shifted to Edith to politely wait for the lady to look in her direction. Lady Kilgour sat on the opposite side of the table, beside her brother, and her brother sat beside Collin and Moira.

She was not surprised to witness the lady gazing at her husband with secret affection. However, the feeling that bubbled up inside her certainly was a surprise. Reissa felt alarmingly protective, nearly hostile. An urge to lash out was overpowering, but she subdued it by trying to seek rational thought. Such intense feeling was confusing, frightening even, but her surging emotions were gratefully distracted when Edith glanced at her.

Guilt for staring at Viktor instantly flooded the lady's round face with color. Reissa dismissed the issue and said, "Edith, I must request your assistance in the village on the morrow. A student's mother appears to be unwell."

In an obvious attempt to compensate for being caught in the act, she nodded vigorously. "Aye, Reissa, 'tis my pleasure to give needed aid."

Hearing their discussion, Viktor inserted, "And I have already informed my wife that you will have an armed escort."

Edith nodded shyly. "Of course."

The weight of her husband's gaze caused her head to turn, and their eyes locked.

"I expect to be informed of the woman's condition upon your immediate return," he ordered quietly.

"I am to seek you out during drills?" she wondered, knowing he did not like to be disturbed while he trained.

"Aye." His gold-flecked eyes moved over the plains of her face before circling to meet hers. "You need not fear raising my ire while I am on the field, Reissa. I am willing to address any legitimate issue you may have."

She could not help but smile. "Legitimate," she repeated lightly, "so if I were to disturb swordplay to inquire of your opinion over the matter of my gown, 'twould raise your ire?"

He chuckled. "Most certainly."

Reissa grinned, thoroughly enjoying the sound of her husband's deep laughter. "You have my assurance of anonymity over such matters, Viktor."

"I am eternally grateful," her husband continued the carefree banter with a jest.

"In the past, I sought my mother's opinion above all others, but as she is gone, I shall seek Moira when I desire an opinion not of my own," she said thoughtlessly.

Several moments passed as he looked on her in a pensive reverie, causing the lady to shift uncomfortably in her chair. Finally, he glanced at Bernard and wondered quietly, "You do not seek your father's opinion?"

Reissa stole a glance at the man seated at her right elbow. He was preoccupied in a discussion with another; therefore, it appeared that he had not heard the abrupt shift in their conversation.

Her head turned back to her husband, but her eyes lowered to the table. She had no desire to speak of her father, but her mother she chose to embrace with open arms. "My mother and I were extremely close, but, sadly, she was stolen from us more than a decade prior. The Black Plague."

Viktor opened his mouth to respond, but Bernard suddenly cut in. Apparently, he had been covertly listening to the whole of their dialogue since the meal began.

"Stolen?" he repeated with thick disdain. His steely eyes touched on Reissa in irritation before moving on to her husband. "Grace's passing was a blessing. My wife was an ungrateful whore. She was a wench who gave away her charms to any male willing to sample them."

Reissa was able to draw strength and courage from the fact that she occupied a room steeped with people. She knew her father would never act on his angry inclinations before an audience of grown men and women. His words had been insensitive, intentionally cruel, and he knew Reissa would be extremely offended by them, yet he cared not. Fury exploded within her, but, ironically, the same keep full of people also hindered her.

"She sought other men because she was unappreciated, disrespected, and unloved by her own husband." Before her father could respond, she turned to Viktor and continued, "I loved my mother above all others," her eyes shifted back to Bernard, and her expression transformed into one of sad accusation, "and she loved me."

"She was a fool," Mr. Maitland bit out, but his voice was only loud enough for Reissa to hear.

"She was an angel."

Bernard was clearly preparing to breathe another vicious retort, but Reissa intruded upon his heartlessness with anger. "And I will hear nothing to the contrary from you, Father." With that, she turned her attention to the trencher before her and began to pick at a piece of chicken.

Moments passed in taut silence as she felt her father quietly simmering beside her. The minutes stretched, and her tension mounted. She knew she had crossed the line where Bernard was concerned, and fear of the repercussions when he cornered her in private were already weighing on her mind. It was likely she would not survive the strength of his abuse this time.

Chapter 26

Observing that Reissa was upset because of her father's disdainful talk of Grace, Viktor did not press her for further conversation during the course of the meal. He was rather cross with Mr. Maitland for speaking the unkind words that had dissolved his wife's amicable mood. He had genuinely enjoyed her humor, and that enjoyment had been furthered because he had actually been the cause of her smiles. But now she sat in silence, her expression sullen. And seeing her revert to her meek, muted nature caused his own disposition to foul.

When people began to rise from the table to return to the games and dancing, he noticed Bernard turn to his daughter, and in a low voice, he commanded, "I will have a word with you, girl."

Without meeting his hard gaze, she nodded and rose from her chair. Reissa preceded him from the dais and marched over to the corner near the fireplace. She stopped directly in her husband's eye line, but she could not have done it intentionally because she stood with her back to him, and to the whole of the room. Bernard rounded her petite form, giving Viktor a clear view of the man's face over her head. He was not pleased to see that Maitland's features were thunderous. Reissa's father grabbed her arm, clearly intending to physically lead her from the keep, but after she glanced at the couples dancing to the minstrel's music, she brushed his hand away.

Moments passed as they appeared to quarrel; however, Viktor could only assume that because he was unable to see his wife's face. Without thought, he drank from the tankard near his elbow.

"Would there be additional rumors of unrest circulating the village, little brother?" Collin put the question to Viktor without realizing he was distracted by the scene unfolding near the fireplace.

"Nay, 'twould seem that our overlord is practicing to be discreet," he returned mindlessly. He was morbidly fascinated by the quiet argument between father and daughter.

"Perhaps we should consider dispatching informants of our own." He followed the direction of his younger sibling's gaze.

"It has been done. Two of my men remain in the village—" Viktor replied monotonously, but the words died on his lips when he saw Bernard gasp in murderous outrage, then raise his hand in the air and ruthlessly strike his daughter with an open palm. The force was so extensive that she was spun around and thrown off balance. Her strawberry blond locks and navy skirts fanned into the air. Slender arms instinctually outstretched to save herself from the pain of the fall.

Viktor did not think; he simply acted. The tankard fell from his hand, crashing onto the dais floor, the contents sloshing onto the stone. He jumped up from his chair, causing it to violently topple backwards, then he literally vaulted over the corner of the table in one fluid motion. As his raging figure stalked across the Meeting Hall with purpose, men and women turned curious eyes to the shocking events playing out before them. The music ceased, and, in a domino effect, a hush moved through the crowd.

Bernard looked up from the beaten form on the floor struggling to rise. His eyes widened in terror. He took a step back in retreat.

Thanks to the helping hand of a nearby foot soldier, his wife stood, albeit unsteadily, but she was on her feet, nonetheless. Long strides carried Viktor past her, and, without hesitation, his fingers curled, and he threw his fist into Bernard's face. The blow was equal to the one Maitland dealt his defenseless daughter. He lost his balance and stumbled onto the stone flooring with a dull thud.

Viktor did not relent for a moment. He hurried forward and fell to his knees, straddling Bernard's writhing figure. Once again, his fist slammed into his father-in-law's face. Then again, and again. He pummeled the man, yet he was acutely aware of his actions. In spite of his fury, he held back, ensuring that he did not knock him unconscious. The bastard deserved to feel the agony of a beating.

As Viktor rained blows upon him, the image of his wife falling to the floor replayed itself over and over in his mind, causing his anger to climb. The force behind his fists intensified, and his intent nearly spun out of control. He became so involved in his need to wound the dissolute cretin that he failed to see Collin and Alden exchange worried glances. They bent down to pry him off his bloodied victim.

The men yanked him to his feet, and when Viktor began to struggle against their intervention, they dragged him a couple feet from the cause of his tempestuous tirade.

"Viktor!" Collin shouted to break through his consuming state of determined wrath.

His thoughts began to merge into an intelligible rationale, and he gained a modicum of calm. Irritated by the hands imprisoning his arms, he pulled them from Collin and Alden's grasp with a snap of motion.

He glanced at both to silently convey that he had no intent to cause the man greater harm, then approached Bernard and roughly lifted him up from the floor. The instant the agonized man was able to stand on his own two feet, Viktor clutched his upper arm and half led, half dragged him across the hall to the double doors. He kicked them open in a grunt of fury and then ruthlessly pushed his wife's father out into the cold. Bernard stumbled and nearly fell to the frozen earth in the bailey, but he managed to catch himself at the last moment.

"Bernard Maitland, I disown you from my family and from my lands. You are banished forever. If you dare to place a foot upon the earth of my estate, I will have you struck down for trespassing. And all rights to your daughter have been dispatched. Never again will you see her; she is dead to you." He drilled him with flashing eyes. "Now begone, afore I have you struck down this instant for your cruelties!" Viktor charged in a resounding shout that echoed throughout the manor's curtain walls.

Through the blood and bruises of his pockmarked face, Bernard sent him a swift scathing glare before he turned and began to hobble toward the portcullis that rose on cue.

Viktor spun around and found that countless people from the dais had followed him. He dismissed the presence of others, and immediately his eyes scanned the vast room for his wife's tiny figure.

"If 'tis Reissa you seek, she fled while you were kindly escorting her father from the Meeting Hall," Moira offered perceptively. "Shall I see to her?"

Viktor was startled by the well of emotion that abruptly overcame his sensibilities in response to her question. The need to comfort his abused wife overwhelmed his being. His gaze drifted to the staircase entrance, and he shook his head. "Nay, I will see to her."

With that, he broke into a hasty stride that carried him the length of the room and up the stone steps leading to the chamber. He marched down the candlelit corridor and cautiously entered into Reissa's antechamber.

***

Reissa's gaze bolted to the door of her bedchamber when she heard the sagging hinges creak, announcing another's arrival. Her eyes touched on her husband's large figure, and she quickly wiped at the salty moisture on her cheeks. The scene below had been mortifying. The whole of the castle's occupants had witnessed her father's brutality, and she would forever be shamed by it.

Following Bernard's slap, a kind gentleman had helped her rise to her feet, but shock surpassed embarrassment when she turned to take in the sight of Viktor ruthlessly striking her father. Paralyzed in a maze of feelings, she could do nothing but observe until Collin and Alden lifted her husband away. Then, overwhelmed by a myriad of emotions, she chose that moment to turn and escape to the privacy of her room.

When she was finally alone, she broke into harsh sobs that shook her to the core. Unfortunately, her miserable solitude was now intruded upon.

"Please leave me, Viktor," she choked while averting an ashen face to hide her sorrow and humiliation, but she heard his steady footsteps approaching. The noise announced that he had ignored her request.

"Reissa, how badly have you been hurt?" he demanded quietly.

The shake of her head from side to side was nearly imperceptible. However, in spite of her muted denial, he halted before her seated figure on the edge of the mattress, bent over, and cupped her chin in his hand. Gently, he raised her face up so he could take stock of her physical condition. The raw, crimson patch on her cheekbone turned down the corners of his mouth.

His fingers fell away, then he erected himself and sighed heavily. He looked down on her hunched, defeated form for a moment, then turned and seated himself on the vanity bench several feet from the canopy. Once again, his eyes sought her out.

Without warning, he spoke. "Your father has raised his hand to you afore this night, has he not?"

Reissa gulped. "Aye." The word was but a whisper.

He grunted unhappily. "I have heard your lies, and I was a fool to believe them."

"I apologize for the falsehoods, Viktor," her eyes remained on the floor, "but I could not speak the truth."

"I know not what truths you have spoken, lady," he grated as he leaned against the cool wall at his back and crossed his arms over his chest.

Reissa grew frantic as he indirectly claimed that he was no longer able to trust her. For some reason, the knowledge that he could not trust her caused her insides to clench in desperation. She could not allow him to believe she was a liar; she simply could not. Overcast eyes lifted and locked with his to make a plea. "I assure you, my lies were restricted to my father's heartlessness."

"I would have an explanation why such is an exception," he demanded, his disposition chilling with subdued irritation.

"I have sought untruths for so long that I know not," she admitted frankly.

Viktor sat forward, braced his elbows on his knees, clasped his hands together, then fixed her in a softened stare. "I am your husband, Reissa, and by rights I am entitled to know my wife. You should have confessed Bernard's fallacy. In fact, 'tis a trait I would know of any man. I do not tolerate such abuse, and I will take any man to task who does," he stated with such conviction that Reissa nearly believed him.

Unfortunately, the knowledge that he had strangled the life from Golly's body reminded her that he was capable of much more than merely raising his hand to a woman. Yet, in spite of that thought, she was prompted to present a question: "I shall never fear your hand?"

He scowled, clearly offended that she felt the need to ask. "Nay. You have already suffered the extent of the direct physical punishments I shall inflict."

"You provide various forms of punishment?" Her insides quivered at the thought.

"Perhaps." His face was impassive as he stood to his towering height, then wandered over to the washstand and wet a clean cloth.

"Will you state an example?" Her gaze followed his handsome figure as it crossed the room and returned with the moistened rag.

"The punishment shall fit the crime; therefore, if you foolishly act insubordinate a second time, I will simply choose befitting consequences," he explained during a leisurely approach.

The butterfly sensation in her stomach that consistently accompanied her husband's presence only increased as he seated himself next to her on the mattress. Gingerly, he pressed the wet cloth to the dried, bloodied scrape on her cheek, bringing his face uncomfortably close to hers.

Her eyes were magnetically drawn to his as he watched his fingers carefully wiping the blood from her flesh. She was so preoccupied by the act of looking upon his attractive face that she was only vaguely aware of his gentle ministrations.

"In fact," he continued their conversation while he worked, "I should choose a punishment for your lies—" The words broke off as he sighed regretfully. His eyes shifted, and her heart skipped several beats when those black, golden-flecked orbs locked on hers.

"Should?" she uttered in a shaky whisper.

"Aye," he returned quietly, "however, I believe your father's hand has surpassed the punishment you deserve."

Unable to meet that penetrating gaze any longer, her eyes lowered to his chest, and she gave a slight nod of agreement. Her limbs began to tremble when she felt the weight of his eyes drop to her lips. Moments passed in pregnant silence, causing Reissa to shift uncomfortably, but, finally, against her will and her better judgment, curious gray eyes rose back up to her husband's face.

She was startled to see a sleepy expression softening his hard features as he stared at her mouth. Intensely aware of his focus, her lips felt painfully dry, so acting without thought, her tongue parted them and smoothed over the bottom first, then the top.

The lady jumped, as did her gaze, when a callused hand curled around the nape of her neck. Viktor's eyes moved over her face as if he was seeing it for the first time.

"Set aside your fear of me, Reissa. I desire a kiss," he warned before he pulled her near, and warm lips claimed hers.

Reissa stiffened immediately, startled and dumbfounded by the unexpected contact. He had taken her twice during the short course of their marriage, but not once had he touched her in such a way. The first time he had—her mind flinched. She had no desire to recall the first time. And the second time he had behaved with passive determination. Neither occasion included a kiss. This was completely new to her. No man had ever pressed his lips to hers before that night. She knew not what to do or how to react.

As his mouth moved over hers in a tender assault, the initial shock began to fade. It was replaced with confusion that climbed to confounding heights. Something stirred deep inside her, something she had never experienced before. It was mildly terrifying and highly exciting. The sensation coursed through her blood, heating it, causing her body and mind to relax against her will.

Desperately, she tried to cling to her thoughts, but they were rapidly dissipating into a void of nothingness as feeling took over. She felt languid and restless at once. An unparalleled need to press closer to her husband engulfed her. She searched the remnants of her mind for rational thought, but when she could not grasp anything tangible, she gave in to the need gripping her.

Trembling arms rose to tentatively circle her husband's neck. The moment she did so, Viktor's hands smoothed down her back, and he folded her in a smothering embrace that took her breath away. His mouth increased pressure, then a lightning bolt of sensation shot down her extremities when his tongue parted her yielding lips and touched her own.

A helpless moan vibrated her throat as she clung to him, lost in her response to his skilled seduction. She was so caught up in their kiss that she was only distantly aware when he hooked an arm under her knees and lifted, shifting her, stretching her petite figure out on the bed.

His weight blanketed her, but the bulk of his masculine body was not uncomfortable. She felt safe and secure even as her senses heightened to an open awareness, feeling the hard planes pressing to every inch of her.

Slender fingers delved into his textured locks as their kiss seemed to explode with fire, their breathing growing labored by the moment. Viktor's booted foot nudged her ankles apart as he continued the curious exploration of her mouth with his tongue. Then his knee pressed between her parted legs.

Reissa tore her lips away to gasp as a throb of pleasure surged through her being. Her husband did not relent. He tasted the skin of her neck and moved on to rake her earlobe with his teeth. His knee slid over the aching area at the apex of her body, causing her to writhe beneath him, filling the room with the sound of her hoarse breathing. An overwhelming sensation was slowly knotting in her stomach, tightening, searching for an enigmatic release.

A sharp rap on the door rudely intruded upon their involved state.

Chapter 27

Viktor uttered a biting curse. And it was the sound of his voice that finally cut through Reissa's haze. She returned to reality with the feeling that the wind had been knocked from her, like taking a hard fall. Startled eyes locked on her husband's face. Humiliation quickly flooded her cheeks with crimson despite the obvious regret shining in his eyes.

"It appears we must delay," he whispered as his gaze slipped to her ravaged mouth. He took a deep, raspy breath, then dropped a chaste kiss on her mouth and rose from the bed. Viktor held out a hand, offering to help her up.

Once again in a perplexed state, Reissa accepted the offer. Firmly, he pulled her to her feet, then he was forced to steady her slight figure when she faltered. After he assured himself that she was capable of holding her own, he sent her a devastating smile. But as he turned and crossed to the door, his expression transformed into one of boiling frustration.

Viktor swung open the door and shot his brother with a murderous glare. "You best have good cause, Collin," he growled with real menace.

The elder sibling looked from Viktor's thunderous expression to Reissa's embarrassed flush, and a glib smile broke out on his handsome face. "I sincerely apologize for interfering.

However, I am forced to retrieve the lord and the lady of the manor posthaste. The king has arrived."

Viktor's brow creased. "Edward has impeccable timing."

Collin chuckled, obviously enjoying his brother's mood, then his thoughts shifted, and his features abruptly fell. "Edward has traveled through the darkness to arrive this night. I sense the crime of Golly's murder falls second to a greater issue."

Viktor gave a curt nod of understanding. Collin bowed slightly toward Reissa and took his leave.

Her humiliation gave way to curiosity when she heard her brother-in-law's statement. "Greater issue?" she asked of her husband as he turned to face her.

"We have not the time to discuss it presently," he returned as he picked up a silver-handled brush from the vanity and tossed it to her.

Thoughtlessly, she pulled the brush through disheveled strawberry blond locks, her head downcast to carry out the task, but her actions ceased when she felt Viktor's approach. Then the accessory fell from her fingers and bounced on the cool stone flooring when his palms suddenly caressed her hips and moved down her skirts, smoothing out the wrinkles in her gown.

Viktor's tall form unfolded, and he stood gazing down at her, his hard features softening as his eyes touched on her face. Gently, he brushed away a stray strand of hair that was clinging to her moistened lips. His gaze locked on hers. "This night you will know the pleasure I have been lax in giving," he sighed, hating Edward's intrusion, "but now we must play host to the king."

More so perplexed by his remark of pleasure rather than the fact that she was about to meet England's greatest lord, she was unable to speak a word as he escorted her to the Meeting Hall.

Her taut nerves stretched nearly to the breaking point when she noticed the room was now brimming with royal soldiers, in addition to her husband's personal army. Her face reddened, recalling the scene that had sent her fleeing to her bedchamber. She sported a raw cheek because of her father, but unable to seek escape, she pushed through her mortification and continued on as if Bernard had not struck her in this room full of people.

She looked at Viktor's place at the head of the table as they climbed onto the platform and was startled to see a distinguished man seated there. She knew instantly that he was the king. Not only would no one else dare to fill Viktor's place, but the elaborate dress and respected air about the man spoke of his position.

His long, dark, wavy locks were sprinkled with gray, as was the beard concealing his mouth and jaw. His eyes were brown molasses, with straight brows and a beak-like nose. Edward's build was average, as was his height. There was nothing remarkable in the man's appearance, but despite the fact that Reissa observed he was as plain as she, she was still intimidated by the simple truth that he ruled their nation.

As Edward became aware of their arrival, he smiled and abruptly rose, causing the other occupants at the table to rise in a hasty flourish. Reissa was preparing to kneel before him, but the king and her husband cordially shook hands as equals.

"Viktor, when we last parted I had hoped it would be quite some time before we met again," he jested in relation to The Hundred Years' War.

Her husband's lips twitched with a grin. "'Tis a pleasure to receive you in my home, Edward."

The king sobered. "Aye, I have heard of your father's unfortunate passing. My condolences."

"Aye, his absence is certainly felt, but my marriage brings an addition to our family. Edward, I would like you to meet my wife, Lady Reissa Colville," he introduced, gesturing to the little woman hooked on his arm.

Reissa was unaware that her arm tightened on Viktor's, seeking his strength when the king turned those brown eyes upon her and smiled with sincere welcome. He grasped her free hand and politely kissed her knuckles.

"'Tis truly a pleasure, Reissa," he said, immediately dispensing with the formalities.

"'Tis an honor to meet you, Your Majesty."

"Ah," the king breathed, "the wife of my greatest, fiercest warrior shall not address me so. I am simply Edward."

"You are most kind," she returned.

Then his smile suddenly fell again. "'Twould be a pleasure to chat, Reissa; however, I have a matter to discuss with my knights. I must ask you to join the women."

It was only after he put forth the order when she noticed the table was void of females. She glanced at the gathering near the fireplace and saw Moira, Edith, and the others casually conversing while the men at the table quietly waited for the return of their king's attention.

"Of course," she agreed dutifully, then curtsied less than gracefully and exited the dais.

Feeling a bit slighted that the women were banished from the conversation, Reissa wandered over and seated herself next to Moira, who opposed Edith in a game of backgammon.

"Who shall be the victor?" Reissa inserted offhandedly as she smoothed away the wrinkles from her navy skirts.

"I foresee Edith as the victor," Moira said good-naturedly. "This sweet girl is positively merciless in competition."

It had been an innocent remark, yet Reissa could not fight the suspicion it aroused. She glanced at Edith, expecting her to be staring at Viktor, but her eyes were cast upon the game board. She gave herself a mental shake and summoned a smile, dismissing her nature of insecurities.

"'Tis the quiet ones we must fear," Reissa spoke with good humor.

Moira turned an inquisitive grin upon her sister-in-law. "Then we shall also fear you."

Reissa laughed, enjoying the lady's wit. "Aye, I unknowingly spoke of myself."

"What have we to fear from you?" Edith questioned lightly, although there was a sense of seriousness that Reissa knew she had not imagined.

"Or more so, what have we to fear *for* you?" Moira corrected as her sky-blue eyes touched on her scraped cheek.

"Let us not speak of my father," she evaded with a tight smile. "Let us only speak of pleasantries."

"Aye, I agree," Edith chimed in as she shook the dice and rolled them onto the game board.

"'Tis your anniversary, Moira," Reissa reminded as she accepted a chalice of wine from a maid carrying a tray.

"Aye, I have not forgotten; however, the arrival of the king must take precedence over our celebration." Abruptly, her eyes widened, and she looked to the small mound of her stomach. A joyful giggle erupted, and she pressed a hand to the bubble of sensation within. "'Tis not fitting to speak of such things, but I care not. My babe has moved for the first time within my belly." She grabbed Reissa's hand with a frenzy of excitement and placed it to the swell of flesh.

The lady's breath stalled in anticipation of movement, and she was graced with a gift unlike any other. She did not have to wait long. She felt a flutter beneath her fingertips. It was faint, nearly imperceptible, yet it caused both women to glow with smiles of wonder over the life Moira carried. Their behavior was drawing stares, but they cared not. Both were too overjoyed to take notice of others around them.

The ecstatic mother suddenly grabbed her companions' hands and said, "Come, we must dance!" She led Reissa and Edith over to the crowd of people skipping before the minstrels, then pulled them into the festivities.

The scene with her father temporarily forgotten, Reissa gave in to the lively atmosphere and kicked up her heels. She laughed and shouted along with the others as her skirts swished about. She linked arms with men and ladies alike, spinning in circles and stomping her feet. Her petite frame moved until her face shone with perspiration and her feet ached from overuse, but in spite of her physical exhaustion, she could not recall the last time she had ever had so much fun.

During one particular rest period, Reissa was sipping from her goblet, and, against her will, her eyes lifted to seek out her husband's familiar form. Her heart tripped when she found him gazing directly at her. After the initial startlement, her lips drew up in a tentatively nervous smile. She was rewarded with a warm rush of feeling that swept through her body when Viktor responded with a beautiful smile of his own. However, the moment was interrupted when Moira grabbed her hand and once again led her onto the dance floor.

Chapter 28

Viktor had watched his wife exit the dais after Edward ordered her to join the others at the fireplace. He seated himself next to his king, but his gaze remained on the tiny figure seated beside Moira.

"I have it on good authority that Bennington and Rynearson have forged an alliance." The king looked at Viktor and Collin, his brow creased with anger. "I must have your confirmation that the both of you remain loyal to the crown."

"I assure you, you have our allegiance, Edward. We are prepared for any necessary actions that must be taken to ensure your position as our leader," Collin confirmed, then slapped the tabletop with feeling.

"'Tis clear by the numbers of your present army that you intend to battle," Viktor indicated with a nod toward the overflowing hall.

The king's expression was grave. "I have dispatched attendants to all territories seeking loyalties, but I must not tarry. Treason I will not abide. I will see those traitors hanged immediately."

"We must take into consideration a margin of error," Alden intelligibly joined in.

Edward gave him a sharp look. "Your doubt is not welcome, boy."

"Are you aware of information that we are not, my friend?" Viktor questioned, tearing his gaze from Reissa to penetrate Alden with his eyes.

"'Twas simply my intention to suggest misdirection," Kilgour explained. "Is it not possible that your sources may be conspiring against you rather than our overlord? Is it not possible that we believe the innocent are guilty?"

Edward emphatically shook his head. "I would place my life in the hands of my attendants. They would never betray me."

"'Tis possible that your attendants have been supplied with false information," Collin chimed in.

"Do you have anything to act on in addition to the word of your informants?" Viktor tested.

"You now require physical proof afore you will act on my behalf?" Edward growled.

"Certainly not," Collin was quick to say, "however, the consequence of this issue would benefit from further investigation."

"Do you volunteer to do so?" the king demanded.

"Aye."

"As do I," Viktor inserted.

"And I," Alden chimed in.

"Name your intent," the king ordered, then gulped from his tankard of ale.

"I believe a visit to Rynearson is long overdue." Collin grinned.

Edward gasped. "'Tis suicide, you fool."

Viktor's grin matched his brother's. "'Tis brilliant."

"I fail to understand your reasoning," Alden spoke for many.

"Rynearson will never suspect if his visitors number two, rather than an army. As the issue of Golly's murder still stands, we have legitimate cause to surpass the exterior. We may bleed the man for information pertaining to my stepmother and his alliances," Viktor explained even as he saw Moira grab his wife's hand and pull her onto the dance floor.

"If Rynearson seeks the throne, and he suspects, you two will not survive to see the light of day," Edward stated, concealing his concern.

"My army will be positioned within miles. Alden shall lead my men," he said, masking the distraction his wife's laughter caused.

He was still amazed by the sudden, overwhelming attraction that had assaulted his every sense not an hour ago. Possessed by the simple intent to clean her wound, he had seated himself next to her on the bed. Then the proximity heightened his awareness of the fact that she was a woman, and she was his wife, and she belonged to him. Abruptly, and surprisingly, he was beaten down with the desire to kiss her.

As a man who did not deprive himself of any want or need, he kissed her. The attraction had certainly caught him off guard, but the feeling that rolled through his body when his lips touched hers—there was no way he could have ever prepared himself for such an all-consuming need.

Now, as he watched Reissa from afar, he could not erase such need from his mind, or his body. His eyes moved over her, realizing that plain face had grown rather lovely during the short course of their marriage.

Once empty gray eyes now sparkled with life and an inner strength he was certain she was not aware she possessed. Her flawless skin glowed, and strawberry blond locks that were once dull and mousy shone with the light of the sun. A figure that had been as slight as a stick had taken on several pounds of weight in all the right places. She was still extremely slender; however, her modest curves were now visible to the naked eye, announcing the fact that she was indeed a woman, not a child.

Collin snapped his fingers before his eyes, breaking him from his silent reverie. "Little brother, would you care to join us?" he inquired a bit irritably.

Viktor sent his brother a scowl, then looked at their king. "Excuse me, Edward."

"I shall repeat," the king voiced, "when will your army be readied for mobility?"

"Two days will be sufficient."

"Marvelous." Edward grinned, then shifted the topic to another issue. "And what will be addressed of Rynearson pertaining to Golly's murder?"

"I believe the lady seduced him to gain approval of my marriage." Viktor clenched his teeth together, the muscles in his jaw flexed with feeling.

"You had no desire to wed?" the king asked with clear surprise.

"Aye."

Edward looked to Collin and broke into a fit of laughter. "Your behavior is certainly contrary, Viktor. Your eyes have not left the lady during the whole of our discussion."

"Aye, I am quickly learning that marriage carries its benefits; however, I do not wish to be chained to one woman for the rest of my days." He caught Reissa's meek smile, and his body tightened. He imagined carrying her up the staircase to her room in the next moment, and he returned a smile that caused her cheeks to blush with pretty color.

"Golly knew of such an aversion to marriage?" Edward quizzed.

"Aye." He went on to explain the finding of her in his bedchamber days after his father's death, his rejection, her announcement of his wedding soon after, and, finally, her death.

The king stared at him, lost in thought before he said, "You admit that the evidence against you is rather damning, Viktor?"

"Aye, I am aware."

"How many maidens were jilted by your marriage? How many would see you punished for taking a wife?"

Viktor's only response was a sour expression.

Edward observed, "Golly is murdered on the day of your marriage. 'Tis likely that many a maid is unhappy with that arrangement."

"Every maid in the charge of Moorestone and Colville Manor has been questioned," Collin supplied.

"'Twould seem more reasonable that a maid seeking vengeance would take it upon the lady rather than Viktor," Alden interjected rationally.

Startled by the knight's words, Viktor's eyes flew to Reissa's dancing form. The need to protect that had gripped him when Bernard raised his hand to her rapidly resurfaced.

"Aye, Alden," Edward agreed one hundred percent. "Therefore, it must be a legitimate enemy rather than a jealous maid. Who have you recently crossed?"

"'Tis where we strike a wall," Collin breathed as he sat back and lifted his ankle to rest on his knee.

"A ready answer is not known," Viktor commented as he ripped his eyes from Reissa. "However, I will not rule out a woman as my opposition. I will not see my wife in danger."

"Excluding your entourage, Edward, every person in this room is well aware of Viktor's nature to protect his family. The demonstration of his anger was witnessed by all earlier this evening," Alden spoke as he shook golden locks from his vision.

"Oh?" their king wondered curiously as he leaned back and grinned.

"Reissa's father foolishly struck her afore all, and my little brother took it upon himself to beat the man until he was unrecognizable," Collin offered with something resembling paternal pride.

Edward spotted the object of their dialogue, and his eyes locked on her cheek. "'Twould explain the injury to her face. You have my applause, Viktor." He scratched at the beard on his face. "And as 'twould seem that Golly's murder will remain unsolved this night, I should like to converse with the lady afore she collapses in exhaustion from her exertions on the dance floor." He picked up his tankard and signaled toward the occupants at the table that they were free to leave if they wished.

Viktor knew he could send a servant to retrieve his wife, yet he chose to grasp the opportunity himself. "I shall collect her," he announced, then arose and descended the dais. His tall form crossed to the dancing crowd and patiently waited for Reissa to notice his presence. Almost immediately, she glanced up, and her eyes lit upon him. The smile on her face fell. She made her excuses to Moira and Edith, then wove through the crowd.

"Is anything amiss, Viktor?" she requested, clearly assuming he sought her out to reprimand her for her out-of-character behavior.

"Calm yourself, Reissa." As he stood looking down upon her, he was instantly moved to touch her. His thoughts surged with longing to bed to her posthaste, but with great difficulty, he tempered his attraction. However, he could not fight his feelings to the extent of keeping his hands from her. A palm cupped her upper arm and then slowly slid down to hook her wrist upon his elbow. "Edward merely desires to know you."

Reissa's cheeks heated with vivid color when Viktor saw the violent shiver his touch produced. Her eyes shifted to the floor as she allowed him to escort her back to the dais.

Collin had excused himself to join his wife in the celebration, opening a seat on Edward's left, so Viktor and Reissa were able to take places across from one another, at the king's elbows. A maid was quick to provide a goblet of wine for the lady, and after checking on Edward's and Viktor's spirits, she made an invisible exit.

The king turned his head, and the childish expression of gaiety on his bearded face inspired Reissa to smile in return. "At last, I am able to chat with Viktor's bride. I regret that the queen was unable to accompany this visit; she would have been delighted to meet you."

"I hope she is not unwell," Reissa said sincerely as she picked up the silver chalice of wine.

"Nay, my girl, she must oversee our court. 'Tis a dreadful duty, but my wife is a pleasant eccentric, and she remains unaffected by the trappings of her station. She is well suited for social functions."

"'Tis a gift I truly admire in others, for I am a social cripple," she admitted rather frankly, then daintily sipped red wine from the glass in her hand.

"You certainly do not appear to be a social cripple," he made reference to her antics before the minstrels.

"I must credit such to Moira; her joy inspires joy within others."

"Aye, she is certainly wrapped in the glow of impending motherhood." His eyes crossed the room and found Moira dancing with her husband. His gaze was openly appraising, but not uncomfortably so. But then, his eyes shifted back to Reissa, and he was pensive for a moment. "You do not share such glow."

Reissa nearly choked on the spirits in her mouth. She swallowed hard, and widened eyes rose to gape at the king. "I beg your pardon?"

"Do not take offense, my girl; 'twas merely a worthy observation." He grinned. "Your marriage is in its infancy. My thoughts of another Colville heir are rather premature."

"Reissa is destined to be a mother," Viktor said thoughtfully. "She loves children."

The lady perked up with life. "I volunteer two days a week at the schoolhouse in the village."

The king's head swiveled to his disciple, obviously aghast. "You condone such demeaning behavior?"

"I am not overjoyed with the undertaking. However, it pleases her to do so. 'Tis why I allow it." His eyes remained locked on his wife's face.

Reissa met his masked gaze, and the words spilled out. "I was forced to act insubordinate and suffer a memorable punishment afore he agreed to my wishes," she spelled out for the king, a resenting inflection in her tone.

"Will the voluntary duty be shelved after you have conceived?" Edward directly asked, obviously uncaring that such matters were not discussed in an open forum.

"Aye."

"Nay." Husband and wife disagreed in unison.

Reissa stared at Viktor's handsome form, first startled, then moved to anger by his response, while he frowned in obvious opposition.

Edward took on a sheepish expression and broke through their combative reverie. "I may be king, but I believe I have overstepped my bounds." He grinned. "May I suggest that you two cross that bridge later on?"

The minute amount of alcohol in her blood seemed to loosen Reissa's tongue. "Our marriage contract dictates the conception of an heir in the first year of marriage; therefore, that bridge may be seen on the horizon."

"As the wastrel who asked for such a stipulation has been banished from our lives, I would like to abandon it; however, I am an honorable man, and 'twill be upheld in spite of his absence," Viktor stated monotonously.

Both men heard Reissa's sharply indrawn breath and looked at her. "Banished? You have banished my father?"

"Aye," he returned with one curt syllable.

A myriad of emotions washed over the lady's face as she learned of his actions: startlement, happiness, relief, confusion, guilt, abandonment, and, finally, sorrow.

***

She knew Bernard felt nothing for her; she knew he only used her for his own gain and a convenient punching bag, but she could not deny that he was her parent, her blood. Bernard was the only father she had ever known, and now he was gone from her life.

She felt tears hovering beneath the surface, and in the effort of self-preservation, her eyes lowered to the slim hands clasped in her lap. Her throat burned as she fought against a sob. Delicately, she coughed, then took a deep, steadying breath.

"'Tis been a taxing day, and my wife is terribly exhausted, Edward. I believe we will retire." Viktor swiftly redirected the conversation and made their excuses when he noticed her solemn reaction. He rose from his chair, as did the king.

Reissa, who had been distracted by her feelings, was only vaguely aware when her husband guided her to stand, then ushered her from the dais. It was only after they began ascending the staircase when she became aware that they had exited the room. She looked up at his devastating profile in the shadows. With the wine fueling her feelings, she easily gave in to the need to vent her frustration.

"You had no right, Viktor!" she cried. "He is *my* father!"

He ground to a halt on the landing between levels and turned on her, his eyes flashing with rage and something she could not define. "And *you* are *my* wife!" he hissed. "'Tis my responsibility to see to your best interests."

"He is the only family I have," she returned with quiet fury. "And you believe removing him from my life is in my best interest?"

"I do," Viktor responded, not a hint of regret in his tone. Then his rage dipped considerably. "And he is not the only family you have, Reissa."

Her eyes narrowed as she gazed up at him. Suddenly the sliver of light from a wall sconce blinked out. The nearest candle had extinguished itself in its own wax, and without the light of day shining through the window embrasure, they were left in virtual blackness.

"The Colvilles do not share my blood," she said with less conviction. The sudden loss of light moderately cooled her fiery temper. Her eyes slowly adjusted to the darkness, yet the only visual was Viktor's eyes shining through with a light of their own. The light of anger.

"We may not share your blood," he grated as his hands firmly gripped her upper arms, "but not one of us would ever treat you so cruelly."

Her laugh held bitter irony. "Your stepmother was brutally strangled to death the morning after our wedding."

He gave her tiny frame a rough shake. "You go too far, lady."

The fear that had dissolved in recent days returned with full force, yet she could not stop the words that whispered past her lips. "Am I to be next?"

"Aye, you shall be next—"

Her heart stopped beating, and her legs completely gave out, positively horrified by his stunning confirmation.

She sagged against his broad form, and he caught her to him. With laughable ease, he lifted her into his arms and began up the darkened staircase, two at a time. "However, 'tis not my intent to kill you," he finally finished in a husky voice.

Chapter 29

They had just quarreled, yet he placed her on the bed with a gentleness that belied the emotion flowing between them. Reissa had instantly understood the intent he referred to on the staircase. As he rapidly made the journey to her chambers, her fierce anger transformed into fierce desire.

Anticipating their lady's needs, the servants had prepared her room. Flames crackled in the fireplace, a candle burned on the nightstand, the coverlet had been turned down, and a clean white cotte and matching bed robe had been laid out at the foot of the bed, but Reissa was oblivious to such details. All she knew in that moment was her husband.

He lay there, his muscled form partially covering hers, yet she welcomed the heavy weight and hard plains of his body. A pair of beautiful black eyes hooded with desire leisurely moved over her face and hair, taking in every last detail. She breathed in the masculine scent of him, was intoxicated by the smell of clean clothing, sweaty skin and a hint of the wine he had consumed following the evening meal.

A callused hand delved into her unbound locks, the biceps in his arm flexing with the effort, straining against the material of his tunic. Reissa took an unsteady breath and met her husband's lingering gaze. His sharp jaw was shadowed with stubble, ebony locks astray, creating an unkempt and dangerously sexy picture. The scene upon the stairs was forgotten, as were all her thoughts. He cast a spell upon her with one smoldering look.

Her chest stalled when his gaze settled on her lips. Her limbs poised with expectation when his head slowly inched closer. Too slowly. He was delaying the moment of contact, increasing her awareness of the need within herself, and the need for his touch.

After an eternity, his mouth brushed against hers. It was a brief, yet electrifying caress that she felt in every nerve ending in her body. Her lips parted, longing for another kiss, but she became distracted when his fingers traced the delicate flesh on the side of her neck, then followed the slope of her shoulder and down her arm.

He lifted her arm, lightly nipped her palm, then pressed her hand to the mattress beside her head. His fingers trailed down the inside of her arm, and, despite the armor of her gown, her skin was stimulated with gooseflesh. He paused when the pads of his fingertips tripped over the line of a rib.

Viktor stared at her with sensual seriousness. She knew he was watching, absorbing her reaction to his skilled ministrations.

His palm suddenly covered the peak of her breast, and a throaty gasp filled the room. Reissa's hands slid around his back, and her arms clenched, pulling him near. His large, work-roughened hand moved in a circular rotation, causing her flesh to swell and tighten beneath his touch.

Her eyes closed to his sleepy stare, and she heard his breathing grow labored. Wine-scented breath warmed her face.

She was unprepared when his lips captured hers in a hungry possession that was nothing like the first kiss. He tasted her as a man starving for affection, drinking her in, unable to quench his thirst. Passions pulsed as he deepened the kiss, then receded to nibbling on her bottom lip. His tongue delved inside, and he teased her by pulling it away when her own moved to meet him. He broke their kiss, but his mouth hovered near, taunting.

Viktor's actions forced her into the role of domination. She lifted her head and pulled his to hers, initiating the contact, renewing the kiss. For a short time, he allowed her to guide him, responding to her instinctual touch. But the man inside him took over, needing to be the one in charge.

His hand strayed, gliding over her abdomen and down to her hip. As he caressed her body, his fingers seeking every curve with intent concentration, Reissa gave in to the fantasy that he was making an attempt to commit every inch to memory. However, she was ripped from the fantasy when his arms wrapped around her tiny form and he rolled over, taking her with him.

Reissa was rather disoriented to find herself lying atop him, looking down on his darkly handsome face. Her features must have shown her apprehension because he smiled, and his deep voice entered into the silence.

"Do not fear, my lady. I merely desire to disrobe you." He did not allow for a response because his fingers combed through her strawberry blond locks, and he lifted his head to connect their mouths. He gave her a thorough kiss that relaxed her body against him, fitting them together so naturally that Reissa sighed blissfully into his mouth.

While she was distracted by his kiss, he easily opened the buttons of two layers of gowns and the laces of her cotte. He slipped her arms from the sleeves, then pushed down the garments. With one well-placed kick, the whole of her attire fell to the floor, leaving her clothed in nothing but him as he rolled her to her back once again.

Reissa felt acute disappointment when he eased his lips from hers, but the cool air that breezed over her skin drew her gaze down to see that she wore nothing at all. Embarrassed by her state, she lifted to gaze to meet Viktor's. He stared not at her face, but at her body.

The insecure woman reacted instantly. She sat up and desperately grabbed for the coverlet to drag over herself, but she gave a whimper of shock when his hand clutched her wrist, denying her intent.

"Nay, woman," he muttered, clearly preoccupied by the sight.

"Please, Viktor, I feel naked!" she pleaded in a panic.

He laughed, and his gaze finally returned to hers. A licentious smile caused the skin around his eyes to crinkle. "I must confess, Reissa," he leaned closer, and his voice dropped to a whisper, "you are naked."

The man's glibness in the face of her self-consciousness succeeded only in inspiring her temper. Slender arms crossed over her breasts, and her legs bent, curling against her stomach to shield herself from his view. "'Tis not fitting!"

"You are my wife, and I fancy giving you a tumble. I assure you, 'tis fitting." He grinned wickedly and easily pried her arms from her chest.

Bared to his eyes, her desperation quickly resurfaced. "But I will be cold."

A single brow crooked sinfully. "'Tis not possible, my lovely wife. I shall take great pleasure in warming you." With that, he firmly pushed her back onto the mattress and straddled a pair of narrow hips.

Pinned to the bed, Reissa could do nothing but watch as her husband's head tilted and his tongue flicked across the tip of her nipple. Alarmed by the powerful thrill that shot through her torso, she gasped. Then her gasp dissolved into a glorious whimper when the heat of his mouth descended on her areola and his lips closed around pebbled flesh.

"Oh dear Lord," she breathed as her body began to writhe beneath him. Her back arched of its own accord, giving him greater access to the small mounds of her breasts. He kissed and fondled until both were tingling with arousal, then a strong arm slid around her back and held her in the arched position. His mouth began to move lower, tasting her, caressing her. He halted momentarily to pull the navy tunic over his head and tossed it on the floor. While he continued on, he unlaced his braies and kicked them off, also leaving him unclothed.

Reissa moaned vibrantly when a deft tongue dipped into her navel, then he drew a line down to the red-blond curls between her thighs. Feeling his fingers easing the soft folds of her flesh apart, her eyes snapped open, and her head rose. His mouth moved toward her.

"Nay, Viktor," she choked, disbelieving his intent.

His beautiful smile returned, then he kissed her in a way her innocent mind never could have conceived. Her head dropped back onto the bed, and feeling took over. A knot of pleasure began to curl in her belly, tightening, growing, until finally it exploded in wave after wave of ecstasy. Violently, she thrashed about as satisfaction wrapped itself around her petite figure and mercilessly shook. Her quiet moans filtered through the room as her hands clutched at the mattress beside her thighs.

Eventually, the gratifying throbs faded, leaving a glow upon her that was nearly as potent. She gasped for air, unaware that an illuminating smile marked her feminine features.

Once again, Viktor straddled her hips, and she began to grasp reality through the haze that held her in its grips. Shining eyes rose to stare up at the man who had taken her to heights she had never known existed.

However, she was caught off guard by the sight that met her. A pair of broad shoulders and a chest covered in a fine mat of black curls dominated her view. Extremely relaxed, Reissa let curiosity prevail. Her gaze roamed over his tanned skin, taking in the thrilling curves of his biceps and pectorals. The strength beneath seemed to be straining for release. A blue map of his veins was visible, especially in his forearms.

Then she noticed the white lines through the hair on his chest and several marring his shoulders. The lady rose to her elbows, and as she focused on a single raised ridge, she realized they were scars.

Of course, this man, her husband, had seen battle on countless occasions. It was only natural that he would possess the scars to give proof to his violent life. Hadn't the king referred to him as his greatest warrior? Even though his wounds had long since healed, a streak of concern passed through her. Many appeared to be deep and gaping at one time. The scar tissue was thick and angry.

Then pride in his obvious ability as a knight swiftly followed. His strength of survival in the face of the enemy was clear. The knowledge added to the sight of his masculine form was volatile. In spite of the unparalleled pleasure she had known mere moments ago, unbelievably, another ache began to build at the meeting of her thighs.

"Cold, my little wife?" he asked with a self-righteous smile.

His arrogance in knowing what she had experienced at his hands prompted a sassiness that surprised even her. "Aye, chilled to the bone." She tried on one of his sinful smiles.

He growled and pressed her to the feather mattress with the bulk of his large frame. "Liar," he accused dramatically, a playful glint in his eye.

Reissa's healthy giggle broke off when he reached down and clutched her ankles. Her hands lifted to his shoulders in uncertainty when he guided her legs to hook around his waist.

Seeing her anxiety, he pulled her into his arms and impressed a kiss upon her that caused her heated blood to boil over. And when she thought she would melt in the fires of their passion, he buried himself inside her with one smooth motion.

As another delighted gasp steeped the space of her bedchamber, his arm circled her back and lifted her slightly, bringing their faces within a hair's breadth of one another. His eyes remained fixed on hers as he began.

Reissa felt the sensation building again, and now knowing what she sought, her hips found and mirrored his rhythm. They climbed the precipice together and then simultaneously tumbled over the edge into the realm of nothing else matters. The moments were pure physical elation, too all-consuming for thought. They traveled the same path across the plateau, and as they traveled as one, they also descended as one.

***

They were left in a mass of perspiration and harsh breathing. Viktor held her to him as he collapsed onto the bed. However, aware of the delicacy of her petite body, he ensured that the bed took most of the punishment as he landed, replete with satisfaction.

Only twice before had he experienced something relatively akin to that episode, and those occasions were also with this woman. True, he recalled little of their first exchange, yet somehow he knew that the pleasure he had sampled was not comparable to others. Reissa had been immobile, merely tolerant of his advances both times, yet he hadn't known such purity of feeling with any other woman. And now that his wife had shared in his passions, he simply could not find the words to describe their union.

He took in the sight of his wife's closed eyes, heaving chest, and beaded brow. Generally, that was the point in time when he made his exit with her and with others he had tumbled in the past. But as he lay there, he acknowledged an unexpected contentment. There was no desire within to leave her bed, or, more to the point, *her*. He accepted the present without thought or analysis, and, in doing so, fatigue quickly enveloped him.

Mindlessly he pulled the coverlet up and over them, then threw an arm over her waist. He was asleep in moments.

Chapter 30

Reissa lay beside her husband, observing his slumber. He had drifted off nearly an hour ago, yet she remained awake and in a state of euphoria. She thought back to his words earlier that day. He had claimed, "This night you will know the pleasure I have been lax in giving." That had been a colossal understatement. The pleasure they shared had been nothing short of miraculous. He had introduced her to Shangri-la.

She stared at his warrior's form, yet did not feel threatened. He was at peace. Unfortunately, Reissa knew that appearances could be deceiving. Her awed disposition wavered. Had she not hidden the fact that her father was a tyrant for years? This man was equally capable of cruelty, and far more dangerous. Bernard had not concealed his faults from her, at least she could give him credit for that, but she could not credit Viktor with the same.

She knew he was guilty of murder, but the fear in this was the truth that he had yet to display such tendencies. Yes, he had an explosive temper, but he also possessed control, and that was a lethal combination. She genuinely feared the day when he chose to unleash the cold-blooded monster within.

The thought caused her eyes to stray to the scars on his chest. The pads of her fingers lightly traced a white line of rough, healed tissue. The man had suffered unimaginable pains at the hands of enemies. If all the wounds were combined, it was likely he had shed buckets of blood, but he survived. It was also likely he had cut down many others in the course of his life. Reissa could not help but wonder if she would eventually fall victim to the man's heartlessness.

Careful not to disturb him, she slipped from the canopy structure and pulled on the white bed robe that still lay at the foot of the massive bed. Dismissing the fact that her feet were bare on the cool stone flooring, she crossed to the window embrasure and gazed up at the sky. The moon was nothing but a sliver, a ghostly apparition that ironically mirrored her exhausted mind. She was married to a man she feared—no, a man she was terrified of—yet he was so adept at concealing his heartlessness that she was growing to care for him.

She climbed up into the window embankment and seated herself, reclining against the unyielding rock. He had banished her father. Reissa wanted to despise him for his presumptuous actions, yet, at the same time, she was grateful for them. He had removed a serious threat from her life.

After her bold rebelliousness in the hall, she had no doubt that Bernard would have gladly beaten her to death when the first opportunity presented itself. So, grudgingly, she had to admit that, yes, Viktor had succeeded in looking after her best interests. However, if that were sincerely the case, he would also have to remove himself from her life.

She could not allow herself to desire him. She could not allow herself to care for him. She could not allow herself to trust in him, only to be betrayed when his true nature finally peeked out from behind the curtain. But, to her great misfortune, she could not escape him. They were husband and wife, together until death do they part. And, unfortunately, there was no way to halt her growing feelings if he continued to behave as he had on that day. What was she to do?

Her thoughts continued on in a maze of confusion until her mind refused to function furthermore.

***

Viktor turned over and instinctually reached out to pull his wife close, but he came alarmingly awake when he felt nothing but empty space. He sat bolt upright and frantically searched the black room for her tiny figure. The fire had burned down to useless ashes, and darkness was still upon them.

His knight's eyes swiftly adjusted to the night, but before he could see clearly, he spotted Reissa slumped in the window embrasure. The white light of the moon caused her matching cotte to glow with supernatural wonder. She had the look of a sleeping angel. She was beautiful.

Immodestly, he stood in his nude state and crossed to her side. As he drew nearer, he saw her shivering with cold, so without reflecting and without pause, he carefully scooped her into his arms. As if she subconsciously knew that he held her, her hands slid around his neck, and she nestled against him, seeking his warmth.

Her actions were minor, done without thought, yet he felt the corners of his mouth turn up in an endearing smile. However, the sentiment rapidly faded when he felt her tempestuous trembling, snagging his anger. Earlier in the evening, he had realized his need to safeguard her from anyone who intended her harm, but now he realized that he also needed to safeguard the lady from herself.

"Viktor?" she inquired groggily.

He looked down as her eyes blinked with consciousness. "Your thoughtlessness is dangerous," he said quietly. "You may take ill for this jaunt without the proper attire."

"Aye, I may," she readily agreed with a pretty yawn.

His smile returned. He had anticipated a stubborn denial. Once again, he placed her on the bed, and once again he chose to join her rather than escape to the solitude of his own chamber.

Chapter 31

Reissa awoke to the wondrous sensation of a mouth suckling her breast. A moan vibrated in her throat, and abruptly the heat was lifted away from her. Passion surged through her veins. She squinted through the harsh midmorning light and found her husband staring down at her with a smile so bright that she had to close her eyes to the illumination of it. In spite of her unhappy musings while she sat in the window embrasure the previous evening, her arms thoughtlessly rose with the desire to pull him close.

The next hour passed in a blur of kisses, caresses, and pleasure. After a climax that only seemed to surpass their previous loving, Viktor rolled over onto his back and pulled her upper body across his chest. She pillowed her head on his shoulder, her bosom heaving from their exertions.

"This day certainly holds promise," Viktor crooned as the tip of his finger trailed down her naked spine.

"This day," the lady repeated, and her brow creased in thought, contemplating her memory. Was there something she needed to do that day? She took a deep breath, and abruptly the task was recalled. "Dear lord, I am not fit to live!" Reissa chastised herself with ease, then sat up and groped for the bed robe that was tangled in the coverlet.

She was in the midst of furiously thrusting an arm into one of the sleeves while muttering beneath her breath when Viktor grabbed her shoulder, stalling her efforts.

"Reissa."

She spared him a glance over her shoulder. "Aye?"

"You will give me cause for this tirade," he ordered firmly.

"Mrs. Michaels is unwell, and I am here, lazing the day away," she said with self-resentment. With that, she pulled from his grip and shrugged into the robe while simultaneously rising from the bed.

However, her efforts were once again intruded upon when an iron arm snaked around her waist and yanked her back onto the bed before her feet could touch the floor.

"Your feet are unadorned, lady," Viktor scolded with a frown. As he shook his head in disapproval, he reached down and collected her slippers from the floor on his side of the bed. "You will wear these." He handed them to her.

She obeyed without complaint. He was right, after all. The floor was freezing, and she was fortunate that she had not caught a chill from her foolishness last eventide. So, she busied herself with the laces that wound around an ankle, and as she did so, she heard Viktor rise and begin to dress. The temptation to turn and watch him was overwhelming, but she forced the idea aside and fought to focus on the simple task of donning her slippers.

At last, she crossed to the wardrobe and mindlessly selected garments to don for the day. Viktor's voice drifted to her from his place near the washstand. He spoke while splashing water on his face, washing away the film of sleep.

"You and Edith will have ten added men to your escort this morn," he announced without consequence.

Reissa looked up from the violet gown in her hands. She possessed intelligence, and the addition of men alerted her to an anomaly in the routine of traveling to the village. "Why?"

He wiped the icy water from his face with a linen cloth, then treated her to a serious disposition that caused an unsettling feeling within. She saw him take a deep, controlled breath, and her apprehension elevated to real fear.

"Viktor?" she prompted.

"'Twould seem that our overlord is a traitor to the crown. He has sought an alliance with our northern territory." He tossed the cloth aside and approached. "And if the man learns of our knowledge of his treason, he will see the Colvilles as a formidable threat."

"We may be in danger?" she croaked.

"'Tis unlikely," he assured as his palms came to rest on her shoulders.

"Our overlord seeks the crown?"

"We believe he may, aye." His jaw clenched in subdued fury. "But I will not allow you to concern yourself over such matters presently. Mrs. Michaels clearly needs Edith's hand posthaste."

She nodded solemnly. Again, he was right.

"Alden shall also accompany you," he decided.

"Do you believe 'tis necessary to inconvenience him, Viktor?"

Long, masculine fingers combed through her tangled tresses as he looked on her with open affection. "Aye, 'twill ease my mind."

"But you spoke of unlikely danger," she pointed out.

He sighed unhappily. "I must be prepared for your father."

"My father?"

"And his vengeance."

She failed to follow his line of thinking, so he elaborated for her.

"He will have been weakened from his wounds and the cold, and the village is the nearest refuge. A kind soul will have offered shelter, or he may have forced his way into a home, but 'tis a certainty that he remains there. And if he attempts to confront you, I shall be extremely unhappy," he growled.

"If the presence of my father angers you to such an extent, why do you delegate the chore to Alden. Why do you not play escort yourself?" she tested, unsure of her feelings in that moment.

Once again, he seemed reluctant to share information with her, but he conceded. "I must remain to gather the armies."

Her mouth dropped open. "I beg your pardon?"

"We have devised a plan to bleed details from Ryncarson. Alden, Collin, myself, and our armies shall depart at dawn." The explanation was vague at best.

"Please elaborate," She requested, feeling a rise of concern.

***

With the intent to distract her from his tale, he began to help her with her dress. "Collin and I will enter his home in a polite guise." He pushed the bed robe from slim white shoulders, holding her gaze with his eyes. Had he thought to distract her? Hell, he was distracting himself.

Never could he have imagined such an alluring little package was concealed beneath her clothing. "We shall manipulate him into sharing the necessary details of his offense, and after he has admitted his guilt, he will be returned to face the king's wrath."

"'Tis insane!" she cried and glanced down, evidently realizing that he had disrobed her. "If he perceives your intentions, he will dispatch you both without a care." He guided her palms to his shoulders for balance as she stepped into an emerald cotte he held out for her. "You shall be trapped in his castle, surrounded by his men."

Viktor slid her arms into the sleeves and turned her to give him access to the laces at her back.

"We are both well versed in the art of combat, Reissa." He finished with the task in record time, then spun her around to face him. Now that she was attired, he was better able to focus, however, only slightly.

The unexpected attraction that ignited inside him the previous evening showed zero signs of dissipating. Quite contrarily, it elevated with every passing moment. As he stared upon the female figure standing in the sunlight with a glorious mane of red-blond tresses, delicate bone structure, and skin like spun silk, he marveled at the fact that he had once considered her plain.

"I do not question your capabilities as a knight, Viktor; however, all such strength and skills are useless when the numbers favor the enemy," she spoke with fierce rationale, her eyes pleading for a reconsideration. "'Twill be Collin and yourself against a castle of men-at-arms."

He could not argue that point. In this, she was the one who was right. Nevertheless, he felt confident in Collin's and his abilities to present a ruse to their overlord. They would stay true to their plan. "Alden shall be in the vicinity with reinforcements." He raised her arms in the air and then pulled the violet gown down over her head.

"You are not guaranteed that your army will arrive in a timely fashion if Rynearson should turn on you, Viktor," she pressed, with fear stamped on her features.

He stood before her. He was safe, yet she was terrified for him.

Her clear concern warmed his heart, but he was growing weary of defending their scheme. "You best be on your way, Reissa. I will not see you returning in darkness," his voice was firm. A pair of hard eyes challenged her to argue.

She nodded amicably.

"I expect to be sought and informed of the woman's state when you arrive this evening," he reminded and brushed a stray lock of hair from her brow.

"I shall."

He gave her a reassuring smile, then bent down and placed a light, lingering farewell kiss on her lips. With that, he spun on his heel and marched from the room with purpose. There was much to be done to prepare for the journey and the inevitable battle.

Chapter 32

Within the hour, Alden, Edith, Reissa, and two dozen mounted soldiers departed the Colville estate. The sun was swiftly rising to its highest point in the sky, but they were unable to see it through the thick cloud cover stretching across to create a gray ceiling bloated with unfallen snow.

Reissa said little during the journey into the village. Her brother and sister companions each made numerous attempts to draw her into polite conversation, but when her responses consisted of distracted, one-word answers, they gave up.

Her thoughts were preoccupied in pondering the present unrest in their nation, and Viktor's part in it. She pictured him plunging headlong into battle, wielding his sword amidst a mass of Rynearson's men. And her fears carried it to a morbid conclusion.

An unconscionable bastard struck him from behind, finding the kinks in his armor. He collapsed where he stood, and blood spilled from the gash in his neck. He coughed and choked until all the life had poured from his body and his beautiful black eyes.

She shook her head imperceptibly against the images in her mind. Rynearson had moved to his winter abode in early December, which was much farther north than his summer estate. It would be a three-day journey to their destination, which meant she would suffer nothing less than a week of such images, and a week without Viktor.

Thoughts of his departure implanted an acute feeling of dread, and further thoughts of his absence caused a void that knocked the breath from her body.

The woman sighed miserably. How had she grown to care for her husband? How had she grown to care for a murderer? She must be insane. Reissa supported strict morals, yet she had allowed an extremely dangerous man to slip past her defenses.

He had lured her with a single kiss and possessed her with a night of passion. She had fallen prey to his handsome face and masculine form. Even as the conservative lady kicked herself for succumbing, she knew she would fall again with one heated glance. He had introduced her to the delights of ecstasy, and now she was hopelessly addicted.

She knew he was destined to hurt her, physically or emotionally. Perhaps a little of both? One day they would argue, and he would he give in to the temptation of eliminating her, as he had with Golly. Or one day they would argue, and he would throw all her faults in her face. Perhaps they would occur on the same day. It was inevitable because he did not care for her. He only truly cared for his blood family. She was merely a tolerable nuisance. And now, a warm body in his bed.

Reissa was in such a deep state of melancholy that she actually welcomed the distraction when they arrived at the Michaels's broken-down shack. She dismounted without waiting for aid and moved to the door with a determined gait. Her damask skirts and matching ermine cloak dusted the frozen dirt. Alden and Edith were forced to hurry in order to catch up with her.

Her knuckles rapped on the splintered, sagging door, then the trio patiently waited in silence. Nearly a minute passed, causing them to exchange concerned glances. Abruptly, the door groaned on its hinges, and Maisie's angelic face peeked at them through a crack.

"Maisie, dear," she said in a soothing voice.

The child's apprehensive expression instantly lifted into one of joy. "Lady Reissa!" she shouted, opened the door, charged out, and threw herself into outstretched arms.

Reissa gave her an affectionate squeeze and then stood from her crouched position.

"Have I missed my lessons?" Maisie's brow creased in confusion.

"Nay, I have brought my kind friend, Edith," she gestured to the woman on her right, "to check on your mother," she explained softly.

"Mama's ill," Maisie returned sadly.

"May we see her?"

The child nodded, then turned and raced back into the shack. They followed her inside and were brought up short by the unkempt residence. Soiled clothing and dishes filled with rotting food were scattered about. And despite the winter temperatures, flies buzzed around, feeding off moldy, crusty scraps. A pathetic fire burned in a makeshift fireplace, scorching thin logs. The smell was pungent, halting their entrance as if a stone wall hindered their intent.

Maisie hurried over and lay down on the earthen floor, attempting to share the pallet her mother resided on.

The woman lay there, staring at them through the fog of disease. Her breathing was frighteningly shallow. Blood splotches were visible on the pillow beneath her head and on the rag in her clenched fist. She appeared racked with fever. She had kicked a woolen blanket down to her feet, and her brow was shimmering with perspiration.

Edith glanced at Reissa. "Please, distract the child while I assess her mother," she requested below her breath.

Reissa nodded readily, expecting this would be required of her. Her short legs carried her over to the pair on the floor, and she knelt to take Maisie's hand.

"Lady Colville, 'tis a pleasure to see you again," Mrs. Michaels croaked through a parched throat and smiled through her eyes.

Reissa summoned the brightest smile she possessed. "The feeling is mutual, Mrs. Michaels."

"I welcome you into our home, my lady. I would—"

"Please, save your strength," she quietly interrupted. As her eyes moved over the woman's ashen skin, she was stricken with empathy. "I have brought a woman to evaluate your condition. Will you allow her to do so?"

Her nod was nearly undetectable.

"She attends all ailments in the castle. I assure you she is kind and competent." Reissa looked to the youth and said, "Maisie, shall we play while your mother rests?" She did not wait for the child's response, merely helped her to stand, then guided her toward what must have been the dining table in the Michaels's shelter. It was a large tree stump accompanied by three smaller stumps for chairs.

"I shall await you and my sister out of doors," Alden whispered into her ear, then exited the shack without another word.

Reissa grinned after his exit. Why were all men uncomfortable around a sickly woman? Then she regained focus and looked at her charge. "What would you like to play?"

Maisie jumped up from the tree stump and bounced excitedly. "Will you tell me another story?!"

Reissa laughed and patted the wooden cylinder, signaling for her to retake her seat. "Of course."

Maisie complied without complaint.

"Once upon a time," she began while Edith examined the patient.

Several minutes passed as she told the tale and Edith came to a conclusion about Mrs. Michaels's condition.

Reissa was just finishing the story when Lady Kilgour stood and crossed the room.

"Excuse me, Maisie." Reissa rose to her full height of five feet and turned to Edith as her stomach clenched with tension.

A head of golden blond curls shook, and her amber eyes were desolate. "She is suffering the final stages of consumption, Reissa." Edith glanced at Maisie, who innocently sat on the stump, restlessly waiting for her teacher to finish the tale. Her voice lowered. "Her death is imminent."

Reissa sighed heavily, hating the world in that moment. "What do you suggest, Edith? Would you like to bring them to the castle so you may care for her?"

"Nay, she is too weak; travel would finish her," she returned gravely.

"How long—" Reissa was unable to put voice to the remainder of the question.

"A week, possibly two with extreme care."

"Very well. We shall stay," the lady announced firmly.

"Reissa, the child is soon to be orphaned," Edith explained patiently. "She must be placed in another home. You must consult Viktor as to his wishes for her, and he—"

"—departs on the morrow," Reissa finished the statement as she began to understand the full extent of the ill-fated situation.

Edith nodded. "I suggest that you return to consult him as to placement for the child when the time arrives, and I shall remain to look after Mrs. Michaels and her daughter."

"I will not leave you here alone to care for an invalid and a child," Reissa emphatically opposed the idea. Maisie anxiously tugged at her skirts, wanting the return of the lady's attention.

"Reissa, I assure you I will be fine. It pleases me to care for others." When she noticed her companion's reluctance, she added, "The hour grows late. You and my brother must be on your way."

With Maisie still tugging on her skirts and the sun lowering in the sky, she unwillingly agreed. "I shall instruct five men-at-arms to remain for your aid and your security," the lady announced in a tone that brooked no argument.

Edith accepted her will with a nod of thanks.

***

Moderate snowfall began during the return trip to Colville Manor. By the time Alden helped Reissa dismount in the bailey, nearly two inches of icy flakes covered the ground. Only an hour of daylight remained.

Hearing the presence of soldiers in the side yard, Reissa turned to her male companion and said, "Go on and fill your empty belly, Alden. I must inform Viktor of the day's events."

"Very well," he acknowledged, then stalked toward the entrance to the manor.

Growing flushed and uneasy at the thought of seeking her husband in front of all of his men, she pushed the fur-lined hood from her head, welcoming the wintry cold. She followed the manor wall and turned the corner to see the side yard filled with her husband's personal army.

They stood at attention, poised with bows and arrows, ready to launch them toward a distant target. Her gaze scanned the crowd and was rewarded with the handsome sight of her husband's profile, standing amongst the first row of his men. His arrow aimed at the stack of hay piled against the curtain wall.

His loud shout rang through the thick silence, "Fire all!" And with that, hundreds of arrows cut arcs in the air, some with such intensity that whistles could be heard. They descended and injured the unsuspecting hay that was now draped in a thin blanket of snow.

After taking stock of the results, Viktor turned to address the congregation. "Well done, men." From the corner of his eye, he caught sight of his wife standing near the manor. He gazed at her for a brief moment, then looked at the army. "Eat heartily and seek your pleasures this night. We depart at dawn." He grinned, and the crowd whooped with joy and raucous clapping and laughter.

Viktor started toward her, and the crowd began to disperse in a disarray of commotion. He cut a direct line of approach, reaching her quickly. His height towered over her. He stood near, his legs brushing her skirts, but he did not touch her.

"What have you to share, Reissa?" he interrogated distantly, glancing at the passersby who were vacating the bailey.

Feeling uncomfortably aware of the man's presence, Reissa hesitated. When she did not immediately answer, he curiously sought her eyes. Their gazes locked.

Something inside the gray depths of her eyes prompted him to act. He reached out and palmed her elbows, drawing her near in spite of the men who remained, chatting to one another in small groups.

"Edith remains in the village, caring for Mrs. Michaels. I instructed five of your men to give her security and aid."

"And the woman?" His brow rose in question.

"Mrs. Michaels is terminal," she said with a soft sigh.

"Edith has determined her illness?" he demanded, then waited in tense silence for her response.

"Aye. She is wasting, in the final stages." Reissa's brow creased when she saw the unmistakable relief in his eyes. "I fail to see the optimism."

"I feared The Plague had traveled north," he justified.

"The Plague?" Reissa gasped. She was struck with images of her mother's tortured death, and panic surged through her being. Her gloved hands pressed against the metal of his armored chest in an attempt to calm herself.

"Be easy, wife, 'tis merely caution," he placated and it appeared he was inwardly reprimanding himself for adding to the weight of her worries. "While breaking a tardy fast, Edward informed me that The Black Death has reappeared in two of England's southern territories. However, he has quarantined such locations, so 'tis not probable that it should expand."

"But 'tis possible," Reissa underlined, her disposition staid.

Unable to assure her to the contrary, he redirected the subject. "Maisie is an only child?"

"Aye."

"Are you aware of any extended family?"

"She has none." The teacher had questioned the girl of her background one evening while escorting her home. It was only Maisie and her parents, rather like Reissa's family in a distant past. She thought of Maisie, soon to be deprived of a mother's unfailing presence. Her heart went out to her. It was not fair. She deserved guidance, she deserved security, and, above all, she deserved unconditional love.

Reissa knew she could provide it all, but as she gazed up at her husband, she also knew she did not have the right to request this of him. It was too grand of scale, too life-altering to seek permission for Maisie. And even though it killed her to do so, she remained dutifully silent.

A callused hand parted the folds of her cloak and slid around her tiny waist, supporting the small of her back with his palm. The crook of his finger lifted her chin, ensuring she could not look away. "You long to be Maisie's guardian, I know it," he murmured. "'Tis clearly written in those beautiful gray eyes."

The shake of her head was slight. "I cannot ask it of you, Viktor."

His gaze roamed over the snowflakes melting in her hair like a reserved child observing the winter phenomenon for the first time. He pulled her closer, pressing her against the body of his armor, and then heaped a tender stare on her. "Do you wish to put forth the request?"

"Desperately," she breathed.

"Ask it of me, Reissa," he urged.

The warm inflection in his tone drew the words from her in spite of her will. "May I be guardian to that child?"

"You may." He grinned.

Reissa was absolutely dumbfounded for a moment. But when his permissive smile continued, her shock rapidly melted away, and she shrieked with pure joy. Bubbling over with gratitude, she reacted without thought for her actions. She palmed his cheeks, drew his face down to hers, and claimed his mouth with her own.

It was meant to be a swift, chaste kiss, but when she began to draw back, a strong hand cradled the back of her head. Her husband held her immobile as he explored the smooth texture of her lips with his tongue, stirring her blood and stimulating her senses. His teeth gently raked over her bottom lip, then he healed the tingle with a soft kiss.

He drew his face away, and she expelled a rasp of air, her limbs trembling as a result of his touch.

"However, I must enforce one stipulation, Reissa," Viktor spoke firmly, engaging her attention.

"Aye?"

"I insist that a nursemaid is acquired for the child. I will not have you driven to exhaustion by catering to your charge, as well as myself." The pad of his thumb smoothed over her mouth. "You may provide Maisie your company during the light of day, but your nights shall be passed in my arms."

Her eyes widened. She was overwhelmed by his candor, yet the sudden flip of her stomach caused a chain reaction of feeling that traveled to the tips of her fingers and toes.

"Do you wish to contest this outline, my lady?" he tested, his demeanor poised for her response.

Presently, he held her in his arms, which caused her feelings on the matter to be strikingly clear. Yet, simultaneously, her thoughts on the matter were muddled. The arms holding her close inspired security, trust, and, above all, passion. But the thoughts racing through her mind shouted danger, liar, and murderer. Nevertheless, Maisie's welfare was her only cause. She would agree to a daily beating if it brought her the child's presence.

"Nay," she squeaked, her cheeks coloring with a flush of embarrassed excitement.

Viktor sucked in a breath, and his gaze slipped to her lips. His golden flecks deepened several shades with the glow of desire. Quickly, he scanned their surroundings. Observing that a handful of soldiers were present, he grabbed her hand and pulled her along the perimeter of the castle walls. They rounded a corner on the south side and descended a slope that proceeded into the servants' entrance in the basement.

Her husband nodded cordially at the guard posted at the door, but Reissa kept her head down, apprehensive, uncertain of Viktor's intentions as he pulled her through the narrow entryway. He kicked the door shut as he pulled her into his arms and captured her lips with a need that clearly relayed his intentions.

Aware that there was a guard on the opposite side of the wooden structure, Reissa tore her mouth away and gasped, "Viktor, we may be caught; 'tis scandalous!"

That wicked smile she was growing to know well returned. He palmed her cheeks and bestowed upon her a kiss that obliterated all rational thought.

His passion ignited her own. Her arms circled his neck, and liquid fire coursed through her veins. She pressed close, but the barrier of his armor denied her access to the hard plains of his body. The lady pulled back and frowned at his metal-clad figure. Viktor glanced down and realized the cause for her frustration.

Once again, his fingers clasped her hand, and he pulled her along toward the steep, narrow staircase that was situated to the right of the door. He guided her to stand on the fifth step, and then seated himself at her feet.

Reading his thoughts, she bent down and, with a great deal of difficulty, lifted the metal casing over his head. She nearly fell back under the weight of his armor in her arms, but he quickly relieved her of the burden and set it aside. Then, just as quickly, he stripped off the remainder of his knight's attire, leaving him clad in a charcoal-gray tunic and sienna braies.

With that done, he pinned her with a hot stare. Wordlessly, he climbed up the steps and firmly pushed her down into a seated position. Her husband pressed her back against the stone with the volume of his broad chest, reigniting their kiss.

Hungry hands roamed over her slender form, finding her most secret places, arousing her to the point of pain. Both still wore full dress, although the lady had divested her gloves and unclasped her cloak.

Reissa was desperate for the gratification she knew he could provide. In an effort to further their intimacies, her palm boldly traveled over his abdomen and down to press to the front of his braies. Her features flared, stunned by the profuse flesh she felt there. During their prior relations, she had not possessed the courage to take in the sight of his lower half, but now, as she felt his member swelling to her touch, she marveled at the truth that her tiny form was able to accommodate his extensive size.

Curiosity prompted her to act. Her hand curled around him, and she could feel the throbbing of his heart through the thin material of his hose. The muddled, tortured groan that sounded near her ear enlightened her to her capabilities as a woman, and as his wife.

Hearing his pleasure, her fingers pulled at his laces, frantic to unite them. And as his lips tasted the sensitive skin of her neck, he drew up her skirts. When Reissa freed him from his material prison, he collected her hands and dispensed them to his shoulders. He clutched her hips, and her legs instinctually lifted to circle his waist, only vaguely aware of the discomfort of the staircase supporting her back.

He plunged into her, sheathing the length of him in her warmth, but Reissa was the one who initiated the measured cadence that lifted them up, up into the heights of explosive ecstasy. As they rode upon the cresting waves, indulging in one another, their impassioned cries echoed up the stairwell, concealing the quiet shuffle of presence that resided there, listening.

***

Mindful of his wife's position on an unyielding structure, Viktor did not indulge in the desire to collapse in his satiated state. He held himself aloft as his breath and his thoughts slowly returned to normal. His muscled arms barely strained as he looked down on Reissa. But as he observed her closed eyes, radiant smile and glistening brow, guilt struck him like a physical blow.

The woman had caused him to lose control of himself, and in doing so, he had treated her as he would a scullery maid. He cursed himself for a heartless bounder. He had not even had the decency to disrobe her before the hasty liaison in the stairwell. He had simply tossed up her skirts and taken his pleasure.

The woman was his wife, not a convenient body to be used for his baser needs. Yes, she inspired the need within greater than any other woman ever had, but that did not justify his thoughtless treatment. Reissa deserved care, respect, and absolute worship in the bedroom. And he had given her none of that.

Viktor adjusted her skirts, then himself, setting them to rights following their impulsive exertions. He knew without a doubt that his attraction for her could not be tempered, and it was inevitable that it would arise when a bed was not near at hand. He had to make amends.

He helped her to stand and collected the ermine cloak, which was now dusted with dirt from lying beneath them. The soiled garment was tossed over his forearm, and then he looked at his wife. Her skin was fused with crimson, and by the way she would not meet his eyes, he guessed she was feeling the effects of her discarded inhibitions.

Viktor could not help but be flattered with the knowledge that he had caused her to lose control. Shockingly, his body stirred with renewed desire. He gave himself a mental shake and voiced his regret.

"I apologize for my impatience, Reissa," he smiled and traced a line down her cheek with the tip of his finger, "but I give you my word, after we have dined with our king, I shall escort you to your chambers and spend the remainder of the night making reparations."

Chapter 33

Viktor was true to his word. They shared a pleasant meal with their family and their royal guest, then they retired to Reissa's chambers and passed a blissful night in one another's arms.

But as the pair walked from the Meeting Hall and stepped into the icy dawn, Reissa's contentment was absent. Only unhappiness remained. She was not prepared for this. She was not prepared to watch her husband ride through the gates into certain danger.

Once again, the bailey was steeped with activity. Knights and soldiers were readying themselves for departure. Others were sharing in conversation, passing the time before the army moved en masse. And yet another group of people were exchanging heartfelt farewells with their family members, much like Viktor and Reissa.

Before they drew too close to his temperamental warhorse, the lord turned on his wife and gazed down upon her with open affection. He took in her distressed expression and spoke to assure her.

"I shall return, my lady," he vowed quietly.

"Unharmed," she added with feeling.

***

He grinned even as he marveled at the reluctance within himself. Prior to his marriage he had always embraced the anticipation of battle, but on that day, he could think of nothing but his return, his return to this woman in particular. Shining black orbs caressed her tiny figure in awe.

"You are truly lovely," he breathed wondrously.

Reissa's eyes began to shimmer with tears. "Viktor, I—"

"Shh." Sensing her intent for sentiment, he held a finger to her lips, halting her words. "Let us speak our farewell in silence." Then his mouth replaced his finger. Uncaring that they could be viewed by countless pairs of eyes, Viktor yanked her into his arms and bestowed upon her a kiss that he wanted to forever be burned into her memory, and her heart.

"Uhhem," a grunt intruded into a world where Reissa and Viktor were the only occupants. They broke apart to find Collin standing there, an amused smile upon his bearded face. "'Tis time, little brother," he announced, but as his eyes moved between the couple, his grin remained.

"Aye." Viktor nodded. With that, his elder sibling gave a cordial nod to Reissa, then spun on his heel and walked away.

Left alone, the masculine arms circling her waist banded tightly, holding her for several drawn-out moments before falling away. Then he too whirled around, mounted his horse, and spurred the animal into a steady trot.

Colville Manor

Viktor did not allow himself to look back at the woman he was leaving behind, because he feared if he did so, he would lose the will to go.

***

Collin and Viktor stood over Rynearson's cold corpse, their faces grim.

A knight was perpetually cautious, but when they arrived to find the portcullis wide open, they feared a trap. Nevertheless, loyal to their plan and to the crown, they forged on slowly, prepared to do battle in the next instant. Warhorses carried them through the empty bailey and directly up to the keep entrance. There they waited, expecting an army of men to charge around the castle and bear down upon them, but minutes passed and still nothing. There was not a soul visible on the property.

Viktor gave his elder sibling a glance, then dismounted. He unsheathed his sword and heard Collin approach his back, also arming himself. With one merciless kick, the double doors swung open, admitting them to an interior devoid of heat.

The body of their overlord lay at the center of the hall, motionless. They entered to take stock of his fatal injuries, but still, no one rushed at them from the shadows or came marching down the wide berth of the staircase. Rynearson's head had nearly been severed from his body. Grossly, the cord of his spine held it on, and blood surrounded him in a sticky, congealed puddle.

"'Twould appear we are too late," Collin stated the obvious, causing his brother to send him a dry glare.

Viktor scanned the surroundings. A fermenting meal sat on the tables, and countless chairs were overturned, speaking of the occupants' sudden interruption. However, the lack of dead bodies told an entirely different tale. The castle had been abandoned, not invaded.

"We have stumbled upon a mutiny," he put a voice to his thoughts.

"I believe you are correct, little brother. He has been betrayed by his own."

The sharp point of Viktor's sword scraped the floor as his mind spun, pondering the abrupt turn of events. "Perhaps his men were persuaded to do so with generous compensation."

"Bennington?" Collin asked, his thoughts running in a similar direction.

Viktor's brow rose.

"Let us assume 'tis so. Clearly, he has not betrayed an ally to possess the estate," Collin's hand waved to encompass the empty castle, "so name his cause."

"The cause remains; 'tis merely the man seeking the throne who has changed."

"Very well, Bennington has gained Rynearson's army in addition to his own. Hypothesize the continuation of his treasonous plan."

"'Tis simple: he possesses the artillery, and due to the fact that several royal heirs exist, he must take the throne by force. Bennington would see Edward dead immediately—"

"—or force him to abdicate to another."

"Edward would die afore agreeing to name an heir he has not chosen. I foresee our king's death—" Viktor broke off, suddenly stricken.

"And Edward resides in Colville Manor," Collin finished his thought with a frown.

Their gazes locked, realizing the consequences of that statement in the same instant.

Collin and Viktor tore from the castle with lightning speed.

Chapter 34

The morning of Viktor's departure, at table, he had expressed his desire for Reissa to learn the management of the castle's affairs. Eventually she would oversee the savings and distribution in the coffers. Food reserves needed monitoring, and meals chosen. The overall cleanliness of the keep must be tended to, as well as the comfort and welfare of their guests.

She was the manor's mistress, after all; it was her duty to fulfill. So, in acceptance of her husband's wishes, and, selfishly, to preoccupy her thoughts from his absence, she did not waste any time in throwing herself into the task.

That same afternoon, after receiving word from a messenger that Edith fared well in her temporary residence and Mrs. Michaels's state had stabilized, she sought Viktor's steward. Hoyt was a man of average height with a lanky, bony build. He was young, not thirty years, yet he appeared no less than fifty. His hair was graying and receding, and his brown eyes were dead.

But he possessed the energy of a child and spoke a mile a minute. On occasion, she was hard-pressed to individuate one word from another, but in spite of her confusion, she found humor in his disposition. Her hand would lift to conceal a smile, or she would be forced to clear her throat to halt a giggle. And as the days stretched, she grew increasingly grateful for that.

Reissa found herself living in a perpetual state of worry. Viktor's welfare was silently questioned with every breath, and she loved him with every beat of her heart. The development was new, and quite unbelievable. It was when he spoke the words, "You are truly lovely," when she was blindsided by the truth that she was in love with her husband.

Overwhelmed by that feeling, tears had sprung into her eyes. Yes, she loved him. She loved a murderer. She resented such emotion, but it was useless to deny, because the emotion controlled her; she did not control it. And his farewell kiss only proved to support her heart's desire. He imprinted himself on her soul with that embrace, and then departed without a backward glance.

Reissa missed him terribly, and while she lay in her lonely bed each evening, she prayed for his safe return. As she had surmised, she was plagued with images of his death. And not only in the evenings when she was alone. She would snap from violent reveries while amidst a Meeting Hall full of people.

She also suffered while she was meant to be concentrating on Hoyt's teachings. The man was high-strung but extremely patient with her and her distractions. When her eyes would blink, returning to reality from such fatal fantasies, he would simply grin knowingly and repeat himself without hesitation. There was only one occasion when she witnessed his obvious reluctance to speak.

They stood in one of the guest chambers. Hoyt was running down the list of necessities that must be tended to before a guest stepped into the room. He extended a finger with every addition. "A fire must be burning, warming the chamber, heated stones placed in the bed, and a steaming bath drawn. If the women do not possess a lady's maid, one must be furnished for them; and similarly with the men, a herald shall be provided, perhaps a valet." He paused, and she was intrigued when his cheeks began to color with red patches. "If our male guest has arrived without a female companion, one shall also be provided."

Reissa gasped. "Hoyt, you jest!"

"I fear not, my lady. Every guest must be made to feel entirely welcome," he explained, obviously uncomfortable in sharing this with her. His speech lagged.

"The married men are also provided this service?" she questioned through her shock.

"If the wife is not present, aye," he responded quietly.

"'Tis positively vulgar!" she choked, longing for a return of her blissful ignorance. That was one detail she would rather have been left unsaid, and unknown.

"'Tis courtesy, my lady. A maid shall be chosen for the man, that is, unless a specific woman is requested."

"The king arrived without the queen; was he also provided such service?" Her curiosity won out over discretion.

Hoyt's brown eyes lowered to the floor, and he nodded distinctly.

As that knowledge settled in her mind, the silence stretched. Then she was abruptly struck with the realization that the same service would be provided on other lands. As she thought of

Viktor's absence from the castle without her, pink lips compressed, causing them to thin with jealousy. Her temper sparked. Reissa gave in to the desire to voice an audacious question. She knew it announced her common background, but she cared not; she needed an outlet for the green haze before her eyes.

"Are the women also provided with that service, Hoyt?"

His eyes widened, scandalized. "Nay, my lady." His cough was faked to cover a smile.

Reissa recognized the act as one of her own, and she could not help but smile herself.

That evening while snuggling in the warmth of her bed, she was assaulted with fresh images. She pictured her husband retiring to a guest room while visiting a friendly estate. A pretty maid awaited him there, and he did not turn her away.

A pitiful sob entered into the darkness. It was near dawn before she fell into a restless sleep. Nevertheless, she rose early, deciding to visit the village on that day.

Reissa made the journey with an escort of a dozen men, and when she entered into the Michaels's shelter, she was astounded by the transformation. The interior appeared to be that of another's. All the filth had been cleansed away. Only order remained.

Edith greeted her with sincere welcome, and even Mrs. Michaels appeared to have gained a modicum of strength. Reissa spent several hours visiting with all three occupants. Maisie's youth was infectious, providing all with entertainment. And Edith's sweet disposition endeared the melancholy lady. By the time she departed, her foul mood had actually dwindled, and a smile graced her lips.

Reissa was slightly fatigued when she arrived at the manor. She climbed the main staircase, needing to freshen up and change her dress for the evening meal. Slender legs carried her down the corridor to her antechamber, but a debilitating wave of dizziness abruptly seized her senses. Her knees buckled, and she stumbled. Instinctually, a hand lifted and pressed to the wall, catching herself from falling face-first into the cool stone. She stood stock-still for many moments, leaning against the wall, waiting for the world to right itself.

Eventually, the oddity passed, and she was once again able to see straight. Tentatively, she continued on, her steps cautious, her thoughts buzzing in confusion. She sought an answer to that unexpected spell with all the knowledge in her mind, but when nothing presented itself, she simply brushed it off as a fluke and carried on with her day.

Two days passed without incident. On the eve of the third, Reissa sat at her vanity, preparing to retire for bed. She brushed out her strawberry blond locks, and after she was satisfied that all knots had been detangled, she rose from the wooden bench. Without warning, consciousness blinked out.

Reissa awoke to find herself lying face-down on the floor near her bed. The lady's figure was racked with chills in reaction to the frigid floor supporting her, and her head ached where it had smacked into the unforgiving stone.

With an agonized groan, she lifted herself off the floor, pressed a palm to the bump on her head, and hobbled over to the bed. She collapsed onto the feather mattress and pulled the coverlet up to her chin, huddling into the fetal position until her shivers subsided. The ache in her head slowly dulled, and she drifted off to sleep.

When she rose the following morning, she felt nothing was amiss. The only proof of her swoon was the shrinking bump on her head.

It was the second abnormality in her health within days, but she decided it must be the effects of stress, concern, and exhaustion. It was not serious. There was not any need to speak of the spells to anyone.

When she descended to the Meeting Hall to break her fast, she became aware of a commotion that was equally great. She hurried down the remaining steps and entered into the massive room. Reissa froze and took in the sight. People hurried about in all directions, countless attired in full armor, and armed with bows and arrows. Shouts could be heard, and what sounded like stone attacking stone rang in her ears. The tension in the air was palpable.

Unnoticed in the uproar, Reissa lifted her skirts and ran to the double doors. She emerged into the shadows of dawn, yet there was enough sunlight to see that the bailey was alive with the king's royal army. Armed men were lined on the battlements of the curtain wall, firing arrows through the embrasures.

There was a frightening sound of rocks smashing against the exterior curtain walls. Every so often, one would miss the mark, charge over the elevated stone walls, and crash into the bailey, taking out anything in its path. Many men sat, staring at large basins of water that had been placed beside the towers, waiting for visible tremors of undermining from the opposite side. Others worked diligently, digging through the frozen earth to meet the opposition beneath.

Suddenly, soldiers appeared on the crosswalks, swiftly moving toward the outer curtains with tubs of boiling water. Reissa watched in horror as they halted and poured the same water over the edge. The agonized screams of men erupted into the air, causing her stomach to clench with nausea.

"My lady, we are under siege. 'Tis unsafe in the bailey; you must take protection in the keep!" a king's footman shouted as he ran up to her. Without waiting for a reply, he firmly grasped her upper arm and tugged her tiny figure through the entrance.

As they rushed into the Meeting Hall, Moira emerged from the enclosed staircase. She spotted Reissa near the double doors with a sigh of relief.

"Reissa, thank the Lord, I have been searching high and low for you," she called as she hastened across the massive space.

Reissa turned to thank the man on her left for his escort, but he had gone without a word.

"We must take precautions, Reissa. If the castle should fall, we will need reserves of food," Moira said with quiet calm.

Reissa nodded in agreement. At that moment, as the gravity of their situation finally sank in, she was grateful Edward's army had not gone with the others. Certainly, the king was never without a mass of constant protection, but never would Viktor and Collin allow the keep to stand without men to defend it.

Her insides quivered with worry and fear, but she had faith in Edward's men. They would do everything in their power to ensure the king's safety, and also theirs.

"The castle will not fall," she announced with stubborn confidence.

But just then, the deafening sound of the north tower falling echoed through the keep. The sound waves radiated through their bodies like a resounding death knell.

Moira looked to the ceiling and breathed, "Dear Lord, heaven help us."

Chapter 35

The Colville brothers pushed their men and their mounts to exhaustion. They traveled day and night, abbreviating a three-day journey to less than two.

As one of Edward's most trusted and most accomplished knights, Viktor's greatest loyalty lay with his king and his welfare, yet his thoughts dwelled on one soul: his wife's. Frantically, he revisited the facts over and over in his head, seeking an altered conclusion to the one they guessed at Rynearson's, but logic always brought him back to their original deduction. The keep and all within were in grave danger.

The state of Rynearson's cold body announced that Bennington possessed the advantage of a day's head start. Mentally, Viktor prepared himself for the worst, but when he struck the point of considering the possibility of Reissa's death… He simply could not visit it. He refused to follow that line of thought.

It was midday, and at long last, they drew near the manor. Viktor grudgingly acknowledged the fact that he was bone-weary, but tension and adrenaline provided the necessary means with which to carry on. His fine-tuned senses were dulled with fatigue, but he would not allow room for error.

Did he hear something? He commanded the whole of his army and his entourage to halt and issued silence.

Viktor and Collin strained themselves, listening, then they exchanged knowing glances. The worst had indeed come true, because the unmistakable roar of a siege sounded at a distance.

"To arms!" Viktor bellowed and unsheathed his sword. With that, they spurred their mounts, initiating a breakneck speed.

When the foe became aware of their opposition quickly bearing down upon them from the rear, not only were they trapped by the manor to which they sought entrance, but they were forced to make an about face and engage in direct combat.

The Colville brothers courageously led the charge, their weapons raised, their throats vibrating with shouts of primal rage. They were the first to confront the enemy, face-to-face, sword-to-sword.

Chapter 36

The resounding roar of battle rang through the keep like a church bell on a day of mourning, constant and agonizing. Distant screams of dying men and the clash of swords were ever-present, seeping through the stone walls that surrounded them.

From their seated places in the pantry, Reissa and Moira exchanged anxious stares. Long ago, a passing footman had informed them of the arrival of the Colvilles' armies, and that had only added to the strain of waiting. Their fears for Collin and Viktor were heaped onto their fears for the castle and themselves.

The ladies had kept their hands busy and mouths preoccupied with inconsequential talk to distract themselves from the conflict on their doorstep. They crated food for emergency reserves while outside the battle raged on endlessly; at least in their fretful minds it seemed that way.

But twilight was falling. Shadows settled around them, emphasizing the stark emptiness of the manor and the noise outside. Drained of their mental and physical resources, they had given in to the need to rest.

Moira looked at her stomach, and trembling hands moved to caress the budding mound, diverting her face. Reissa grew distressed when she noticed the tears dripping onto her sister-in-law's lemon skirts. She shifted to seat herself on the crate beside the weeping woman and curled an arm around slumped shoulders.

"Collin is safe, I assure you." Reissa hid her cringe, knowing she spoke out of turn, despite her best intentions.

"I know my husband is seasoned in combat, yet I cannot dismiss my fear. Reissa, 'tis possible our child may never know his or her own father," she choked.

An idea occurred, and Reissa was able to speak with total confidence. "Viktor would never allow that."

A pair of beautiful sky-blue eyes rose, and the foreboding there communicated the thought behind them.

What if Viktor fell in battle?

Understanding the unspoken words, Reissa's head began to shake, and a surge of frightful hysteria shot through her being. Rather than give in to the need to seek an outlet of tears, she forced a smile. "The devil himself could not blow out Viktor's fire."

Moira gave a curt laugh through her sorrow. "Aye, the man could battle the devil and find victory, but we must face a cruel reality, Reissa. He is not infallible."

Reissa's mind did a collective summation of her knowledge of the man. Her laugh was bittersweet. "Aye, Moira, I believe he is," and she was quick to add, "and he *will* watch over your husband."

Moira sighed and wiped the moisture from her cheeks. "'Tis not as it should be. He is the elder sibling, yet Viktor knows greater favor. The king, their mother, and even a father with a cold heart showed the younger brother more attention. Collin's comedic disposition is a direct result of that. He sought attention through humor, while Viktor was molded into the mirror image of Collin

Senior. 'Tis clear that Viktor feels responsible for the whole of the Colville family in spite of the presence of an elder brother, and I believe that is also a result of unbalanced care."

"I have not observed an inequality in the king's favor," Reissa returned with a frown.

"'Tis subtle," Moira attempted to smile, but it fell flat.

"Perhaps a result of Viktor's aggressive nature," she provided an excuse, although she felt a sliver of pity emerging for Collin.

"I love my husband beyond the depths of my heart, but I resent his parents," she looked to the ceiling, "Lord rest their souls," her eyes returned to Reissa's, "for failing to give Collin the care he deserved. I shall be sent to Hades for speaking this, but the absence of Collin Sr. and Margaret is truly a blessing for him. Please, do not misunderstand, my husband adored his parents; 'tis I as an observer who has decided this conclusion.

"Collin is capable and strong, in every aspect of his life, equally as capable as Viktor. His act as the elder brother is present, perhaps not clearly visible, but Collin looks after him as well."

"'Tis a detail I would never doubt, Moira. 'Tis also obvious that Collin loves his brother much."

The lady shook off her distress and grinned. "Collin adores his brother, and I must admit Viktor has found a small place in my heart, but I am unable to decide your feelings for your husband. It appears you have surpassed your fear of him, but I am uncertain of the emotion beyond that.

"Nevertheless, I shall be bold and venture an educated guess. He has cast his spell upon you, and you have fallen prey to the wand." She laughed when Reissa was unable to stifle a revealing gasp. "'Tis clearly written in your eyes, my dear."

"My emotions are transparent?" she wondered in dismay.

"Oh, Reissa, your innocence is endearing," she said with warm affection. "I find the trait rather refreshing. We live amongst a dwelling of envious, conniving, and spiteful scullery maids. You must not allow the presence of such immorality to jade you." She lifted her yellow skirts and rose from the crate.

"How so?" the naïve lady wondered as she clasped her hands in her lap.

Moira brushed a piece of lint from her bosom. "You must prepare yourself for the ruthlessness of envious women. Servant girls grow rather attached to their lords after years of faithful service, and they resent a mistress when she enters onto their territory. I learned early on in my marriage that a wedding band does not hold female vipers at bay. I have watched maids lust after my husband while I sat at his side."

A slender hand fluttered up to her throat. "Oh my," Reissa breathed, quite taken aback.

"Viktor is an attractive man, and 'tis inevitable that headstrong women will chase after him regardless of his wedded state, but you must not give in to the hatred you feel, dear, or you shall be tempted to react in accordance with their deceit."

"On the eve of our wedding, Viktor instructed that I must turn a blind eye to such faithlessness, Moira. He will not tolerate a jealous shrew," she voiced even as the thought of him with another woman left a sour taste in her mouth.

"Viktor cares for you, Reissa. Perhaps his feelings for you have changed the rules."

"The Lord himself could not convince this lady," she pointed at her chest, "that he would favor myself over a lovelier woman."

Moira gave an unladylike snort. "Reissa, look at me," she gestured to her ample figure and blinding yellow gown, "I am a walking banana, yet Collin would favor me over any other. You must give yourself more credit, my dear."

"Your husband loves you," Reissa felt her bottom lip quiver, and she stared at the floor, "but my husband merely tolerates my presence."

Moira returned to her side. "His eyes tell a different tale," she whispered.

Warm tears streamed down her cheeks, wishing her sister-in-law's words were true, yet deep inside, she knew it was not possible. A beautiful noble could not love a plain commoner. It was not a design of life.

Through her quiet sorrow, they heard the final clang of swords, and to their everlasting horror, it was followed with resounding silence. The hush seemed to move through the dwelling like a frightening entity, invisible and hair-raising.

Not a word was spoken. The ladies communicated their desperate pleadings to one another through locked eyes, and their conversation was forgotten. They needed answers. They needed to know if their husbands had survived.

Unable to wait another moment longer, they jumped up in unison and raced from the narrow room. With their skirts held high in their hands, they ran across the extended distance of the Meeting Hall. However, when they met the double doors that firmly shut them away from the outside world, they drew to an uncertain halt and once again exchanged worried glances.

They knew not what lay on the other side. If the Colvilles were victorious, they had nothing to fear, but if their husbands had been defeated, certain death may meet them on the other side.

Abruptly, the double doors were ruthlessly yanked open, stealing choice from them. But they didn't care because the familiar forms that nearly trampled over them in their haste to enter provided proof that the Lord had answered their prayers.

"Collin!"

"Viktor!"

As Reissa stared up at her husband, she was struck with four simultaneous thoughts. One, his presence announced that the Colvilles had indeed been victorious. Two, his standing form also announced that he was alive. Three, his armor had been discarded, leaving him in nothing but a rumpled gray tunic and matching braies. And four, grotesque blood spatter covered his face, neck, and hands. In numerous places, there was so much red that she could not be sure if it was his or not. Dear Lord!

"Are you hurt?!" She did not hesitate to put a voice to the fourth thought as she stepped forward and pressed a palm to a sticky patch of crimson that had run down his neck and onto his chest. The intense eyes boring into her tiny figure and a bailey full of men-at-arms awaiting entrance went unnoticed in her distressed state.

Reissa's fears were instantly forgotten when his strong arms gathered her against his chest. Her eyes squeezed shut, and she buried her face in his shoulder, allowing the protection and contentment of his secure embrace to wash over her. She didn't care that blood transferred onto her figure, ruining her olive-green gown. All that mattered in that instant was Viktor, and the fact that he was holding her close.

She clutched his tunic at the small of his back and squeezed, wrinkling the fabric in her tiny fists, giving silent thanks to the Lord that Collin and Viktor were safe.

"You two must be famished. Let us get some food into your bellies," Moira spoke to the men, then grabbed her husband's hand and waited for Viktor's reply.

Reissa reluctantly began to pull her from husband's arms with the intent to allow him to cross to the dais, and also to allow the men patiently waiting in the bailey to enter. But he refused to let her go. He held her in a firm embrace and gazed down into her pale face.

"Aye, I shall have food, but first I shall have my wife," he announced with such serious regard that Reissa's mouth fell open in astonishment.

As he swept her into his arms, she heard Moira, Collin and several of the men in the yard laughing softly. A mortified blush crept up her neck and heated her cheeks, causing the lady to hide her face in his neck as he carried her toward the staircase.

"Moira, have the servants draw a bath in my chambers and have the food sent up as well," he called over his shoulder, then entered into the enclosed stairwell.

When Reissa was certain of their solitude, she lifted her head and stared up at a jaw shadowed with several days of black stubble. "I would complain about that scene below, but the joy that we have all survived this ordeal overrules such pettiness."

"'Tis over, Reissa; your fears may rest," he said in a soothing voice as he ascended the top step.

"The king is safe?"

"Aye, Bennington is dead, thereby vanquishing the threat of unrest."

"And Rynearson?"

"Murdered by his own men." He looked straight ahead as he moved down the corridor with a determined gait.

The lady grimaced. "How dreadful." She rambled on, her tense excitement growing with every step he claimed. In the Meeting Hall, he had spoken plainly of his intimate intent, and the mere thought of it made her tremble.

"Mrs. Michaels's state of health?" he tested distantly and pulled her close to enter his antechamber.

"She clings to life... with the will... of an angel," Reissa answered, effectively distracted when he placed her on unsteady feet in his bedchamber, pressed his soiled palms to her cheeks, and gazed deep into her eyes.

"For hours, men fell at my feet in supreme agony, struck down by my hand, but my only thoughts were of you, Reissa. The north tower had fallen, the perimeter breached. I knew not if you were dead or alive." His breath was shaky. "When we opened the doors to the keep, I saw a beautiful face afore me," Viktor whispered, a finger tracing the line of her cheek, "this face." Then his mouth brushed over hers in a feather-light kiss.

Chapter 37

They ate together and bathed together. Then Viktor carried his wife to the canopy and made love to her with a passion unlike any she had previously experienced in their marriage bed. And with their breathing still labored and perspiration dotting their brows, they fell into an exhausted sleep, blissfully curled in each other's arms.

Viktor continued on in a deep slumber when Reissa rose early the following morn. Quietly, she donned her gown and returned to her chambers to prepare for the day.

Mrs. Michaels's time was growing short, and she intended to spend much of the time with the sick woman and Maisie. And, in addition, she continued her voluntary work at the schoolhouse. It was Thursday. She needed to tutor her children when the sun rose to its peak in the sky.

After Gert aided her toilet, she descended to the Meeting Hall and collected an entourage for the journey. Anticipating her plans, Alden approached and requested to accompany her into the village. It had been days, and he longed to visit with his sister. The journey to and from the village was rather tedious, so Reissa was delighted for the friendly companionship.

The lady's appetite was absent, so she declined to break her fast. Upon her insistent orders, they all departed posthaste.

The date was February first. They were entering the dead of winter, yet it was unseasonably warm. The snow on the ground was melting away beneath the morning sun, and the air was still. Reissa closed her eyes and lifted her face to the brilliant rays of light with a welcoming smile.

Following the perfect evening with her husband, she felt her insides glowing with wonder. It was certainly visible on the outside because her mouth was stamped with a perpetual grin. The previous night, while munching on the meal Moira had sent up to them, they had an involved conversation that included talk of their parents, their friends, and their childhoods.

Then Viktor disrobed them both, and they climbed into the large wooden tub that had been filled with buckets of steaming hot water. Viktor lathered her entire body with soap bubbles, and even massaged her scalp when he washed her hair.

Reissa returned the favor, but when her hands moved below the water line and touched his most intimate part, he groaned and lifted her from the tub. He hastily dried their dripping bodies, then, with a licentious smile, he tossed her over his shoulder and playfully swatted her behind. When he dumped her onto the bed, both were burning with desire.

Her husband took her once, then twice, and finally a third time. During each occasion he introduced another position, while equally introducing his never-ending need for her feminine figure. It was nearing midnight when at last he pulled her back to his chest and draped an arm over her waist.

And while his heavy breathing fanned her ear, he issued an order that she would never consider disobeying. "You will not depart, Reissa; you will pass the night in my bed, in my arms." With that, he kissed the sensitive flesh of her naked shoulder and promptly fell asleep.

The woman thought of her husband remaining nestled in his bed. She longed to be there, and because of that, she began to resent her obligations. Reissa gave herself a mental slap and opened her eyes to reality. She must see to Maisie and Mrs. Michaels and her charges.

"Viktor has informed me that the child shall find permanent residence in Colville Manor," Alden's voice abruptly sounded.

Reissa snapped from her quietude and sent her companion a luminous smile. "Aye. The circumstances leading to such a joy are tragic, but his allowance is an unexpected gift."

"Aye, unexpected," he repeated. The knight shook his head with obvious disbelief, and a humored grin tugged at the corners of his mouth. "Viktor is certainly selective in his favors, lass. 'Tis an awesome responsibility to take in an orphaned child, and his willingness to agree to such speaks volumes."

"I fail to understand your meaning," she returned with a frown.

"I have known Viktor as long as memory serves, but never has he shown any of his women such care. You have changed him, Reissa," he stated.

"Have I received an insult or a compliment?" she demanded lightly.

"A compliment, to be sure," he confirmed quickly. "His spirits have soared. When he believed the occupants of the castle to be in peril," his head shook again, "I have never been witness to such ruthlessness."

Reissa shifted uncomfortably in the saddle. It was the second time in two days that another had spoken of Viktor in relation to her. Clearly both Alden and Moira believed her husband genuinely cared for her, and she wanted so badly to accept their words as truth.

But she couldn't allow it. She would not raise her hopes, because to do so would mean she was opening herself up to certain disappointment. She would like to continue on in blissful ignorance rather than learn that all Viktor felt for her was obligation.

They had a contract to uphold, which may have been the only reason for his elevated attention in their marriage bed. She must have been insane when she nearly voiced her love for him on the day of his departure.

Unwilling to confront the subject directly, she downplayed Alden's comment with a dismissive wave of her hand. "Viktor was merely protecting his family and his home."

"Aye, *Lady Colville*." There was no mistaking the lilt in his voice.

Her husband had pointed out the same while they stood on the staircase one evening not so long ago. Yet the fact that she was a member of the Colville family still seemed to be an illusion.

Reissa was growing desperate to take the focus from herself, so she mentioned the first thought that entered her mind. "You are aware that your sister is in love with him?"

His nostrils flared, then he sighed unhappily. "Aye, I am aware. However, I was unaware that others knew she possessed such feelings."

"I stumbled upon her in Viktor's quarters, smelling his clothing, many weeks hence," she admitted, realizing the topic was equally discomforting.

"I am ashamed to confess that I have exerted little effort in negotiating a match for her. She is miserable in her current state, but, selfishly, I would miss her more than I am able to comprehend if I arranged her marriage. She is my only remaining family, and I love her. I cannot consciously let her go," he remarked with overt honesty.

"The Colvilles are also your family," Reissa returned, her words heartfelt. "You will not find loneliness."

"Of course," Alden agreed.

Her gaze turned on him curiously. "Perhaps you seek a wife of your own?"

He chuckled heartily. "The Lord has not granted me the fortune of marriage," his brow rose optimistically, "as of yet."

"Do you favor one particular lady, Alden?"

"Nay, but I shall not wed for love. I shall wed to advance my dependent state to one of independence."

Reissa glanced at him from the corner of her eye, and her brow creased. "Is that not a paradox, sir?"

The man gave her a glib grin. "Aye, 'tis that, my lady."

"Do you care to elaborate?"

He brushed a golden curl from his vision and gazed at the distant horizon. "The Colvilles have been mine and my sister's sole support for many years. When I marry, it shall be to a woman who may advance my station into one of independence from this family."

"You are certain to sweep a woman off her feet with that sweet talk, sir knight." Reissa's laughter was melodic and contagious.

Alden's deep voice joined hers in a quiet roar of comedy. "I cannot afford the luxury of romance, my lady. I shall not take advantage of a friend's generosity forever."

"As a woman who possesses a background of poverty, I certainly understand your reasoning, Alden; however, I do not believe that Viktor defines you as charity," she explained her own logic.

"'Tis likely you speak true, Reissa, yet the matter stands. I must resign myself to the fact that Edith must wed, as must I." He groaned quietly with the prospect. "A rather unpleasant chore."

"I cannot imagine the will one must possess to choose a spouse for a loved one," she returned with a pensive stare.

"Aye, Edith's welfare resides in my hands, and I know not if I shall ever find a man worthy of her. The added bonus of her feelings for Viktor will only cloud my judgment. Inadvertently, I will measure every candidate against him, and as we are both aware, Viktor cannot be equaled."

"'Tis a certainty."

"'Tis also a certainty that I shall not stumble upon your fortune."

Her confusion was acute. "How so?"

"Viktor and you entered into an unwanted marriage, a marriage arranged for means, but you have grown to genuinely care for one another. I believe we have all witnessed the Lord's will."

The humor was absent in Reissa's laugh. "You have witnessed an enforced contract, Alden, 'tis all."

He smiled. "In time you shall surpass your denial, my lady." The village became visible over the rise. "Now, we must cater to others in need."

She returned the sentiment, "Aye, sir."

They descended the rise in silence.

Reissa felt it the moment they entered the village pass. Everything appeared to be in order, yet she could not explain it, something was amiss.

"Something is terribly wrong," she said below her breath, but Alden had heard her nonetheless.

"I feel it too." A gloved hand instantly moved to the hilt of his sword.

Without turning around, Reissa knew their entourage had executed the same gesture. All were alert with caution. Their pace slowed.

Suddenly the bell topping the structure of the schoolhouse chimed loudly. Initially, the lady jumped in her saddle, startled by the noise, but as her mind swiftly connected the meaning, she began to fill with dread.

The schoolhouse was also used as the village's church. It was too early in the day for lessons, and it was certainly not Sunday mass; therefore, a single explanation remained. A person had been laid to rest in the cemetery yard.

A collection of headstones was tucked away in a far corner of the lot behind the small building.

"Dear Lord, let my assumption be incorrect," Reissa prayed, then spurred Hornet into a breakneck gallop.

"Reissa, nay!" Alden shouted, but she disregarded his order.

Her heart pumped with denial, and her skirts lifted on the momentum of her reckless ride. The equestrian rounded the south corner of the building, and the sight that met her gray eyes caused her to tug on the reins. Instantly, her mount ground to a halt.

Her fears were confirmed. Edith held Maisie's hand, and they stood looking down upon a fresh grave.

Reissa jumped to the ground and rushed over to the solemn pair, burgundy skirts lifted, indigo cloak flying. Edith and Maisie lifted their heads and gazed at her profile in stark silence. The soldiers who had remained behind mutely watched from their position on the far side of the freshly upturned earth.

The moments stretched as Reissa readjusted her mindset to accept the tragedy, her head bowed respectfully.

Finally, "'Tis over," Edith whispered with tears in her eyes. "She was gone when we awoke this morn."

Alden approached quietly and draped a supportive arm around his sister's shoulders. "My condolences," he offered.

Edith turned, seeking an embrace to allow her to give full rein to her mourning. His arms muffled her weeping, hiding her crumpled face of sorrow from Maisie.

Observing Alden's enduring strength, Reissa was struck with an urgent need to feel her husband's arms around her, comforting her pain. But it was not to be. She must gather her own strength and offer it to the orphan standing quietly at her side.

Without pause, the lady knelt down to offer solace. When she saw the tears streaming down an ashen face, she folded the girl in a motherly hug. She murmured words of assurance, speaking of her mother's place with the Lord in heaven and that they would be reunited one day. Reissa had to bite her lip so she would not give in to the need to cry herself.

At last Maisie and Edith regained a semblance of composure. After a final farewell to Mrs. Michaels, they all set out for home. Unable to attend her commitment to the schoolhouse on that day, Reissa scribbled a message of excuse for Maisie and herself and left it on Mrs. Sandborne's desk.

Maisie doubled with Alden, and following an hour without speech, she fell into an emotionally exhausted sleep.

Reissa glanced at the child and sighed heavily. "I have not adequately prepared for this. I have yet to secure the nursemaid Viktor insisted upon."

"I would like to offer myself for that position."

"Edith, you would?"

"Aye, in our days together, we have grown close. Maisie and I get on rather well, and I care for her. 'Twould be a joy to continue looking after her, Reissa."

The lady raised her brow, pleasantly surprised by the convenience. She knew Edith was more than capable of filling the position. The Scottish lass was patient, knowledgeable, and compassionate. But more importantly, Reissa trusted her. She grinned, ever so grateful. "Very well, the position is yours."

Chapter 38

As they approached the castle, Reissa observed her husband and many of his men diligently working to rebuild the tower that had fallen as a result of the siege. In spite of the season, their labor had heated them to the point of perspiration. Three had actually discarded their tunics, leaving them naked from the waist up. However, Reissa's eyes sought only one. He was one of the three who sought to cool himself by partially disrobing.

Noticing his alluring state, her stomach tugged with attraction. But the lady knew such feelings at that time were inappropriate, so she shifted her gaze and gave herself a mental slap for the instant response of her body.

Reissa glanced at Maisie's sleeping figure, and pity quickly replaced desire. Her mind was filled with decisions and details pertaining to the girl as they crossed the distance to the manor. Her eyes were averted from Viktor, who paused in his work to watch them draw nearer.

Unable to distract herself any longer, Reissa looked up to find her husband casually wiping the sweat from his face and chest with his tunic. His gaze settled on Maisie. A dark brow creased, and his eyes jumped to Edith, then finally, his wife.

He tossed the garment aside and moved away from the pile of stones. Callused hands grabbed the reins to help pull Hornet to a halt. He peered up at her withdrawn expression, clutched her waist, and aided her dismount.

Reissa hastily removed her hands from his bare shoulders and stepped back from his lingering hold, her eyes steady on the ground at her feet.

"Mrs. Michaels has passed," he stated with an empathetic sigh.

"Aye," she confirmed. "This morn."

"Reissa." He gently gripped her chin in an effort to look into her eyes, but she successfully evaded his attempt by closing them. "Are you all right? Why do you refuse to see me?"

"Viktor, please be kind enough to cover yourself," she responded as two spots of red heated her cheeks.

Her husband's understanding immediately dawned, and he chuckled quietly, exuding that it pleased him to know that she was so affected by his state of undress.

As Viktor pulled on his damp tunic, Edith approached with Maisie at her side, holding her tiny hand. "I shall take the child in to oversee a bath and a meal."

"Of course," Reissa returned, giving her permission to do so. With that, the pair entered through the open portcullis, and Alden joined the men who continued to erect the tower.

A frown creased Viktor's smooth brow as he stared after them, and it did not lift when his attention returned to her. "Edith as nursemaid, 'tis an unexpected development."

"She offered, and I accepted," she said simply.

"Edith is a noble; 'tis below her station to play nursemaid, Reissa." There was disapproval in his tone as he stared down at her.

"And I am a commoner, yet I have been married to a noble," the lady was quick to defend, "a massive misconduct that has been accepted by the whole of your family and your men. I do not believe Edith's intent to care for that girl will create a scandal."

He nodded, knowing she spoke true, so without another word on the matter, he dismissed it entirely. His gaze abruptly narrowed on her. "You appear rather fatigued. I insist you rest yourself afore the evening meal." He dropped a kiss on her brow and urged her to go inside with a playful swat to her backside.

Aware that his men were covertly watching them, she threw him a suffering look, then dutifully obeyed his order.

***

March arrived without incident.

Maisie quickly adjusted to castle life. She accepted her mother's fate without question, and with the exception of quietly mourning the loss of Mrs. Michaels, she flourished under Edith's competent care. Because of the distance to the village, Edith provided the necessary lessons of learning. But that was also divided with periods of playtime, to indulge in a childhood that was quickly diminishing due to tragic events causing her to grow beyond her young years.

And Reissa found her days filled to the max with domestic chores, voluntary work, and surrogate parental duties. As promised, her nights were spent in her husband's arms. In fact, it seemed she had found permanent residence in her husband's chambers. Her own rooms simply provided home to her wardrobe and her toiletry items. However, several of her garments anonymously appeared in Viktor's bedchamber without her knowledge as to how. But she did not question it, merely accepted it without another thought.

One afternoon, after a particularly grueling morning spent taking inventory of the manor's kitchen supplies, Reissa snuck up to her own bedchamber to nap. She lay down on top of the coverlet because she did not have any intention of indulging in slumber for more than an hour. She closed her eyes, and sleep claimed her within minutes.

Creaking hinges waded through the haze of her slumber. Reality struck, and she came awake instantly. She bolted upright, and through the shadowed interior, she caught sight of her husband standing in the open doorway, his expression exasperated as he looked in on her.

Realizing darkness had fallen, she cursed under her breath.

"Have I done it again?" she demanded with self-directed irritation. Reissa had missed six days of dining since the battle had taken place over a month ago, and as the king was still their guest, it was not fitting for her to do so without excuse. And as the king had plans to depart in the morning, to do so on that night could be considered close to a criminal offense. The weight of guilt bore down upon her shoulders when Viktor verified her assumption with a curt nod.

"You will apologize for your disrespect posthaste," he ordered, his features hard with anger.

"He has not retired?" she questioned.

"He has not."

Reissa simply sat there, aware that her fatigue had not lifted.

"Make haste, woman!"

"Aye, of course." She jumped up from the bed and crossed to the wardrobe to collect a gown worthy of their king. The cherry wood doors were flung open, and she scanned through the extensive array of garments.

The colors swept over her vision, and the world tilted without warning. The dizziness was so sudden that she was unable to save herself from collapsing. She fell, crumpling to all fours and bruising her knees and palms on the cool stone at her feet.

"Reissa?" Viktor's footsteps pounded the floor, and he knelt at her side. A muscled arm circled her shoulders, and his free hand clutched her wrist, giving support.

She sat back on her haunches, closed her eyes, and pressed a palm to her spinning head. "'Tis inconsequential, Viktor. 'Twill pass in a moment."

His concern elevated along with his fury. "'Tis not the first occurrence?"

She hesitated, mutely allowing the lightheadedness to pass.

Viktor waited patiently, giving her time to heal, but as the moments stretched, panic pinched his features, frightened by the blemish in her health.

At last, when the color began to return to her ashen cheeks, he hissed, "Reissa? There have been others?"

Slowly her eyes opened, and her face was filled with the shame of omitting the truth. "Aye."

"Lord's teeth, lady, how long?!" he demanded as he easily helped her to stand.

Reissa wobbled a bit, and, seeing that, Viktor acted without thought. He lifted her into his arms and carried her to the bed.

"I am able to walk," she opposed, but did not attempt to struggle.

"How long?" he repeated through gritted teeth. Gently he placed her on the coverlet.

"I experienced the first while you sought Rynearson," she tentatively confessed. "And numerous since then."

A string of expletives steeped the room and burned her ears. "You should have sought Edith at once!"

"'Tis merely fatigue, Viktor." Her hand flicked, dismissing the spells. She began to rise, but an unrelenting palm pressed to her chest and forced her back onto the pillows.

His dark eyes bore into her with suppressed rage. "You are confined to that bed until Edith has seen to you."

"But the king—" She sat up.

"I have ordered you to stay in that bed, Reissa. Do not disobey me," he warned, his tone unyielding, his expression black. With that, he stormed from the room.

Chapter 39

Viktor paced in the antechamber. The through the open door he was able to glance in and see that Edith gave Reissa a thorough physical exam and drilled her with personal questions. A half hour passed, and he was finding it extremely difficult to remain calm. He had the urge to pull his hair out and bite at his blunt nails, but finally Edith approached and beckoned him into his wife's bed chamber.

He stalked into the room, and his gaze instantly landed on the figure in the bed. She wore a simple white cotte that was snug and rather fetching. Her strawberry locks were unbound, fanned about narrow shoulders. She sat upright and was completely alert. Noticing her color had returned to normal, Viktor felt only a modicum of relief.

He crossed to stand at her side and placed a supportive hand on her shoulder. Both looked to Edith, awaiting a report of her condition.

"Viktor, Reissa, you shall be parents in August," she announced with a smile that appeared forced.

Viktor turned to her and grunted in elation. Without pause, he sat on the edge of the mattress and pulled her into a firm embrace.

***

Reissa registered the news with mixed emotions as she rested her head on his shoulder. Great joy was her initial feeling. She was going to birth a child at last. She was going to be a mother.

But her happiness was fleeting because she realized that this information fulfilled the contract. It would not be necessary for Viktor to welcome her into his bed any longer. He would seek his pleasure elsewhere. She knew he had only gifted her with such lavish attention because of the contract.

Yes, she was aware that he had overcome his distaste for her appearance, but the necessary toleration was over. More than half the maids in the manor were prettier than herself. Certainly, he would choose more appealing liaisons now that she was with child. And the knowledge of it was so heart-wrenching that she directed herself to focus solely on the positive, on the child growing inside her.

She lifted her head with the intention to thank Edith for the wonderful declaration, but the lady had wordlessly slipped away. Only Viktor and herself remained in her bedchamber.

"You have made me a father, Reissa, thank you." He grinned, and the tenderness in his eyes only magnified the pain she had not successfully banished.

She attempted to reciprocate his satisfaction with a grin of her own, but she failed miserably.

His face fell, and his dark gaze narrowed perceptively. "Your sorrow is most disconcerting, Reissa. You are carrying our first child. I am overjoyed; why are you not?"

"I am delighted," she assured while brushing her hair onto her back.

"Extremely unconvincing, lady," he grated, his temper rising.

"What do you require of me, Viktor?" Reissa demanded brusquely as she crawled to the opposite side of the bed and stood. She crossed to the wardrobe and once again began searching for a gown to don.

"I require an honest response, Reissa." He rose and folded his arms over his chest as he stared at her back. "I will not tolerate lies."

His comment recalled another statement he had issued immediately following their wedding: "I will not tolerate disobedience, disrespect, possessiveness, or jealousy. I expect promptness in my requests and a tight lip to my faithlessness."

Hurt inspired an abrupt outburst. "And I am to tolerate your extramarital affairs with a closed mouth?" the question erupted without thought.

"I beg your pardon?" his voice sounded at her back.

She whirled around, more afraid than startled. But she fed off her pain and recklessly forged on. "I have been ordered to tolerate your faithlessness, but I will not!"

Reissa was surprised when his brows creased in confusion rather than fury. "I have not followed the transition, lady. How is this related to the previous matter?"

"You questioned my lack of joy." She told herself not to, yet her mouth did not obey her brain. "'Tis because you shall now turn me away, Viktor. I shall be forced to turn my head while you actively practice faithlessness." When she felt tears forming in her eyes, she turned back to the open wardrobe.

He circled her dejected figure and lifted her chin with his thumb and forefinger. Reissa's confusion continued to rise when she saw the radiant smile on his handsome face. "You are jealous, my lady?"

"I am not allowed to be jealous," she whispered.

Her comment did not register. He was too distracted by the unexpected display of feeling. "I have not sought another woman," he explained, his smile remaining.

"But you will." She swallowed over the lump in her throat.

"You condemn me for a crime I have yet to commit?" A single brow rose with open curiosity.

"The contract has been fulfilled; 'tis inevitable that you will stray," she voiced her fears aloud.

"I seem to recall issuing an order on the eve of our wedding, Reissa, of possessiveness and jealousy—" His thoughts clearly began to travel the path hers had.

"'Tis that precise comment which has assured me you will seek extramarital pleasures." She stared up at him, prepared for him to explode with rage because she continued to push the matter, but her jaw dropped when his grin expanded.

"Remove that comment from your mind, Reissa." His callused palms slid around to her nape, warming her scalp with the slight pressure he exerted.

She closed her eyes for a moment, then opened them, disbelieving his words. "Viktor, are you unwell?" she wondered quite seriously.

Deep laughter filled the room.

"I fail to see the humor in this, you heartless man," she scolded and began to pull away, but he denied her action. In fact, he drew her closer, and a head of ebony locks dipped.

His mouth was mere inches from hers, and he gazed into her eyes. "Calm yourself, woman." Then his mouth claimed hers in a kiss that instantly ignited her passions.

Bare arms circled his neck, and she pressed her body to him.

Finally, he tore his mouth from hers in order to catch his breath. Sleepy eyes pinned her with a possessive stare. "'Tis you I want, Reissa." His hands sought the laces of her cotte as his mouth returned to hers and he breathed against her lips. "*Only you.*"

After he removed their clothing, he effortlessly lifted her into his arms and started for the bed.

"But the king?" Reissa suddenly recalled with a gasp.

He placed her on the mattress and covered her body with his own. "He will simply have to wait."

Chapter 40

Reissa arched her back and extended slim arms and legs, stretching her tiny figure like a cat as she roused from a deep slumber. She sighed in contentment and turned over, expecting to find her husband in an unconscious state, but he lay there with his head braced on his palm, silently watching her actions. She startled, and he chuckled happily.

"We have slept the day away, my lady," he murmured, then reached out and drew her near for a sensual kiss.

Following an unparalleled union in her bed the previous evening, they had descended to the Meeting Hall and announced their wonderful news to all. The king was so delighted for them that he decided to extend his stay several days in order to share in the celebration.

The Colvilles, Kilgours, and the king socialized while relaxing by the massive fireplace in the Meeting Hall. And after a respectable amount of time had passed, Viktor sought his wife's hand and announced their retirement of the scene. He escorted her to his bedchamber, where once again he provided physical proof that he wanted her. Only her.

Now, as he accompanied their kiss with heated caresses, Reissa reveled in the knowledge that her plain form fired his passions. Never could she have imagined that a man of his stature and his unrivaled looks would ever feel anything for her but obligation.

However, as his lips tasted the skin in the valley between her breasts, and his hands worshipped her buttocks, she knew he had confessed the truth. Yes, she was well aware that attraction was not love, but as a woman who came from nothing, and possessed nothing, she was more than grateful for his declaration of desire. Their first child was growing in her belly, and Viktor craved her presence in his bed. How could she ask for more?

The lady's thoughts were distracted when his arms circled her back and he rolled over, carrying her with him. She looked down into his smiling face as her body rested atop his muscled frame, and strawberry blond locks fanned forward, tickling his bulky chest. Her legs parted, she straddled his hips, and her fingers curled into the thin mat of black hair blanketing his chest.

He shifted the curtain of shiny blond tresses to fall down her naked back, and his hands slid down her arms, brushed over her breasts and touched the line of ribs visible there.

"Your weight has fallen, Reissa," he mentioned as his eyes traveled over her figure.

She sat up straight and summoned a sleepy, licentious expression. As her palms traced over her slight curves with wantonness, she uttered, "Soon I shall grow thick with child, Viktor, so you must value the sight afore I grow monstrously large."

He shook his head. "'Tis an impossibility, Reissa," his voice became husky with feeling as strong hands firmly gripped her narrow hips and pressed her against his hard flesh. "You shall only grow more lovely as your belly swells with our babe."

Reissa groaned as he increased the contact, then cried out when he lifted her hips and impaled her, sheathing himself deep inside her with one smooth motion.

She instantly exploded with convulsions of pleasure. And as she rode the tumultuous crest, she braced her hands on his chest and threw her head back in wondrous ecstasy.

Mere moments later, Viktor joined in her climax as he experienced his own.

The couple shared in mutual pleasure as primal nature shook them to the core. They soared higher and higher, crested the greatest wave, and then drifted back to reality like a feather falling to the earth.

Reissa's bosom heaved, and her brow glowed with perspiration. She looked down on Viktor, and her grin was the picture of ultimate satisfaction.

The corners of his mouth lifted, his expression mirroring her own. As she still straddled his hips, he sat up, and an arm banded around her waist, pressing her chest to his. His kiss lingered, but at long last, he retreated several inches and gazed into her eyes with obvious regret.

"My men will be waiting," he said softly.

"Aye, and I would like a ride afore I check in on Maisie," Reissa mentioned as she shifted to the edge of the bed and immodestly rose in her disrobed state. As she stood in the open space, her eyes scanned the floor for the gown that had been hastily discarded the previous evening.

"Nay," Viktor returned.

She spotted the rust-colored underdress near the foot of the bed and picked it up. "Nay?" The lady did not understand his command. She pulled the gown over her head and smoothed the wrinkled garment over her curves.

Without warning, powerful arms swept her from her feet and deposited her on the bed.

Reissa looked up to find Viktor scowling down at her. "Do you never protect yourself from a chill?" he demanded, referring to her bare feet. But he did not allow her time to give a response because he continued on without pause. "And, nay, you will not ride, Reissa. I forbid it."

The lady was so shocked by his emphatic order that she simply sat there for several moments and watched as he knelt, uncaring about his nude state, and slid slippers onto her feet.

Finally, as he tied the laces around her ankles, she put a voice to her confusion. "Excuse me? Did I hear you correctly? I am not to ride?"

"Aye. 'Tis too dangerous. You could be thrown." He erected himself, plucked his braies from a nearby chair, and stepped into them. An attempt was not made to fasten the ties. He merely crossed his arms over his chest and studied her.

Her pretty face scrunched in irritation. "And I could stumble down the staircase, or trip over my skirts, yet you do not forbid me to walk." Suddenly struck by such a possibility, she stared up at him in question. "Would you?"

"'Tis a temptation, lady," he snapped, then collected the soiled tunic from the floor and tossed it on the chair.

"I am expecting, Viktor; I am not an invalid," she defended, offended by his tone.

"The matter is not open for discussion, Reissa. I will not yield," his voice rose equal to his temper.

"You have personally selected my mount, Viktor. I am not in danger of being thrown," she rationalized as she inched to the edge of the mattress and stood before him.

"Reissa," he warned and glared down at her, his eyes flashing, announcing that she had pushed him beyond his limits.

Yet somehow, the fear she should have known did not present itself. She gained courage, and with it, a voice. "'Tis an unfounded order, Viktor, and I will not obey it."

"You dare to defy me, lady?" he demanded with a frightening calm.

"I dare to stand up for my rights." Her chin lifted with a notch of pride.

"You are certain to recall a previous punishment for insubordinate behavior."

"Aye, I recall, and I shall endure," she took a deep breath, "if necessary. I am determined to gain a compromise."

"Compromise," he spat the word like an epithet. "I am your husband; I need not compromise. I speak, and you obey; 'tis simplicity."

"'Tis insult, Viktor. I manage your affairs, shelter the growth of your child, and share your bed, yet I am unable to choose the luxury of a leisurely ride." She scowled as her spirits rose with negative energy. She began to pace in the open space of his bedchamber.

"I shall be forced to act if you continue to pursue the issue, Reissa," he notified and took a warning step toward her.

Her eyes closed for a moment, summoning strength. When she opened them, she pinned her husband with an intrepid stare. "Do so if you must."

He grunted his rage and stalked directly up to her.

Reissa's limbs trembled, but she stood her ground, her fists clenched at her sides.

His masculine frame halted one foot from her, but he did not act. He merely stood there, glaring. The rage emanating from him was palpable, gripping her like a physical assault.

The moment she witnessed his hesitation, she knew she was not in danger of being struck. He had assured her he would not raise his hand to her, and, as of yet, he had not.

The realization of that took her to another place and time, emphasizing the itch of curiosity. And the anger burning within only spurred her into speaking of it. "Many a time I have wondered the words Golly spoke to cross you. She must have pushed and pushed, because I have borne witness to your temper on several occasions, yet I have failed to provoke you to murderous violence." She cringed inside with every utterance, but she could not stop herself. It was a subject too long endured without answers. It was a shadow constantly hanging over her head, and her heart.

His hand rose.

The threat was clear. Reissa squeezed her eyes shut in anticipation of the blow. Horror rippled through her body in the form of a shiver as she breathlessly waited for the pain that accompanies brute force. But when the slap did not materialize, her eyes tentatively opened. They flared with surprise when she saw his fingers were clutching his hair, palms pressed to his head, eyes closed with clear self-disgust.

Viktor threw his hands down and pinned her with an unforgiving glare. "Golly chose her vengeance well," he growled with open menace.

"I beg your pardon?" Another shiver shook her as she failed to understand.

"You are my punishment, Reissa. The plain, meek commoner. When I denied my stepmother's advances following my father's death, she chose a bride for my lifetime, a bride I was certain to dislike. She chose you," he gave in to his wrath, unleashing it to the fullest extent.

His declaration was devastating. But even as her heart was breaking, she sought to save face. "'Tis punishment for the monster you are. She must have foreseen her murder in your eyes," she seethed. "I am pleased I could aid in her vengeance. I am pleased my lowly person fleshed out her plan to perfection. But more so, I am pleased that the illusion has met its end."

"Aye, it certainly has. The contract has been fulfilled. Therefore, we need not continue on in pretense," Viktor gritted as his fists flexed with suppressed savagery. "You shall return to your chambers, and I will remain in mine. Our evenings together have concluded, lady." A sneer appeared. "I shall find my pleasure elsewhere."

Reissa snatched her sienna overdress from where it was slung over the foot of the bed and pierced him with her eyes. "Do as you please, my lord. I care not how you pass your evenings." She hurried over to his wardrobe, flung open the doors, and began to yank her garments from within.

"Perhaps you shall lie awake in the night and wonder if I intend to visit murder upon you." There was bitterness in his deep voice.

She spun around, her features alight with fright. "Do you issue a sincere threat?"

"Fear not, lady, my child grows in you," he shot over his shoulder as he trudged to the washstand in the corner.

"Oh," she gave a dramatically fake sigh, "'tis such a relief." With that, her tiny form crossed to the dressing table that had been brought in to accommodate her toiletry items. She puddled a gown in the crook of her arm, fashioning a dip with the material, and began to toss vanity objects into it.

"Make haste, lady," Viktor mumbled irritably.

Her movements quickened. Not only was she battling her husband, but she was also battling tears. Forcefully, she threw the last of the items into the makeshift satchel and hurried to the exit. Reissa longed for the courage to make a biting retort before her departure, but the tears were coming, and she was unable to deny their arrival.

The moment she entered the corridor, she broke into a run. Her legs carried her all the way to her rooms without breaking stride. She carelessly threw the gown aside, and the toiletry items scattered across her antechamber floor. But the lady did not give the mess a second thought. She continued on into her bedchamber and threw herself on the canopy, giving her sobs full release.

Chapter 41

Reissa waited until she was certain Viktor had vacated to the bailey for daily drills before she descended to the Meeting Hall. The lady had cried rivers as she mourned the truth behind her marriage.

Desolate, she had given in to self-pity, and every insecurity she had known in her short lifetime returned with extreme force. She blamed herself for her common station, for her weak resolve, and above all, her unextraordinary face. She was not born into privilege or wealth. And, sadly, it was evident that she possessed nothing and no one.

When she grew weary of condemning herself, she mourned the loss of her husband's superficial affections. Yes, it was reality that he had never truly desired her, but he had certainly played the part well. It was because of that that she longed for the return of such ignorance.

She longed for the return of his kindness, his protection, and his arms holding her all through the night. She longed for the precarious happiness that had caused her to shine. Now, it was gone. Viktor had scorned her with the truth, and she hated him for it. Reissa hated him for informing her of Golly's revenge. She hated him for committing murder, but more so, she hated him for caring nothing for her.

Presently, as she lifted her wool skirts to take herself down the staircase, her eyes were dry, but if one looked close enough, the jagged red lines and puffiness proved the truth that she had been weeping. Her head remained downcast, and she pasted a soft smile on her lips to distract people from taking stock of her false disposition.

As she took each step slowly, a familiar ache pulsed in her right leg, speaking of harsh weather on the horizon. Outside, the temperature hovered near freezing, yet the skies were blue, belying her body's intuition.

The Meeting Hall was virtually empty. Two maids occupied the kitchen, diligently cleaning dishes from the midday meal. Moira sat by the fireplace alone, needles in hand, creating a security blanket for her babe.

Following a request for a modest meal, Reissa seated herself by Moira and continued the pretense that nothing was amiss. It was extremely difficult, but she must have successfully accomplished the chore of actress, because Moira did not make mention of signs that she appeared troubled.

They chatted, and Reissa ate, needing the sustenance to maintain her strength. As she finished a bowl of creamy venison soup, she studied the empty container and could not help but be reminded of her husband's comment that she was growing too thin. So, she signaled to a servant, and the bowl was refilled.

The women continued their light banter for quite some time. As they talked, outside an overcast sky rolled in, creating a daunting ceiling of gray. The hour grew late, twilight was falling, and soon the men would seek the refuge of the evening meal.

In an effort to avoid her husband, Reissa excused herself with the intent of checking up on Maisie. As she climbed the staircase, she acknowledged the emotional fatigue gripping her and decided she could not uphold the pretense of happiness in the child's presence. So, rather than taking a right at the top of staircase, she turned left and sought the solitude of her bedchamber.

Reissa pushed the bed curtains aside and crawled onto the mattress. Unable to summon the motivation to carry on with the day, she lay there for hours, her mind in action, her body immobile. She revisited every thought that had plagued her before visiting the Meeting Hall, and then branched off into different territory.

She thought of the one and only person who had ever genuinely cared for her, her mother. She recalled her voice, her smile, her eyes. She recalled the animated stories Grace told her at bedtime, and her endearingly terrible singing voice as she worked in the kitchen, preparing meals for a man who never appreciated them.

As Reissa indulged in the temporary break from the present, an abrupt downpour sounded beyond the window embrasure. She was only distantly aware when the weather began. But she finally drifted off into a dreamless sleep when the rain transformed into an unforgiving sleet that pelted the manor's exterior with freezing drops all through the night.

Reissa awoke at dawn to find a world of ice. The land gleamed with a beautiful shine under the sun, but the temperature had dropped, leaving a frigid cold that could be felt from her place on top of the coverlet. She shivered, chilled to the bone without Viktor's body heat to warm her.

Recalling yesterday's turn of events, she was hit by a lightning bolt of sadness. She rolled over, giving her back to the shimmering scenery at the window, and hugged the unused pillow next to her. Her eyes closed, and, against her will, tears began to zigzag down pale cheeks.

She dreaded going below to break her fast. Viktor was certain to be present, yet she resigned herself to doing so. She could not avoid her husband forever. In spite of the events leading to their union, they were married, and they would remain married.

Divorce was simply not an option, and there was not a location to which Reissa could escape to find permanent separation from the manor and her husband. Of course, there was one exception, but suicide was not an option either. Death would certainly be a welcome release from her miserable life, but she would never consider it. It was a natural process to the grave, and she would not disrupt it.

With a groan of regret, she rose from the bed and summoned Gert to aid her toilet. The young girl helped her into a rich royal blue underdress of velvet, and a deep navy blue overdress of brocade. It was sleeveless, allowing the tippets of velvet to fall to the floor at her sides. Her shining strawberry locks were braided in a crown around her head, with tiny ringlets dusting her temples and nape. The finished product was a lovely vision, yet her expression was dour.

Reissa descended the staircase alone and entered into the bustling hall with her gaze averted. She stared at the stone flooring as she crossed to the dais and climbed the steps up to the platform. As she approached the head of the table where Viktor was seated, she was overcome with a flush of nerves.

She halted at her place, and her cheeks went up in flames as she waited to see if Viktor was going to pull her chair, as was their routine. When he simply ignored her presence, her throat began to burn with unshed tears.

She was about to give in to the urge to flee when Collin, seeing her distress and his brother's rudeness, jumped up and rounded the table to pull her chair for her. She knew the grateful smile she bestowed upon him was pitiful, so she silently sat down and stared at the hands clasped in her lap.

A maid approached and deposited a trencher of bread and cheese on the table in front of her, along with a chalice of cider. She looked at the food, but out of the corner of her eye, she caught sight of a grin on her husband's face.

A bud of hope sprouted in her chest, and she looked up. But that hope was instantly dashed when she saw that the elated expression was being bestowed upon the pretty young servant on her left, rather than herself. Green blurred her vision, and she swallowed over the lump of emotion in her throat.

The girl continued refilling empty tankards even as her gaze returned to Viktor again and again. Reissa kept her eyes downcast, but she felt the shared looks between her husband and the help. Her skin itched with disgust, and her stomach twisted with nausea. One would have to be blind not to realize that her husband and the servant now shared an intimate rapport.

Desperate to remove herself from the agonizing scene, Reissa covertly began to shovel food into her mouth. As she attempted to be invisible, the occupants of the table spoke of Edward's late night of spirits with his knights, explaining why the king failed to appear for the meal. Edith and Moira were also absent. Edith was tending to Maisie, and, unbeknownst to Reissa, the babe in her belly had kept Moira awake for the whole of the night, and now she slumbered on.

Viktor was involved in talk with Alden and Collin, so Reissa remained unnoticed and uninvolved in the discussion of world events. Because of that, she was able to glance in her husband's direction and take stock of his sober condition.

He appeared rather weary. There were smudges under his eyes, and his tanned skin possessed an ashen tint. Clearly, it had been a late night, but as his eyes strayed to the servant girl on the far side of the table, she was made to wonder if the tale of indulging in spirits with the king was an outright fabrication. Had he passed the evening holding another woman in his arms?

The nausea in her stomach sharpened, causing her to stand without a thought. "Please excuse me," she said to no one in particular, and then hurried from the Meeting Hall without another word. She raised her skirts and bolted up the staircase as fast as her petite legs would carry her. She reached the chamber pot in her suite without a moment to spare. The lady collapsed to her knees and suffered the misery of uncontrollable retching.

The food she had forced down mere minutes prior resurfaced. Her brow grew damp from the convulsive strain to her body. She was grateful for the fashion of her hair, which allowed her to relieve the condition without having to hold it aside.

When the nausea finally subsided, she sat back on her haunches and wiped the sweat from her brow with the back of her hand. She sighed heavily in effort to calm her taxed breathing. She felt positively wretched.

Once her breathing returned to normal, she gingerly rose to her bed and crawled beneath the coverlet. A dreamless sleep claimed her almost instantly.

There was not a hint of illness when the lady awoke two hours later. And rather than going below to tend to the task of pantry inventory, which needed to be done, she chose to spend the evening with Maisie.

Edith was allowed a hiatus as Reissa indulged in playtime with her surrogate child. She even took her supper in Maisie's chamber and tucked her into bed following the sunset. The mother in her waited until the girl had fallen asleep before she slipped from the room.

As she quietly closed the door, she acknowledged the fatigue that engulfed her mind and body. She knew she should put in an appearance while the king remained their guest, but as she recalled

Viktor staring after one of the maids, she decided she couldn't confront another such scene that day.

With that decision made, she retired to her bedchamber and sought the ignorant bliss of slumber.

Chapter 42

Reissa was rather refreshed as she stood before the window embrasure in her bedchamber the following morning. The sun had barely risen, and once again the air was unseasonably warm, so warm, in fact, that a fog was forming as the previous day's ice melted. Because of the temperature change, a slight breeze disturbed the trees beyond the outlook of the window. The sky was streaked with burgeoning blue, clouds entirely absent.

In terms of weather, it was going to be a beautiful day.

She breathed in the fresh air and felt her spirits stir with good will. In her optimistic state, she was struck with the impulse to build a bridge over the rift Viktor and she had opened in their marriage. Yes, she was still extremely hurt as a result of their quarrel, but they were husband and wife, and she could not continue on in that fashion.

They could not ignore one another forever. Certainly, she did not expect a return of their affections, but she could hope for a civil exchange. Because he cared nothing for her, and because they were both well aware of it, the rift was sure to remain. But if they built a bridge, it would ease the path across the vast emptiness in their relationship.

And, in addition, if they mended their animosity, Viktor may take her feelings into consideration in relation to his adultery. He would not wound her with open displays of dissoluteness, as he had the previous morning. She believed he would conceal his lecherous ways so she may maintain a thread of dignity. Yes, he would. Would he not?

The decision was made. Reissa would go apologize.

Following a leisurely bath, Gert arrived to help her don a snug emerald underdress of silk with floor-length tippets at the elbows, and an equally snug overdress of navy velvet, minus the sleeves. Her damp locks were brushed dry. Shimmering strawberry blond tresses were left unbound, allowing them to swish around her waist. However, there was an exception of two strands around her temples that were pulled back into a single braid, effectively framing her oval face.

Reissa tucked several errant strands behind her ear and rose from the vanity bench. She dismissed her lady's maid and simply stood at the center of the room, breathing deeply in order to gather her courage.

Her hands were trembling with nerves, and her legs felt like lead weights. She forced herself to exit her suite of rooms and entered into the extensive corridor that also contained the doors to her husband's rooms. It was a straight shot to Viktor's chambers. The hall ran the length of the castle, which was two hundred yards, but it was only fifty yards that separated the locations of their individual chambers.

Her gaze peered down the dim corridor as she slowly walked toward her goal. The space was drafty and cool. A violent shiver tore through her body, causing the lady to vigorously rub her arms to ward off the chill.

But the cold was instantly forgotten when a familiar feminine figure caught her eye and froze her gait. The maid Viktor had been ogling the previous morning appeared in the hall outside of his chamber. Her head was downcast as she shut the door in her wake, but Reissa had seen enough to be certain it was the same girl.

The pretty head began to lift, and, out of desperation and misery, Reissa sprang into action. She spotted the nearest door and bolted for it. The handle turned easily. She rushed inside without taking stock of the quarters and softly closed the wooden structure, shutting out the ugly truth of Viktor's infidelity.

"My lady?" a male voice questioned at her back.

Reissa spun around to find Alden standing directly in front of her, fully clothed, an expression of surprise lighting his modestly attractive face.

"Oh my," she uttered, and her cheeks burst into flames of mortification.

"If this was a show of affection, Reissa, I would be more than flattered by the offer; however, I know 'tis not." He gave a grin to ease her embarrassment. "Clearly, you sought immediate shelter. You are hiding. From whom?"

She spoke the first lie and excuse that entered into her mind. She knew her actions had been childish, and she knew Alden would not take her to task for them; nevertheless, she felt the fool. "I do not hide; I merely sought to request your company for a morning ride,

Alden." In knowing her husband had shared his bed with that wench, she felt a surge of rebellion through her pain, which was why the urge to ride was so great.

Viktor had ordered her not to do so, but her husband be damned, she would not obey that letch, not a moment longer. "If you care to join me, meet me in the stables in one quarter of an hour." She flashed him a forced smile, then turned and cautiously stepped into the corridor. Seeing that it was empty, she returned to her antechamber to collect gloves and a white ermine cloak for the impromptu ride.

As she descended the narrow servants' staircase, the one in which Viktor and she had made love mere weeks ago, she found herself fighting tears. The consideration of apologizing to that monster had been incredibly stupid. And now she was mutely scolding herself for thinking of it.

"Damn you, Viktor," she mumbled and wiped a solitary tear from her cheek. For several moments, she stood at the door in the basement, collecting herself and her raging emotions. She had been introduced to the presence of his extramarital affairs yesterday, but her previous knowledge did nothing to ease the disturbing image of a woman slinking from his bedchamber.

Her head fell into her hands, and a depressing shudder shook her shoulders, but she refused to give full rein to the sorrow that threatened. The minutes stretched as she cleared her mind of all thoughts pertaining to her husband.

Finally, she took a deep breath, pulled the hood of her cloak over her head, and stepped out into the light of day.

***

"Do you care to discuss the real cause for bursting into my bedchamber this morn, Reissa?" Alden prodded as their mounts set a slow pace.

Her gaze settled on the distant horizon. The dawn fog had dissipated, allowing her to scan across acres of earth. The world of ice that had existed the previous day was now nothing but condensation on brown, dormant grass. Bark on nearby trees possessed dark patches where water dried, and the air was humid, yet it held a chill that worked its way into one's bones. Reissa pulled her cloak closer around her tiny figure as a bitter smile lifted the corners of her mouth.

"Nay, I do not."

They continued on in contented silence for quite a while before curiosity prompted Reissa to put forth a question. "My husband will certainly anticipate my absence from the morning meal, as at present we are not on speaking terms, but will you not be missed?"

"Viktor allows my every freedom, Reissa," he returned monotonously. "Nay, I shall not be missed." Then his gaze shifted to her, and an inquisitive expression lit up his face. "And am I to understand that you and Viktor have shared a difference of opinion?"

"A difference of opinion, Alden, 'tis an understatement. We have shared the ultimate quarrel. I have learned—" the words abruptly cut off as she decided it was not wise to discuss the relationship between Viktor and herself with her husband's closest friend.

"You have learned?" he prodded with an accompanied wave of his hand and a raise of his brow.

"I believe 'tis a matter best left between Viktor and myself," she said gently.

"May I venture a guess, Reissa?" he wondered in a childlike manner.

She glanced at him, dreading his venture, yet equally driven by curiosity. Tentatively, she nodded.

"You have learned," he repeated, "of Golly's manipulation of your marriage."

The lady sucked in her breath, startled by his perception. "A direct hit, Alden." Her brow furrowed. "Are the servants gossiping," then she was struck with the thought of Viktor's intimate relationship with the maid, "perhaps one woman in particular?"

"Pashaw!" he dismissed her suspicions with a flick of his wrist, "'tis a simple matter to determine, Reissa. You knew all but for Golly's vengeance; therefore, 'twas nothing else to learn."

"Incorrect, sir knight. I know not the lady's motive for such vengeance."

"Viktor failed to elaborate?"

"Aye. The confession was thrown at me in the midst of rage; therefore, I was not inclined to request an explanation. He made mention of rejecting her advances," Reissa spoke as she lifted her face to the sun's warmth.

"Do you desire an explanation?"

Reluctantly, she said, "I admit to curiosity."

"Golly concealed her attraction for Viktor during all her years of marriage to his father. Then, mere days following Collin's death, the lady boldly made advances toward her stepson," he paused, allowing the information to register in Reissa's mind.

"Oh my," she sighed, assuming the worst, "he gave his stepmother a tumble, then rejected further interludes."

"Nay, my lady, rather the opposite," his disbelief sounded in every word.

"He denied her initially?"

"Aye."

Utterly stunned, Reissa tugged on the reins, and Hornet drew to a halt. She simply sat there, incredulous.

"Scorned by his rejection, she sought to marry him off—"

"I am well aware of the tale's conclusion," the lady interjected, still stung by such knowledge.

Alden's mount restlessly pawed the earth as they sat in silence. Sensitive to her pain, he did not attempt to continue the conversation.

At last, Reissa spoke up. "Despite the insult I give to myself with this statement, I must declare that Golly was a horrid woman." She turned her eyes to the sky. "Lord, forgive me for speaking ill of the dead. She chose a wife Viktor would detest simply to slake her revenge. Her miserable pride upset far too many lives. Viktor and I are forever joined, two people who do not belong together, because she could not suffer the humiliation of rejection."

"Aye, she was certainly an original," he mentioned as he looked to the horizon.

"She was extraordinarily beautiful," Reissa complimented despite her aversion to the lady.

Alden waved off her comment and made an odd disclosure, "But ultimately flawed—she snored."

Reissa sent him a dumbfounded frown. "I beg your pardon?"

He was quiet for a moment, then, realizing his statement, he chuckled. He pinned her with an informative stare. "The whole of our entourage knew precisely when that woman slept because she could be heard from the carriage during travel."

His explanation drew her understanding, and she sent him a smile. "I shall forever be afeard of slumber in a carriage now, Alden, thank you."

He roared with laughter and then grew rather sober. "You may be compared to her, you know."

Reissa spurred her mount into a trot, and another frown turned down the corners of her mouth. "'Tis your intention to offend me, sir?"

"Nay, never. I merely meant that, comparatively, you and Golly are rather unlike one's first impression. She was beautiful and kind, yet the woman we grew to know was ugly and cruel. You were plain and meek, but 'tis not you a'tall. You are truly lovely and caring." His words were sincere.

As always, the compliment made her feel uncomfortable, so she abruptly changed the subject.

Chapter 43

The pair parted in the Meeting Hall. Alden announced his intent to join the men in the bailey for drills, and Reissa ascended the staircase to check after Maisie's welfare.

She found them in the instruction room. Edith stood before the blackboard filled with chalky numbers, and Maisie sat at a tiny wooden desk in the front row of thirty. She was the only child in the room, with the exception of the babe growing in Reissa's belly.

Unwilling to disturb their lesson of addition, she folded her petite body into one of the desks at the back of the room. Edith glanced up from the chalkboard and noticed their visitor. She smiled but did not make mention of her presence.

Lady Kilgour continued quizzing her charge for many minutes, and then finally directed a question to Reissa. "Lady Colville, would you care to join us?"

Her mouth turned up. "I would be delighted." She shifted to the desk next to Maisie's, and after Edith had pulled up a chair, the trio indulged in a recreational game of jacks.

As the morning wore on, Reissa's stomach began to rumble loudly, reminding her she chose to ride rather than break her fast. Well aware she was not only responsible for herself but also for the life growing inside, the mother-to-be excused herself and sought the kitchen. She collected a glass of chilled milk and two slices of buttered bread and turned to scan an empty Meeting Hall.

Rather than dine alone in the vast space, she took to the staircase, deciding to seek the solitude of her antechamber. The silence was deafening as she entered, but somehow the quiet was calming. She welcomed it as she placed the tray on a side table and crossed to the fireplace. Coals still smoldered there, so it was an easy task to throw a couple of logs on the orange embers and ignite flames.

As the wood crackled and emitted a soothing heat, she seated herself on a bench before the fire and diligently ingested the meager meal. As she chewed, she stared into the jumping flames, and her thoughts wandered.

Her thoughts could not help but touch on her father. Following the eve when Viktor banished him from the estate, Bernard seemed to vanish into the wind. When Reissa learned of his forced exit, she had consoled herself with the confidence that she would learn of his travels, whether through rumor or conjecture, she cared not, but not a single word had been spoken of him.

His fate was unknown. Did he remain in the village, or had he sought refuge in distant lands? She did not have any doubt that he would survive wherever he had gone, because monsters always survived. He was in need, and she knew he had gained help through violence rather than kindness. Sadly, it was his way. She pitied those who had most certainly fallen into his path. Her mother and herself had known the brutality of his hand, but now others would share in the misfortune of knowing him.

Bernard was ruthless when striving to gain his desires, but when she thought of him in desperation, she feared the worst. She may have never been witness to it, but she knew he was capable of murder.

Bernard a murderer?

Her hand slackened with shock, and the tankard of milk fell to the floor. It crashed loudly, and the white liquid sloshed across the stones. But it went unnoticed as it puddled and seeped into the cracks.

Had she assumed the worst of her husband when he remained innocent of the crime? Bernard was a beast of the worst sort, unfeeling and unconscionable. Could he have found reason to cause Golly's death? Could he have found reason to frame Viktor for the murder he himself had committed?

She recalled Bernard callously taking over Golly's seat at the table, days after her body had been found. His actions spoke of conceit. Had she overlooked guilt as well?

Suspicion had been born, and questions grew. Reissa needed to find her father and demand his knowledge of the woman and the events leading to her death. She needed answers. She needed the truth.

It would not wait. Slender hands lifted her velvet skirts, and she stepped over the spilled milk. She hurried into her bedchamber and pulled on the cloak she had tossed on the bed before going to the instruction room.

As she slid her hands into the white silken gloves, her eyes caught sight of a tankard on the bedside table. She frowned. It was not hers. Who had placed it there?

Reissa crossed to the table and looked down upon the heavy mug. It was filled with a brown, murky liquid. The frown deepened.

Suddenly a glint of metal flashed before her eyes. Two crushing arms snaked about her shoulders and waist from behind. A horrified gasp escaped her mouth as she was pulled against an unyielding chest. The bite of a blade touched the sensitive skin of her throat.

Her limbs began to tremble with terror when a smooth cheek pressed to her temple, and she heard a familiar voice. "Drink it, Reissa."

The initial shock of her attacker's identity slowly faded, and her eyes settled on the tankard with calm fear. "Do you intend to kill me?"

"We have not the time for an explanation. Drink it posthaste!" was growled into her ear.

Anticipating death, she stared at the tankard as if it were a snake, coiling and ready to strike. It was not only her life at stake, but the babe in her womb was also foremost in her thoughts. Protecting her child was her first and only priority.

An impatient sigh filled the room. "I assure you, 'tis not poison, Reissa. 'Twill not kill you. Drink it." The blade at her throat increased pressure, painful, threatening.

"My child," she uttered, despair in her voice.

"Drink it."

"Nay. Please reconsider whatever intentions you have. I beg of you."

A heavy, frustrated sigh met her rebellion. "I supplied Viktor with the same herb on the eve of your wedding. It will not harm the babe. You have my word."

Utterly helpless, Reissa could do nothing but comply. Her hand reached out and reluctantly lifted the tankard to her lips. She squeezed her eyes shut and tipped back, swallowing the bitter liquid against her will. The mug was only half full.

She only dared to take a few sips of the bitter liquid.

As she returned the tankard to the table, she noticed a growing sluggishness in her limbs. A daunting haze began to muddle her mind.

"We will go for a ride," he ordered as the arms around her figure fell away.

Irrationality tugged at her thoughts, preventing her from putting up a fight as she was led from the bedchamber. She was only distantly aware as they took to the servants' staircase and exited through the basement, the precise route she had followed that same morning.

Hoyt and Dax were deep in discussion when they entered into the stables and collected their mounts, which had already been saddled for them. Reissa waved at the men to gain much-needed attention in her perilous state, but neither noticed their entrance. They continued with their talk. It was only after Reissa began to turn when Hoyt glanced up and saw the pair exiting the stables with the horses.

Confusion swirled in her mind as she clumsily guided her mount away from the manor. Her vision began to blur, and she found herself overcompensating for every minor movement.

She was on her own mount. Would it be possible to attempt an escape? Immediately the idea was dismissed. Negotiating the horse while she was in such a perilous physical state was not possible. A breakneck ride would be dangerous for the tiny life inside of her, and she certainly didn't trust her own abilities while under the influence.

They rode for several minutes, side by side, but the moment they lost sight of the manor, the reins were tugged from her hands, and Hornet was pulled to a halt.

When Reissa felt the arms close around her waist, the abrupt violence brought her to life. She struggled and kicked and clawed, but her efforts were useless. Her petite figure was roughly yanked onto her unwanted companion's mount, and her combat was easily subdued in a merciless embrace.

Helpless once again, Reissa stalled her battle. The sun shone down on them, and the bright light burned her eyes, allowing a hint of reality through her drugged state. She searched her mind, but she simply could not fathom an explanation for this unexpected turn of events.

"Why are you doing this, Alden, why? I need to know why," she pleaded in a whisper.

He sighed regretfully and spurred his horse into a swift trot. "I do not hold you accountable, lass, but because of my fool mouth, you have learned too much."

"I know nothing!" she shouted in defense.

"Currently you are unaware, but you are an intelligent woman, and 'tis a certainty you would eventually question my slip. Eventually you would realize that Golly and I shared a relationship beyond acquaintance." His tone grew lifeless and unfeeling.

The comment about Golly's snoring entered her thoughts. She had not known it then, but it *had* aroused an unconscious suspicion. He was correct. In time, she would have questioned it. Yet the knowledge did not provide an explanation. She still didn't know why—

His words cut into her disjointed reverie. "Viktor has known dozens of women intimately. I have watched him turn them away, discarding them after taking his fill, while I am passed over again and again. My own sister has fallen prey to his charms. Never has he taken advantage of her feelings, yet 'tis equally insulting." The inflection in his tone had grown venomous.

"Then Golly entered into our lives—a beautiful, vibrant woman—and she did not seek Viktor's bed. She sought mine. I believed it to be a miracle. Our midnight liaisons were magic. I had never known a woman with such passion, such spirit. We met in secret for months, and not a soul suspected, not even her husband."

Reissa she could hear the twisted affect in his smile.

"But alas, my happiness was not to last. I learned of her obsession with your husband only after he had rejected her advances. I knew not that she came to me from his quarters." His arms tightened painfully about her shoulders, nearly crushing her.

"I knew not that that eve was to be our final liaison. Viktor revealed her secret obsession the following day, leaving me with nothing. I was infinitely pleased when he was forced into marriage. I thrived on his unhappiness, but 'twas not enough. Golly needed to be punished for her betrayal, and Viktor appeared as the perfect patsy.

"'Twas almost effortless. I drugged him, then visited Golly's chamber. For a lass of such passion, she gave in to death with little fight. After I had successfully throttled the life from her, I simply waited. When I was certain the herb had taken its full effect, I carried the body to Viktor's chamber and placed her beside him. The illusion was complete. And I believe you are aware of the result," he concluded, his tone hollow.

"Aye, Golly has been punished, but Viktor remains free." Reissa took a deep breath. "You have failed, Alden," she said with a degree of pleasure.

"Incorrect, my lady. In time, Viktor shall meet an unfortunate fate; you may depend upon it."

Reissa snapped. She renewed her struggle with more will than strength. Her slender figure bucked and kicked against the arms holding her still, but the drugged haze was all-encompassing, suffocating. Her effort was ineffectual, like an ant battling an elephant. Slender arms and legs grew lax, and, finally, immobile.

"May I also depend upon an unfortunate fate for myself and my babe?" she demanded as her eyelids drooped, dizzy.

"Regretfully, aye. Reissa, I adore you, truly I do. There is nothing but goodness within your heart. And your babe is pure innocence. However, 'tis that precise reason why you cannot be trusted to keep my secrets. You must be permanently silenced," he declared quietly, his breath fanning her ear. "'Twill be painless, Reissa. I give you my word."

"Your word is meaningless, Alden," she mumbled.

His cold laugh shook her.

"Consider the child in my belly," she pleaded as her eyes closed.

"Viktor's child," he spat.

At long last, she was unable to fight the fog any longer. Her head bowed, and she slept.

Chapter 44

Viktor wiped the perspiration from his brow with the back of his hand as Collin and himself pushed through the doors into the Meeting Hall. He had dismissed his men one quarter of an hour ago to dine for the midday meal; therefore, all were seated and in the midst of eating when the brothers entered.

Generally, they discarded their armor in the privacy of their chambers, but on that day, due to the heat of the sun, they had left their armor in the bailey, under the protection of their heralds. Of course, their swords were ever present, belted at their waists. A true warrior wore his side arm at all times. The only exception was the confines of one's bedchamber.

It had become habit for Viktor's eyes to settle on Reissa's place at the table, hungry for the sight her. But when they found her chair empty once again, he made no attempt to hide his black scowl. She had dined with the whole of the castle's occupants only once since their quarrel of two days hence, and even then, she had rushed away from the table the moment she had finished her food.

Well, he would not stand for her hiding, not for another day. She would join them in spite of the ongoing battle between them.

He knew the pantry's inventory was to be done; therefore, Hoyt would be privy to her current whereabouts. Angry eyes scanned the room, and when they found his steward in the kitchen supervising the servants, he waved him over.

"The most courageous of men would flee from that dark expression, little brother. Is anything amiss?" Collin wondered as he continued to stand at his side.

"My wayward wife has chosen not to attend another meal," he said with quiet menace.

"Perhaps she is unwell. Moira still suffers spells of illness, and she has surpassed months of conception," the elder sibling offered an excuse for the lady.

"Perhaps." But in his anger, he clearly disbelieved that possibility.

"You have been a bear for two days. What has passed?"

Viktor's eyes filled with bitterness. "Reissa believes I am guilty of Golly's murder."

Collin scratched his beard and shook his head in disappointment. "She does not yet know you as we do, little brother; she does not know you are incapable of such stark immorality. You must grant her latitude."

"'Tis the greatest of insults," he growled under his breath as Hoyt closed the distance. "I will not. I cannot."

"And the maid? Have you truly bedded her, or 'tis merely a ruse to punish your wayward wife?"

Viktor shook his head, feeling his own self-disgust. He was loath to admit his actions. "Simply a petty ruse on my part. However, the maid thought it to be truth. She entered my bedchamber this morn, seeking a tumble."

"Did you comply?" Collin tested.

Viktor could hear the apprehension in his brother's words. Their father may have strayed from the marriage bed, but Collin remained faithful to his wife, and he knew he expected the same of his little brother.

"Nay. My interest in others has waned. Reissa provides my only pleasure." He turned eyes to the steward, who crossed the remaining yards to stand before them.

"My lord?"

"Hoyt, where has my wife taken herself off to?"

"My lady and Sir Alden have gone out for a second ride this day, my lord," he provided.

Viktor's fists clenched so hard, his knuckles whitened. "A recent departure?" he demanded through gritted teeth. Reissa had intentionally disobeyed a direct order. He was absolutely irate.

The small man nodded while mutely observing the flash of anger in his lord's eyes. Instinctually, he stepped back. Finally, he spoke, "Aye, my lord."

"Thank you, Hoyt, you may go," Collin dismissed the servant when he saw that Viktor was so enraged, he was unable to speak.

Hoyt scurried off.

"Why would they venture on a second ride?" the elder brother wondered, his brow creased in confusion.

Viktor crossed his arms over his chest, pensive. "That is certainly a valid question. Their actions are unusual, to be sure."

The brothers stood there for many moments, lost in their own thoughts on the matter.

"Another unusual act by our friend," Collin mentioned as he searched his memory.

Intense eyes settled on his sibling, suddenly overwrought with unease. "How so?"

"On the eve of your wedding, I noticed he poured your ale himself. I had dismissed it thoughtlessly and forgotten about it thereafter, but I'm suddenly beaten down with a disturbing thought." His gaze was intense as he asked his brother, "Why would he do that?"

"There would be no innocent cause. There could only be an ulterior motive—"

"'Twas the evening you were drugged, Viktor."

"You are certain?" he demanded desperately.

Collin nodded and scratched his dark beard.

Viktor clutched his brother's forearm as the pieces of the puzzle fell into place. And, as such, Alden's actions spoke of his probable guilt in choking Golly and placing her in Viktor's bed to displace the suspicion.

The men spoke in horrified unison. "He murdered Golly."

Collin shook his head in disbelief. "Why? Why would he commit such an act of betrayal?"

"I believe the better question would be, why did he take Reissa out on a second ride? 'Tis also an unlikely event. And now we are aware of his lethal capabilities." His breath was strained, his shoulders trembling.

It was likely Reissa had gone for the first ride as an act of insubordination and politely invited Kilgour along. But she must have surmised the truth or learned a token that cast her in a threatening light, necessitating Alden to act. It seemed the only likely possibility for an abrupt second ride.

Suddenly Collin jumped onto the same page, and his eyes widened in terror. "Good gracious, I am a blind fool!" And he hurried on, putting Viktor's thoughts into words. "Reissa may be in serious danger."

Without pause, both men broke into a frantic run.

Chapter 45

As their mounts raced from the stables, Viktor was gripped with unparalleled fear. His heart beat rapidly in his throat, and his fists clenched the reins with such ferocity that his knuckles were a ghastly white.

"Where would he have taken her, little brother?" Collin's voice was rigidly calm, his eyes searching the land in hopes of spotting two familiar figures.

"'Tis logical that he shall seek Willingham Castle. 'Tis the perfect location for a convenient accident." Vivid images of his wife bloodied and beaten floated across his vision, causing him to spur his warhorse into a reckless speed.

As the men crossed the sun-kissed earth, they noticed a horse on the distant horizon. The brothers exchanged concerned glances.

Rapidly, they drew nearer, and the horse came clearly into view.

"'Tis Reissa's mount, is it not?" Collin questioned breathlessly.

"Aye," his voice was curt and anguished.

The prospect of Reissa in danger was now a certainty. The lady would never abandon Hornet—never. The knowledge caused the men to redouble their efforts, and, because of that, they arrived at the suspected destination in record time.

Alden's horse grazed near the moss-covered castle walls. Viktor sent a silent prayer into the skies, asking for the Lord's mercy for his wife. She was so tiny, easily overcome by physical strength. It would take little effort for Alden to dispatch her with his bare hands.

The knights jumped to the ground and drew their swords as they carefully picked their course across the rocks surrounding the opening of the corner structure. The sight of Alden standing at the edge of the second level with Reissa's limp figure in his arms drew both men to an abrupt halt. Collin cursed, and Viktor felt his heart stop.

"I hope she has been drugged rather than rendered unconscious in some brutal fashion," Collin mentioned to his brother under his breath.

Viktor's lips thinned, considering the possibilities. Aware of Reissa's extreme fear of heights, he was moderately grateful that she was unconscious in her state of peril. Seeing the risk to her person was horrifying enough, but if he'd witnessed the terror that was certain to mark her face if she were awake, he feared that would have caused hysterics within himself. Yet the idea that Alden could have struck her unconscious caused an overwhelming urge to kill as a matter of retaliation.

"We know of your guilt, Alden. Murdering my wife and babe will not aid your secret campaign," Viktor said urgently, slowly moving forward.

There was a hint of madness in Kilgour's laugh. "I knew you would surmise my crime one day, but I had not expected such swift perception." The laughter transformed into an ugly threat. "Halt, Viktor! Or I shall be forced to drop this precious package."

Viktor froze.

"My crimes are revealed, but Reissa shall still provide an outlet for my hatred of you." He pinned Viktor with a detesting glare. "You care for the lass more than you are aware. The apology for your actions in the basement stairwell gave testament to that, my friend, and her death will bring about a grief equal to the loss of your mother." A single brow crooked as he looked to Reissa's unconscious face. "Perhaps more so." He grinned. "The knowledge of that is infinitely pleasurable."

"You harbor resentment for me, Alden, so take your vengeance upon me. Reissa need not take any part in this." He gazed up at a man he would have entrusted his life to before that day. The fresh knowledge that the bastard had shadowed an intimate moment shared between Reissa and himself, and perhaps other moments, caused his hands to curl into enraged fists. Nevertheless, he maintained the appearance of calm.

Kilgour seemed to ponder the matter of redirecting his murderous intent for several agonizing moments, and Viktor began to hope. But then a sinister smile raised the corner of Alden's lips, and he declared, "Farewell, my lady." With that, he heaved her tiny figure into the vast space, sending her into a freefall toward the solid flooring below. Without waiting to witness the results of his actions, he turned tail and fled.

"Christ!" Collin cried while Viktor dropped his sword and sprang into immediate action. As the heavy metal clanged against stone, he rushed forward, dove to his knees, and his hands lifted to catch his wife, one foot from certain death.

He stared into her lovely face, feeling her figure safe within his arms. Then, abruptly, his head bowed against her chest, and to his everlasting amazement, warm tears of relief seeped from his closed eyes.

Assured of Reissa's safety, Collin ascended the open staircase, taking two steps at a time in his haste to catch the assailant. Viktor remained kneeling, clutching her limp body against his own. His masculine frame trembled from the shock of nearly losing her.

Above, pounding footsteps echoed throughout the deteriorating structure as Collin gave chase. The noise of their movement faded, but suddenly the distinct sound of a primal scream ripped through the vast space. It was followed by an eerie silence, announcing an end to the pursuit.

Uncertain of the screamer's identity, Viktor raised his eyes in search of answers. Footsteps echoed. The footsteps slowly grew louder, but it was a single set. His breath stalled, anticipating the worst.

Collin rounded a freestanding wall, and Viktor's mouth turned up with a grateful smile.

"I am afraid Kilgour has taken an unforgiving fall. He tripped over rubble on the back staircase and cracked his skull on a window embrasure."

"Dead?" Viktor asked and easily stood with Reissa in his arms.

"Aye."

"Justice has prevailed," Viktor announced without regret as he looked at his wife's slumberous face.

The brothers returned to their horses. Viktor temporarily handed Reissa into Collin's care, but, following a graceful mount, he reached down to retrieve her. It was a simple matter for him to position her comfortably. He straddled her petite figure across his lap and guided her head to rest upon his shoulder. An arm circled her waist, holding her close, then he set a slow pace for their travel back to the manor.

Chapter 46

The weight of an arm resting on her waist caused Reissa to come awake in a combative panic. She was surrounded by the darkness of night, forcing her to blindly strike out at the hard figure tracing her back. But once again the effort was ineffectual because mere moments after she began to fight, the arm tightened about her waist, and a leg was thrown over her skirts, caging her in human bonds.

"Shh, Reissa."

The familiar voice broke through her disoriented state, immediately calming her opposition.

"You are safe," Viktor said quietly, giving her a reassuring squeeze.

Relief flooded her being, and her eyes slowly adjusted to the lack of light. As the shadow of objects became visible, she determined that they lay in his bed in Colville Manor.

"Oh, dear Lord," she breathed with an appreciative sigh. "Thank you." She twisted about, turning to face her husband, then threw her arms around his neck and held on with all of her might. "I never expected to wake again," she sobbed, "I never expected our babe to enter into this world."

"Do not fret, Wife, I would never allow that." His lips pressed to her hair. His expression was pained with feeling as his arms pulled her close.

"How did you learn of Alden's intention?" She swiped at the moisture wetting her cheeks but did not relinquish her hold. As far as she was concerned, her arms would remain around his neck forever.

"Hoyt informed me."

"Lord grant that man great fortune." She smiled.

Viktor chuckled. The sound of his rich voice soothed the tremors in her body. "I shall be certain to commend the man for his unwitting aid. However, that reminds me of an order that you failed to obey, Reissa."

The lady's tears of relief transformed into tears of frustration.

The callused hand stroking her hair contradicted his latter statement of anger. "But I am in a forgiving mood, and I believe the trauma you have suffered this day will suffice as punishment for another act of insubordination. You will not ride again, not while my child grows within you."

She pulled back, gazed at the glitter of his eyes through the darkness and wiped the moisture from her cheeks. "And I am also reminded of the scene I witnessed earlier, which prompted me to disobey your order."

"Scene?" he wondered with a frown.

"Aye, your maid failed to see me in the corridor when she stole from your bedchamber this morn," she announced, vigilantly studying his reaction, her bottom lip quivering with feeling.

"She is not *my* maid, Reissa, and the scene you witnessed this morn is not as 'twould appear. Aye, the woman sought my affections, but I turned her away." He pressed her onto her back, and his fingers delved into her hair.

"The smile you bestowed upon her during the morning meal belies your words," she whispered even as she welcomed the warmth of his body and the caress of his hand at her nape.

"'Twas merely for your benefit," he confessed with a devilish smile.

"A ruse?" Her eyes widened with the possibility.

"Aye." A gentle kiss to her brow accompanied the confirmation.

"You bastard." The knowledge filled her heart with such joy that she could not find true anger there. But the corners of her mouth twitched with a smile.

" It was petty, I confess, but 'twas consequence for your belief that I murdered my stepmother," his tone was clipped, and his fingers clenched upon her hair.

Her humor vanished, and once again she threw her arms around his neck. "I shall forever be shamed for disbelieving the sincerity of your innocence." The lady retreated many inches. She stared into his eyes, and her palms pressed to his cheeks. "Please forgive me."

"The matter is forgotten, Reissa, as is the cause of our marriage. Let us lay to rest our misgivings and continue on in contentment."

Tears of joy blurred her vision. "Even as I condemned you for murder, deep within my heart, I prayed that I was wrong. But the abuse I suffered on the eve of our wedding was real; 'twas a personal endurance; therefore, I could not dismiss the possibility that you were capable of harming Golly. However, after experiencing for myself the effects of the drug you were given, I understand the state of your mind during consummation. Your actions were not your own; thereby, I do not harbor any ill will for that horrid evening."

Tender eyes traveled over the plains of her face, then lowered to the flesh of her throat. His fingers slid from her nape to touch the delicate pulse below her jaw, causing a pleasurable sensation to shoot through her limbs. "'Tis a certainty that Alden plundered Edith's herb kit for that damnable drug."

"Tis a minor matter compared to his extensive crimes. Tell me, Viktor, will his neck stretch?"

His heavy sigh caught her attention. "A hanging will not be necessary, for he is already dead," his tone was monotonous, yet emotion charged his eyes with fire.

Reissa gasped, startled by the morbid declaration. "You killed him?"

His head shook, causing ebony locks to fall across his smooth brow. "He stumbled in flight. 'Twas an unavoidable accident."

A satin hand caressed her husband's stubbled cheek, and her expression softened. "Are you repentant?"

"'Twas his intention to murder you and our babe, Reissa." His eyes rose to meet hers, and his head shook again. "Nay, I am not sorry."

She brushed stray locks back from his brow and was overcome with a hint of melancholy. "Lord grant him peace."

"'Tis the devil you must request for Alden's mercy."

The idea was pushed aside for a more pressing curiosity. "How is Edith? She must be devastated."

"The lady possesses more strength than she is given credit for. I am told that she cried quietly, and currently Moira watches over her sleep. He removed his thumb from the pulse at her throat and lowered his lips to taste her skin.

A flush of feeling spread through her body, and Reissa spoke before her thoughts scattered like leaves in the wind. "And what of Alden's defection? How much did he share with you afore his death?"

"Beyond the truth that the man harbored a secret loathing of me and thought to punish me by ending your life, I know nothing," he spoke against her neck, then pillowed his head on her bosom.

"I see." Reissa did not offer further explanation, reluctant to relay Alden's ugly story. It was muddled in her mind because of the herb, but there was enough there to tell the tale.

"Your silence speaks for itself, Wife. Share his confession," Viktor ordered gently.

The lady curled a leg over the back of his thigh, settled into the mattress and told the whole of Kilgour's tale. When she finished, the quiet was filled with a string of oaths. He straddled her hips and rose to look down on her, his eyes alight with the fire of fury. "If I had known of his hate, I would have challenged him long ago. I could have prevented Golly's murder and your near-death."

Reissa's heart skipped with fear. "Near death?" She sat up, and her hands moved to her body in a frenzied search for unnoticed injuries.

He caught her wrists in a firm grip and his expression relayed that he was kicking himself for mentioning her plight. "Reissa, you have not been harmed."

She gazed up with an impassioned expression and demanded, "Tell me. I would know of the events during my forced slumber."

Viktor hesitated, obviously reluctant to share the tale.

Her palm caressed his cheek. "I need to hear it."

He sighed heavily. "Collin and I arrived at Willingham Castle to find Alden on the chamber level, staring down at the entrance with you in his arms. I attempted to reason with him, but my attempt failed. Without warning, he threw you into the air. 'Twas only a miracle that allowed me to move forward with enough speed to catch you. Alden fled, and Collin pursued; 'tis when he stumbled and struck his head."

The woman's breathing grew shallow with feeling, and her eyes lit with wonder. "You saved my life."

"I would not see your death," he dismissed his heroism without a second thought.

Reissa could not withhold the tears that spilled onto her cheeks or the voice that sounded in her throat. "I love you, Viktor."

The man blinked, obviously startled by the statement, but then his expression transformed into one of awe, and the smile that followed was radiant. His fingers threaded through her hair, and he captured her mouth with a kiss that quickly progressed to the heights of ecstasy.

Chapter 47

Reissa had been awake for quite some time, enjoying the reality of Viktor sleeping beside her, when an abrupt knock on the door broke the spell of contentment. She startled, and her husband sat bolt upright in bed, fully conscious.

After glancing at her, he jumped up and hastily donned his braies. As he crossed to the door, the lady tugged on slippers, then tucked the coverlet around her nude figure and stood. She moved near the wall, and when Viktor was certain she could not be seen from the open doorway, he addressed the person patiently waiting on the opposite side.

From her place behind the door, Reissa was able to distinguish the voice as Collin's.

"I have rather disturbing news, Viktor."

"Aye?"

"Maitland has arrived at the gates, and he sends a message to the lord of the manor." The elder Colville paused, clearly reluctant to repeat it. "He insists upon the immediate return of his daughter."

Reissa covered her mouth to stifle a surprised gasp. That was most unexpected. Viktor turned turbulent eyes on her, and his jaw clenched. He stared at her, but he spoke to his brother. "I shall be but a moment, Collin."

"I will await you in the bailey." With that, he departed, and her husband firmly closed the door.

Reissa watched in silence while her husband swiftly dressed, her distress mounting to a fever pitch. The arrival of her father suddenly threatened the fabric of her contentment.

In the dark of night, she had confessed her love for Viktor. It was true he had failed to return the sentiment, but she could accept it, grudgingly. Certainly, it would make her happiness complete if he shared equal feeling for her, but she knew it was too much to ask. Clearly Viktor did care for her in some form, and they could have continued on in their present relationship, but Bernard's demand forced her to question the depth of Viktor's feelings for her.

He had never wanted the marriage, and now an opportunity presented itself, allowing him to discard her. Would he embrace her departure, or would he fight for her on the principle that he fought for all of his family? If he chose to act on the latter, she realized it was possible that her father may risk serious injury for his greed.

Bernard had not returned because he was her father and he loved her. He had returned in hopes that he could marry her off to another for pure profit. The man was as predictable as the sunrise.

Viktor pulled his sword around his waist.

Reissa was moved to speak. She lifted the coverlet and crossed to stand before him. A hand settled on his forearm, drawing his attention. "Please, Viktor, do not hurt him."

His only response was to snap the belt firmly in place.

"He is my father," she pleaded.

"I am well aware of that fact, Reissa." He dropped a chaste kiss on her cheek, then started for the door.

"Shall I accompany you?"

The man whirled around so quickly that she retreated a step. "Nay, Wife. I am ordering you to remain here. I expect to find you in this room when I return," he issued in a hard tone. Then stalked from the bedchamber without looking back.

Helplessly, she gazed about the room, her nerves fraying with each moment. Then she recalled the window embrasure. It looked out upon the bailey. She could see nothing beyond the curtain wall, but it allowed her to watch as Viktor and Collin marched to the gate towers with purpose. Their figures grew smaller and smaller, and finally they entered into one of the massive stone structures that upheld the portcullis.

She kicked off her slippers. Clothed in only the coverlet, she seated herself in the window embrasure and waited, her stomach a mass of knots, her hands shaking with apprehension. Her eyes were fixed on the doorway her husband had entered.

The minutes stretched.

The morning was warm for March, sun shining brightly. But she could feel herself trembling, her future hanging in the balance.

Finally, after all her nails had been bitten to the quick, Viktor and Collin emerged into the bailey. As they drew nearer to the castle's entrance, she was able to distinguish smiles upon their handsome faces, but she knew not whether it was a good sign or bad.

Reissa climbed from the embrasure and moved to the center of the room, facing the door. Once again, she waited.

At last, the hinges creaked, and her husband stepped into the room. He closed the door and turned to face her, but he did not approach.

"Well?" she prompted as she clutched the off-white coverlet tightly to her naked chest.

"He has gone in peace, Reissa." His hands sought the belt buckle at his abdomen, and the sword was removed from its place around his waist. With care, he set it aside.

"Am I to vacate as well?"

Startled eyes shifted to her, and he moved into the room. "Do you wish to depart?" He halted and looked down on her from his extensive height.

"I am happy here, Viktor. Nay, I do not wish to depart." She brushed a stray lock from her vision. Tentatively, she wondered, "Do you wish for me to depart?" Her breath stalled in anticipation of his response.

"You are my wife, Reissa; you belong to this family." The weight of his hands pressed on her bare shoulders. "*You belong to me.*" His mouth pressed to hers in a lingering kiss, and when he pulled back, she gave him a blinding smile that inspired one of his own.

A callused hand scratched at the stubble on his cheek, and he frowned. He crossed to the washstand and began the routine of shaving.

Delighted with the knowledge that Viktor desired her permanent presence in his life, she collected her clothing from the floor and began to dress.

"May I inquire as to the conversation between my father and yourself?" she questioned as her hands moved to her lower back and tightened the laces of her wrinkled cotte.

"He reaffirmed his intention for your return. And I informed him that I would never allow him to hurt you again. That clearly angered him, for he drew the sword at his hip and demanded I reconsider."

A blade scraped at the white foam on his chin as he explained, "In defense, I was forced to draw my weapon, and as we faced off in combat, I informed him that I would never give you up. I spoke of my love for you, and, with that, he reluctantly retreated. He gave his word that he would never return, then departed in peace."

Reissa had been smoothing the wrinkles in her emerald underdress as he told his tale, but now she stood still, stunned. "Your love?" she choked under her breath.

He wiped the last of the shaving cream from his face and neck and nonchalantly looked up. When he saw her frozen state, he tossed the rag aside and hurried around the bed that separated them. "Reissa, are you unwell?" His hands caressed her shoulder blades, and he gazed into her face for answers.

"You love me?" she tested in a whisper.

His black brows creased. "Certainly. I have known for quite some time. It became clear to me when we made love, and I did not possess the desire to leave you. Even in slumber, I knew you rested beside me."

"Why did you not speak it?" She clutched his tunic in a state of utter disbelief.

"I believed you knew." His confusion was genuine. "I believed my actions spoke for themselves."

The lady laughed, overwhelmed by the feeling sweeping over her heart and soul. "A woman must hear the words, Viktor."

He grinned. "I love you, Wife."

Her laughter was positively giddy as she threw her arms around his neck and pressed her lips to his. Her happiness was now complete.

Epilogue

August 1360

As a result of the beautiful weather, many of the guests for Edith's wedding had gathered out in the bailey, rather than enduring the stifling heat in the Meeting Hall. The bride and groom stood near the keep's doors, accepting congratulations from a never-ending line of nobles.

The bride was positively radiant as she bestowed a loving smile upon her groom. She wore a stark white gown shot through with royal blue threading. The color offset her blond curls to perfection and set her amber eyes to shining. Her husband wore a black mantle that possessed the same blue threading, announcing their match by way of attire. However, not only were they a match in clothing, but they were also a direct match by way of hearts.

Viktor had chosen Edith's groom well. Lady Kilgour met the modestly attractive, slightly rotund, kind-hearted Scotsman, and the love she had felt for Viktor transferred to her husband-to-be. It was not because she was forced to marry the man, but because she was given the choice to marry the man. If she had not cared for the foreigner, Viktor would have simply continued the search; however, the first man he introduced as a prospect won the lady's love. And by the way the Scotsman looked upon her with his heart in his eyes, clearly the feeling was reciprocated.

Reissa mused over their happiness.

Her gaze shifted to the group gathered on a linen blanket that had been spread across the plush green grass in the shade of the manor's structure. The nursemaid she had recently hired, a pleasant older woman with graying hair and tender eyes, was reading from a storybook to Maisie. The girl sat at her side, listening intently. On the other side was Moira and Collin's beautiful little daughter, who was deep in slumber. Linley was a dark angel, with her mother's ebony curls, her father's black eyes, and the sweetest disposition one could find in a child.

Her eyes shifted once again to the babe who was currently sleeping soundly in her own arms: her happiness, her joy, her son. Rather than keeping in line with tradition and naming their firstborn son after his father, they chose to give him his own namesake.

Slender fingers gently brushed raven locks from his brow. "I love you, Fulton." His eyes creaked open, revealing ash-gray depths. He gave her a lazy smile, then snuggled closer and drifted back into dreams.

She grinned and looked up to find Moira approaching.

"May I take him?" the lady wondered with a hopeful smile.

Realizing her arms ached from holding him for far too long, Reissa agreed to temporarily hand him off to her dearest friend.

Moira gently took him into her arms, careful not to disturb his napping. She settled on the blanket next to her daughter and tuned into the story being read.

A roar of boisterous shouts suddenly sounded from the men who had taken up an archery contest near the outer curtain wall, gaining Reissa's curious attention. She stared at the group, and her lips turned up with pride when she saw that her husband struck the center of the target, gaining a victory over the others.

"My lady?"

She turned to find a messenger standing before her, holding a sealed parchment. Overcast eyes narrowed with a start when she saw *For Lady Reissa Colville* written on the exterior of the scroll in a familiar hand.

Reluctantly, she took it. As she stared at the black ink lettering, she offered, "Please, sir, avail yourself of the feast in the Meeting Hall. You may linger as long as you like."

He nodded his gratitude then vanished into the crowd of mingling guests.

Reissa glanced at the occupants on the blanket, checking on the welfare of all. Seeing that they remained as they were, contented in recreation, she directed her attention to Moira.

"Reissa, are you well?" the lady asked from her seated position. "Your color has gone."

She nodded distantly. "Will you excuse me for a moment?"

"Of course."

With that, Reissa quietly followed the wall of the manor around to the solitude of the basement entrance. She temporarily dismissed the guard posted at the door, then waited for him to depart. Following a hasty glance to assure she was alone, she opened the parchment.

A glint of gold flashed as an item fell from the parchment onto the grass. With a confused frown, Reissa lifted the outer layer of her burgundy gown and knelt on the ground, searching for the object she knew to be there. As her palm brushed over spiky green tips, she realized her hand was trembling with an overabundance of feeling.

Her hand balled into a fist in effort to gain control of her emotions, then she continued her intent search of the earth. Minutes passed. When she was unable to locate the object she had clumsily let fall from the parchment, she gave a frustrated sigh and returned her attention to the letter.

To my only daughter,

The letter in your hand is notification that I have succumbed to Influenza. You are certain to thank the Lord for His justice in this, as I believed 'twas a blessing that your beloved mother also succumbed to a diseased fate.

Following Grace's death, you foolishly requested the possession of her wedding ring, and, as you are aware, I denied it. Now, in my impending death, I am finally inclined to grant that request.

Bernard Maitland

Reissa felt tears threatening as she rolled up the parchment. Yes, she had despised her father, yet she had loved him in spite of herself. It was a matter of mourning, and a matter of freedom from the fear that he would one day return and insist on entering into his grandson's life. The lady embraced the latter more so than the sorrow.

Bernard had made his departure from Colville Manor months ago, and in that time, she had learned to accept his absence in her life. His death merely solidified the truth and relieved her of the burden of worry.

Nevertheless, her tears remained. At last, he had given her the ring she had desired for so long, and now it seemed it was lost to her. She tossed the parchment aside, and, in a respectable calm, she took up the search once again. When the ring continued to elude her, her tears broke into frustrated sobs.

"Dear Lord, Reissa, what has passed?"

The lady swallowed over the lump in her throat and rubbed at the water in her eyes when she heard her husband's voice break into her emotional state. With her blurred vision partially relieved, she looked up to find him rushing toward her, his face a mask of concern. He dropped to his knees and clutched her shoulders in a firm grip.

"My father has passed," she sniffed.

Briefly his eyes closed with regret, then his arms circled her figure, folding her in a close embrace in an effort to soothe her tears. "'Twill be alright, Reissa."

"You misunderstand, Viktor." She pulled away and gazed into his handsome face. "I inherited my mother's ring, and, fool that I am, I lost it." Her eyes shifted to the ground, explaining her fallacy.

He glanced at the grass, then back to her as she spoke.

"'Twas hers and hers alone. The gold band was passed down from my grandmother; 'twas not a gift from my father." She swiped at the moisture on her cheeks.

Seeing her torment, he pressed her hands between his, and loving eyes locked on her quivering face. "Do not fret, Reissa; we shall find it," he vowed.

With that, they both moved to their hands and knees and began a thorough examination of the area surrounding them.

Her eyes strained against the green background, her fingers deftly threading through the grass.

"'Tis there!" Viktor abruptly spoke.

She looked to his pointed finger and followed the line of his eyes. Near the hem of her gown, a gold glint appeared. Her heart leapt into her throat, guided by the shine. She plucked the ring from the grass and held it to her breast. Her eyes squeezed shut to the world as she sent a prayer of gratitude into the heavens.

Once again, strong arms banded around her. Viktor's strength allowed her to give in to the need to weep. Her brow dropped to his chest, and her shoulders shook with feeling.

He held her as she indulged in a river of tears that cleansed her of the weight of Bernard's death. Then she wholeheartedly embraced the joy of owning the one possession she had longed for for so many years, and the sentimentality attached to it.

At long last, she stared up at her husband and gave him a resplendent smile. "Thank you, Viktor."

"'Tis my pleasure, my lady." He dropped an adoring kiss on her lips.

Reissa opened her palm and stared at the ring resting there, her expression one of utter awe.

Suddenly, Viktor plucked the ring from her hand, causing Reissa's mouth to open in opposition, but the words stalled when he gripped her left hand and began to remove the wedding band from her finger.

"Oh, Viktor, nay, you cannot," she argued, guessing at his intent.

"Shh, Reissa, I insist you wear it." He exchanged her mother's ring for the one he had placed on her finger the day of their wedding. It was a perfect fit.

"But," her eyes pinpointed the gold band now held between his thumb and forefinger, "you gave me that ring. 'Tis representative of our marriage, our love."

Viktor's grin was luminous. "You do not need the ring, Wife." His mouth moved within inches of hers. "You have me."

His kiss held a lifetime of promises and happiness.

Other Titles by Shalene Marie:

Scandal

Ocean of Fate

Widow Wilkes

Echoes From the Past

Treasures

Justice

A Stranger's Vow

The Storm Breaks

The Spring

A Breath In The Rain

Secrets

Secret Sins (18+ Dark Historical Romance)

Amazon Link:

https://www.amazon.com/author/shalenemarie

Author Website Link:

https://www.shalenemarie.space/